Fict

$2^{\underline{00}}_{QE}$

$6^{\underline{80}}_{C}$

6D/JL

148520

 W9-BOB-329

BETRAYALS

ALSO BY CHARLES PALLISER

THE QUINCUNX
THE SENSATIONIST

BETRAYALS

CHARLES PALLISER

BALLANTINE BOOKS
New York

Copyright © 1994 by Charles Palliser

All rights reserved
under International and Pan-American Copyright Conventions.
Published in the United States by Ballantine Books,
a division of Random House, Inc., New York.

Originally published in Great Britain in 1994 by Jonathan Cape.

Library of Congress Cataloging-in-Publication Data

Palliser, Charles, 1947–
  Betrayals / Charles Palliser.
     p.   cm.
  Includes index.
  ISBN 0-345-36959-9
  I. Title.
PR6066.A43B48   1995
823'.914—dc20   94-22769
                                                                      CIP

Text design by Ruth Kolbert

Manufactured in the United States of America

First American Edition: January 1995

10 9 8 7 6 5 4 3 2 1

FOR

L, appropriately

"alas for both his victims and his readers!"
AUBERON SAVILLE

CONTENTS

1
An Obituary from *The Daily Scot*   *3*

2
The Wrong Tracks   *7*

Mrs. Armytage's Story: "The Masque"   *13*
The Parson's Story: "The Scapegoat"   *22*
The Major's Story: "The Stairs"   *35*

3
"The New Surgeon at St. Oswald's"   *49*

4
The Medicine Man   *60*

5
The Trap   *92*

6
The Accusation   *97*

7
An Open Mind   *106*

8
A Nice Touch   *234*

9
The Catch   *270*

10
A Review from *The Daily Scot*   *323*

APPENDIX   *329*

INDEX OF NAMES   *339*

ACKNOWLEDGMENTS

For "William Herbert Dugdale," "Graham Speculand," "Angus MacMaster," "Sholto MacTweed," "Ramsay McCoo," "Drummond Gilchrist," "Jeremy Prentice," and "Auberon Saville."

Thanks for your help with this novel—unwitting though it was. Don't read "your" chapter out of sequence or you'll be even angrier with me. Read the chapters in the right order and then decide who has been betrayed by whom.

Thanks, also, to Ruth, Judy, Frank, Ronald, Marcus, Shira, and Chris.

17 January 1994

BETRAYALS

1

An Obituary from *The Daily Scot*

William Herbert Dugdale,
M.B., Ch.B., M.A., Ph.D., KCB, FRS, FRCP

PROFESSOR RITCHIE WRITES: SO SMALL IS THE WORLD OF immunotoxinology that it is not surprising—though somewhat ironic—that it should fall to myself to write the obituary of William Herbert Dugdale. The fact that I have outlived him is an irony that his mordant sense of humor might have equipped him to appreciate.*

William Herbert Dugdale was a man of rare qualities. In simple terms, he may be said to have enjoyed a successful career by finding ways of using natural venom to good effect.

He was born in Perth, Scotland, on March 11, 1916, the son of a railway guard who died in an accident just a few months before his birth, and rose far and fast, though he was affected by his early experiences to such a degree that it could be said of him that in later life he never betrayed his working-class origins. Seizing the opportunities provided by the local high school, he obtained a scholarship to Balliol, Oxford, and on graduating with a (disappointing) Second, made his way to Cambridge, where he quickly became part of the circle of young immunotoxinologists who were drawn to the brilliant but unstable Max Spitzer in the years just before the war. Taking from Spitzer and the others what he could, Dugdale left for the U.S.A. shortly after Spitzer's tragic death with its well-known repercussions within the Cambridge scientific community. He embarked at

3

Stanford University on a well-publicized career that had, perhaps, more than its share of ups and downs.

Although his warmest admirers—and in the media, public administration, and government he found many of those—always claimed that he never behaved dishonorably except when he believed it necessary to achieve the aims he held most dear, even they conceded that he was excessively susceptible to the belief that his own success was essential to the advance of science.

Happiest when fronting a team of talented and hardworking colleagues, Dugdale was seen at his best when publicity was required. He was not one to shun the limelight nor overly self-effacing when it was a question of sharing with others the credit for an important discovery, and this quirk often poisoned his relations with fellow researchers. Outside his band of fiercely loyal subordinates many found his style of leadership somewhat disconcerting. Never one (as he often boasted) to suffer fools gladly, he had a ready and a sharp tongue, which some called venomous. It is only fair to say that many tolerated his idiosyncrasies with more or less composure. Even his most devoted colleagues, however, found their faith tested in the scandal involving the death of a laboratory technician, which cut short his career in the U.S.A.

It was on his return to the U.K. and to an unusually precocious and controversial chair in my own department at Imperial College in the early fifties that he and I first crossed paths. Dazzled from the start by the reputation of this slightly younger man—for he was possessed of considerable natural charm, whenever he chose to exercise it—I eagerly invited him to take part in my current research project. It was now that we undertook the work on the clinical implications of the toxins derived from spider venom with which his name—and I might add, without undue immodesty, my own name, too—will always be associated. I have no wish to rake over the smoldering ashes of the controversy that was provoked when Dugdale alone was awarded the Nobel Prize for Medicine despite the fact that many of those best qualified to know the facts believed that I myself had made the crucial breakthrough. Nor is it my intention to discuss the web of allegations and insinuations into which many of even the most responsible commentators were lured.

The abrupt ending of our scientific partnership, and of what I had always thought to be our friendship, coincided with the breakup of my marriage. Despite persistent and malicious rumors, I bore no particular ill will toward either party when my former spouse became Dugdale's third wife in a marriage that was not a success and was fated to be cut short by the early death of that last-mentioned individual—an event that had for Dugdale the happy consequence that it released him (very opportunely as some said at the time) to marry his fourth wife.

In later life honors and distinctions came to him with little effort, for his scientific achievements were widely respected by public opinion, if less so by fellow specialists. He was awarded a KCB in 1975 and became an FRS in 1979. From 1973 to 1982 he was a member of the Adverse Reaction Subcommittee of the Committee on the Safety of Medicines. And from 1981 to 1986 he was secretary to the Advisory Council on the Misuse of Drugs. In 1984 he returned to his native land to become Pierre L'Angelier Professor of Immunotoxinology at the University of Glasgow.

Throughout his life Dugdale dabbled with inventions and discoveries in areas other than his speciality, and had a number of successes. The "electronic cat," however, whose failure had such tragic repercussions, cannot be counted among them.

Dugdale's capacity to stimulate controversy was recently displayed when he published a provocative—some called it outrageous—paper suggesting that there was immunological evidence to support the belief of the Ewe people of northwestern Africa that an individual who survives the highly toxic sting of the red sand scorpion (my own speciality for the last decade) thereby acquires immunity to the otherwise fatal disease of rabies. He claimed to have discovered evidence for this by experiments using the live form of the virus rather than the less dangerous attenuated form. With this Parthian shot, he threw down the gauntlet to the rest of the scientific community working in the field. It remains to be seen whether anyone will have the courage to pick up the poisoned chalice he has left behind.

William Herbert Dugdale died suddenly on February 4th

under mysterious circumstances, following a series of controversial and much-publicized incidents at Glasgow University. He leaves a widow and five daughters by his four earlier marriages.

*In point of fact Professor Ritchie did not outlive Sir William but died just three months ago, and the final paragraph was written by this newspaper's obituaries editor. Professor Ritchie died, by what was presumably a macabre coincidence, of rabies, on which he was apparently working in secret during his retirement. (Editor.)

2

The Wrong Tracks

I T WAS AT THE MAIN-LINE STATION THAT WE SET EYES ON EACH other for the first time.

The train had two carriages and, as it happened, we had entered different compartments in each of them. *(The ladies were, of course, in the "Ladies Only" compartment.)* There was then a deucedly long wait. The weather was cold and there was thick snow on the ground, but it was not snowing at that time. If it had been, events might not have turned out as they did.

The delay occurred because of an animated discussion among the employees of the railway company—for the most part stupid old men brought out of retirement—who were gathered on the platform to argue about whether or not the train should depart. The Driver was in favor of departing, while the Guard was raising objections on the grounds that there was a blizzard blowing ahead. (It seems that he was in communication by telegraph with a signal box farther up the line.)

At last the view of the Driver prevailed. Of course we were delighted and certainly had no reason at that time to suspect his motives.

The reason why, having boarded different compartments of the train, we ended up sharing a single compartment is really very simple: The Guard, presumably having realized that we were likely to endure an arduous journey (though quite how arduous it seems impossible to believe

7

he could have imagined), was so courteous as to bring a lighted brazier and place it in the middle compartment of the front carriage. He then walked down the length of the platform—for the train had no corridor, of course—inviting all of us to move into that one.

Once we were all in the same compartment, we did not speak for some time, and then only to comment on the late departure. The old lady, who I later learned to be Mrs. Armytage, remarked that the line had always had a reputation for lengthy delays.

Certainly—to the best of my recollection—no one asked anyone where the other was going nor volunteered that information on his or her own behalf. And no names were uttered since no introductions were made. The Parson was the first and indeed the only passenger to mention his business, for he frankly and openly said very early on that he was going to visit a friend for the festive season. Another clergyman. An Episcopalian, of course.

The train moved off at last. It was still only about four o'clock, but already growing dark because of the snow, which was falling fairly heavily now. We therefore couldn't see much through the windows. Once the train was in motion, such conversation as there had been came to an end. Mrs. Armytage, naturally, spoke to the young lady. She did not, of course, reply. Not in speech, at least.

Frankly, she seemed to be mentally incompetent. Her subsequent allegations confirm that fairly conclusively.

There was thus no general conversation until, about twenty minutes later, the old lady suddenly exclaimed that we were on the wrong track. There was some dismay expressed at this rather remarkable proposition, and she was invited to clarify it. She explained that in order to take the branch line, the train had to halt and the Driver dismount and himself turn a point to redirect the train. She insisted that this should have oc- curred by now. The Major dismissed this idea in rather robust terms, and when the old lady indignantly insisted that she was correct, he sug- gested that she was remembering a practice that must have been discon- tinued many years ago. The points were now controlled, he insisted, by a signal box rather than manually. The old lady stuck to her guns, and the more the Major sneered at this idea, the more convinced she became that she was correct. The Driver, she maintained, had neglected to stop at the correct place on account of the darkness and the snow. The Major invited her to look out of the window and she would see that we were now running along a single-track line, which indicated that we were al- ready on the branch line. She said it proved no such thing since the main line itself consisted of only a single track. He snorted derisively at this and said that on the contrary it had had a double track for at least thirty years.

Mrs. Armytage asked him if he had traveled on the line before this. He answered that he had studied a map of it before leaving Edinburgh. The old lady made a remark implying skepticism toward a claim to knowledge derived from maps rather than direct experience. The Major, clearly stung by this, was quick to defend the usefulness of the art of cartography, which the old lady's remark had insulted.

He pointed out somewhat indignantly that as a military man he knew how to read a map and was trained to remember what he had seen. Lives might be lost or saved, he pointed out with considerable gravity, depending on the ability to find one's way through territory one knew only from a map one had seen just once.

Mrs. Armytage riposted by saying that if we had indeed turned on to the branch line and entered Killiecrankie Glen, then we should soon see its famous landmark, Meikle Jock's Yeird. The Major laughed angrily and said it would be much too dark to see it. She insisted that in spite of that we would soon know whether or not we were in the glen, for if we were, then the train would start to climb an incline—from the top of which the landmark would normally be visible—that was much steeper than any on the main line. The Parson asked her at this point if she was familiar with this terrain, but she failed to answer, apparently not having heard his question. Or she chose not to answer. *And the Major was surely correct about the impossibility of seeing the landmark, for the density of the snow, and therefore the darkness as well, increased within the next few minutes.*

When, after about ten minutes, the train was still running along the flat, the old lady announced triumphantly that she had been proved right: We were still on the main line. The Major insisted, with some asperity, that we had failed to reach the incline only because the train was traveling much more slowly than usual. The old lady answered that the sound of the engine indicated, to the contrary, that the train was running at normal speed. The Major answered that the engine was indeed functioning as usual, but the train was going more slowly than under normal circumstances. When the old lady smiled sarcastically at this and asked him what he meant, the Major explained with some heat that this anomaly was caused by the snow, for as it formed drifts across the rails, it offered resistance to the passage of the locomotive and so slowed it. He said he understood these matters and described a similar observation he had once had occasion to make in Waziristan.

As it transpired, the Major was correct.

The Parson, attempting to distract the disputants (who were exhibiting a surprising degree of hostility), now pointed out that whatever speed the train had been making, it was now getting slower and slower. All four looked out of the windows and agreed that this seemed to be the case, though it was difficult to be sure. This was because the violence with which the snow was being hurled at the windows made it impossible to see anything very clearly. We seemed, moreover, to be ascending a gradient.

All doubts were cast aside when the train began very suddenly to slow down and then stopped. The Major lowered the window and put his head out. At that moment the Guard came hurrying past from the rear coach, which was the brake-car. He seemed to be bent upon passing without speaking, but the Major called out to him to ask why we had halted. He merely jerked his head insolently and didn't answer. Mrs. Armytage commented that this must be where the branch line diverged and that the Guard and Driver were going to change the points. The Major rejected this without ceremony.

A moment later we heard the sound of an argument from the front of the train. It was between, on the one hand, the Guard and the Stoker, and, on the other, the Driver. The Major kept his head half out of the window—despite the protests of Mrs. Armytage that with the window open the compartment was growing even colder—but he could make out nothing.

It later transpired that the Guard was angry that the Driver had continued to take the train along the track when the snowdrifts were becoming so deep. Until the train stopped, he could not, stuck as he was in the Guard's-car at the rear, speak to his colleague. He wanted the Driver to take the train backward until it met the main line (for the Major had been correct about that as well) and then communicate with the signalman at the box near there and obtain leave to return to the station. The Driver, however, insisted on going forward on the grounds that going backward with the engine at the rear of the train was much more dangerous in deep snow than going forward. There was a halt at the top of the gradient, he had pointed out, where the passengers could wait more comfortably and in greater safety than in the train. The Guard had angrily given way.

We knew nothing of this at the time, of course. The Guard passed us

tional Christmas story the presence of a ghost was optional, but what was essential was that the story should have a surprise or "twist" at the end. Or at the very least it should turn out not to be quite as straight-forward as it seemed. The rest of us readily consented to this condition.

Mrs. Armytage then asked if the stories had to be true, and the Major asked what else they should be if not true? The Parson concurred, and this condition was accepted, though it was conceded that the story need not have been experienced by the person telling it so long as he or she could vouch for its having happened.

When we came to decide who was to tell the first story, it occurred to the Parson as somewhat embarrassing that the poor young lady was nec-essarily being left out of this. But there was no remedy.

Mrs. Armytage offered to go first, saying that she had a story that was highly appropriate to tell in the situation in which we found ourselves.

Nobody objected, and so she began.

M R S .   A R M Y T A G E ' S   S T O R Y :   " T H E   M A S Q U E "

This story was told to me by my aunt many years ago when I was hardly more than a girl.

My aunt, whose name was Gwendolyn, was then unmarried. You must understand that she was at the time these events occurred quite a young woman. One summer she attended a house party in the highlands of Scotland. Her hosts were a very good family, whom I will call the Fordyces, though that was not their name. Sir Archibald—he was a baronet—and Lady Fordyce moved in a very fast set and were connected with a Most Eminent Person. I'll say no more about them here be-cause they don't matter to this story, but what does concern us is that they had a son, the only son and therefore the heir to the fortune and the title. This young man—who was extremely good-looking and whom I shall call Randolph—was a talented amateur artist and already a member of the British Society of Painters. Randolph was engaged to be married and, indeed, the young woman concerned was a guest at that house party. (None of you, of course, is old enough to remember that world at the height of its glory—that world that has now vanished completely. The War has finally closed that chapter.)

Another of the guests was a young woman of about nineteen

or twenty, who was, I suppose, the heroine of this little anecdote. I shall call her Mona Elliott. My aunt was not more than ten years older than she, and since they were on intimate terms with none of the others in the party, they struck up a friendship. They enjoyed comparing notes on their fellow guests, for Mona had a lively and sharp wit—as did my aunt.

The engagement between Randolph and his fiancée—whom I shall call Isadora—was considered a strange match, for she was from a family that, though once fairly distinguished, had lost most of its position and all of its money. Randolph Fordyce was, of course, rich enough to make up for the lost fortunes of Isadora's family. My aunt thought the whole affair rather odd, however. And the more so since the happy couple seemed to take very little pleasure in each other's company. She was not handsome, though she had a good figure and was of a height with the young woman whom I have called Mona. I think I may go so far as to say that Mona was a much better-looking girl, a few years younger and with finer features. Not that the fiancée was plain exactly. Her one glory was that she had flame-red hair—if you consider that to be an attraction. I confess I don't, but I am aware that some gentlemen do.

Throughout the period of the house party the weather remained extremely hot. There is the heat you asked for, Reverend. How strange it seems to think of it in this bitter cold. Probably it was because of this unseasonable mugginess that the occasion passed off badly. Everyone was unaccountably listless, and conversations petered out soon after beginning or turned into long, rambling disagreements that never quite became open arguments. The guests sat for hours at a stretch sprawling in front of the great open doors into the garden, fanning themselves. They found themselves as irritated by the attentions of the servants as on other occasions by their fancied neglect. They were, I suppose, directing onto them the annoyance they felt with each other but could not express openly. What we call civilized intercourse among well-bred people always, I believe, skates on the thin ice of barely concealed dislike and rivalry. Sometimes worse things. On this occasion the ice—perhaps because of the heat!—was wearing thin. I believe all those present half knew that some kind of rupture of the appearance of civility was about to take place.

And so it was that, only a day or two after the party had assembled, my aunt thankfully escaped from the oppressive company of her fellow guests and went strolling late one afternoon in the enormous grounds. And it was now that something happened that didn't seem significant at the time—didn't seem, that is to say, likely to have any further consequences.

The grounds were very extensive, and she wandered a mile or more from the Castle toward the west. (I call it a castle, but in fact the original medieval fortress formed only a very small part of it, and the rest of it was a modern house in that barbarous style the Scots adored sixty or seventy years ago.)

My aunt wandered as far as she could in that direction, for, following a path through a little wood, she came to a high cliff. Along its foot there ran a stream—a burn, as they say here—and my aunt pursued its course along the bank where the path continued. After a few hundred yards she came to a little wooden bridge across the burn that seemed, queerly, to run straight into the cliff. But as my aunt peered at its face, she saw steps cut into the rock that descended perilously from the cliff top. Untempted, she walked on and a few yards farther came to a place where the burn had been dammed to form behind it a small lake that extended some thirty or forty yards to the foot of the cliff. The lake was fed by a small but spectacular waterfall that came tumbling down from the top of the cliff from beside a tall rock that thrust up strangely from the top of the cliff. This, with its romantic Scotch name, was a well-known landmark. It was truly a wild and most picturesque spot—though largely contrived, of course, by human ingenuity. And how cool the water looked in that oppressive heat! My aunt walked along the edge of the lake, and all sorts of literary associations, as far as I remember, came into her mind. At least, so I imagine. Suddenly she saw a figure some twenty or thirty yards ahead of her at the edge of the lake. She was quite surprised, for she had believed she was alone in so remote a spot. The figure was that of a woman, and when my aunt went closer, she saw it was Mona. She was standing quite still facing the cliff and seemed to be looking intently at something. As my aunt advanced, she was struck by the fact that Mona seemed quite pale. Now that she was almost upon her, she was able to see what it was that she was looking at. There was somebody standing beneath the waterfall on the other side of the lake. He was about thirty yards away. He had his back turned towards us and he was letting the cold water run off his body.

My aunt saw that it was a young man and that he was quite, quite naked. Well, in those days one was brought up so differently from young girls these days that it was really a most extraordinary shock. My aunt wondered if he were one of the gentlemen in the house party, so—rather wickedly—she advanced a little closer, while taking care not to be seen either by him or by Mona—for a kind of prospective embarrassment had come upon her so that she dreaded to be caught watching the other young woman observing the naked youth. At that moment he turned, and she recognized him as one of the Castle servants. It was a young footman she had seen waiting at table and whose handsomeness she now believed she had noticed. Well, the lake was so remote that it was quite reasonable for him to assume that he would remain unobserved, and my aunt had no intention of getting him into trouble by reporting what she had seen. The young man had no apparent consciousness that he was being observed—and observed not even by one but by two ladies. And, across the lake and shielded by young trees and high shrubs, it was not likely that any of the three of them would be seen by anybody else. *The youth was a very handsome lad with a fine frame, his skin not completely pale but slightly golden as if he were accustomed to occasional exposure in the sun, and with strands of dark hair curling about his chest and below it.* After a few moments my aunt turned back and left Mona standing there.

During the next day or two my aunt, though tempted to tease the younger woman and perhaps share their little secret, said nothing to Mona about what she had seen. She noticed the servant a few times after that, though it was some time before she was able to identify him in his somewhat unflattering livery of a footman and smiled at the memory of how beautiful he was when the ugly uniform was off.

It was a few days later at breakfast that the next incident occurred. (I should mention that, of the ladies, only my aunt and Mona were in the habit of taking breakfast downstairs with the gentlemen. The other ladies breakfasted in their own rooms.) When Mona entered the room, my aunt was struck by her appearance. She was quite pale and during the course of the meal was unusually quiet. She looked as if she had been deeply upset by something. My aunt asked her in an undertone if she were unwell, and she admitted that she had hardly slept the previous night. Randolph happened to overhear this remark and teasingly demanded to know if she had been kept awake by "the banging of the bogle." When she looked alarmed and asked in dismay what he was referring to, he explained that he was wondering if she had seen or heard the Castle's famous ghost—a "bogle" in the Scotch dialect—which accompanied its appearances with a thumping noise. She seemed disconcerted by this reply, and to fill the silence, Rudolph's friend—whom I shall call Valentine Fanshaw—begged him to narrate the story. He happily obliged.

The story was simple enough and a fairly characteristic piece of Scotch history. A wife who had married into the Fordyce family in the sixteenth century had been accused by her husband of having formed an improper relation with a manservant while he was away at the wars. And, indeed, of having borne a child by him. When the husband had returned, he had tortured both her and the servant in the hope of making them confess. They had both died without admitting the offense. The surviving portion of the old Castle was haunted by the tortured—and perhaps guilty—wife.

"Why," Mona said rather strangely when she had heard the legend, "I believe I may have seen the ghost." Instantly the gentlemen desired her to tell them the story—but she would say no more and made an excuse to withdraw soon afterward, looking so pale that my aunt was quite alarmed.

Well, the rest of the day passed, as far as my aunt was concerned, without anything untoward occurring. The next morning at breakfast, however, she was surprised to discover that nobody was down. Neither of the two young men who had spoken to Mona about the ghost the previous morning was present, and Mona herself was not there. Stranger things were to come. During the morning it became known that the engagement between Randolph and Isadora had been broken off. This was an extraordinary occurrence at that time and among people of Randolph's kind. And gradually it emerged that something— something possibly of a scandalous nature—had come to light the night before that had precipitated this. And then by the time luncheon was served—a meal for which only a handful of the guests and none of their hosts were present—my aunt learned that Randolph's former fiancée had left for the station earlier that morning.

Most of the guests found an excuse for terminating their visit earlier than intended and departed that day or the next. For various reasons Gwendolyn was unable to do this. (Mona, too, was one of those who stayed on.) Randolph departed for a shooting lodge in a remote part of the estate, where it was announced that he intended to spend a few days. His parents, of course, maintained the formalities, but it was an awkward situation. My aunt was dying to know what had occurred. At last, she found herself alone with Valentine, who had remained for some reason, and pressed him to tell her what he knew. He needed some persuasion, but at last he consented to confide in her on terms of the strictest confidentiality. (I might say that only the fact that these events occurred so long ago and the participants must nearly all be dead licenses me to betray that confidence now.)

Valentine began by reminding her of how Mona had implied that she had seen a ghost at breakfast the day before the breaking off of the engagement, but had seemed to be hiding something. Now he told her that later that morning he and Randolph had encountered Mona in the library and there they had, very gently and tactfully, prevailed upon her to tell them the story of how she had—apparently—seen the ghost.

This was the narrative she had given them:

It had been a hot night and she had been unable to sleep. She had therefore dressed and gone downstairs and then let herself out into the garden. Now, I know that this must strike you as rather rash, and the more so since I am speaking of a time more than fifty years ago when young girls were expected to behave more decorously than our present very lax manners permit. However, she was a headstrong young woman and had rarely failed to act upon her impulses. She therefore roamed around the gardens for a time gazing up, she said, at the great black bulk of the unlighted tower of the Castle. It was a cloudless night and there was a bright moon.

Now, in order to comprehend the point of what I am going to say, you must understand the disposition of the buildings concerned. At the rear and to the side of the Castle there was the

toward the young one and said that she was unwilling to make her meaning more precise beyond saying that gross and scandalous misconduct was the cause. The Parson was now extremely embarrassed that his obtuseness had forced her to be so explicit. (Though it was hardly the poor man's fault that the old lady had been so circumspect.)

The Major said it was a most intriguing story and he only wondered at the ability of Mrs. Armytage to recall it in such detail so many years after hearing it from another, and to make it so vivid that you'd think she had been there herself. Indeed, he pointed out, at one moment she had become so carried away that she had forgotten that she had not been present. He wondered if the young girl whom Mrs. Armytage had called Mona had indeed seen—or believed she had seen—a ghost that first night?

Mrs. Armytage did not reply but contented herself with looking mysterious.

The Parson asked whether, supposing she had seen nothing supernatural—indeed, he had to say, something only too natural (not that he wished to be understood to be condoning the frailty of the flesh)—but whether in that event she were justified in doing what she did?

Mrs. Armytage said she would be most anxious to know his own views, as a clergyman, on this matter.

Before the Parson could speak, however, the Major pointed out that quite another explanation was possible given the presence near at hand of all those costumes—and, he assumed, wigs—*which were used for charades, but when the Parson, apologizing again for his stupidity, which must be such a bore to the others, asked what he meant, he declined to say any more.*

And then the Major announced that he would give a great deal to know whether Mona had eventually married Randolph? Mrs. Armytage appeared to be taken aback by his acuteness (which was nothing more than a deuced thrust in the dark). *She said nothing and after that fell silent for several minutes, glancing at the Major occasionally.*

The Parson now invited the Major to tell the next story. He, however, declined and insisted that the Parson take precedence. The Parson was not anxious to do so, and the two were engaged in a courteous battle of pleasantries when the train, with a violent jerk, suddenly shot backward. It traveled a short distance, stopped, and then started forward again. The Major once again peered out of the window but could see virtually nothing. After traveling no more than a hundred yards the train began to slow down and then to be buffeted by the rear carriage running up against it, presumably as its forward progress was impeded by the drifts. It was now making no more progress than a man walking. After a few minutes of this most unpleasant mode of travel, it came to a halt again.

The Stoker now came back and told us, as far as we could understand his thick accent, that the reason why the train had moved off so suddenly was because the Driver—despite the earlier discussion and the Guard's departure in search of assistance—had decided to make another attempt to get through the snow to the halt. The Stoker said he had wanted to wait for the Guard to return with the plow and was obviously very angry. After saying this he went back to rejoin the Driver, commenting that it was a great deal warmer on the footplate.

It was certainly getting much colder in the carriage now that the brazier was almost extinguished. When Mrs. Armytage quite brusquely urged the two gentlemen to decide which of them was going to tell the next story, for otherwise the cold was going to kill her, the Parson mentioned that his anecdote was set in Africa. Instantly the old lady insisted that an African narrative was exactly what she needed to "warm her old bones up." So the Parson began.

THE PARSON'S STORY: "THE SCAPEGOAT"

I was out in the Northwestern Territories as a very young man more than twenty years ago and I heard this story from a district magistrate, who, though as old as I am now when I knew him, had been a young man himself when it occurred. It had made a profound impression upon him, for he had found himself faced with a hideous situation at an early age and had ever since reproached himself for failing to resolve it satisfactorily.

You must understand that it happened in an area that was under British protection but not under our rule. The tribes who inhabited it were untouched by civilization, and Christianity had barely begun to reach them. The D.M. whom I have mentioned was based at the provincial capital of Sansanne Aissa, about five days from the coast by river steamer. One day a young Englishman came to him from far in the north of the Zanfara district. His name was Huxtable and he was known to the D.M. by reputation as an anthropologist, though it happened that he had not met him before. An anthropologist was an unusual person to en-counter in those days.

Huxtable was living with a tribe about a day's journey from there and had been with them about two years. He was collecting material for an ethnographic monograph on their religion and was close to the end of his stay. Indeed, had an unfortunate occurrence not taken place, he would have been within a few weeks of leaving the tribe altogether.

He first asked the D.M. if he might be allowed to have a hot bath and then to put some things in the bag for the official post, which went off to the coast every couple of weeks on the steamer in the custody of a special messenger. It was due to go in a couple of days. When this had been done, he said there was something that he wanted to tell the D.M.

He explained that he had had a young servant attending on him. This boy was the reason why he had come to appeal for help. The youth was from a different tribe from the one the anthropologist was studying, which had in itself been a cause of friction with the tribespeople. But now the boy had been found guilty by the tribe of having done something very foolish and dangerous, though he denied it. Huxtable was concerned because the boy was in grave danger, and he felt a degree of responsibility.

He was a good boy and reliable, though occasionally careless and even mischievous. He had sometimes been late serving his master's dinner and once or twice he had been caught wearing his djellaba. But these were no more than the high-spirited pranks to be expected of a good-humored youth. Now, however, he had been found guilty of something much more serious. He was accused of having stolen the most sacred part of the tribe's idol.

I should explain that this barbaric object was some kind of fetish or totem that the tribe believed gave them potency in battle and in the rais-ing of their crops and in various other matters. It was a hideous thing made from ivory and wood, taking the form of a grotesque human figure with certain elements, certain parts, hugely magnified. And it occupied the largest and most ornate of the villagers' huts. It looked like nothing so much as an elephant's head with the head of a pig stuck on top.

The tribe believed that their god spoke through the particular part of the idol that was hideously enlarged. On ceremonial occasions the pop-ulation of the village assembled before the idol's hut and performed var-ious dances and rituals under the direction of the medicine man or high priest or witch doctor or whatever you choose to call him. (This individ-ual was, in effect, the village's chief, although it had a nominal king, who was a very fat old man who rarely spoke—and never without con-

sulting the medicine man.) Huxtable had been permitted to watch, though from a distance. He had then seen and heard how, at the climax of these proceedings, the tribe's god gave its commands to the people for the next few months. It "spoke" through the idol, which was hidden by a screen from all its worshipers except a very few. In fact, the medicine man, as Huxtable had established beyond reasonable doubt, stood behind the idol and spoke through this particular part of it, rather as if through a speaking trumpet. Huxtable had heard the high-pitched voice of the medicine man rising and falling from where he stood.

As long as the idol was intact and was worshiped according to certain rites, the tribe believed that they would continue to thrive. Should it become lost or damaged, then the tribe would know that their tutelary deity had deserted them. They would be without a god, without anything to protect them and give purpose and meaning to their lives—unless some new divinity were to be made manifest to them. Perhaps a divinity that would show them a way of life that was not founded upon superstition and ignorance. A divinity that might, in rescuing them from the mire of sensuality in which they were immersed, show them a prospect of eternal bliss in the life hereafter.

The hut occupied by the idol was in the center of the village. Apart from the medicine man, only a very few elders were allowed into its presence, and profane eyes—especially those of women or strangers—were not allowed to look upon it under penalty of death. And within its hearing—what was conceived as its hearing—women had to remain absolutely silent. (At certain times, moreover, they were not allowed even to come within hailing distance of it.) Although it was guarded during the day by a succession of worshipers drawn from among the elders, at night it was left quite alone and unguarded because of the tribe's curfew.

For it is very important for understanding the story I am telling to know that the tribe believed that evil spirits took over the village at night. This was a barbaric and primitive superstition that the young anthropologist had labored—alas, in vain—to eradicate. Consequently there was a kind of curfew under which it was strictly forbidden for anyone to leave his hut during the hours of darkness.

So much Huxtable had to explain. He now told the D.M. that the allegation made by the elders of the tribe was that a couple of nights ago his servant boy had gone to the hut of the idol and stolen the crucial part. He told the D.M. he had no doubt that the boy was guilty, but he had come to request official intervention in order to save him.

The D.M. asked how the anthropologist could be so sure the boy was guilty. He answered that one of the tribe—an ancient man who was too old to do anything at the time and too frightened of evil spirits to leave his hut at night in order to raise the alarm—saw the boy leaving the hut of the idol and carrying something during the very night when the sacred part disappeared.

When its disappearance was discovered in the morning, the old man had described to the elders of the tribe what he had seen. The boy was seized and his hut was searched. Nothing was found. (I should explain that he had his own little hut some way from his master's in which he slept at night. I mean, the boy slept in his own hut. And the young anthropologist slept in his own.) The medicine man and the elders of the tribe then began the customary proceeding in such cases. They invited the boy to confess, and when he maintained his innocence, they cast the bones to decide what to do. So—Huxtable told the D.M.—the chief necromancer, directed by the medicine man, chanted his superstitious nonsense for a few minutes while he danced and skipped around in a circle, and then he flung a handful of bones on to the ground. He, the medicine man and the other elders, pored over them for nearly an hour while Huxtable and the boy watched. At intervals the elders glanced toward the two outsiders somewhat threateningly. Huxtable was somewhat perturbed, although he knew he was fairly safe since he was under the protection of the British authorities.

When they had finished their deliberations, they announced to Huxtable and the boy that they wanted a confession that would reveal the whereabouts of the missing object. They said that if they gained the object, they would not punish its thief. When Huxtable and the boy both indicated that they could not or would not provide what was sought, the elders explained that in order to extract a confession, the boy would be stripped naked and tied down in the middle of the village and that bits of his body would be severed—one part every day at sunset—until either a confession were forthcoming or he died. His tongue would be cut out first.

This, the anthropologist admitted to the D.M., seemed at first sight a strange proceeding, since the intention was ostensibly to make the victim confess and reveal the hiding place of the stolen object, but you had to have an insight into the childish concepts of the savage mind in order to understand the assumptions behind it. The tribe believed that when a person was charged with an offense that he refused to admit but that he was known for certain to be guilty of, then it should first be made plain to him what his fate was to be. If he still refused to admit it after he had been given every opportunity, then the mutilation began. The point was that the tongue was cut out first because the tribe believed that in such cases it was for the gods to speak and not the merely mortal tongue of the accused person. The tribespeople held some sort of belief that the crime that was denied would be brought to light by means other than speech.

The D.M. agreed it was a horrible business. He had heard of the savage customs of that particular tribe. In the quite recent past even European missionaries had been brutally killed by them—sometimes without even the pretext of a justification. He mentioned that the tribe had a particular abhorrence of unnatural practices, which they were inclined to suspect in the case of all men and boys from outside the tribe, especially Christians and Muslims. *If the tribe were to repeat such atrocities against British subjects, the authorities would have no hesitation in taking punitive military action and extending British dominion over that district.*

Even so, the D.M. said very reluctantly, he had no authority to intervene at present. At least, he had no standing in the matter if the boy was truly guilty. Was Huxtable absolutely certain that that was the case? The anthropologist seemed strangely upset at this. So the D.M. followed this up by asking him where, if the boy had taken it, was the stolen object since it was not found in his possession? Could he have hidden it somewhere? Could he even have hidden it in the anthropologist's own hut? The anthropologist showed great emotion at this. He nearly wept. In fact, I recall that he did weep. Then he said that his own hut had been searched minutely in the hope of finding the missing part and being able to save the youth—to whom he was devoted—by returning it to the elders. It seemed to the D.M., however, that the anthropologist was holding something back. He continued to press him.

Well, it appeared that the D.M.'s instinct was correct. The other man was indeed holding something back. For eventually he admitted that there was more to the story than he had so far revealed. In fact, he conceded, the boy was in a sense innocent. At least, he had not stolen the part for personal gain but out of a kind of excess of enthusiasm or as a kind of prank. The truth was, the anthropologist said—and he begged the D.M. to treat this in the utmost confidence—the truth was that he himself had asked the boy to visit the idol that night in order to be able to describe it to him. It was crucial to his work to know what it looked like, and the tribe had never given him permission to see it at close quarters. The anthropologist had asked the boy to do this since, being himself black-skinned, he had a better chance of not being seen in the darkness than he, a white man. The boy had done so but in an excess of misguided loyalty, he had foolishly and, on an impulse, stolen the most easily detachable part of the horrible object. He had done so without realizing the significance of his action, for he had not understood that the part he was taking was not incidental but essential and so its loss would bring about these terrible consequences. In stealing it he had, to put it in the mildest terms, exceeded his instructions. But that was because, the anthropologist explained, the boy adored him, almost worshiped him in the way that the savage often did a white man because of his superior intelligence, education, and morality. The D.M. could see what a difficult situation the boy's action had placed him in. He couldn't admit to the elders what had happened because to confess to having spied—even at secondhand—into the mysteries of the tribe would undermine his own position there. Several years of work, he explained, would be thrown away if he were unable to complete his study. At best it would hamper the work he was trying to do there by destroying their trust in him. At worst he might have to depart immediately. And he would have been lucky to get away without being punished himself! *The D.M. saw this and also had a larger responsibility to consider, for he saw that such a revelation would undermine the tribe's faith in British authority generally at precisely the moment when an attempt was being made to bring the whole area under the protection of the Empire. He realized that vital trading and military interests were at stake.*

The D.M. said that the one possibility he had of exercising any authority lay precisely and paradoxically in the fact that the boy was from another tribe. Unfortunately, this was not a firm basis on which to base a claim of jurisdiction, since the other tribe was not under British rule either, though it was under our protection. But this might at least give him the chance to argue that the tribe should not treat the boy in the way they would do an offender from among themselves.

He agreed to accompany the anthropologist back to the village and use his good offices to persuade the tribe not to continue with the torture and, in effect, the execution of the boy.

So they went back to the village. They traveled more slowly than the D.M. could have done alone, for the anthropologist was small and slightly built. Quite a puny little fellow, in fact. *By the time they got there the next day, the boy had lost several fingers from one hand and also a foot. He was staked out on the ground with a canopy over him to keep the sun off, and some of the village women were giving him food and water, presumably not from any compassionate motive but in order* to preserve him from complete insensibility so that the torture would be the more effective. As the two Englishmen approached him, he gestured toward his master in a way that the D.M. took to indicate gratitude and devotion, pointing with his bleeding hand as far as he was able, and nodding his head while grinning painfully round at the villagers who were watching.

Once the news had got about that the D.M. had arrived, the elders began to assemble beside the mutilated youth. When they had all gathered, a ritual exchange of courtesies and gifts took place.

The medicine man came forward. He was tall and thin with a high, sharp nose and deep-sunken black eyes that were glittering and humorless. He wore an elaborate cloak of exotically colored feathers, and a tall headdress, also adorned with feathers. He obviously felt frustrated and angry at the prospect of losing the power he had exercised because of the way he had been able to speak through the idol. He now made a long speech, the burden of which was that the tribal god had fallen silent now that its part had been stolen. It could be made to speak again only by an act of confession involving a sacrifice to atone for the blasphemy. The part it had lost must be given back to it in one form or another. If the actual part could not be restored, then a substitute would have to be provided. (While he was speaking, he stared intently at the two white men, and it occurred to Huxtable that he was trying to put a spell on them.) The medicine man, reaching the end of his speech, now began to curse the thief, promising that he would develop sores all over his body and suffer so horribly that he would eventually kill himself.

When he had finished, the D.M., speaking through his interpreter, asked to be allowed to speak to the old man who had seen the boy leaving the hut of the idol. The old fellow was brought before him.

The D.M.'s examination, as he modestly admitted to me, was a masterly process of drawing coherence from the savage mind and of attempting to demonstrate to the tribespeople in the most practical form the concepts of justice, from which they were far removed.

In the course of his examination of this witness, the D.M. discovered that the old man could not have seen—and, indeed, did not claim to have seen—the boy actually leaving the hut of the idol. He could not have done so since from his own hut that of the idol was not visible. The D.M. recalled that the anthropologist had summarized the evidence against the boy as if it were much more conclusive than turned out to be the case and felt, he told me, encouraged by this at that stage in the proceedings.

In his calm, rational way, the D.M. first of all established to his own satisfaction the position of the huts. There were two rows of them parallel to each other. Of the four that concern us, three were aligned in the same row in this order: the hut of the idol, that of the boy, and finally that of the anthropologist on the outskirts of the village. In the next parallel row was the hut of the witness, which was level with that of the boy. This meant that he could see the boy's hut but could not see either of the other two.

What the old man insisted he had seen was the boy moving about the village at night—which was, it had to be granted, in itself both highly suspicious and absolutely taboo. Moreover, the boy had looked as if he had been coming from the direction of the idol's hut and was certainly carrying something. It was because the part of the idol was missing the next day that this evidence was held to be damning. Having established that the boy had not actually been seen coming out of the idol's hut, the D.M. continued to question the old man. He told him to recount precisely what he had seen. The old man began to say that he had seen the boy creeping along carrying something. The D.M. insisted that he describe what he had actually seen rather than what he believed he had seen. It took some time for him to convey this distinction to his savage interpreter, but at last he succeeded and eventually the old man was made to grasp the point. He said that he had seen in the light of the bright moon a fairly small figure dressed in the distinctive long black garments of the boy, moving away from the direction of the idol's hut. He admitted that he had not seen the face of this figure.

So the D.M. had considerably weakened the case against the boy: rather than it being the case that he had been seen leaving the idol's hut, it was only admitted that someone closely resembling him had been seen coming from that direction. In a European court—or at least, a British court—the case would have been dismissed at this juncture.

Now the D.M. pursued another line of questioning. He asked whether it was less unusual for people to move about the village at night than might be supposed, granted that it was contrary to the law of the tribe. The old man admitted that it was not uncommon. The elders nodded at this. One of them made a remark—at which there was laughter—which the D.M. interpreted as a reference to irregularities of a kind that are all too frequent in our own society and to which the story we have just had the pleasure of hearing itself alludes. He asked the witness and the elders if the boy had ever been seen moving about the village at night. The old man admitted that he had seen him a number of times leaving his own hut and then toward dawn returning to it. Was he going toward the idol's hut? No, the old man admitted. He was going in the exactly opposite direction, as on the night of the blasphemous theft. In that event, he was going along the row of huts toward the outskirts of the village.

This gave the D.M. a great deal to think about, and a number of ideas came to him. Yet whatever the real truth of the matter might be, he still could not see a way out of the dilemma he was in. After some reflection he decided to make an appeal to the natives' sense of natural justice, of which he believed even the most savage breast to have some intimation. He said that in his own country the boy would not be found guilty without more evidence than this. For example, the missing object would need to be found in his possession or in a place where he might be assumed to have concealed it. The elders admitted that nothing had been found when the boy's hut was searched. He asked them about the search of the anthropologist's hut, and they conceded that nothing had been found by Huxtable when, following their request, he had searched his own hut in case the boy had hidden the part there.

Failing all else, the D.M. now used the argument that the boy was from a different tribe as a reason for exercising clemency. The answer of the elders was that this made no difference. Indeed, it made his profanation of the idol even more serious. To a youthful member of their own tribe mercy might be extended. In the case of an outsider there was a responsibility to act in a way that would deter other strangers from such blasphemy.

The D.M. told me that he was horrified by the pitilessness and primitiveness revealed by this reply. He began to feel that the tribe, by its display of callous indifference to the fate of the boy, had forfeited the right to be treated decently and he began to contemplate the propriety of a punitive expedition. (This was, indeed, carried out a few months later, and the protection of the British authorities was extended over the survivors.)

This "trial"—if that is the right term for such a barbaric proceeding—had taken the greater part of the day. And now that the dusk was approaching, the time had come for another of the wretched youth's limbs to be amputated. The D.M. was in an agony of indecision and perplexity, for, as he told me, he had by now come to suspect that it was not the boy who had committed the sacrilege at all but someone for whom he had been mistaken.

Yet if this was so, there remained at least one puzzle: How could the witness have seen somebody whose appearance was so different from that

*of a black boy and yet have believed that that was whom he was seeing?
Part of the reason was that he had seen the boy surreptitiously creeping
about the village at night a number of times in the past and so had assumed that he was seeing him again. But it still remained puzzling.*
You'd need more than a d——d wig this time! *The D.M. looked at
the boy as he reflected on this.*

*The poor lad was quite naked and bleeding profusely from his severed
limbs, despite the crude attempts that had been made to staunch the flow
of blood. The D.M. noticed that he had an athlete's body, slender with
narrow hips and wide shoulders—though now twisted into exquisite con-
tortions like the body of the youthful Saint Sebastian in Guido Reni's famous painting. As he looked at the youth and pondered, the D.M.
realized the significance of the argument he had just used, so unavail-
ingly, based on the fact that the boy came from a northern tribe. This
meant that, when clothed, he was most likely wearing a long black
garment—the djellaba—which was traditional in those districts because
of the influence of the Arabs. (Indeed the boy was a Muslim rather than
an animist—not that that has any relevance, since one set of supersti-
tions is much like another.)*

*So the D.M. put his hypothesis to the anthropologist, explaining in de-
tail and at length his interpretation of the evidence and the conclusions
he had drawn from it. Huxtable looked at the ground all the while. And
the D.M. told me—twenty-five years later—that he was not in the least
surprised (but neither was he shaken in his conviction) that the other
man, when he had finished what he had to say, refused either to look up
or to speak. The maimed boy, who was within earshot of this conversation between the two men although he had seemed not to be fully conscious, now opened his eyes and appeared to be listening.*

*At this moment the smoldering fire that was a few yards from the boy
was made to flare up by one of the women, and at this signal that dusk
had arrived, the medicine man's assistant advanced toward the boy
carrying his knife. At a sign from his superior, however, he paused some
distance away from where the boy and the two white men were.*

*The rest of the elders, watching from a few yards away, looked on ex-
pectantly. Despite the D.M.'s persistence, however, the anthropologist continued to remain silent, and after a few minutes the boy seemed to have
lapsed back into unconsciousness. The D.M., however, was by now convinced that the artifact was more than a day's journey away and he
therefore saw that there was no means to save the boy except by
repeating—but this time in the hearing of the elders—an accusation*

that, even though it would be denied, would destroy the authority of the white race and the dignity of the white man's religion.

He was spared the necessity of making a hideous decision, however, for while he was actually debating within himself what course of action he should take, the medicine man's assistant came forward and began to cut off another part of the boy. The pain made the poor fellow regain consciousness, and now he seemed to be trying to speak, although his condition of tonguelessness made this impossible. All he could do was hold his mouth open and wiggle the obscene stump of his severed organ. After a few moments he closed his mouth and seemed to be swallowing. Then he choked several times while we looked on in utter horror and helplessness. And then, in less than two minutes, the poor fellow died. (He either bled to death or died of shock.) Within the hour the anthropologist was packed and had taken leave of the tribe. He returned to the provincial capital in the company of the D.M. Almost no words were exchanged by them during the course of the journey, and they parted as soon as they reached the little town. Before doing so the D.M. mentioned that he would have to send an official report on the incident to his superiors, who would probably pass it on to London. The anthropologist said he had already dispatched to London his own—necessarily partial—account of the events prior to his leaving the village to seek help from the D.M.

The D.M. pointed out, too, that the anthropologist would have to wait nearly two weeks for the next steamer to take him downriver to the coast. (For the fortnightly steamer had, as was mentioned at the beginning of this story, just sailed a couple of days earlier, carrying the official mailbag.) He did not, as was customary, offer him the hospitality of his own quarters but recommended him to a boardinghouse in the town.

By the time he had reached the end of the story, the Parson was close to tears. There was a silence. When he had somewhat composed himself, the Major said he had enjoyed the story but was puzzled by several aspects of it. For example, he was surprised that Huxtable was able to describe the appearance of the idol so precisely when no outsider was supposed to have seen it. And when the Parson pointed out that the boy must have described it to him, the Major persisted in his view that the description was more vivid than one might have expected, given that the anthropologist was describing it secondhand.

Mrs. Armytage then commented that she was disappointed that the Parson's story had not obeyed the requirement for a "surprise." The Major merely said that he was astonished that she should say this, but she took offense at this innocent remark and withdrew into an angry silence.

The Major commented that Huxtable's behavior was unusual for an anthropologist. And then he asked if an anthropologist usually wore a long black garment.

The Parson looked upset, but they were unable to pursue the point because there was an interruption at this moment.

At this point the Stoker and the Driver suddenly appeared at the side of the track. The Major opened the window and talked to them. The Driver was in favor of all of us leaving the train and going forward to the halt, which he calculated was no more than five hundred yards up the line. Being at the top of a hill, it would provide much better protection against the snow, he insisted, than the train, which—because we were in a cutting on the hillside—could quite literally be buried under drifts if the snowstorm continued for many more hours. (He said that such a thing had happened on that very line a few years before.) The Stoker insisted that it was much safer to remain with the train so that the rescuers, who must soon be on the way—assuming that the Guard had managed to raise the alarm—would be able to find us. And he maintained that the halt was more like a mile and a half away than five hundred yards. The passengers were thrown into confusion by this—*except for the Major, who strongly supported the Driver. He cited his long and frequent experience of blizzards and deep snow on the northwestern frontier and described similar incidents that had occurred involving himself and others. Mrs. Armytage, however, expressed in the strongest of terms her terror at the prospect of leaving the safety of the carriage for the danger represented by the wind and darkness and driving snow. The Major, nevertheless, insisted on the course of action he had advocated.* And that had been suggested by the Driver. And so eventually it was decided that the Driver would lead us to the halt while the Stoker would stay with the train in order to tell the rescuers where we were.

Taking the two lanterns, we set off. The Driver walked at the front carrying one of them, and the Major brought up the rear. It turned out that the Driver had indeed underestimated—either deliberately or inadvertently—the distance to be covered.

Stumbling through the driving snow, our hands, faces, and feet numbed by the cold, it took us more than half an hour to cover the distance.

We were then horrified to find that the halt consisted of no more than a small, half-ruined brick building comprising a single apartment. Some harsh things—*perhaps unnecessarily harsh*—were said to the Driver on this account, for he had led us to believe that we would find secure shelter there. All we found was a bare room with no fire lit and no means of procuring one. A few chairs were its only furniture, and it had no means of illumination. The door was off its hinges, and several panes of the window were broken so that snow was piling up inside through both the door and the window. Mrs. Armytage—*doubtless weakened more than any of us by her journey from the station*—was particularly angry with the Driver for luring us away from the comparative safety of the train. She virtually promised, in fact, that she would undertake to have him dismissed.

It was apparent that we were no safer than we had been in the train. Indeed, we were in a more dangerous situation, since the broken window and unfastened door gave us even less protection against the bitter wind than we had had in the carriage. There was obviously, however, no question of our attempting to go back.

We seated ourselves in the darkness around one of the lanterns, extinguishing the other in order to conserve the oil. The Driver sat at the edge, almost out of earshot. Now it was that the Major offered to tell his story—*although the rest of us had wholly forgotten our story-telling agreement. Mrs. Armytage was clutching the arm of the silent young lady.*

Mrs. Armytage, in fact, objected to his proposal on the grounds that it was quite inappropriate under the new and much more dangerous circumstances in which we now found ourselves. She suggested that we should be thinking of saving our souls and asked the Parson to lead us in prayer.

The Major commented that two of the party had made their confessions and now it was his turn. Nobody made any remonstrance at this remark. Then he said he would like the Parson to tell him if it was possible to confess to a crime that one had not yet committed. The Parson suggested that he should say a prayer before the Major began his story, and this happy thought was accepted by both parties to the disagreement.

The Parson therefore recited from memory the most appropriate prayer he could think of from the Book of Common Prayer, *which was one of the "Prayers to Be Used in Storms at Sea." ("We confess, when we have been safe, and seen all things quiet about us, we have forgot Thee Our God, and refused to hearken to the still voice of Thy word, and to obey Thy commandments: But now we see how terrible Thou art in all Thy works of wonder.") And since, by a happy accident, he had in his possession a vial of water from the River Jordan, which had been blessed by the Archbishop of Jerusalem and which a friend of his had brought back from the Holy Land, he sprinkled it on his hearers while he recited the prayer.*

Afterward, when it became clear that the Major was going to tell his story, Mrs. Armytage insisted that she would not listen to it and moved a little distance away from us. Within a moment or two, however, she had moved back—whether to hear the story or to be closer to the light and mild warmth cast by the lantern it was impossible to judge.

THE MAJOR'S STORY: "THE STAIRS"

This is a story about a man called Durrands, whom I met when I first went out to India as a young subaltern some twenty-five years ago. He was my senior by about fifteen years when I reported on station. Durrands told it to me and, since he was a straightforward man, this is a straightforward story. Except that I'm just a plain military man, so I don't know how to tell it. I can mar a plain tale in the telling, as Kent says.

Some years before I first met him, Durrands had been accused—quite ludicrously, as you shall hear—of having conspired to bring about a man's death. Indeed, he came close to being court-martialed for murder. The evidence against him was, on the face of it, overwhelming, for it was nothing less than an accusation by the dead man to the effect that Durrands had killed him, an accusation that was written in his own blood while he lay dying. Nevertheless, the charge was absurd, as I'm sure you'll agree when you've heard my tale.

Whether a man was murdered or not remains for you to judge. But a man was undoubtedly dead. He was a fellow officer of Durrands's called Appleyard, and he was considerably older. Appleyard was a man who thought rather too well of himself.

Like many of his kind, he was better liked by the ladies on the station than by his fellow officers, who regarded him as rather a cad. And also thought he was somewhat *too* well liked by the gentler sex.

Durrands was about twenty-five at the time of these events and a bachelor. He came from an old Indian Army family of the utmost respectability (for such do indeed exist), and was born out there in the Barrackpore cantonment in Bengal. His mother had returned to England when he was a child. I believe the climate did not suit her. And there were various other circumstances. *In fact, she died in very sad and shocking circumstances. Most distressing.* Durrands was the most decent, upstanding sort. A truly honorable English officer and gentleman. He regarded Appleyard with scarcely concealed contempt, for the man was a bounder without background or breeding. Those are good reasons for despising a man but hardly an adequate motive for killing him.

When Durrands joined the regiment on his return from a few years in England, it had been on station at Chattargarh for less than a year. It had just been posted from Edwardesabad in northern Waziristan—that's in the Northern Frontier Province. (It's important to note that he had not been stationed in Edwardesabad as most of the other officers had.) A few months later it was learned one day that Appleyard had disappeared. He had gone on leave telling everyone he was going to Poona. When he didn't come back at the end of his period of leave, which was a month, as far as I recall, enquiries were made, and it was established that he had not been seen in Poona during that time. He had, it was eventually learned, taken the train from the nearest railway station and traveled toward the northwest—the exactly contrary direction—but beyond that he could not be traced.

Well, nothing more was heard of him, and although his disappearance excited a great deal of speculation at the time, as the months passed, it was forgotten. (I might mention that a number of husbands on the station were only too pleased by his absence.) Then, when he had been missing for three years, his body was discovered. It hadn't been found before because it was in the most devilishly remote and inaccessible spot. This was in the Khost Mountains of northern Waziristan, right up in the district from where the regiment had been posted less than a year before his disappearance. The body was found about three days' journey from the former station, Edwardesabad. And as if that wasn't remote enough, its position was so extraordinary that it was miraculous that it was ever found at all. It came to light when a peasant who was doing something or other on the side of a cliff—gathering samphire, perhaps, for all I know—found a skeleton (all that the vultures had left) on a narrow ledge half-way up the side of the cliff. He recognized it from the boots as that of a pukka wallah, poor fellow. And there was a military telescope lying nearby. And certain precious objects.

He informed the authorities—for the sake of a reward, and I hope it was a decent one—and the body was recovered. It was identified as Appleyard's by documents found with it, and the death was investigated by the local military authorities.

You'll never understand this story at all if I don't describe the site where the body was found. The cliff was the edge of a high plateau and was about two hundred feet high. Near where the body was found there were steep steps down the side of it. (That must have been how the fellow who found him got up there.) *But the steps were virtually hidden, and you had to know they were there before you would ever find them. And the only indication of their presence was an oddly shaped rock nearby rising from the top of the cliff.* Now, the point is that in one place just above the ledge where the poor devil's body was found, the steps appeared to have been deliberately undermined. In fact, the chaps who were investigating the affair very nearly fell victims to the trap themselves. I use the word *trap* because several of the steps had been hollowed out in such a way that if someone put his weight on what looked like solid stone, it would give way. It seemed clear that this was what had happened to Appleyard and that he had fallen onto the ledge about thirty feet below. Whether the miserable wretch starved to death or died of injuries sustained in falling or perished in some other way was never established. The significant thing was that the steps were very ancient, but the undermining appeared to have been done much more recently— three or four years ago. In other words, not long before Appleyard had been killed by it.

Clutched in the dead man's hand was a piece of paper. He had cut himself with his knife and written on the back of it in his own blood: *"Durrands has killed me with this accursed paper and . . ."* Nothing much more could be made of what was written on the other side. It looked to the chaps investigating the case like a kind of map or diagram and had some script on it in what looked like Hindustani—but it had been rendered almost illegible by the exposure to the sun and the frost.

Well, an account of all this was telegraphed back to Chattargarh, and Durrands was summoned by his C.O. and told to take himself up to Edwardesabad pretty damned quick. When he got there, he was shown the piece of paper. He flatly denied that he had ever seen it before. When he was asked why the dying man had accused him, he said he had no idea. His inability—or refusal—to give any explanation of this fact was held against him, of course, and certain conclusions were drawn from it.

In fact, as he told me all those years afterward, he did recognize it, but chose to assert the contrary. It wasn't his own skin he was trying to save by lying. It was out of reluctance to incriminate another.

He was told by the chaps investigating the case that a white man had been seen in that district just a few weeks before Appleyard had arrived there. (Such a thing was so unusual in such a remote place—particularly after the departure of the regiment from the province—that it would be remembered for many years.) The witnesses who had seen this man were brought into his presence. They were fairly sure that Durrands was not the European they had noticed, though after three years they said they could not be absolutely certain.

Someone else who knew the story told me later that the reason why this mysterious accusation against Durrands by the dying man was taken seriously was because it was known that he had a grudge against Appleyard. It was over the kind of thing that on a station in India nobody speaks about and yet everybody seems to know even when, as in this case, it had occurred many years ago and on another station. *It had been when he was a child, in fact. Appleyard had been a young officer stationed at Barrackpore, and there had been some sort of ill-will between him and Durrands's father.*

In fact, Durrands had an unimpeachable defense. He was able to prove that he had not gone off station for many months previous to the date of Appleyard's disappearance, and so it could not have been he who had prepared the trap. He could establish this beyond any doubt, for there were records and logs showing that he had fulfilled his military duties during the whole of the period in question and had not taken more than a few days' leave. (Since the site of the cliff was three days' journey beyond the regiment's former station—itself several days by train from Chattargarh—he would have needed at least ten days to get there and back.)

Apart from the mysterious accusation written by Appleyard, there was no evidence to incriminate Durrands, and so he was told that no further action would be taken against him. However, the accusation of a dying man carries a great deal of weight, and as a result the shadow of suspicion hung over him. (To jump forward to the time of my own acquaintance with him, it dogged him for the rest of his life and blighted his career so that he retired early. He died quite young, and I think I can say that the business killed him.)

Well, this was the story as it was widely known at the time he and I first made each other's acquaintance. We became friends, and one day he told me in strict confidence what it was that he had chosen to conceal from the investigators.

You're probably wondering why Durrands wanted to confess all this to a young subaltern. I suppose that after brooding about it for all those years, he wanted to see how the story would be interpreted if he confessed to someone who hadn't been involved. But I don't really mean "confess." That's the wrong word. After all, the whole point is that he wasn't guilty. But I suppose you can feel the need to make a confession even when you don't feel that you're to blame. The worst thing must be to have something preying on your peace of mind and to find yourself incapable of speaking about it—as effectively as if you were struck dumb—and therefore unable to relieve your guilt by some kind of even veiled disclosure.

However that may be, Durrands admitted to me that not only did he recognize the map that poor Appleyard was clutching but he knew its whole history. Indeed, it was through him—though indirectly—that Appleyard had acquired it.

This is the story of the map that he told me. He had acquired it in Bombay while on his way to his posting at Chattargarh. He had bought it from a native trader, who had claimed that it indicated the hiding place of buried treasure, as the Hindustani inscription suggested. This man said he had obtained it from a dying Parsi, who had owned it for many years but had never dared to trust anyone to try to retrieve the treasure whose whereabouts it recorded. The map had supposedly been made by the Parsi's grandfather, who had been the treasurer to a rajah who had had to flee from the British and in doing so hid his wealth in a cave. The Parsi had sold the map to the trader when he knew he was dying, in order to provide for his only child—a daughter—after his death. Whether or not he believed this, Durrands had bought it from the trader. Well, all that sounded to me like something out of *The Arabian Nights* or Wilkie Collins. You know the kind of thing. A terrible crime is committed that cries out for vengeance. The offender thinks that he—or she—has escaped the consequences, but many years later finds herself being pursued by a descendant of the person whom she has wronged.

Durrands was not much of a scholar in the vernaculars, but he believed he could read the inscription on the map. He deciphered it thus: "Go to the Rabbit and walk south along the top of the high cliff. After three courses [*kuroh*] and two hundred gudges [*gaz*] you will come to [*The?*] Zakar. Go twenty gudges farther and you will find steps. There is a cave halfway down the cliff, where you will find what your merits have earned you."

The word *Zakar*—if that's what it was—was difficult to decipher and to interpret. Durrands assumed that it referred to some kind of landmark, presumably a rock of the particular shape suggested by the word. A shape I think I need not specify. Suffice it to say that it was of a highly indelicate nature.

For months during his spare hours on station Durrands made an attempt to identify the place described by the map. He searched dictionaries and gazetteers but could not find any topography that corresponded to these place-names or anything similar to them. At last he showed the map to another officer on the station. This was a rather older man called Maddocks. He had the reputation of being something of a scholar in various of the native tongues and had even published translations. Durrands was not a friend of his, for he was a gloomy, difficult sort of chap who drank too much. He wasn't generally liked. And he had a pretty young wife, whom he was said to neglect shamefully and, on a station full of unmarried officers, foolishly. Maddocks took the map and a little later told Durrands that he had failed to make anything of it. When Durrands asked for it back, he said that it was missing. Durrands didn't believe him, for Maddocks was a sly and somewhat secretive fellow, but he thought no more about it.

Well, that was Durrands's story of the map's history. And when Appleyard's body was found with the map, he recalled that the poor devil's disappearance had taken place a few months after Maddocks had claimed to have lost the map. And now Durrands also remembered that Maddocks had taken several weeks' leave at just about that time. As Durrands turned over in his mind the puzzling fact that the map had ended up in Appleyard's possession, he suddenly realized that it was Maddocks who had killed him.

And yet Durrands said to me that he himself had precipitated the murder, and this is what he meant.

When he had shown the map to him, Maddocks had presumably recognized the terrain to which it referred. He had recognized it because it just so happened, by one of those strange coincidences, that the cliffs were three days' ride from Edwardesabad, where the regiment had been based until recently. (You'll recall that Durrands had only joined the regiment after it had been transferred to the Chattargarh station.)

In my view, by accepting the map without admitting that he knew what it referred to, Maddocks was cheating Durrands, to say nothing of what else he did. I don't know whether it was the treasure that interested him or the other thing. Whether the whole devilish contrivance occurred to him then or later I cannot say, but Durrands explained to me that he had worked out what must have happened. Maddocks realized that if *he* could recognize the topography referred to by the map, then so would Appleyard who had also been stationed in Edwardesabad. And so he must have gone to Edwardesabad on his next leave. He knew that the Rabbit was a steep pass leading to the plateau. Having correctly interpreted the word *Zakar*—presumably because he knew the feature it referred to—he had found the steps down the cliff. He had then constructed the trap in order to kill anyone who used the steps.

When he got back to Chattagarh station, Maddocks presumably showed the map to Appleyard and claimed he could make neither head nor tail of it. Appleyard, as Maddocks had anticipated, recognized the area just as he himself had done. But just as he had done, he pretended not to, thinking, presumably, that Maddocks had merely failed to perceive what seemed obvious to him and hoping that the treasure—if it existed—would fall into his hands. So it was Appleyard's desire to cheat Maddocks that led to his walking into the trap. And it must have given him a particular pleasure to think he was going to outwit Maddocks, since there was already bad blood between them on account of the other man's wife.

Now it didn't all turn out as Durrands *(That is, surely, Maddocks!)* had expected. For it had presumably not occurred to him that Appleyard might approach the trap by climbing up the steps from the bottom rather than descending from the top of the cliff. That was because the map gave instructions for finding the landmark—and therefore the steps—by walking along the top of the cliff, and Maddocks hadn't realized that the landmark could be seen from its foot. But from what was found with the corpse, Durrands was able to work out what must have happened. You'll remember that a telescope was found by Appleyard's skeleton. So it seems that he had walked along the bottom of the cliff and used it to espy the landmark at the top. Then he had found the steps where they ended at the foot of the cliff and had climbed up.

Because he had climbed up rather than down, Appleyard succeeded in reaching the cave indicated on the map, and this, of course, was quite contrary to what Maddocks had expected.

The extraordinary thing is that it appears that he actually discovered treasure in the cave, for some silver trinkets were found there and on the body. These took the form of small silver scorpions. It seems that there was a nest of them in the cave, for two were found there and another in one of Appleyard's pockets. Of course, there might have been others and perhaps even more valuable objects. For the fellow who reported the finding of the body might have stolen them first. But then, if he had done so, he would probably not have dared to report his discovery of the remains. Other thieves might have taken other objects, but in that case they would probably not have left three silver pieces behind. And I believe the natives' superstitious horror of and respect for the dead suggests that the body had not been looted. *It's also possible that Maddocks found treasure there and left only a few pieces behind.*

Then for some reason—perhaps because he intended to make his way back by the shorter route—Appleyard had climbed farther up the steps, and that is when he was caught by the trap. He fell and landed on the ledge. Finding that he was badly hurt, he must have realized that he was doomed. Nobody was likely to pass by that place for months, if not years. But he had time to work out what must have happened and to leave a note on the back of the map, written in his own blood, making the accusation against Durrands.

Why he had accused Durrands rather than Maddocks I leave for you to ponder. It might have been a slip of the pen, understandable under such extreme circumstances. Or he might have intended to write Maddocks's name after Durrands's and lost consciousness before he was able to.

But there you have it. A simple enough story, really.

When the Major's story ended, there was a silence. Mrs. Armytage sat staring into space with one hand clutching the young lady's arm. She had been doing so ever since a moment in the story when she had suddenly gasped and stared at the Major, who carried on as if he had noticed nothing. (It was the moment when he had talked of a guilty person being pursued for the sake of vengeance by a descendant of the individual he or she has wronged many years before.) The Parson broke the silence by saying he was entirely baffled by why the wretched victim had accused Durrands rather than Maddocks, for it was the latter who had set the trap for him. The Major shook his head with a little smile.

The Parson then said he was also puzzled by the fact that there really was treasure hidden in the cave. The Major replied that either it must have been hidden there by mere chance or else Maddocks had gone so far as to put it there in order to lend the story plausibility—though it was not clear to him what purpose could have been served by this. The Parson replied that it was apparent from the Major's reply that he believed the map had been forged since he ignored the most obvious possibility: that the treasure was there in conformity with the inscription. In that event, it was presumably Durrands who had forged it. The Major looked somewhat surprised and then laughed. After a moment he pointed out that if the map was a forgery, then the perpetrator might have been the Parsi or even the trader who had sold it to Durrands.

The Parson wondered if Durrands really was unacquainted with the district of Edwardesabad. He might have visited it and then forged the map. Or if he had not forged the map, perhaps he had recognized the landscape to which it referred and had set the whole trap up from the very beginning.

The Major smiled and asked Mrs. Armytage if we might be permitted to know her view of that interpretation. But the old lady shook her head slowly as if stunned and neither looked at him nor made any reply. Still looking into her face, though she held it away from him, the Major asked her in a very serious tone if he might address a question to her. She now looked at him with an expression of alarm. Indeed, I might even say, of terror. When she made no answer, the Major put to her slowly and solemnly the question whether she thought a man had a duty to defend the honor of his mother as much as that of his wife? She turned quite pale. Her mouth dropped open and she turned away and gripped the young lady's arm even harder.

The Parson, with the innocent intention of changing the subject, quickly remarked that he believed he had been told that the scorpion was an ancient symbol of vengeance, and that it was used in that sense within Masonic rituals—of which, of course, he thoroughly disapproved. To his astonishment, the old lady uttered a cry of alarm or despair at this apparently harmless remark.

At this moment the Driver stood up and came closer to where the rest of the party was seated. In doing so he recalled us to our increasingly desperate plight. It was now late in the evening and had got even colder. The snow was being driven with increasing ferocity through the door and the broken window and was accumulating on the floor of the room around us.

The three men in the party now discussed the situation. The Driver said that it was most unlikely that our rescuers—assuming the Guard had succeeded in summoning them—would be able to reach us until the following day. We therefore had to consider the dangers involved in staying there overnight, when the temperature would drop even further. It was obviously pointless to attempt to return to the train, which might by this time be buried under several feet of snow. Now the Driver suggested that we should make for the shelter of the nearby Castle Killiecrankie, which he insisted was within a mile or two of where we now were. Mrs. Armytage and the young woman looked at each other as soon as the name of the castle was uttered.

The Parson asked what the Castle was and whom it belonged to, and the Driver said that it had been shut up for many years, ever since the old laird, Sir Rudolph, had been taken away. He had left no heir, and his widow had married again and moved south. He added that it was said that her second husband had recently died and that she was coming back to live in the Castle, but as far as he knew, she was not in residence yet. But he believed that a housekeeper and small indoor staff were living there and preparing it for occupation.

The Driver strongly urged that we should make for the Castle. Mrs. Armytage, suddenly abandoning her silence, joined him in advocating this course of action. The Parson, however, resisted the proposal on the grounds that we were comparatively safe where we were and would face all manner of dangers outside. The Major then gave his opinion, which was that, on balance, it was safer to make for the Castle than to stay. At this moment Mrs. Armytage suddenly changed her mind and insisted that the way to the Castle would be far too dangerous. We had only two inadequate lanterns and none of us knew the path, she asserted. The four of us (leaving out the young lady, who expressed no opinion) were now equally divided, and so the proposal to leave the halt was abandoned in the face of the old lady's vehement opposition, despite the Major's strongly expressed irritation. For about an hour there was virtually no conversation as we listened to the howling of the wind and strained our ears for the sounds of rescue that none of us really expected. At the end of that time the Driver went outside and came back a moment later to warn us that the blizzard was so heavy that it was threatening not merely to engulf the shelter entirely but to crush it. The Major went outside to look at the situation and came back to confirm the truth of what the Driver had reported. The rickety wooden shelter was close to collapse under the weight of the snow building up on its roof.

The Driver and the Major therefore renewed their insistence that we should make for the Castle. Mrs. Armytage objected strongly again. She seemed very frightened indeed. She suddenly said that she wanted to say more about the story she had told us. She wanted to explain something. She had not quite told us the truth. She wanted to apologize, even to confess.

The Major interrupted her, however, saying that the time for stories was over. Now it was time for action. The old lady looked at him in frank terror. The rest of us stood up and prepared to depart, but she remained seated, even though her companion rose to her feet. She almost shouted, saying that it was madness to leave the safety of the station and *entrust our lives to a dangerous path through deep snow and across rugged and treacherous terrain.*

The Driver insisted that he knew how to reach the Castle even though he had never approached it from this direction. We should follow the track a little farther along the top of the hill. Then we had to turn down to the left through a small pine wood until we came to the edge of a cliff, beyond which were the grounds of the Castle. We had only to get down the cliff—the most difficult part of the journey—and we would be half a mile from the Castle itself across gentle parkland.

The Driver spoke with impressive authority, and so, despite Mrs. Armytage's protests, it was agreed that we should set off. The old lady had to be pulled to her feet by the Driver and the young lady, but then she seemed to resign herself to what had been decided. When we left the building, the snow was swirling about so thickly that we could see ahead of us no more easily than in the most impenetrable London fog. We advanced along the track in single file—the Major in front with one lantern, then the Parson, the young lady, Mrs. Armytage, and finally the Driver with the other lantern. At times we had to hold on to the person in front because we could see so poorly. We walked for a period of time that could not be determined—something between five minutes and half an hour. Then the Driver called out that we should leave the track and go down the hill to our left. We did so and passed, with considerable difficulty, through the pine trees of which he had spoken. As we were making our way down the slope, the Major stopped suddenly and saved the rest of us from certain death. For now as we peered into the white mist ahead of us, a gust of wind blew the eddying snow back for a moment and we saw to our horror that we were at the very edge of the cliff. It was almost as if he knew the district. What a wonder to be a military man! The Driver admitted that he had not expected the cliff to be where it was and that he was confused about the direction we should now pursue. Then to the astonishment of all—or most—of us, Mrs. Armytage suddenly cried out that she knew where we were and insisted that there was a landmark a few hundred yards to our right that indicated where there was a waterfall, and a little farther on we would find steps down the side of the cliff. We should look for a tall, narrow rock that stuck up from the top of the cliff, she said. We cautiously made our way along the top of the cliff to the right and indeed found the landmark the old lady had described. We had no leisure to speculate on how she had known it was there. Here a little stream—or burn—did indeed run over the cliff edge and form a cascade. A few yards farther along we came to the steps of which Mrs. Armytage had spoken. Now we were faced with a choice between going down the steps and following the cliff edge.

Mrs. Armytage spoke for the steps. She argued that at the foot of the cliff we would find a bridge over the stream and then a path would lead us straight to the Castle a short distance away.

The Major argued strongly for continuing along the edge of the cliff, which, he said, gradually sloped down until it reached ground level. At that point we would be only a couple of hundred yards away from the Castle.

The old lady angrily insisted that this was wrong. The Castle was to our left, not to our right. And the cliff continued a long way. If we took the Major's advice, we would have to make a lengthy circuit of several miles through the park with no path to guide us or landmarks to steer by. Anything could happen, she said. And the edge of the cliff was the most dangerous place to walk.

The Driver said he thought Mrs. Armytage was right, but he wasn't certain. At last, however, he and the Parson decided to take the Major's advice and follow the edge of the cliff. With hindsight, the other way would have been safer, but all our instincts were against entrusting ourselves to those perilous steps. We felt this, I believe, all the more powerfully after hearing the story that the Major had told us. Mrs. Armytage was apparently so frightened at the prospect of taking the long route that it was only with great difficulty that she could be dissuaded from venturing down the steps in the dark on her own—an absurdly dangerous undertaking. Though as it turned out, it might have been safer for her.

We set off again. And now Mrs. Armytage, who was very frightened and angry, insisted on bringing up the rear. It seemed to the Parson that she was determined to be as far away as possible from the Major. So when we began to make our way along the cliff edge, the Major was once again the leader, with the Parson behind him, then the Driver carrying the second lantern, and finally the young lady and Mrs. Armytage brought up the rear.

Somehow it happened—perhaps because the Major was going so fast (though at no point did the Major get so far ahead of the Parson that he was lost to the other man's sight)*—that Mrs. Armytage was left behind. For after ten or twenty minutes the young lady came hurrying up and by means of gestures and facial expressions indicated that her companion was some distance to our rear.*

The Major immediately offered to go back. The young lady, however, pointed at him and frowned, shaking her head all the while. Then she pointed at the Driver and the Parson and nodded and smiled. Looking very unwilling, the Driver went back with his lantern. After a short time he reappeared saying he could find no trace of the old lady. So now, despite the young lady's unease, the Major retraced his steps.

He was away for some time. It was impossible to judge how long. Perhaps five minutes. Or perhaps twenty. One or two of us thought we heard raised voices and a scream, but with the sound of the wind in the trees it was impossible to be sure. Though nobody at the time mentioned hearing anything of that nature. The truth is quite simply that the Major went back the way they had come, following the tracks in the snow and calling out. There was simply no sign of the old woman at all. So after a time he turned back and rejoined the others. *Then he came back saying he could not find her. The Driver now went back yet again, but he too returned—after a much shorter time—with the same conclusion. We felt we had no alternative but to continue along the edge of the cliff, for our own lives were in grave peril. The difficulties we experienced in making our way across the park to the Castle—for Mrs. Armytage had been right about its position—considerable as they were, are not relevant to this account.*

The old lady's death was most unfortunate, but there seems no obvious reason to suppose anything but that in attempting to follow her young companion when she had gone ahead to ask the rest of us to walk more slowly, she took the wrong track in the darkness and the driving snow and fell over the edge. The discovery of her body on the frozen lake at the foot of the cliff the next day supports this, though admittedly some of her injuries seem somewhat inconsistent with this explanation.

CHAPTER

3

"The New Surgeon at St. Oswald's"

Editorial Department: Romance
Title: The New Surgeon at St. Oswald's
Author: Lavinia Armitage
Reader: Morag McCoo
Date: November 23, 1957

Recommendation:

This manuscript, by an author that I understand we haven't used her before, shows a high degree of litterary competance but is unacceptably marred by it's wholly inapropriate ending, which seems to come from a novel of a quite a different genre. In this part of the market one simply cannot afford to confuse genres. But a simple rewriting of the final chapter would solve these problems, and provided that is done satisfactorily—and also that a few smaller revisions are made—I would recommend this manuscript for publication as a potentially very commercial proposition. For the future, it must be made quite clear to the author that she is wasting her time and ours if she offers us work in this condition. That being said, she clearly has a degree of ability that, rightly directed, could make money for the company and herself.

Or, on the other hand, the manuscript might be referred to

49

the editor of our *Gothic Horror* list, and then the author will have to be asked to substantially revise it.

The opening is good. The setting is a large hospital in which a young nurse, Marie Kelly, finds herself strangely attracted to an older surgeon, Mr. MacQuarrie, who is new to the hospital when she sees him for the first time.

She first saw him while she was in Surgical D with some of the other girls.

One of them whispered: "Who's he?" And another of them, it was June, said she'd heard he was the new surgeon.

"They say he's Scotch. Isn't he a dish?" she had said.

And then that stupid girl, April that thinks she's so pretty and so sophisticated, had the affrontery to say, "Oh, do you think so? I think he looks cruel. And he's old!"

Marie bit her tongue and said nothing. All right, he was well over thirty. But anybody that had eyes in her head could see that he was awfully handsome.

The new surgeon soon gets a reputation for being demanding and short-tempered with his nurses and for showing scant sympathy toward his patients, but Marie finds him increasingly intriguing, even though he has so far hardly even noticed her. She quickly realizes that he is romantically interested in a more senior nurse, Sheila Bartlett, who has always behaved spitefully toward Marie and who is obviously very taken with the handsome bachelor surgeon.

Marie couldn't help overhearing their conversation as she worked at the instrument cart. They were discussing books they had both read. From the number of books she mentioned, Sheila Bartlett, who was obviously showing off, must of spent a lot of time reading. And no wonder, thought Marie. For the life of her, she couldn't imagine what man would want to go out with her.

Yet Mr. MacQuarrie seemed to enjoy her company!

Marie could see how shamelessly she was flirting with him, and to her dismay he seemed to like it. How could he be interested in someone so plain and so dowdy!?

Just at that moment Sheila Bartlett glanced toward her and said sharply, "What are you doing here, Nurse Kelly? Be about your work. Quickly."

Just before she hurried out of the room, Marie looked at Mr. MacQuarrie and noticed that he was smiling in her direction, as if he was amused at her discomforture. Her eyes pricked with tears. Of course, he would find an older and more sophisticated woman attractive. She herself, she reflected ruefully, must seem no more than a schoolgirl to him. Then she tossed back her hair, and as she walked quickly down the corridor, anyone that was watching her would have seen a smile appear on her face and may have asked themself why the girl was grinning from ear to ear.

Marie talks to the surgeon for the first time when she assists while he is operating. (Here and in other places, incidentally, the manuscript will have to be rewritten to comply with house standards of taste since the language—which is too disgusting to quote—shows a complete misjudgment of what our readers are entitled to expect.)

As young Marie was removing his surgical gloves at the end of the operation, she was so nervous that she let the fingers slip and they flew back against his hand. "Ouch," he said softly, and the girl felt herself blush.

Then he leaned his head forward and said, still wearing his mask, "Clumsy wee girlie. But mebbe it's your time of the month?"

She nearly died. She was so embarrassed, she didn't know where to look. Luckily there was nobody else within earshot. Dumbly, she carried on tugging at the glove.

"Is it your time of the month?" he repeated. "Come, come, don't be shy. We're both medical people. Are you bleeding, girl?"

She lowered her eyes and nodded dumbly. She knew she had flushed bright red.

He reached out the hand that was now free of the glove and gently tweaked her gown.

"Blood," he breathed softly. She looked down and saw the green material was streaked with red smears. Then he brought his head closer to her and almost whispered, "The proper red stuff."

He turned away. And now Marie noticed Sheila Bartlett, who had been watching them curiously and must of seen her blushing. The older woman scowled at her maleviolently.

The more senior nurse, now deeply jealous of the girl, gets Marie into trouble deliberately by telling her to disconnect an intravenous tube from a patient just before Mr. MacQuarrie is due to commence operating.

"Do you mean this one?" she asked.

"Just do as I tell you, nurse," Sheila Bartlett said without looking in her direction.

She did what she had been told. A moment later Mr. MacQuarrie came into the operating room. He smiled at Sheila Bartlett and said, "Are my knives nice and sharp?"

She nodded with a stupid smile.

Then he turned toward Marie, and she felt her heart pounding. She couldn't look at him.

Then he spoke, "You, girl. What's your name?"

She told him in a firm but small voice, "I'm Marie Kelly, sir." (In fact, she had been christened Mary Jane but had always called herself Marie Jeanette.)

He said, "Speak up. I cannae hear you."

She repeated it more loudly, hoping he couldn't hear the tiny quaver in her voice.

Then to her dismay he shouted, "What the hell do you think you're playing at, Nurse Kelly?"

It sounded all the harsher in his Scotch accent.

He pointed toward the I.V. line, and Sheila Bartlett hurried over self-importantly and reconnected it.

The girl wanted to explain. It hadn't been her fault. But before she even had a chance to speak, he waved her out of the operating room and without glancing at her got on with plying his knife. As she ran down the adjacent corridor, she felt her eyes fill with tears. It was unfair. So unfair. But then the girl paused and said to herself, "Pull yourself to-gether, Marie." She resolved that she would keep her chin up and just show them all. And so with head held high she walked on down the corridor.

She becomes disallusioned with the surgeon, particularly now that she hears rumors about his insensativity toward his patients.

She told herself she had been a fool ever to let herself daydream about him. He was above her in almost every way. On his salary he must have a good lifestyle, she reflected. And he would want to marry someone that had the same sort of lifestyle. How silly she had been. Why, he was almost old enough to be her father. Well, not really. But not far off it. And yet she couldn't help telling herself that he was a lot more handsome and young-looking than her dad.

Now she let herself listen when the other girls gossiped about him, and she learned that his stern manner was making him enemies everywhere in the hospital. People said, as well, that too many of the patients he operated on died. And they told spiteful stories about the way he carried on in the operating room. She didn't—she couldn't—believe them. "Jock the Ripper" they called him, she heard. She was upset at that and was dying to refute these rumors, and yet she felt a sort of thrill of excitement when she heard such things.

Then one day Mr. MacQuarrie meets her when they are alone in one of the long corridors of the hospital and teases her by telling her that he has noticed that she always seems to avoid him now. He asks if she's afraid of him? After this he talks to her whenever they meet, but only so long as nobody else is present. In the presence of others he speaks to her only when necessary and very formally. So she thinks he is ashamed to be seen with her because she is just a junior nurse. In one of their brief conversations, they discover that they both live in adjacent districts of the city, and then one day, when she has finished at the hospital and is waiting at the nearby bus stop in the rain, he stops his car and offers to give her a lift home. She gets in and they have their first real conversation. Now his sensitivity emerges and he reveals a bit of himself to her when he tells her about his passion for painting. And he warns her to be careful because there is a sadistic murderer on the loose in the city.

"I love my work," he said. "But I know I'm not liked. My trouble is that I set myself the highest standards."

He paused for a moment and then went on quickly as if he'd decided to trust her.

"Let me tell you something. I'm an artist. Oh, I don't mean a proper one. I'm what they call a weekend painter. But once, when I was much younger—about your age, in fact—I really wanted to become a painter. But then I realized I hadn't got enough talent to be among the very best. And I'd settle for nothing less than the very best."

Marie realized that he was allowing her to see a wistful, thoughtful side of him that she had never seen on the wards or in the operating room.

He went on suddenly, as if embarrassed by how much of himself he had betrayed: "I was trying to explain to you about my high standards. You see, my problem is that I expect other people to measure up to them. I cannae suffer fools and mediocraties. I'm a fine surgeon. A damn fine surgeon. Despite what they say about me. Oh, I know all about that, don't you worry. What they don't say is that I take risks none of them would dare to take. I suppose the truth is that you need to be a bit of a brute to be a good surgeon."

She felt herself blushing at his words and didn't for the life of her know why.

After a moment he resumed the topic: "But I was talking about my art. I like to clear my head after an operation and I find that painting calms me down. One day you must see my work. That is, if you'd like to."

If she'd like to! She was dying to say how much she'd like to, only she couldn't trust herself to speak.

They drove for a few moments in silence and then, as he drew up outside her house, he asked, "Do you live alone?"

"No. I share a flat with another girl, Gail."

"Do you often go home at night on your own?" he asked, and she wondered if she was deceiving herself when she thought his voice vibrated tenderly.

She said she did. She wondered if she should get out or stay because he seemed to want to talk.

"You must be careful," he said. "You know about those incidents involving young girls around here?"

Of course she did! Everybody was talking about the sadistic sex murders that had commenced taking place recently.

Just as she commenced to reach for the door handle, he spoke: "Look," he said. "I know it's late, but there's a charming wee pub I know adjacent to the reservoir. It's called the Ten Bells."

Marie felt herself flush and her heart commence to pound. He was asking her out! Her, little Nurse Kelly! What would Sheila Bartlett think about that! At that moment she saw in the distance her friend turning the corner of the street. More to give herself time to think than for anything else, she said, "There's Gail now!"

It was a nuisance because she knew her inquisitive roommate would want to know who the car belonged to if she saw her getting out of it.

"Well, mebbe another time," Mr. MacQuarrie said brusquely, and reached across her to open her door. She found herself on the pavement, and the car drove off quickly.

Marie was left standing there stunned and baffled by the mixture of tenderness and rudeness Mr. MacQuarrie had shown toward her.

At that moment the wretched Gail came up.

"Hello," she said. "Did you just get off the bus?"

After this Marie tries for several weeks to bring about Mr. MacQuarrie's giving her a lift again by leaving the hospital at the time she knows he is going home. But each time he passes her, he fails to stop, and she fears that it is because she is in a line with other girls in nurse's uniform. And noticing that whenever they meet in front of other people, he gives the impression of barely knowing who she is, she decides that he is ashamed to be seen with her. Then Marie is brought in to assist at an important new operation that Mr. MacQuarrie is masterminding and that the other surgeons are known to be skeptical about. In the middle of it Marie has to take over her rival's job when the older nurse breaks down, and her good sense and calmness help to make the operation a success. (Again, some of the language here is quite unacceptable.) Mr. MacQuarrie is so pleased with her that he offers her a lift home.

*When she went into the scrub room later that afternoon to scrub up
for the operating room, everyone was talking about the nurse that had
been found the night before. Marie didn't know her at all because she
had worked in an adjacent part of the hospital.*

*While one of the operating-room nurses was giving a graphic descrip-
tion of what her friend had seen when she went out with the ambulance,
Marie noticed Sheila Bartlett looking pale and sickly.*

*When the girl had finished her account, Mr. Worsdall, the senior reg-
istrar, said to Mr. MacQuarrie, "Did you know her, MacQuarrie?"*

*He answered, "I barely knew her by face. I didnae know her name."
Then, in an undertone so soft that Marie thought that only she must
have heard it, he added, "Poor wee lassie."*

*"Her injuries were quite unusual," Mr. Worsdall commented. "I
thought they might interest you. I thought of you when I heard about it.
It was almost as if the killer had botched an abdomenal operation."*

*Sheila Bartlett uttered a little gasp at this. The Scotchman, however,
said nothing.*

*"Is anything wrong, Nurse Bartlett?" Mr. Worsdall asked. "You look
somewhat ill."*

*"It . . . it's just that I knew the girl quite well," she stammered. "But
I'll be all right, I'm sure."*

They went into the operating room and the operation began.

*As scrub nurse Marie's task was to work under the nurse dealing with
the instruments and swabs. Sheila Bartlett, as a more senior nurse, was
helping the anesthesiologist by monitoring the patient's condition. At the
same time, she was holding the retractor to keep the wound open for Mr.
MacQuarrie.*

*She was having difficulty doing both things at once and, only a few
minutes into the operation, when her hand slipped on the retractor and
it nicked an artery, Mr. MacQuarrie had to reprimand her quite sharply.*

*"Keep your mind on the job, will you?" he demanded. "Or do you
want this one's blood all over the damned floor, too?"*

*Sheila Bartlett started at this, and Marie thought she saw her literally
blench beneath her surgical mask. But Mr. MacQuarrie's words didn't
seem to have any effect on her because before long the same problem occurred again.*

*This time he turned to her and almost shouted, "Can't you manage
to concentrate for five minutes, woman? You're not reading one of your
damned whodunnits now. If you don't buck your ideas up, we're going
to have a real corpse on our hands in a moment."*

Sheila Bartlett gave a cry and burst into tears.

"Out," Mr. MacQuarrie ordered, pointing toward the exit with his bloody scalpel. "You're no damn use to me in that state."

Sheila Bartlett rushed out of the room in tears.

Mr. MacQuarrie watched her go and then remarked, "Nurse number one squealed a bit."

It was so funny the way he said it that Marie laughed in spite of herself. He glanced at her and said, "Have you ever monitored the patient's blood pressure during an operation, Nurse Kelly?"

She shook her head dumbly.

"Or used a retractor?"

She had to shake her head again.

Despite the presence of the other and more senior doctors, he was taking control in his typically masterful manner.

"Damn," he exclaimed. "Are there nothing but kids here? Well, you'll just have to try. Do exactly as I tell you."

Though she was somewhat awed at first by the hissing valves and numerous counters, Marie forgot her fears once she found herself absorbed in the demands of the complicated machine. At the same time she found she had the requisite manual dexterity to quite satisfactorily operate the retractor as well. And yet, even though she was concentrating wholly on her task, all the time as she worked she was thinking about Mr. MacQuarrie with a part of her mind—his strong hands in the rubber gloves cutting, stitching, tying, squeezing. And when their gaze met, she was sure that his eyes above the surgical mask were smiling encouragement at her.

Then suddenly it was all over.

Mr. Worsdall pulled off his surgical gloves and mask, said something she couldn't catch to Mr. MacQuarrie, and strode out of the room.

Suddenly she was very tired. She followed Mr. MacQuarrie out. In the postoperative tension, there was silence in the adjacent scrub room. The others hurried away. And in a few moments she and Mr. MacQuarrie were alone.

Mr. MacQuarrie looked at her and said gently, "You kept your head. That's the main thing."

She felt her face and neck burn with pride. She raised her chin and smiled at him.

She saw the weariness in his face and suddenly realized how tired he must be. He had worked for hours and hours with maximum concentration. He must be exhausted.

Then he said, "The operation works, young Marie."

He knew her Christian name!

"It works, and I've proved that it works. It's a crying shame we didnae manage to bring the patient with us, but next time we will. I'm sure of it."

He had said "we"!

He looked at her with those burning, intense eyes of his and said, "You were more than adequate. You did well. You have a natural talent for anesthesia."

With the exhaustion and now this display of his interest in her, she found her legs giving way and slid suddenly onto a bench.

"How selfish I'm being," he exclaimed. "You're exhausted! And if my calculations are right, it must be that time of the month again, mustn't it?"

Too tired to be embarrassed, she nodded.

He gave her a dazzling smile that lit up his tired face and said, "Tell you what, I'll run you home. Only don't tell anyone, or they'll all expect the same treatment. Meet me at the corner of Corporation Street in five minutes."

Once they are in the car, Mr. MacQuarrie suggests they go to a pub to celebrate the success of the operation. There Marie has a little more to drink than she is accustomed to and agrees to his suggestion that they should drive to a beautiful spot he knows with a lovely view. When they reach it, he parks the car down a lane on a hill overlooking the city. It's a warm summer night and by now it's about midnight. They get out of the car and as they walk a little way down the hill to a small wood situated nearby, he takes her hand. He states that he has found himself thinking about her the whole time. When she asks him if he doesn't care for Sheila Bartlett, he informs her the older nurse is nothing to him and he has been amused by watching her try so hard to win his attention. I quote the final page, all of which is fine and in tune with what our readers would expect, down to the very end, where something highly distasteful occurs that is wholly inappropriate in the context. This is the only part of the manuscript that needs to be rewritten—apart from a few minor revisions that I've already mentioned about—but the revision need only affect the final three or four sentences:

"But let's not talk about Sheila Bartlett," he said. "Let's talk about us."

As he said these words, he drew her gently toward him.

"About why you're here, Marie. Just you and me in this lonely place. And nobody else even knows." She saw his smile in the moonlight. "Nobody saw you get into my car."

She was so dazzled by his smile that she said nothing.

"Did they?" he added. "Did anyone see you?"

"No, Mr. MacQuarrie," she murmured.

Was he so afraid of anyone finding out that they had been seeing each other outside the hospital? Had she been wrong when she thought he was ashamed to be seen with her? Was the truth that he was seriously interested in her?

"Call me Jack," he said gently.

They were now just inside the trees. The foliage rustled gently in the warm breeze. At that moment the moon passed behind a cloud.

"Turn around, my darling," he murmured with his mouth pressed against her ear so that his breath was warm.

She obeyed. In the next instant his hands were on her, so strong, so masculine. One arm was around her neck. He was fumbling at his trousers and pulling something out. He was behind her now.

He was skillful and so experienced that she hardly felt it when he did it to her. She wouldn't have known what was happening if it hadn't been that just before she lost consciousness, she saw her own blood spurting down the front of her nicely cleaned and starched uniform.

The Medicine Man

Introduction:

Everyone has read about the scandal—*l'affaire Galvanauskas,* as the French press has called it—that has recently overtaken and in the eyes of some people discredited one of the leading theorists of Post-structuralist psychoanalysis.

Much has been written on the subject—articles in popular magazines as well as essays in scholarly journals. Much of it by people who knew nothing of either the facts or the ideas at stake. Galvanauskas himself has, of course, remained characteristically silent and has offered no explanation or defense. I am writing this because I believe him to be—in all but the most grossly literal sense—entirely innocent of these charges.

I myself have now been accused of serious offenses, both by Galvanauskas's supporters and by his detractors. I am writing now to offer a defense against the charges of plagiarism, deception, and theft that have been unfairly and vindictively brought against me by some of my former associates.

As is well known, I am the author of the first authoritative account of Galvanauskas's work, *Unmasking Strategies of Desire: Texts, Power, and the Phallus in the Work of Henri Galvanauskas.* That book is a lucid account of Galvanauskas's work and is designed to be read in conjunction with *Dits,* my collection in three volumes of the Master's crucial essays in their first accurate translation. (I have also edited a collection of the *Aphorisms*.)

I want to explain here the circumstances in which I wrote that book and show that, although I did so without his explicit consent and knowledge, I acted with the best of intentions toward Galvanauskas and in order to publicize and explain his work and teachings. I wanted to rescue him from his own closest admirers and even, in a sense, from himself. In doing so I have suffered quite unfairly from attacks orchestrated by his inner circle.

I am therefore writing this as a factual account in order to put an end to the circulation of grotesque rumors about the sequence of events that led to the Institute's most recent removal.

I should make it clear that I am still profoundly sympathetic to Galvanauskas's ideas, even though he and his circle have disavowed and condemned me.

The Fragmentary Transmission of Galvanauskas's Work:

Galvanauskas is, of course, famous in the world of literary theory, psychoanalysis, and philosophy for having never published a single word under his own name. He is also famous—or even notorious—for his so-called silent sessions. (Numerous lurid rumors are in circulation about these occasions. Having attended many of them, I am in a position to assert that with two or three exceptions nothing controversial ever took place in my sight.)

There were many rumors in circulation about the reason for his unwillingness to publish. His refusal to be photographed or interviewed on television has, since the publication of Gicquiaux's book, also been given a sinister interpretation.

Whatever the reason, the effect was that his work was only known in fragmentary form. His ideas were passed about by word of mouth by those who attended his seminars in Paris. And since transcripts and recordings of any kind were strictly prohibited during Galvanauskas's sessions, one might assume that only an oral tradition existed.

Nevertheless, there had circulated from the 1950s onward transcripts of a number of his seminars that appeared to be verbatim accounts that had presumably been surreptitiously recorded during the seminars. These were known and referred to by the place they had been given or the date or the topic: "The

Dijon Seminar," "The December 1968 Seminar," "The Seminar on Worship and Sacrifice in *The Black Heart*." These transcripts were photocopied and circulated in the most corrupt form: faintly printed, sometimes incoherent, mostly in very poor English, but with long passages and lengthy quotations left in French or sometimes German.

Incoherent though they were, these mysterious pieces of paper were eagerly passed about, discussed, and quoted in learned articles and books, where their meaning was fiercely debated.

Few could seriously deny that Galvanauskas's work represented an exciting and provocative conjunction of ideas. Yet many scholars and theorists working in the same field, while acknowledging the originality of his work, were anxious to see the articulation of the whole, how the various elements of his thought fitted together.

His many detractors argued that his work was muddled, fantastic, trivial, and that the most interesting ideas were plagiarized. His defenders attributed the lacunae and apparent inconsistencies in the transcripts to the fact that the material was dealing with the most complex and subtle ideas and that it existed only in such a fragmentary form. Much could be gained from a close study of the transcripts, but they insisted that the only way fully to comprehend his work was to enroll as a member of the Institut des Recherches Galvanauskasiennes and attend his teaching and therapeutic sessions.

It was an extraordinary situation that in the modern age—the age of the fax, the word processor, and the database—work of such importance and originality should be known only by such unreliable and outdated means. But there was a further twist that made it even stranger.

The transcripts that existed had been pirated. That is to say, some unknown person or persons had on a number of occasions over a period of thirty years managed to record Galvanauskas's seminars in secret either by tape-recording them or by taking shorthand notes. There also remained, of course, the possibility that the documents were complete fabrications. It was all very intriguing and had contributed to the intense public interest in Galvanauskas.

Galvanauskas had disavowed all of the transcripts as grotesque misrepresentations, vulgarizations, and oversimplifications of his teaching. They were, he asserted, full of errors and distortions both in general and in detail, being riddled with mishearings and slips of the pen by the transcriber, mistranslations and mis-understandings.

He himself was said to be working on a distillation of his work in ten volumes that would show how the different elements of his thinking were articulated and would reduce his detractors to a state of complete silence—or, to be more accurate, wordless-ness. (I might mention that this work, which is eagerly awaited, has still not appeared.)

My First Encounter with Galvanauskas's Work:

My own involvement with the Institute came about in this way. It happened that toward the end of 1986, I was senior lecturer (the equivalent in U.S. terms of an associate professor) in the Department of English Literature at Glasgow University. I had been finding its provincialism somewhat stifling after six years away from London, where I had previously been employed at University College. Few of my colleagues were interested in the exciting new ideas, loosely known as Theory (or Critical Theory or Post-structuralism or Deconstruction), that were sweeping through what used to be called the humanities but were now be-ing called cultural studies. I am referring, of course, to the work of thinkers, sometimes called the Parisian Post-structuralists, such as Derrida, Lacan, Foucault, and Barthes.

Shortly, the work of these theorists has to do with interrogat-ing the dominant culture in order to reveal the contradictions and paradoxes on which its ideology rests, and then going on to unmask the strategies by means of which it attempts to conceal these internal conflicts and gaps.

I had been working for several years on a Theory of Pleasure in relation to reading in an attempt to account for the problem of why people read. In doing so, I was following up the implica-tions of some of the theoretical work of Roland Barthes on read-ing as *jouissance*, orgasm, in which the reader finds a kind of sexual pleasure in the play of the signifier. By that last phrase is meant the idea that language does not "communicate" in any straightforward and simple manner. Instead, anything in language which offers signification—the signifier—holds out the promise of full meaning but teasingly delays it. In this respect it functions in a manner analogous to the longings of sexual Desire, in which gratification is endlessly delayed. And this is more than a metaphor: The search for meaning is indeed a sexual quest. And the basic signifier is the penis, which is the mark of sexual difference—the most fundamental of all distinctions. Barthes was attacking the traditional "commonsense" notion of the text as having some sort of definable meaning that is placed in it by the author and imposes limitations on the free play of the signifier by means of this "authority." Barthes was wholly convincing in his dismissal of the claims of the author to be the source of this authority, and this had become one of the most firmly held tenets of Post-structuralism.

It seemed to me, however, that in looking for and finding meaning, the reader necessarily accepts that the text has some degree of authority that limits his freedom to adopt a divergent reading. Barthes's model of reading as a kind of sexual congress, attractive though it was, took no account of the reader's engagement with at least some kind of authority constituted by or through the text, without which no meaning at all could be communicated. For Barthes, reader and text were on all fours, taking turn and turn about in a game of dominance and submission between equals. So much was clear enough. But there was, I thought, a crucial question that needed to be answered in relation to the text-act—that is, the act of reading: Who is the dominant partner—the text or the reader? And how is this relationship established? And if the reader submits to some degree of authority, how can this be pleasurable?

It was now that I encountered Galvanauskas's famous essay "Lo(o)sing the Signifier: Silence, Wordlessness and Desire in Kipling's 'The Tongueless Boy.' " My introduction to it came about like this.

I had organized and run for several years an interdisciplinary seminar to discuss the exciting new developments in the arena of Theory that were breaking upon us almost weekly. It was now that I presented a paper to that seminar on my work in progress, at the end of which a colleague accused me in the most crushing terms of failing to take into account the crucial work of

Galvanauskas on the role played by the unconscious and by desire in the process of reading.

This individual, whom I knew only very slightly, was called William Bentley and was a young lecturer in the Department of Philosophy. Talking to him after the seminar, I confessed that I was only vaguely familiar with the name of Galvanauskas, whom I knew to be the leading figure in the psychoanalytical tendency identified with the Post-Freudian Hermeneutics of Desire.

Bentley explained that Galvanauskas had succeeded in nothing less than welding together Marxism, psychoanalysis, linguistics, and philosophy to produce a materialist theory of language and the unconscious. And he had then succeeded in linking this with the Holy Grail of Theory—a persuasive Theory of Pleasure.

Bentley then gave me a barely legible photocopy of the transcript of the seminar given by Galvanauskas in which a story by Rudyard Kipling was being discussed. I read it that day and was astonished by it. Everything I had been working on was transformed. Some problems disappeared and new approaches were opened up. Before I go on to offer my version of recent events, I must give some account of the impact this essay had on me.

Galvanauskas's "Lo(o)sing the Signifier":

Though I did not realize it at the time, this was Galvanauskas's most famous reading of a text and the one that most succinctly exemplified the ideas on which the whole of his theory was founded. (In what follows I use my own revised edition of the transcript as reprinted in *Dits I* [pp. 123–58], edited by myself. I am grateful to Johns Hopkins University Press for permission to quote from this material.)

The subject was a novella apparently written by Kipling called "The Tongueless Boy," whose setting is a far-flung province of British India in the late nineteenth century.

Essentially, this is the story. (I should mention that since I have not been able to trace Kipling's original text, I have had to retranslate into English the somewhat unsatisfactory French version that Galvanauskas was working with.) A young English anthropologist, Huxtable, comes to a departmental subprefect in the capital and explains that he has been studying and living for several years among a remote tribe in a village in the hills. For the past year or so he has employed a boy as his servant and it is on account of this youth that he is here. He says he wants the subprefect's assistance since this young servant is being punished by the tribe for having stolen a crucial part of their totem. It is important to note that the story makes it clear that the boy has stubbornly remained in denial despite his master's attempts to persuade him to confess. The text is not, of course, concerned with the question of whether he is guilty of the theft or entirely innocent.

The subprefect returns to the village with the anthropologist and confronts the high priest of the tribe. His attempt to save the boy by means of logic and reason having failed, he admits defeat and gives way to the anthropologist. Huxtable now finds himself in confrontation with the high priest, who appears to be triumphant and wholly in control of the ritualized torture and execution being enacted. But in the last movement of the text, the anthropologist makes a decisive and successful intervention and defeats his opponent.

A fuller account of this important essay by Galvanauskas is to be found in the appendix at the end of this volume, and those interested in Theory should read it now (see pp. 329–37). I summarize it baldly and inadequately here, conscious that in being crudely shortened in this way, it loses much of its richness of reference and its persuasiveness.

Galvanauskas showed in the essay that both a reader and a text are always either "phallic" or "emasculated." The phallic text is dominant and duplicitous while the emasculated is submissive and unambiguous:

> What is this gap, this silence, from which the phallic text speaks and yet is silent? What is it but the text's phallus? What but, precisely and exactly, that phallic moment from which it has spinned himself like a disavowal, a lay [lie]. For what is a phallic text if not a lay [lie] which has to be demasked, his strategies witted out? [That is, "outwitted."]

The Kipling story, Galvanauskas demonstrated, is phallic. The boy is, like the text, rebellious and deceitful. He has tried to steal the idol's phallus/tongue and usurp his master's authority.

There is therefore not merely a contest for authority between Huxtable and the high priest but also one between the master and his boy. Both these contests are analogous to the struggle for authority that takes place either when a phallic reader reads and attempts to dominate a resisting phallic text, or when a psychoanalyst attempts to deal with a patient. In each case the interrogation that takes place is a struggle for possession of the phallus as the determinant of meaning.

It was to meet this situation that Galvanauskas had devised a form of interpretation/interrogation that depended upon the use of "silence" (a phallic strategy) and the imposition of "wordlessness" (a form of emasculation). In its classic form, the interrogee is not permitted to talk—and is sometimes even gagged —while the interrogator demands speech of him, even shouting and making threats of physical violence, which are sometimes acted upon. Galvanauskas had in the past had opportunities to put these ideas into effect in the most practical way and found them to be largely effective. For empirical proof of the success of his technique, Galvanauskas cited this work, which was carried out during the Second World War under conditions that were far from ideal for the conduct of scientific research. (Gicquiaux was to make much of this period of Galvanauskas's life by describing it out of context in his controversial biography.)

Galvanauskas showed how authority, at its most phallic, resolves an act of rebellion or betrayal by means of the "voluntary sacrifice" on the part of the text or the patient. This acceptance of authority is the basis of Galvanauskas's Theory of Pleasure, which rests on the idea that the phallic text deliberately allows itself to be entrapped by the phallic reader. So in Kipling's story Huxtable perceives what needs to be done and brings about the necessary "voluntary sacrifice" on the part of the boy by the decisive exercise of "phallic silence," which brings the story to its climactic resolution.

My Contribution to the Galvanauskasian Theory of Pleasure:

Galvanauskas was clearly reading Kipling in a translation into either French or German—and, from the passages quoted, which had been retranslated into English, the translation must have been a poor one. But the essay was itself badly translated from another language, and so it was hard to tell. Despite that, I was profoundly excited by it, for it was precisely what I needed to be able to go forward with my own work. Through the lacunae and incoherencies I sensed that Galvanauskas was formulating a theory of the utmost importance and persuasiveness.

It was in the first flush of excitement that I did the work in which I can modestly claim to have contributed an original idea to Galvanauskas's Theory of Pleasure. My suggestion was that in addition to being entrapped by the phallic reader in the way that Galvanauskas illustrated in his paper, the phallic text always betrays, entraps, and unmasks itself and does so precisely because it is evasive and duplicitous. It is, in effect, too clever for its own good, or, putting it idiomatically, too clever by half.

It happened that I had been working on a text that, I now perceived, very aptly illustrated this point. It was written by a medieval Arab writer, Haroun al-Saddiqi, but is known in the West because Washington Irving plagiarized it for his *Tales of the Alhambra* under the title "The Reflection." Irving distorted into a crudely anti-Muslim tract an original text that could not by any stretch of the imagination bear that interpretation.

Inspired, then, by this essay, I wrote a paper that, as it turned out, played a small role in the events that occurred in connection with the *affaire Galvanauskas*. It was entitled "Pleasure, Authority, and the Phallic Text: A Galvanauskasian Reading of al-Saddiqi's 'The Bait.'"

The text concerns a sultan who discovers that a member of his bodyguard is fornicating with one of his harem slaves. Just as the fornicating guard tries to conceal himself, so the phallic text hides and disguises itself and tries to evade the reader-critic (the sultan). The sultan, however, like the phallic reader, ingeniously traps and unmasks the text by making it reveal itself. He outwits the text because he has anticipated its moves and because the phallic text always betrays itself. In my reading I showed how the text/patient/guard attempts to hide and remain silent but is first lured into entrapping itself/himself, then forced into speech by the realization of being entrapped, and finally required to make a "voluntary sacrifice" before the authority of the sultan.

The Beginning of My Involvement with the Institute:

When I had read the essay on the Kipling story, I told Bentley how gratified I was to have been introduced to Galvanauskas's work. He asked me if I knew that he was coming to Glasgow in a few weeks to reside permanently?

I had no idea and was utterly astonished and had to be told the whole story. It turned out that Bentley had gone as a post-graduate student to Paris in the mid-1970s, largely in order to study under Galvanauskas. He had become a member of the Institute and had risen from trainee to counselor. In the last year he had qualified himself (in some way that I did not at that time understand) for further promotion, and Galvanauskas had recently appointed him to be associate director in recognition of his role in bringing about the Institute's removal to Glasgow.

A few months before, certain well-known events at the Sorbonne had occurred, and Galvanauskas had had to find a new base for the Institute outside France. Bentley had already formed a nucleus of young people dedicated to a study of his teachings in his own department. He suggested to Galvanauskas that he transfer the Institute to Glasgow and as an inducement procured for him a position at the university as a visiting professor.

When Galvanauskas accepted this invitation, Bentley had acquired on behalf of the Institute the leases on two adjoining flats near the university. (These were at the southern end of Otago Street—a dark and somewhat dilapidated street of old tenements by the river Kelvin.) Galvanauskas and his wife were to live in one of them, and across the landing would be the offices of the Institute and Galvanauskas's teaching and clinical rooms.

I was very excited by these developments and eagerly looked forward to the Institute's arrival. Bentley put my name forward for membership, it was accepted, and when I had paid the first annual membership dues, I became a member.

In the meantime, Bentley supplied me with all the transcripts of Galvanauskas's sessions that were in his possession. I read them a number of times with close attention. They were very difficult to understand, but I became increasingly convinced of the importance of what was being said.

At last I met Galvanauskas. One day early in 1987 Bentley took me to the offices of the Institute in Otago Street shortly after his arrival. I had no idea what I would find since he had always, as is well known, refused to be photographed or interviewed on television or even to let his voice be recorded.

As soon as I entered the room, I knew I was in the presence of a remarkable man. I was struck first by the hooded, watchful eyes with their intense stare that seemed to penetrate deeply into you. The head was held low and slightly forward as if craning to hear your slightest whisper. He was smaller than I had expected and burlier. He had a reddish, broad face and usually wore tiny rimless spectacles. His personal appearance was always meticulous—he was on virtually all occasions dressed in beautifully tailored suits and handmade shirts. He was immaculately shaven and—in a little betrayal of personal vanity—the thin wisps of hair were always carefully brushed over his otherwise bald head.

He was a man of quite astonishing presence, and one of the most striking aspects of this was the way he exhibited his notoriously sudden changes of mood from affability to barely suppressed anger. One would receive a warm, almost overwhelming reception and then be the victim of a sudden, impatient and even brutal dismissal.

On this first occasion he came forward and greeted me with considerable warmth, holding my arm in both hands for several minutes as if reluctant to let me go. We spoke in French, for Galvanauskas's English was poor.

Bentley introduced me with the words "He is a professor, *cher maître*. He teaches at the university."

"A teacher!" he exclaimed. "Ah! That it is possible to be. But to be a philosopher. To be Galvanauskas."

He shrugged charmingly as if to imply that he was amused by his own dismay at the magnitude of his responsibility.

"And so, my friend," he went on with a twinkle. "You are one who teaches, and you therefore imagine you have something to teach me?"

I said that on the contrary I believed I had a great deal to learn from him.

He smiled and said, "No, I see in your face that you believe you know things I do not know. You are wrong, as you will find out. You will find out that you have been wrong about many things. And let me from the first be absolutely clear. If you wish to understand my thinking, you must accept my discipline. My thinking is not to be taken in samples like a lucky dip. It is a whole. A seamless whole."

I told him I fully understood that and said that I had begun, in my reading of the fragmentary transcripts, to perceive how the various elements of his theory fitted together, and said that this was something I hoped to grasp better now that I would have the opportunity of hearing him speak in person.

He looked at me with great intensity for several seconds. And then, as if speaking to himself, he said, "I wonder. Dare I think that you might be the one to carry on my work? The one I have been looking for ever since I became aware of my own mortality?" Then he hesitated and added, "I think perhaps not, for although, my friend, you have rare qualities of intellect and dedication, you are arrogant and ambitious and you carry betrayal deep in your heart."

Strangely upset by this reproach, I told him that he was wrong about me.

He smiled and said he had expected me to say that. It merely proved the truth of what he had just said: that I was both arrogant and evasive.

He said this with such a charming smile that it was impossible to be offended.

On this first occasion as on all later ones, I found there was no way to outflank him. It was as if he had anticipated my every move even before I had thought of it.

I told him I hoped his stay in Glasgow would be long and fruitful and that I would endeavor to further his work with all my resources.

As I was speaking, he was smiling. Suddenly the smile disappeared and he snapped, "We shall see. I have work to do."

He turned and seated himself at a desk with his back to us.

I was astonished by this behavior, to which I later became, if not inured, at least accustomed. Bentley tugged at my sleeve to indicate that we should depart.

As we left the room, we were accosted by a tall, lean woman of quite striking appearance. Bentley introduced us, and I learned that this was Madame Galvanauskas. She had a high, sharp nose with deep-set and glittering, almost black eyes. She wore (at all times, as I was to discover) clothes that were in the style of the 1920s, made in material that had a glossy sheen like the plumage of some rich, exotic bird. And as if to confirm this effect, she wore a feather boa and elaborate feathers in her hat. She explained in quite good English that in order to attend a seminar, I had to sign the usual pledge of silence. She produced a formal document undertaking to reveal nothing of what passed at the sessions, and I signed it.

I might as well admit here that I never established good relations with Madame Galvanauskas, and many of the difficulties I later experienced can be traced to this fact.

My First Seminar Therapy:

A few days later I went to the first of Galvanauskas's seminar therapies. I use that term since one of the most controversial aspects of his work was the way in which he combined teaching with therapy. I had been warned by Bentley that Galvanauskas imposed certain conditions. As I already knew, nobody was permitted to take any notes or to use any sort of recording device. To this end one of his circle searched everyone at the door, removing pencils and pens and frisking for hidden devices. Galvanauskas also imposed absolute silence on those present. Except on rare occasions, nobody ever spoke except himself, and often he, too, remained silent. There might be silence for several hours, at which point he might begin to speak, or on the other hand he might walk suddenly from the room as a signal that the session was over. Another unusual rule was that until the moment when Galvanauskas left, nobody could leave the room during the session for any reason at all including the needs of nature. Anyone who did so was banned from ever attending another session because, it was reasoned, to leave the room was to give way to a fundamental desire of the id to destroy Galvanauskas by silencing his flow of speech and, in effect, "evacuating" him.

On this occasion there was complete silence for about an hour. Then Galvanauskas suddenly began to talk. I say "began to talk," but the words are inadequate to describe his speech. He spoke with an intensity and a power that held the listener in fascinated awe, even though actual understanding came and went only in flashes. I felt all the time that I was teetering on the edge of a deep abyss of comprehension, dizzy with the anticipation of falling though I never did quite fall. It would be impossible to summarize in retrospect the content of his lecture, so mercurial and elliptical were the shifts from one topic to another. He was speaking French most of the time but occasionally went into German, which I could follow only imperfectly, and sometimes into a strange version of English, which I found almost as difficult because of his thick accent and unidiomatic phraseology. Sometimes I wasn't sure what language he was speaking. He seemed to be inventing words, making puns from Greek into English, French, Latin, or German in a way that few if any of his listeners could follow.

Another of the factors that made his speech difficult to follow was the way he would refer allusively to his own work with phrases like "As I proved in 'The Bordeaux Seminar' . . ." "As my analysis of Freud's notion of *Missbrauch* showed in 'The Riposte to Derrida' . . ." "As I demonstrated in the 'Dismissal of de Man' and again in the 'Evacuation of Foucault.' "

His talk ranged over the whole field of Western philosophy and thought, making subtle distinctions, brilliantly encapsulating a complete philosophical tradition in a phrase, or brushing aside whole centuries of error.

As I listened, I was filled with the absolute conviction that this man had the insight to penetrate the deepest recesses of humanity even though I was unable to follow him the whole way. I was overwhelmed by the profundity of his thought. It was clear to me that his thinking was profounder than even Heidegger's. Shortly, it was some of the profoundest thinking I had ever encountered.

Galvanauskas's starting point on that first occasion was a novel by the British writer Joseph Conrad called *The Black Heart.* The text takes the form of a confession in which someone is telling some unnamed and undescribed listeners (one of whom is presumably recording the occasion) the story of a man who goes into the jungle of Africa to search for his father and his brother, who have gone on an expedition and are now missing. (The story takes place at the close of the last century.) He makes his way up a long and dangerous river into the heart of the continent. There he at length succeeds in locating a heathen tribe who were the last known contacts of his missing relatives. He lives with them for some months, but they will tell him nothing about the fate of his father and brother. Yet he is sure that they know something. They have an idol that is kept in a certain isolated hut that he, as an outsider, is not allowed to visit. He once or twice glimpses the idol from a distance while it is being carried around the village during rituals, from which he is excluded, and sees that it resembles a human figure but is only about three feet high and is weirdly painted in bright colors. One night he sneaks to the idol's hut since he knows that during the hours of darkness it is guarded only by an old man. By the light of his lantern he is astonished to discover that the idol is alive, is, in fact, a human being. And then, to his utter horror, he recognizes the idol as his father. His limbs have been amputated, his tongue cut out, and his body hideously tattooed and painted, but the man is still alive and fully conscious. He has become the tribe's god—worshiped, sacrificed to, but in pain and mute.

At this point I recall that Galvanauskas lowered his voice and said in a gentle, almost reproachful tone, "My friends, I am that idol. You worship me, but I am in pain, powerless, and if not literally mute, I can tell you nothing." One of the younger women, Sonia, began to weep softly.

To return to the story, the man tells the elderly guardian, who of course is terrified at the white man's intrusion, that the poor creature is his father. And the old African explains to him that it is because his father has done something hideous that he has been elevated into a god by the tribe, who both venerate and fear him for having broken some crucial taboo. (The nature of the taboo is not revealed within the text.) To satisfy and placate him, the tribe carry out before his eyes once every year the most horrific ritual sacrifices of young girls. The man tries to interrogate his father, but he cannot communicate with the poor tongueless and armless wretch. The narrator of the story writes, "With the dark, vivid hush and yet soft whisperings of the jungle behind them, the man demanded to his father what he had done, why had this happened to him, and what had become of his brother? From the mutilated and garish face the agonized eyes stared back at him, illustrating the truth that the guilt which cannot be uttered is the most terrible." Unable to endure the sight of his staring eyes in his speechless face, the man kills his father. He makes no attempt to escape, and the next morning he is found by the natives beside the dead body. The idol's elderly guardian is killed in the most horrible fashion for having permitted this desecration. Expecting to die at their hands in the same way, the man finds himself instead elevated into a god. By committing the terrible act of killing his own father, he becomes himself the thing he kills—a god, an all-powerful idol before whom girls will be tortured to death. The price he pays is the amputation of his limbs and tongue.

That is the end of the story—except that someone asks its narrator how he knows the story since the central figure presumably ended his days unable to communicate. The narrator merely stares at his questioner, the text records, "with all the misery and sadness and guilt in the world."

That first seminar lasted six hours. (I was to discover that they could vary in length from a few minutes—if Galvanauskas dismissed his audience at the very start—to all day and sometimes all night as well.) At the end of it Galvanauskas reached a kind of climax. Then he suddenly dropped his voice to a whisper and said very gently and with a sweet smile, "Everybody leave me now except Sonia." Sonia was one of the youngest of the postgraduates in Bentley's department whom he had recruited to the Institute. And I was to learn that it was usually his practice to require one of the younger students—usually a girl but sometimes a young man—to stay behind at the end of a seminar to go over some of the things that had been raised.

The Work of the Institute:

In the months that followed I became increasingly familiar with the work of the Institute.

This mainly took place at the somewhat shabby offices in Otago Street rather than at the university, which Galvanauskas rarely if ever visited. There was some effort on the part of the philosophy department to persuade him to do some teaching, but he insisted that he was doing at the Institute the work he had agreed to do for the university.

Much of the Institute's work was also conducted in a nearby restaurant, where Galvanauskas lunched and dined and in effect held court. He would occupy a seat by the window, and when he saw someone passing—usually a student—who he thought looked like a suitable candidate for the Institute, he would indicate this to Madame Galvanauskas, who would run out into the street and attempt to interest the passerby in membership. Most of the candidates for admission to the lowest level of membership were young women. He would often generously waive or reduce the fees for young trainees whom he was anxious to admit. When taxed for his excessive indulgence, he would say, quoting himself, "The young are, in the end, the future" (*Aphorism 37*).

I should perhaps say something here about Galvanauskas's attitude toward women. First, the charge that he was hostile to them is nonsense. He adored women. In fact, he was only too fond of them. This is shown by the fact that they comprised nearly eighty percent of his trainees. Toward them he was almost invariably tender and gentle, the mild father whose occasional sternness derived from love. (Toward men he could display much harsher feelings, although here, too, he had his moments of tenderness.)

It is true that women were not permitted to speak at the seminar therapies. But it would be a gross misconception to assume from this fact that Galvanauskas undervalued or despised them. The important role played in his work and its promotion by Madame Galvanauskas suffices to expose that as a slander. Not to mention the time and attention that he devoted to his female disciples.

Apart from the routine administration—collecting the fees, disbursing salaries and expenses, expelling members for failure to pay, and so on—most of the work of the Institute involved taking candidates through the various degrees of affiliation: member, trainee, associate fellow, full fellow, counselor, and associate director. (Galvanauskas himself was the director.) I might add that all three of the first degrees were open to women. The administration of the initiation periods and the tests by which one proceeded to the next degree occupied a great deal of Galvanauskas's time and energy.

I will say something later about the allegedly more controversial practices involved in these procedures when I come to repudiate some of the wilder allegations made by renegades—like Gicquiaux—inspired by motives of spite and vengefulness. But I will state now that, far from encouraging sexual activity as has been alleged, Galvanauskas punished severely any male who attempted sexual relations with one of the female members. This, like all his actions, was part of a considered strategy by which, like Freud's original father of the primal horde, he placed himself between the younger males and the females in order to make himself the object simultaneously of fear and of veneration for the group.

It is not surprising that rumors were spread about Galvanauskas by his enemies, for he had many of them and was proud of this. As he liked to remind us, the more someone resists either Theory or the psychoanalyst, the more it shows how profoundly right the Theory or the psychoanalyst is because such a strong defense mechanism has been provoked into a response. Anyone who disagreed with Galvanauskas was, in effect, expressing the desire to murder him, and since he believed passionately in the need for revenge against someone who had offended, he kept a "Book of Enemies" in which a name was ceremonially inscribed during one of the seminar therapies, or from which a name was deleted when news came that the enemy concerned had died. (He often said that he was delighted to find that *"Nemo me impune lacessit"* was the national motto of Scotland and that that was why he felt so at home there.)

Opposition to the Institute:

A topic that was often discussed among the circle was the fact that somebody inside our circle was a secret enemy of Galvanauskas.

"One of you," Galvanauskas would say, looking around at us, "is a traitor to me and all of my work. One of you will betray me. One of you is as bad as that thieving asshole, Levavasseur, who betrayed me all those years ago. Or that bag of shit, Gicquiaux."

At the mention of the name of an enemy, we would all stand up and make evacuating gestures accompanied by appropriate sound-effects.

Levavasseur, as is well known, had been an early disciple who had plagiarized some crucial ideas from Galvanauskas for a book of his own that was published about five years before. He had been expelled in circumstances of considerable acrimony and had founded a rival school on the basis of the ideas he had stolen. Gicquiaux had been one of Galvanauskas's most trusted disciples and, in the reorganization of the Institute consequent upon the departure of Levavasseur and some of his friends, had shown such conspicuous loyalty that he had, once he had satisfied the necessary conditions, been raised to the degree of associate director. He had suddenly resigned about a year before, which was about the time when the decision to transfer the Institute out of Paris was made.

"For one of you," Galvanauskas would go on when everyone had protested his innocence, "betrayed me to those mediocrities at the Sorbonne with a pack of lies about that miserable, confused young woman. And that same individual has been recording and distributing versions of these sessions without my authority."

New transcripts were indeed circulating with accounts of the Glasgow seminars. And since I had attended them, I could see how distorted and partial they were.

Distortion seemed to shadow Galvanauskas. Many of the myths that have accumulated about his actions have arisen from a misunderstanding of his belief in the importance of keeping his disciples "up to the mark." He believed that we had to be kept from falling into the lazy habit of making assumptions on the basis of past events. So he would suddenly swing around in opposite directions and appear to contradict himself.

He used unpredictability as a ploy, and it was best seen as a kind of playfulness—though some of his disciples took it too seriously. So he would announce new programs and projects suddenly and arbitrarily—often choosing not to mention them again—and would declare every few months that the approach he had been pursuing was finished and that some entirely new direction was to be explored. Often he would identify an entirely new group of enemies. And anyone who failed to follow his new lead quickly enough was jeered at and even on occasions unmasked as himself an enemy and forced out of the Institute.

There were many occasions when he demonstrated the efficacy of anger as a pedagogic device. And his famous "silences" were often deployed in this way. During these periods—which sometimes lasted for several weeks—he would sit in silence while Madame Galvanauskas, standing just behind and beside his chair, read out his written instructions. Sometimes the authority of his silence was directed against a specific individual rather than the whole group. He would neither look at nor address this person and if the offender spoke would pretend not to have heard. This policy usually preceded the evacuation of the individual from the Institute—if he had not already taken the hint and resigned. Occasionally, however, Galvanauskas would reverse this policy dramatically by suddenly making a point of demonstrating his affection toward someone who had just been the object of one of these silences.

In the autumn of 1987 the first signs of the eventual crisis began to become apparent. For several months Galvanauskas had been engaged in a fierce quarrel with the university over its demand that he do some teaching in return for his salary in addition to the onerous and time-consuming duties involved in carrying on the work of the Institute.

The head of the philosophy department, Professor MacMaster, had always been deeply hostile to Galvanauskas and to the Institute. He was a traditionalist in every sense and was deeply opposed to Theory, which he insisted had nothing to do with philosophy. He called it the bastard offspring of an unholy alliance between literary critics and psychoanalysts. And he was fond of quoting an infamous and wholly unfunny spoof of Post-structuralist Theory called *Deconstruction for the Handyman.* Bentley had fixed Galvanauskas's appointment while MacMaster was abroad on sabbatical leave, and he had been furious to find a *fait accompli* on his return. He had then set about requiring Galvanauskas to fulfill the usual teaching duties of a visiting professor. Galvanauskas had resisted, and there had been some very frank exchanges on the telephone between himself and MacMaster.

Galvanauskas blamed Bentley for the fact that he was in this situation and made it clear to many of us that he believed that Bentley had induced him to come to Glasgow under false pretenses in order to increase his own prestige at the price of Galvanauskas's own. (I know that Madame Galvanauskas felt particularly bitter toward Bentley over this.) I remember that I wondered if he was about to become the object of one of Galvanauskas's silences.

The situation was resolved—for the time at least—because Bentley and I managed to rally enough support inside the department and the faculty of humanities to make it clear to MacMaster that he would make himself look very stupid if he persevered in his attempt to treat a world-famous figure as if he were a junior lecturer. (Despite Bentley's efforts on his behalf, relations between himself and Galvanauskas remained uneasy after this.) MacMaster had apparently abandoned his attack, but Bentley, who knew him of old and had had many battles with him, warned me that he was likely to try to achieve his ends by more devious means. As evidence of this, he told me that MacMaster had been reported to him as having said to some of his closest cronies that he would try giving Galvanauskas and his Institute "enough rope to hang themselves." From that moment onward he made no further objection to Galvanauskas's refusal to teach, nor to his involving students in the work of the Institute. Bentley and I suspected—and were later proved correct—that some of the students reported back to him on what occurred in the flat on Otago Street.

Treachery and Unmasking:

This lay in the future. The first warning signs of the crisis that was ahead came from quite another direction. One day in the middle of a seminar therapy that had been in progress for three or four hours and in the course of which several candidates for advancement had been processed, Galvanauskas suddenly rapped on his chair and, rising to his feet, told us he had an announcement to make. I remember how he stood looking gravely around the room and then began by saying solemnly, "I warn you that your loyalty to me is about to undergo a severe trial."

He then told us in a low voice that he had just found out that someone had been making visits to his former friends and family in France, Germany, Poland, and even Lithuania in an attempt, presumably, to dig up facts about his past that this individual hoped would discredit him. He said he had not yet been able to find out who it was.

As he began to expatiate on this person's venomous hostility, his voice rose. Suddenly he reached toward a pile of books nearby and hurled it to the floor. Then he pulled bundles of files off the shelves and threw them to the ground and kicked them around the floor. He was now red in the face and shouting as he knocked over a chamber pot, tore up a sheaf of papers he snatched from a trainee's hand, and kicked some of the underclothes lying on the floor, ripping them into rags with his feet. Then he hurried out of the room, leaving us to make our way from the Institute as quickly as possible.

The next day when, wondering whether it would take place, we all assembled for the scheduled seminar therapy, Galvanauskas came into the room and, in a low-key, almost wry tone, announced that there would be no ordinary session that day. Instead we would all receive an education from someone far more qualified to instruct us than he himself was. The subject would be disloyalty, and the lesson would come from a master of the art. For he had, he said, at last identified the long-feared traitor who had been betraying him and plagiarizing from him by recording his seminars and distributing them in a grotesquely incoherent form. The same person had also helped the enemy who had been investigating his past in Germany and Lithuania. Galvanauskas now told us that the enemy was none other than Jacques Gicquiaux.

At this there were groans and hisses from some of his hearers. Gicquiaux, Galvanauskas now reminded us, was a former disciple who had turned into an enemy. He was about to publish what he claimed was a biography of Galvanauskas called *The Mystic Medicine Man: Henri Galvanauskas in Lithuania 1940–41 and Paris 1977–84.* The traitor among us whom Galvanauskas was about to unmask had helped him to write this book by giving him a grossly slanted version of the events surrounding the Institute's departure from Paris. None of us dared look at anyone else.

After about an hour of detailed denunciations and warnings about the fate of the traitor, Galvanauskas stopped and said, "I invite the traitor to unmask himself and confess."

Nobody moved or spoke.

"Then I address you now," Galvanauskas went on. And so, as we sat in shocked silence, he said, "You are already mentally disturbed and now you will go on to develop a severe psychosis. Your psychological breakdown will be accompanied by a physical deterioration, and you will have painful sores all over your body. When you realize the magnitude of what you have done, you will kill yourself."

When he had finished, he remained silent for over an hour as we all sat there with our own thoughts and suspicions. Then he announced that he would hold an audience the next day in which he would ask those of us who were under suspicion to undertake a voluntary sacrifice as a test of our loyalty.

So we all assembled early in the morning in the seminar room in the Institute's apartment, from which we were to be summoned by Madame Galvanauskas, in the order determined by her list, to go across the landing and into the private apartment of the Galvanauskases. From here each of us would be required to enter his private study alone. As the procedure got under way, it emerged that the order was apparently random with the different degrees of affiliation being selected arbitrarily. Some spent only a minute or two in the room, and others—some of them the least prominent among us—were in there for more than an hour. Late in the afternoon Bentley and I were still left. A few others were with us. Then Madame Galvanauskas beckoned to Bentley, and he passed into the other apartment.

Only fifteen minutes later she returned and pointed one of her beringed fingers at me. I followed her across the landing and into the private apartment. She led me to the door of Galvanauskas's study. At her signal I entered the room, and she closed the door behind me without herself entering. I found I was not alone, for across the room I saw Bentley's face staring straight at me. I realized to my surprise that he was kneeling on the floor. Galvanauskas was squatting behind him and grunting as he moved rhythmically. Both were clothed, though now I saw that my colleague's trousers were down to his knees. The expression on his face when he saw me is something I shall carry to my grave. Galvanauskas gave no sign that he had seen me. As I watched, he paused, brought out the large red-spotted handkerchief which he always carried, and mopped his brow. Then he resumed his regular motion. I softly shut the door.

Immediately I was accosted by Madame Galvanauskas. She greeted me with the first smile I had ever seen on her face. She asked me to wait outside the door of the study and then disappeared. Rather unwillingly, I did so.

A few minutes later Bentley came out. He glanced at me and then looked away quickly and hurried out of the flat.

When I went into the study Galvanauskas told me he was appointing me as acting associate director of the Institute to replace Bentley. I was to keep silent about this because nobody yet knew—not even Bentley himself. My appointment would be ratified, he explained, after certain formalities had been completed.

The next day we assembled again. Galvanauskas gave the traitor another chance to confess. After a long silence he said, "In that case I will denounce him now. Step forward, William Bentley."

I was astonished at this. I think we all were. I looked at Bentley. He appeared to have been struck speechless with amazement.

Then he exclaimed, "I wasn't prepared for this."

Instantly Galvanauskas pounced on him: "Who should have prepared you? Was it the CIA? Or the Psychoanalytical Institute of France? Or MacMaster?"

Bentley stared back open-mouthed. He had no words to defend himself. Galvanauskas dismissed him from the room with a wave of his arm, and he slunk out.

When he had gone, Galvanauskas explained to us that Bentley had been the traitor for many years. Not only had he helped Gicquiaux to make trouble with the Parisian authorities over the death of the girl, but he had even earlier helped Levavasseur to plagiarize some of Galvanauskas's best ideas and to set up his alternative school.

Later that day Bentley telephoned me at home. He was clearly in great distress. He insisted on telling me his version of events. He admitted that he had indeed worked on transcripts of Galvanauskas's sessions and circulated them—though only for the last three or four years. But, astonishingly, he claimed that he had been instructed to do this by no less a person than Madame Galvanauskas! He maintained that he had been doing it on her orders and under her supervision! She had provided him with the basic transcripts, and he had not secretly recorded them himself.

This was the last communication between Bentley and any member of the Institute, as far as I know. A few days later he was found dead. He was discovered in his own flat near the university with his throat cut. There was no note. His death was thought at the time to be suicide, and it was believed that he

had taken this course of action for a reason entirely uncon-
nected with Galvanauskas's Institute and his dismissal from it. After the exhumation of Bentley's body that took place some
months later, rumors began to circulate about an earlier injury
found during the postmortem examination, but—perhaps unwisely—I paid no attention to them.

My New Responsibilities:

It was only a week after Bentley's death that Madame Galvanauskas took me aside after a seminar therapy and asked me
to follow her into her own office in the couple's private apartment.

When we were alone there, she made it clear that she wanted
me to assist her with editing transcripts of her husband's sessions! I was astounded at this. So Bentley had not been lying!
She explained that her English was not adequate to the delicate
task of preparing the final versions for circulation.

She showed me a stack of typewritten transcripts of the sessions going back over the last three years. She explained that
they were taken from tape recordings that she herself had made
using a microphone that was concealed in the seminar room
and linked to a tape recorder in a small locked room next to it.
Bentley had worked on about the first half of these, and looking
at the manuscripts, I could see that the revisions were of an unusual nature.

This became clear when I found the original transcript of the
seminal essay on Kipling's story. This was the text before
Bentley's changes:

> What is this gap, this silence, from which the phallic text
> speaks and yet remains silent? What is it but the text's phal-
> lus? What but, precisely and exactly, that phallic moment
> from which it has spun itself like a disavowal, a lie. For what
> is a phallic text if not a lie that has to be unmasked, its strat-
> egies outwitted? Behind it lies the desire, which is not the
> desire of the author, for the author, as Barthes has told us,
> is dead. (See also *Aphorism 28*: "Barthes is dead.") Nor any
> more the desire of the analyst-master, for the analyst-master
> has no desire other than, precisely, the desire to unmask

the text. It is, rather, the desire of the text [*le désir du texte*]. In what, then, does it consist, the defeat, the mastering of this desire that we have designated the desire of the text? It follows that it is by means of a wound, a rupture. From this wound, this gap where the analyst has unmasked, has emasculated the text, or rather has extorted the text's own voluntary sacrifice, the text now, tongueless and aphallic, utters its truth-which-is-only-that-by-being-manifestly-a-lie. So much is self-explanatory.

Overwhelmed with amazement at what I had discovered, I agreed to what Madame Galvanauskas asked. There seemed to be no alternative.

Now began one of the most extraordinary periods of my life. Every week I went surreptitiously to the Galvanauskases' flat late on Sunday evening, was admitted by Madame Galvanauskas, and worked until after midnight. (I never saw the Master on these occasions.) My rewriting of the transcripts, then, involved a process of revision in which ambiguity, ellipsis, equivocation, and even obfuscation were to be privileged over clarity, explicitness, and logicality.

For several reasons—one of which was the Master's growing impatience at my failure to complete the formalities for the ratification of my promotion as associate director and, more specifically, to submit to the ultimate voluntary sacrifice, which was required as proof of my loyalty—I began to suspect that my period of being in favor was destined not to last long. In October 1988 this was confirmed. For now my article on the story of the sultan was published in the journal *Diaeresis*, which is one of the most respected outlets for new work in Theory.

It was clear that Galvanauskas was not pleased. He himself, as was his practice, said nothing to me about it, but other members of the Institute were not slow to insist that I had misunderstood the point of the Master's essay on "The Tongueless Boy."

One of them accused me of "the idiotism of lucidity." And gradually I found myself being ostracized by the rest of the group. Particularly when my unwillingness to comply with certain of the requirements that needed to be completed before my taking up the post of associate director became known.

It was now that I approached Johns Hopkins University and

began to negotiate for a chair—an action that has been widely misrepresented and misinterpreted. The truth is that I realized that the Institute was threatened from within by errors of judgment on the part of certain individuals and that my association with it was therefore coming to an end. The American university agreed in principle to my appointment but set certain conditions—with which I did not think at the time it would be possible for me to comply.

The Institute in Crisis:

Now there occurred the event that Galvanauskas had anticipated when he warned us to prepare for a test of our loyalty. In November 1988 details of what Gicquiaux had allegedly discovered, and was about to publish in his biography of Galvanauskas, first appeared in the French press and were quickly picked up by the British and American media.

In the light of these so-called revelations about actions that might or might not have occurred in a remote part of Lithuania or Poland (for even this was unclear) many years ago and whose alleged victims, by definition, are not alive to give evidence, a lot of people have rushed to make self-righteous and emotional judgments. Several points need to be stated. One is that Galvanauskas has not admitted that he was the man known as the Silent Torquemada. He has adhered to his practice of remaining silent and thereby shown his contempt for the accusation. But even if he was that man, the manner and circumstances in which he first developed his ideas for making interrogees speak the Truth of Desire do not devalue the usefulness of those ideas when appropriately adapted for the very different contexts of therapeutic practice and textual analysis.

As for the revelation of more recent events, nothing is revealed by this book that was not already known to Galvanauskas's associates. Gicquiaux, however, has twisted and selected the evidence to present it in the worst light. The incident that led to the Institute's departure from Paris, for example, involved a young woman who, far from being the innocent and martyred figure that Gicquiaux's so-called "biography" presents, engineered a trap that then blew up in her face. Feeling that she was being denied the share of Galvanauskas's attention that she required, she got herself pregnant by him in order to establish a claim on him and, when this failed to work, committed suicide in what was probably a bungled bid for further attention. Similarly, the allegation that a candidate for membership of one of the higher degrees of affiliation to the Institute died from a self-inflicted injury during the ratification ceremony was fully investigated by the French police at the time, and whatever might or might not have been found, the fact remains that no charges were ever brought.

While I am on the subject of the rituals for initiation and promotion that Gicquiaux makes so much of, I challenge him to explain why, if he witnessed such events while he was a trusted counselor of the Institute in Paris, he made no attempt either to intervene at the time or to report them to the police. To avoid ambiguity, I want to put it on record that I never saw any of the more lurid scenes described by that author. In particular, I never witnessed—nor indeed ever heard anybody claim to have seen— the ritual insertion of the Signifier into the Woman-as-Other. I did, however, several times witness the ceremony in which Galvanauskas gave his disciples the opportunity to acknowledge the power of his Signifier. All of those present, including the woman involved, accepted this as a legitimate if unconventional means of demonstrating certain truths and impressing them upon those present. If, on other occasions, things once or twice got a little out of hand, I can truthfully say that no violence was ever used beyond a few mild kicks and punches. Certainly no serious injuries were ever inflicted. At least, not intentionally.

The effect of Gicquiaux's allegations and the storm of publicity that followed placed all of us in the Institute under great pressure. A number chose to leave and in some cases began themselves to spread absurd rumors about its activities.

It was at this moment that Professor MacMaster launched his long-plotted attack on the Institute in the University Senate. In going over the head of the faculty to appeal to the University Senate itself, he had the support of the formidable Professor Dugdale, head of the Department of Immunotoxinology. Dugdale and MacMaster were friends and, as profoundly committed Scottish Nationalists, allies in the politics both of the university and of the city. MacMaster now made in the Senate a series of grotesque charges—by carefully veiled innuendo—

about Galvanauskas and some of his associates. Bentley's death was linked by him with these alleged goings-on, and I myself was not exempted from his cowardly campaign of character assassination.

Professor Dugdale injected his own brand of venom into proceedings during the so-called impeachment of the Institute that MacMaster managed to engineer. Now we discovered the extent to which his agents had penetrated the Institute, for it emerged that many of the students—and even some of the affiliates—had been reporting back to him. How MacMaster succeeded in making people betray their trust must remain open to speculation for the present. The scandal arising from the so-called malfunctioning of Dugdale's electronic cat at about this time fortunately served as something of a diversion, for it discredited and turned into a laughingstock the man who had been MacMaster's main ally in his campaign of vilification against Galvanauskas and the Institute.

The reprieve was only temporary, and I saw now that the enemies of the Institute were likely to achieve their ambition to destroy it and in the process ruin the careers of any who had been associated with it. I gradually realized what I had to do. It would be something that would look—superficially—like betrayal, and at first I shrank from it for fear of the odium I might incur. Yet at the same time I believed it was my duty to scholarship and truth to ensure that Galvanauskas's work would be widely known and understood, especially since there was a serious danger of its being lost to posterity. Putting my reservations aside, I therefore reopened negotiations with Johns Hopkins in the hope of finding the necessary encouragement and resources for what I had in mind.

Now it was that I succeeded, during these difficult weeks, in making a copy of the complete set of unedited transcripts of Galvanauskas's seminars—the most accurate records in existence of the Master's own words. I used a miniature camera to photograph them at the desk in the flat on Otago Street at which I worked, for I was not allowed by Madame Galvanauskas to remove them. And so paranoid and suspicious was she that she would occasionally creep into the room silently as if to try to catch me copying them.

My Resignation from the Institute:

Events came to a climax late on the night of Easter Sunday 1989, when I was working on the transcripts in the private apartment on Otago Street. The Galvanauskases, as pious Catholics, had told me beforehand that they would be at church when I arrived (for I had a key and was able to let myself in), and I was listening for the sound of the front door that would indicate that they had returned.

I was taking photographs of the last transcripts when, to my horror, I heard a noise just outside the door. I quickly slipped the camera into my pocket as Madame Galvanauskas came gliding into the room. They had been at home all the time! I hoped she had not seen the flash of the camera. She bent and picked something up from the floor, and after we had exchanged a few words in explanation of the fact that they had changed their plans and not gone to mass, she left. A few minutes later I heard a weird, high-pitched, mad voice speaking in a foreign language in one of the other rooms. I crept out of the room and along the corridor and listened. I thought at first it was German spoken in a strange accent. But then I decided it must be Lithuanian. I had heard similar sounds a number of times while I had been working there, but never so loud or so distinctly.

I peered cautiously around the half-opened door. Galvanauskas was sitting in his usual chair and with his gaze fixed upon his wife. She was striding melodramatically up and down the center of the room clutching something in her hand and speaking with obvious rage. To my horror I saw that she was holding one of the bright yellow packets in which the tiny flashbulbs for my camera were sold and which I must have dropped earlier that evening while changing the bulb.

In the midst of this voluble stream of what I took to be Lithuanian, one word was repeated with emphasis a number of times. It sounded like *kastratsity*. As her voice rose to a climax on this word, she threw the packet across the room and picked something up from a sideboard. It was a wicked-looking knife with a long blade.

As quietly as I could, I crept toward the front door of the flat and let myself out. I hurried toward home with many glances over my shoulder. As far as I could tell, nobody was following me. But just as I was passing along Athole Lane—a dark, cobbled path between the back walls of the gardens just off Byres Road in the West End—I became aware that someone was just behind me. Whether he had followed me into the lane with extraordinary stealth or had stepped out of the shadows as I passed, I do not know.

Suddenly a man's voice said, "Excuse me. I think you dropped this."

I turned and he was right behind me, holding something out. I hardly noticed him as I took the object from his hand. In order to see what it was, I moved toward the streetlamp, turning my back to him. In an instant I was seized from behind and half throttled. I was so terrified that I think I must have blacked out for a moment. As it turned out, this saved me, for my attacker, sensing that I had gone limp and assuming that I had lost consciousness, relaxed his grip—as I discovered when I regained my senses a moment later. My attacker seemed to be fumbling for something, which is why he had let go of me. I now know he was getting out a knife, for when I began to struggle, a blow struck my ear and I later found it was bleeding profusely and had, in fact, been partially severed. I broke free and began to run.

I have never been so terrified in my life as those moments when I ran along the dark lane, frightened of tripping on its uneven cobblestones and sprawling at the feet of my would-be murderer. I truly expected to die. It was not until I had gained the safety of a crowded street that I dared to look behind me. My attacker had disappeared. I found a policeman, who summoned assistance. I was taken to the police station, where I made a statement. The police searched the site of the attack but found nothing. The object that my assailant had held out to distract me was no longer there. The police have asked me not to divulge its nature.

I was cautious from that moment on because I remembered some of the hotheaded discussions within the Institute about how to deal with opponents such as Gicquiaux and Levavasseur. I particularly recalled Madame Galvanauskas talking in somewhat veiled terms of the robust measures that younger members of the Institute had in the past taken against some of her husband's enemies in Paris. I had paid little attention to her words at the time.

That night I made the decision to resign from the Institute and to sever completely my links with it. I did so by letter and will say nothing here of Galvanauskas's and Madame Galvanauskas's intemperate reaction, which they exhibited in a series of telephone calls and letters. I never went to Otago Street again or communicated with either of the Galvanauskases.

When, three months ago, I published my book on Galvanauskas's work, *Unmasking Strategies of Desire: Texts, Power, and the Phallus in the Work of Henri Galvanauskas,* together with *Dits,* a number of absurd accusations were leveled against me by Galvanauskas's most fanatical adherents. Madame Galvanauskas wrote telling me—among other and wholly irrelevant accusations—that she had always suspected that I was too rationalistic and simplistic to understand Galvanauskas's ideas. In short, she said, I was too English. (In fact, I am a Scot, but that remark, at least, was not intended as an insult.) Her husband was too generous and trusting, she said, to have guessed at my limitations. She told me that Galvanauskas believed that out of rivalry and hostility toward him, I had attempted to emasculate his texts. Her task, she said, had for many years been to preserve the complexity and opacity—the "necessary obscurity," as she called it—of his ideas. By clarifying them and unveiling them to the uninitiated I had made them seem shallow and confused. I need not, I imagine, state that it was certainly not my intention to discredit Galvanauskas's work by presenting his ideas in a clear and ordered form. The decline in his reputation that has taken place in the last year was owing not to my book but to Gicquiaux's.

Following the recent discovery about the circumstances of Bentley's death, the later murders that have terrorized Glasgow over a period of months, and the death—apparently also by murder—of Professor Dugdale, I have naturally wondered if there could be a link between these events and the attack on myself. I am still receiving some protection from the police, though it has been stepped down since the recent and sudden removal of the Institute and its members to Spain.

Graham Speculand, Johns Hopkins University, December 16, 1989

CHAPTER

5

The Trap

AT THE CENTER OF THE SULTAN'S PALACE IN THE ALHAMBRA of Granada there is a courtyard, containing a series of elegant pools and fountains, around which his apartments are disposed on two floors.

On the upper story are the women's quarters, and on this floor no man except for the eunuchs may venture on pain of death. It has a gallery running right around the courtyard, from which the women are permitted to watch the comings and goings below.

On the ground floor, the largest of the sultan's apartments is his justice room. This lofty chamber has a fountain with a pool, and the pool is connected to those in the center of the courtyard. In this apartment, it is told, he once beheaded thirty-six men of his guard one after the other in such a way that their blood ran into the pool and the fountains in the courtyard ran red, and all because he saw one of them kissing his favorite concubine.

That is a terrible charge and almost wholly untrue. This is the true story of the sultan's action, and it exonerates him from the charge of needless cruelty and shows that on the contrary he acted with the Moor's love of justice, with political ingenuity, and with all the compassion that his religion enjoined.

The key to understanding the story is that when you are in

the sultan's justice chamber, you can see, in one of the pools surrounding the fountain, a reflection of part of the raised gallery
on the opposite side of the courtyard. So limpid and still is the
water that it bears the image almost as clearly as a mirror. But
you can see this only if you are sitting on the sultan's throne and
from nowhere else. And from that position you can see it even
when the door into the courtyard is closed, for the gate is low
enough not to obstruct the line of sight between the gallery and
the pool. And therefore only the sultan knew of this strange
means of seeing a part of the gallery that was apparently invisible to him.

The sultan was sitting there one evening dispensing justice
when he looked into the pool and saw two figures reflected
therein who were standing on the gallery in the precise position
in which they could be seen by him. The sultan saw that one of
them was his favorite concubine. And to his utter astonishment
and horror he saw that the other figure was a man and that he
was kissing her. Moreover, the man was looking in his direction
and laughing at him over the maiden's shoulder. The sultan
could see this and yet he did not know his face because of the
very slight distortion of the reflection in the pool, but he knew
by his garb that he was a member of his Nubian bodyguard.

At that moment the sultan involuntarily uttered such a cry of
rage that the man turned and looked down and saw over the top
of the door of the chamber the reflection in the pool and knew
that he had been seen by the sultan, for he could see his master's angry face in the water. Although the sultan shouted to his
courtiers in audience before him to catch him, the guard had
time to run down a staircase and escape, although the concubine was seized. The courtiers, of course, had no idea of how the
sultan had learned of the girl's infidelity, but they were accustomed to obey him absolutely and unquestioningly.

The sultan, hastily taking up a lighted taper—for dusk was
falling swiftly—followed the offender, who had hastened toward
the guardroom. When the sultan stole in, he found no light and
all the guards sleeping—or apparently sleeping, for he knew
that at least one of them was feigning sleep and suspected that
others were doing the same, for the hour was still early and
there was a smell as of lights that had just been extinguished. He
went from one man to the other and placed his hand on each

man's breast. Each was still. Then he found one whose heart was pounding. While he rested his hand there, the man opened his eyes very slightly. He and the sultan exchanged a look. But in the little light shed by his dying taper, the sultan could not recognize him.

The sultan took out his dagger. He was about to stab him to the heart, but then he hesitated. What if the rest of the guards should awake and find one of their number slain? Could the sultan rely on their loyalty? He decided that he could not, for in recent months he had had occasion several times to suspect that there were traitors among those who were entrusted with the maintenance of his safety. Since he needed to have a bodyguard strong and fierce enough to crush his enemies, that meant that they were also likely to constitute a threat to him. In order to bind their fate to himself, the sultan had wisely encouraged them in acts of severity and injustice against the common people so that they were more hated than he was. Thus they needed him to protect them even more than he needed them. Despite this, he had noticed signs of disaffection among them. Reflecting on this, he decided that he would not risk angering them by killing one of their number while he was in their midst. And then an idea came to him, and with a single swift blow of his dagger he cut off a large piece of the man's ear.

In the morning the Sultan ordered all of his guards to assemble before him. But imagine his feelings when he found that he had been outwitted, for each man had severed a part of the same ear, and so he could not distinguish the malefactor.

He was very angry and, moreover, very apprehensive, for he saw now that he was right to suspect them all of disaffection, and not just the single man who had offended him before his very eyes. Looking at the ranks of men with bleeding ears, he saw insubordination in their eyes.

The sultan now remembered the concubine, so he dismissed his guards and had her brought before him. Since she was a woman, he had little expectation that she would utter anything to his purpose, but he made every effort to extract from her the name of her lover. She remained stubborn, however, and finally cheated him of the opportunity to learn the truth by dying without speaking only a few hours after his attentions had begun.

The sultan decided that he had to remove the threat posed by his disloyal guards. Yet he could not think how to do so without provoking them into rising up against him. He was also anxious to find and punish the particular man who had crossed him. And then, after much weary effort of mind, he bethought him of an ingenious means of achieving both ends.

He announced that he intended to hold an audience with each of the guards in his justice chamber in order to recompense each according to his deserts. Each man, therefore, entered the chamber unaccompanied.

Alone with each guard, the sultan first asked him if he were the malefactor who had kissed the girl. Each denied it. Then he asked him to name the offender, and each insisted that he did not know. Thus from their rebellious silence the sultan learned how far he could trust his bodyguard. He told each man that he was going to reward him for his loyalty and ordered him to kneel beside the pool. Expecting, perhaps, that some jewel was to be given him, or fearing, it may be, some punishment, each man knelt as ordered.

The sultan drew his scimitar and, giving the man a last opportunity to speak, undertook that if he remained silent, he would qualify him for a position of trust among his harem staff—a position that was not coveted by any of them.

When the guard still kept silent, the sultan, going beyond his undertaking, brought the scimitar down and beheaded him, carefully ensuring that the blood went into the pool and so drained away. The blood flowed out of the justice chamber and made the fountains in the courtyard run red, but none knew what was taking place inside. When, after each decapitation, the blood had ceased to flow, the sultan dragged the body behind the screen that divided the chamber, not forgetting to retrieve and conceal the head as well.

The door was, of course, closed behind each man so that nobody in the courtyard could see in. Once the water had run clear after being reddened by the flow of blood, the sultan glanced into the pool, which, as you will recall, reflected the view over the gate's top of the women's gallery opposite. For he guessed that the offender would not be able to resist the temptation to try to find out what was happening inside the chamber. He alone knew of the reflection in the pool.

When the sultan had questioned twenty-three of the guards,

he looked into the pool, and now at last his eyes met the eyes of another man, and in that instant they both knew the truth: the sultan that this was the offender and the man that he was doomed. For, anticipating that the wrongdoer would attempt to see what his fate was to be, the sultan had posted courtiers whom he trusted up in the gallery, and they now seized the guard.

The sultan dealt with the remaining twelve guards as mercifully as with the others—for the manner of their death was equally swift and private. But to the offender the sultan was not merciful.

Translated from the Arabic by Richard Fawcett Maddocks, 1887

CHAPTER

6

The Accusation

IT'S ODD HOW CONFIDING ONE BECOMES TO A GROUP OF chance-met strangers whom one expects never to set eyes on again. Precisely for that reason, one confesses to them things one would not admit to one's closest friends. Nor, for that matter, under interrogation by the authorities.

I am going to give you an example that illustrates what I mean. In effect, what I am going to tell you is a confession to having, quite without justification, brought about someone's death.

I was staying at an inn in a small assize town in the west of England a few years ago. It was February or March—certainly out of the tourist season, so there were only three or four other guests. It was a highly respectable, comfortable old place, though slightly run down. Like many such establishments in England, it was more expensive than it should have been, since we were paying for the tradition and the respectability rather than any more tangible amenities. You felt safe there from any sort of unpleasantness.

After dinner (a pretty mediocre one, I might mention) I went into the coffee room, and there I fell into conversation with a number of other guests.

One of them was an old gentleman who, after a while, announced somewhat abruptly that he wanted to tell us a story. It was something that had happened, he said, in that very inn in the room we were sitting in now. He was, at the time I am speaking of, a judge who was on the verge of retirement and was actually making his last circuit.

When he had told his story, we—I mean the judge and the other guests—discussed it and speculated about it. In the course of our conversation, one of the party in effect suggested that he had been lying—or at least suppressing or distorting the truth. When the old gentleman had left the room to go bed, this individual cited as evidence of what he had alleged the fact that the judge had betrayed himself by a slip of the tongue. Whether that was so or not remained unclear—to myself at least. In fact, an argument about this broke out and kept us out of our beds for several hours.

But first, you'll want to hear the story the old judge told. And I'll use his own words as far as I remember them.

This happened about forty years ago. I was a young barrister traveling on circuit for the first time. I was in this town for what were still called at that time the quarter sessions. I had dinner—no better than tonight's—and afterward I found myself with my fellow guests in the coffee room—this very room we're in now—reading newspapers and drinking coffee and whiskey.

There were only two other guests in the room. One was a man who was a few years older than I. The other was considerably older and seemed to me to be quite far advanced into middle life—though I suppose he was a great deal younger than I am now! He was a small, balding man with the sallow complexion of someone who has lived in the tropics. He looked timid and retiring and also deeply troubled and unhappy. I found out the next day that he was a cleric, so I shall refer to him as that. He was reading—or perhaps pretending to read—a newspaper and apparently taking no interest in the conversation that ensued.

It was the other guest with whom I struck up a conversation. I found out that he was a medical man. (And I recall that when I said that I was a barrister, the cleric looked up for the first time. Apart from that he appeared to take no interest in our conversation—though as I was to find out he had in fact almost certainly been listening closely.) Finding an area where our professions overlapped, the doctor and I began to talk of murder and the various means by which it may be effected. We discussed some fa-

*mous cases—in particular, the Whitechapel killings and the then fairly re-
cent Croydon poisoning. Both cases had remained unsolved and the murderer—whether identified or not—never brought to trial. This reflection led
us to talk about how and why some murderers get away with it, and we
argued about whether luck or ingenuity played the greater role. The doctor
insisted that luck was the crucial factor. Murderers had to be astonishingly
arrogant in believing that they could outwit the authorities, but the truth
was that the lucky ones—however stupid—succeeded in carrying it off,
while the unlucky ones—however brilliant—did not.*

*I argued for ingenuity and offered to tell the story of a perfect murder.
I explained that I knew about the case because I had been involved in
the trial of the murderer. Oh yes, I call him that, for although he was ac-
quitted, he was certainly a murderer. And he had committed the perfect
murder, for his wife, who had the best reasons to hate him, had to give
evidence that in effect exonerated him even though he had killed her lover
in front of her very eyes.*

*The murderer was a chap called Robertson, who was an accountant.
He found out that his wife was deceiving him with a colleague of his,
and he conceived a means of murdering the man, whose name was
Edwards. Pretending that he had no suspicion of the adultery, Robertson
invited Edwards, who was unmarried, to join himself and his wife at
their cottage near the Solent one weekend where they often went to sail his
yacht. At first Edwards declined, but when the invitation was repeated,
he accepted, probably because he and his mistress were afraid that a continued refusal might arouse her husband's suspicions. They did not
know that he had already discovered their guilty liaison.*

*So one weekend Edwards, who, as Robertson was well aware, knew
nothing about boats, came down and stayed with them. The next morning they all three went out on the yacht.*

*The sea became quite choppy once they were out in the bay and had
raised the sails and switched off the engine. At the same moment,
Robertson surreptitiously turned off the fuel supply from the tank.
Edwards had never sailed before, and Robertson, taking the helm with
his wife beside him, instructed him to go forward, where he calculated he
would become splashed by spray and would feel most vulnerable. After a
while, he called out to him that he could see a loose halyard—which he
had himself left in that condition, of course. He asked him to secure it
and shouted his instructions to him.*

*When Edwards looked utterly dismayed at the idea of going farther
out onto the edge of the boat, Robertson called out, "Come back and take*

the wheel, then. You'll be safe here. I'll go forward and secure that hal-yard."

Edwards gratefully came aft and took the wheel. Sitting beside Robertson's wife—herself only a slightly more experienced sailor—he pre-sumably felt secure, assuming, as a landlubber would do, that he was much safer than when he had been out on the deck.

Meanwhile Robertson went forward and made himself busy with the lines while the boat was heeling and bouncing, smashing into the waves as a yacht does when it's close-hauled and going to windward.

Then, watching the sea and choosing his moment carefully, he called out to Edwards rather imperiously, "You're not steering up to the wind. Come to starboard."

He did a pantomine with his arms to indicate what the other man should do, and Edwards obediently turned the wheel hard in the appro-priate direction so that the boat tacked through the eye of the wind. In-stantly the mainsheet snapped quickly across and caught Edwards off balance. He only had one hand on the wheel. Then as the boat came through the wind, she heeled suddenly the other way, helped by a timely gust.

Just as Robertson had hoped, Edwards was pitched overboard. You see, people who know nothing about boats have no conception that the helm is actually the most dangerous position to be standing in. As he went over, his hand flailed wildly for the guardrail but missed, and he plunged into the icy water. Robertson's wife screamed, but there was nothing she could do to save her paramour.

In apparent horror, Robertson called out to his wife to start the motor. The terrified woman began to turn the starter motor, and it coughed into life for a few seconds but then quickly died. She tried again and again without success. Since Robertson was taking a long time—understandably panicking under the circumstances—to bring the headsail sheet across to the winch and haul it in, the boat was still hove to. Robertson shouted at his wife to get the sails down while he went below to try to start the en-gine. The poor woman was inexperienced and, panicking as she was, made a pretty poor fist of it. All the while, of course, the boat was drifting away from Edwards. By the time Robertson had got the engine running, given the helm to his wife while he finished taking down the sails, and then taken the helm again, the poor wretch was several hundred yards be-hind us and completely invisible in the heavy seas. Robertson now tried to get back to where the victim had gone overboard, but with the best will in the world—which, despite his apparent efforts, he most certainly did not have—there was no way of identifying the precise place. Moreover, as Robertson knew very well, since he had carefully worked out the tides, poor Edwards was being carried swiftly by the west-going tide into the race in precisely the opposite direction. Robertson estimated that he would be drowned in the heavy seas somewhere off the Portland Bill—assuming he survived the cold that long—and this seems to have been the case, for the poor devil's body was washed up a few days later on a beach around the headland.

The beauty of it was that when Robertson was brought to trial for murder—most unwisely on the part of the authorities, in my opinion— his wife had to go into the witness box and testify to the efforts he had made to save his victim. The judge found that there was no case to answer and dismissed the charge. Robertson was criticized for having failed to make Edwards wear a lifejacket, but it was a venial enough error given that he had not realized how choppy it would be once they were beyond the breakwater. And people were less concerned about safety in those days anyway.

So you might say that Robertson got away with it and had committed the perfect murder. And yet in a sense he didn't, for he was tormented by guilt and had to keep on telling the story over and over again—in slightly disguised form, of course.

When I had finished my story, the clerical gentleman remained as silent as he had been since I had entered the room, and continued to look at his newspaper, though without turning the page. The doctor said that he had been intrigued by my story. He still believed that all the ingenuity in the world could be defeated by bad luck. (In fact, ingenuity could defeat itself even without bad luck, and to illustrate that, he recalled Mark Twain's remark to the inventor of an elaborate mousetrap: "It's brilliant. But is there a mouse clever enough to figure out how to get into it?") Then he said that my story had reminded him of another in which ingenuity had played a crucial role.

Addressing his question to the cleric as much as to myself, he asked if we would like to hear it. I remember that while I agreed with enthusiasm, our fellow guest did not speak or even look up.

The doctor then told his story. Frankly, I couldn't see why mine had reminded him of his own anecdote, for the parallels seemed tenuous or banal. Moreover, it was merely a story he had read rather than something that had really happened to him. I'm afraid I don't recall it very precisely, though I have certainly retained its broad outlines.

The story was set in the distant past and took place in some Arabian or Turkish city. Possibly it was taken from The Arabian Nights. *I don't recollect. It concerned a* mosaddegh, *or magistrate—to use an equivalent term—who found out that his wife was committing adultery. But despite his best efforts, he could not establish who among his extensive acquaintance was the guilty man. The point of the story was that the magistrate found out who the adulterer was in a very ingenious way. That's right! It comes back to me now. The point was that he trapped him by means of his own curiosity.*

The magistrate lived in a large house that had some clandestine and ingenious means of entry that only he and his wife knew about. He guessed, however, that his unfaithful wife had told her lover about this secret so that he could come and go without being detected. I think it was a secret door or perhaps a staircase. Or was it a mirror? Now that I think about it, I believe it was a mirror. And so it couldn't have been a means of entry but something else. I'm afraid I don't quite call the details to mind. And there was something to do with the magistrate nearly catching the fellow but only managing to cut off a lock of his hair. I don't remember that very well. But I do recollect that what the magistrate did was to invite a succession of his friends to a meal in order to lure the guilty man into incriminating himself. In some way that I can't call to mind now, this involved asking the guests a number of questions. I suppose their wives must have been present as well, so it must have been very tricky.

And so at the climax of the story, after a series of such feasts that passed without incident, the magistrate entertained the guilty man. In a way that I don't recall, the host maneuvered his guest into doing something that betrayed his identity as the secret lover. But what I clearly remember is that the way this individual betrayed himself was that he looked into the mirror at this crucial juncture and thereby identified himself to the jealous husband. I believe the magistrate didn't kill him. I'm almost sure that he merely had him seized by his servants and beaten and then thrown into the street. Well, that was it. It wasn't a very interesting or edifying story, though I'm sure it was more interesting than the way I've remembered it.

I don't know what effect it had on the third member of our company, for he said nothing and made no movement throughout the narration, but continued to hold up his newspaper. However, when the doctor had concluded, I noticed that he had lowered the paper and was now staring at us in horror.

Half jokingly and with a touch of devilment—for, after all, I was very young—I told him it was now his turn to tell us a story. I said it be-cause I was annoyed at his keeping himself so aloof from us.

He looked aghast and shook his head without speaking.

Then in my best courtroom manner, I said, "Come, no holding back. It's your turn."

Then—goodness knows whether in response to my suggestion or for some other reason—he began muttering some confused story about some-thing he had done or not done many years before. It seemed to be some-thing that had happened in India or perhaps Africa.

He began, "I was out there as an anthropologist. No, as a missionary."

To my eternal shame and regret, I then made my fatal remark. And, quite honestly, I think I only said it as a kind of parody of the most ag-gressive barrister's manner.

"Well, that's not a very encouraging start," I said. "Are you going to tell a true story or lie to us?"

He looked at me in terror and said, "I want to tell the truth at last." Then he made a remark about seeing himself in the mirror and then added something like, "I let them kill him. I was too frightened. I was too ashamed. I killed him!" Then he broke off, got to his feet rather un-steadily, and almost tottered out of the room.

Well, you can imagine how surprised my fellow guest and I were by this behavior. And we could find no way of accounting for it in anything that either of us had heard or seen.

When I came down the next morning, there was no sign of the cleric. The doctor and I breakfasted together and then parted, he to continue on his way and I to attend the assizes.

When I got back from court in the evening, I found the hotel in a state of discreet uproar. It emerged that earlier that day a chambermaid had found the clerical gentleman lifeless in his bed with his throat cut. His razor had fallen from his hand, and there was no doubt that he had taken his own life. (There was a great deal of blood.) He had not left a note, and his motive remained a complete mystery. The fellow was dead. We couldn't ask him why he'd done it. He couldn't tell us anything.

No light was thrown upon his reasons when more information emerged about him. He had for twenty years been a country parson in East Anglia, and before that he had served overseas as chaplain to var-ious postings in Africa and the Indian subcontinent. He had never mar-ried. His only living relatives were a sister and a brother. He had a close friend in Scotland, whom he visited every year at Christmas. When the brother came to collect his effects and make the necessary arrangements a couple of days later, I spoke to him briefly. He was a sensible and shrewd man, a stockbroker as far as I recollect. He confessed himself completely baffled by his brother's action. He had always been of a melancholy temperament, he told me, and particularly so on his return from his final overseas posting, which was in Africa, where his health had been broken by the climate. He had seemed to have something on his mind, but he had never spoken of it. I refrained from mentioning his mysterious words to myself and our fellow guest just before he had left this room.

Among the dead man's possessions was nothing that made his action any the more explicable.

He had left, apart from clothes, toilet articles, a prayer book and Bible, only two possible clues. One of these was a newspaper clipping. But the deceased's brother, after examining these, had not been able to think of any solution to the mystery of the suicide's motives, he told me.

When I heard of the clipping, I wondered if the dead man had read something in the paper while he was apparently listening to us that had driven him to this course of action. But his brother showed it to me, and it turned out to be from an ancient paper and seemed to have nothing to do with him. It gave an account of an accident that had occurred many years before in the Highlands when someone fell over a cliff during a blizzard.

The second possible clue was a book left open with a passage heavily marked in ink. It appeared to be an adventure story set in Africa and was therefore rather unlikely reading matter for a clergyman of melancholy temperament and scholarly tastes. His brother and I assumed that it was the African connection that had engaged his interest. The passage marked occurred in a description—a very horrible description—of the hero's reflections when, having found someone known to him hideously mutilated by tribespeople, he decides to put him out of his misery by ending his life. It was, as far as I recall, a passage about guilt and the additional misery of not being able to utter it. It was to this desire to end the misery of his existence that we assumed the deceased had wished to draw attention. But his reasons for his misery still remained mysterious.

That was the judge's story. When he had finished, the little group of us who had been listening asked him a few questions. Nothing much emerged from these. For a while we speculated on a possible explanation for the cleric's conduct, but we could think of nothing that satisfactorily accounted for it. The judge informed us that he had narrated this story dozens of times in the hope of one day hearing a solution. He believed he had told it for the last time, and, appropriately in the very room in which it had occurred.

I noticed that one of the group—a young man of somewhat saturnine appearance—had said nothing. I asked him if he had a theory. He merely shook his head. I was a little annoyed at this, for his demeanor betrayed a certain arrogance and super-ciliousness, as if the solution to the mystery was clear to him but he could not be bothered to share it with people as stupid as the rest of us.

I asked him again, unfortunately.

He said at last, "It's possible that the poor man was moved to destroy himself by something he heard in one of the stories nar-rated in his hearing. Or perhaps both. But as the man's past is unknown to us and also in view of the fact that our informant has not told either of the stories fully or correctly, we haven't enough evidence to know."

To my surprise the old judge did not angrily deny the charge, though I noticed that he flushed. He said nothing else of sub-stance, and a few moments later he gave us his good-nights and left the room.

As soon as he had gone, we asked the young man if he would explain what he had meant, but he refused to say any more, merely shaking his head in an irritatingly knowing manner.

We kept up the pressure, however, and after a while he said, "He betrayed himself." We asked him what he meant and he said, "Didn't you notice his slip of the tongue?" None of us knew what he was referring to, and we continued to interrogate him.

Eventually he conceded, "I think he heard his own story told."

When we pressed him to expand on this remark, he refused to say any more and shortly afterward himself left the room.

I was destined never to know any more of the story, for the judge was taken seriously ill the next day. This was most incon-venient for those taking part in the trial that he was presiding over, since it had to be abandoned and then begun again with a new judge and jury. I believe he died soon afterward.

An Open Mind

SEPTEMBER

Sunday
Raining. Nothing.

Monday
Raining. Nothing.

Tuesday
Raining. Nothing.

Wednesday
Dry spells. Gardiner St. 9:15. Top right.

Thursday
Raining. Nothing.

Friday
Dry. 19 Kelvinside Ct. Second left. 12:15.

Saturday
Dry. 57 Fergus Dr. Ground left. 9:40.
23 Dowanhill Cresc. Second right. 10:30.

Sunday
Raining. Nothing.

Monday
Raining. Nothing.

Tuesday
Fine evening but nothing much.

Wednesday
Fine but nothing much again.

Thursday
Raining. Nothing.

Friday
Dry. 14 Montague Dr. Top left. 10:30.

Saturday
Beautiful night. Several excellent sightings. 84 Caledonia St. Ground left. 10:00.
19 Victoria Crescent Dr. Middle right. 10:45.
6 Gardiner St. Top middle. 11:15.

Sunday
Raining. Nothing. Rather a dull day generally.

Monday
Raining. Nothing. Jerry quite impossible again. Fussing about the place. Seems to think paying me a few measly quid entitles him to give me a lot of stupid instructions. Full of silly ideas for reorganizing the stock.

Tuesday
Raining. Nothing much otherwise either.

Wednesday
Raining. Not much to report. Jerry fussing about, as per usual. Pointlessly rearranging the stock.

Thursday

Fairly routine day. Too wet for fieldwork. Jerry still trying to reorganize the stock, but really stupidly. Though I knew there was no point, I had another go at him about reorganizing my section (as I call it). I hate the way "Crime" covers "True Crime" and "Crime Fiction." It makes me very angry. I just can't understand why people want to waste their time on reading things that are made up when there's so much interesting factual material in the world to read. B---ming Jerry won't give way on it, though.

Friday

Not much doing. Rain.

Saturday

Showery.

Sunday

Raining. Nothing. Felt a bit low all day.

Monday

Wettish. Nothing.

Tuesday

Wet again.

Wednesday

Rain held off. Fieldwork very disappointing, though.

Thursday

Wet again.

Friday

Raining. Went out anyway. Nothing to record.

Saturday

Drizzling.

Monday

Something astonishing happened today! Utterly unbelievable!

This man came in and browsed for a bit in the Crime section. He was tall and quite thin and he was wearing one of those strange hats. One of those thingummies. Like what's-his-name. The famous detective.

He was obviously English. As was confirmed when he spoke. He asked Jerry if he had anything on Madeleine Smith. Of course, I pricked up my ears at that. Naturally, b---ming Jerry didn't have the foggiest notion what he was talking about. So I came over and told him we didn't have anything just at the moment, but that I was hoping to build up the stock in that area since it had always been my intention to go in for murder on quite a large scale. (Of course I mean real murders, not those dreadful made-up ones!) He inquired what we did have on actual Scottish murders in the way of documentary material. I asked him if he knew *The Right Lines*, which was a sort of history book about the Killiecrankie Mystery and which had just been published and was very good. I showed him a copy that had just come in. (That dreadful Ramsay McCoo, the books editor on *The Daily Scot*, brought it in a few days ago in a stack of review copies he was selling to raise money for his next drink. Of course he hadn't reviewed it or got anyone else to, but he claimed he'd read it and said it was very good.)

He laughed and said he did indeed know it and that he agreed with my assessment of its quality and then he apprised me of the fact that he was the author! He was Horatio Quaife! Well, you could have knocked me over with a feather! I didn't know what to say. I've never really spoken to an author before. Not a proper conversation. Not with a real writer. (I don't count those scruffy layabouts, McConville and McAlweenie, who come in and browse for hours and hardly ever buy a thing.)

It was really embarrassing because I had to admit that I hadn't read it. I have so little time for reading outside my main interests, since I have to be out while the lighting conditions are right.

But I told him I had, of course, read Mr. Roughead's account of the Killiecrankie Mystery in his *Unsolved Scottish Crimes*. I was going to tell him about my own connection with the case, only I didn't get the chance because what he was saying was so interesting. Now we had a most fascinating discussion. Mr. Quaife said he had set out to demolish Mr. Roughead's theory about what had happened. It was ingenious and elegant, but that didn't make it correct. He reminded me that Mr. Roughead's theory is that the Major killed Mrs. Armytage by luring her into following the wrong tracks in the snow. The idea was that when the Major retraced his steps to find her, he went first to the edge of the cliff and then walked backward in his own footsteps until he regained the track and then went back and found her. Then he led her, following his own false tracks, to the edge, where he attacked her and pushed her over the cliff.

We both agreed that the problem with this theory is that no motive has ever been found. And then Mr. Quaife pointed out something that hadn't occurred to me or, as far as I know, to any of the people who have written about the case: that at his first opportunity to go back to murder Mrs. Armytage, the Major did not immediately offer to go and look for her but let the Driver try to find her. Mr. Quaife said that this meant one of two things: Either the Major was innocent of any intention to kill her or he knew that the old lady was already dead.

I was intrigued by this, but when I asked him what he thought had happened, he wouldn't be drawn and he said, *Read my book and next time I come in I'll be interested to see what you think of my own Theory!* Now there's a real compliment! Someone as clever and important as him actually cares about humble little me and my ideas! As soon as he'd gone, I popped the book into the private case while Jerry was out—just in case anyone else wanted to buy it. (I put it between *The Fortunes of Nigel* and *Peveril of the Peak*. Nobody ever looks there. I had to take out some of my observation records and photographs to make room.)

Tuesday

Fairly light day at work, since Jerry spent the day unpacking that load of new stuff from *Fricatives* that I never have anything to do with, so I was able to start on Mr. Quaife's history book. It's really interesting and has lots of new information that Mr. Roughead didn't include. I don't know how Mr. Quaife found it out. Basically it's about this philosophy don from Cambridge who is a man on terms of easy familiarity with More, Russel, and Witgenstien, with all of whom he exchanged ideas as an equal.

He's called Clarence Titheradge, and it seems he was on a walking tour at the time of the old lady's death and happened to be staying at the same hotel as the witnesses (or suspects, perhaps I should say) while they were waiting for the procurator fiscal's inquiry to take place. By chance he saw the silent young lady in the dining room of the hotel and instantly fell in love with her. She first caught his attention when his gaze fell upon her sweet young face that was so incongruously filled with a gentle melancholy. He was horrified when he discovered that she was involved in the inquiry and was considered by some people to be a suspect, since it was rumored that she had inherited some money from the old lady. He found her so intriguing, so sad, and so beautiful that he knew he had to save her at whatever cost to himself. And so he decided to give up his walking tour and try to resolve the mystery in order to clear her of any shadow of suspicion. Her name was Marcia Latimer.

Well, all of that was completely new to me. I got so engrossed that I didn't take the three-and-a-half-incher out tonight!

Wednesday

Found it so gripping, I started reading it over the Branny-Brekkers.

During the next few days Dr. Titheradge attended the inquiry and watched the witnesses in the bar of the hotel. One of the things he learned was that the old lady was found clutching a silver brooch in the form of a scorpion. I wonder if anyone has ever discovered that before!

Dr. Titheradge started to get into conversation with the witnesses. He began with the Major. It was straightaway apparent to him that he was dealing with a very choleric and brusque individual. The Major was a tall man of about fifty with a long, sallow face, a big beaked nose, and hooded, staring eyes. It was a face that was clearly quick to anger and slow to forget a grudge. A face that conveyed a sense of brooding malevolence. The Major, who had a harshly grating voice, refused to talk to him about the case, expressed no remorse for the old lady's death, and was very rude about the Parson and the young lady. Talking of the Parson, he quoted Kipling: *Fighting is like making love: Each man does it in his own way. Some like the bayonet and some like the butt.* And then he said, *I've always been a bayonet man, but I suspect the Parson prefers the butt.* As for the silent young lady, Miss Latimer, he said she was insane.

Thursday

Dr. Titheradge decided that the Major was so clearly uninterested in charming him that he could have nothing to hide. His suspicions fell on the Driver, since he had been the one who volunteered to go back to look for the old lady and might well have killed her. (Of course, all of this had a particular interest for me.) He managed to have quite a long talk with the Driver, who he plied with drink. (Well, that can't be right!) But he learned nothing new from him.

Dr. Titheradge couldn't talk to the guard because he had been found dead not far from where the train had been abandoned. He had presumably got lost and died of exposure in the attempt to summon help. (I hadn't known that, either. Mr. Quaife has found masses of new stuff!)

Then Dr. Titheradge talked to the Parson, who was very unwilling to discuss the case with him. He was extremely nervous. He told Dr. Titheradge without being asked that the Major had never been out of his sight during the time the party was walking along the clifftop. His eagerness to volunteer this alibi for the other man made Dr. Titheradge suspicious.

The young lady agreed only very reluctantly to meet him and was chaperoned at their meeting by an elderly aunt. She answered his questions by writing notes. She added nothing to her written statement, which had been what initiated the inquiry, since at first the authorities had assumed Mrs. Armytage's death was entirely accidental. She broke off the interview after a few minutes. Dr. Titheradge was left with the strong suspicion that she was holding something back.

Fairly dry. Managed to get out for an hour or two. 56 Livingstone Cresc. Top middle. 10:45.

Deer stalker! That's what I meant. Sherlock Holmes.

Friday

I've decided to start a separate list of observations.

When Dr. Titheradge had spoken to the witnesses, he visited the scene of the incident, where he made some notes and sketches. Once he had accumulated all the relevant evidence, the don sat down and simply used his trained mind and proved to his own satisfaction by the exercise of pure logic that Mrs. Armytage's death was neither an accident nor suicide but murder.

In some way that, frankly, I didn't really follow, he established that the victim had been knocked unconscious and then thrown over the cliff. (Nothing about her throat, I notice.)

Moreover, this logical exercise showed him not only that the Major must have committed the murder but also the method he had used. Now I see what Mr. Quaife meant by saying the Major did not offer to go back and find the old lady because he knew she was already dead. His astonishing Theory is that the Major walked on so far ahead of the rest of the party (despite what the Parson said about never losing sight of him) that he was able to circle right around and come up from behind to attack his victim, who was straggling at the back of the line. He hit her and pushed her over the cliff. Then he made another huge circle to get back to the front of the line and simply waited for the others to catch him up and tell him the old lady was missing.

Dr. Titheradge could not, however, find a motive and knew that without this vital element his only hope was to frighten the Major into making a confession. And he had to get the Parson to withdraw the evidence exonerating the Major that he had already given to the inquiry. If the Major had never been out of his sight, then he could not have committed the murder. Dr. Titheradge therefore confronted the suspect with his theory and the evidence for it. The Major angrily denied the allegation and challenged him to find a motive. Then he went on to the attack and, in some way that I didn't quite understand, he hinted that he could blackmail Dr. Titheradge about something he had apparently learned from one of the waiters at the hotel. (This bit was very vague.)

At this point, Dr. Titheradge had to admit that the Major had turned the tables on him, and so he made a strategic withdrawal.

Saturday
Dr. Titheradge remembered his feeling that Miss Latimer, the mute young lady, was keeping something back. From seeing her giving evidence to the inquiry, he discovered that her inability to

speak had begun when she had learned of the death of her brother and her fiancé in the same action in Flanders. After hearing this he spent an hour or two with a copy of the *Army List* in the hotel's library.

Later that afternoon he managed to find an opportunity to speak to her once again while she was having tea by herself in the hotel lounge. He told her how he had worked out that the murderer was one of the party, who had circled around to attack his victim from behind, and invited her to conceive of the state of mind of the old lady at finding herself left alone at the back of the line in fear that she was being stalked by a madman bent upon killing her. (He guessed that she must have felt guilty for having let her fall behind the rest of the party.) And then he asked her to imagine the old lady's terror at seeing someone loom up at her suddenly from the snow and darkness, and realizing that she was about to be killed. Miss Latimer became very upset but still insisted that she had nothing further to tell him.

In a desperate last shot, he decided to tell her frankly that he believed the Major was the murderer. She still refused to reveal anything. And she remained stubbornly unyielding—though obviously deeply upset—even when he asked her, in a reference to the deaths of her brother and fiancé, whether she didn't think that there had been enough pointless killing recently? When she persisted in declining to reveal what he was increasingly sure she knew, he told her that he had found out that the Major had been one of the officers who had ordered into action the regiment in which her brother and her fiancé were serving, and he gave her names and dates to support this. (In fact, he had made this up. And I must say that I take a pretty dim view of that myself. The truth is the truth, after all.)

At this she broke down and told him something which she had kept from the police: Mrs. Armytage had told her just before they left the shelter of the waiting room that she was frightened of the Major because she had recognized him as the son of a lady who had had a grudge against her. This was apparently because the Major told a story that involved a man being found murdered and clutching an image of a scorpion. Moreover, the story he told was one in which there appeared the idea of steps down the side of a cliff that had been turned into a deadly trap. This was why nobody in the party—except for the old lady herself—was prepared to climb down the stairs to the safety of the castle. In fact, that would presumably have saved her life because it was much safer than walking along the top of the cliff in the darkness and swirling snow.

Sunday

Miss Latimer now told Dr. Titheradge the whole story as she had heard it some time ago from an informant in the service of the Armytage family, who had no reason to like her employer. Briefly, Mrs. Armytage was alleged to have tricked her first husband, Sir Rudolph, into marriage by discrediting the fiancée he was originally engaged to. (It had all happened, of course, many years before the young lady was even born.) Mrs. Armytage had somehow managed to convince her first husband that the fiancée had had criminal relations with a servant in his house. He had broken off the engagement, and the other young lady had been publicly disgraced. Mrs. Armytage had realized, during the time she spent in the Major's company because of the blizzard, that he was this lady's son. She had understood this because of things he had said and the story he had told—apparently in a deliberate attempt to frighten her.

This is fascinating. It's remarkable how Mr. Quaife has managed to unearth all this new information!

Dr. Titheradge now talked to the Parson again, because in order to prove that the Major was the murderer, he had to break his alibi. At first the Parson stubbornly resisted his interrogation, but eventually the don's superior intellect and stronger personality triumphed, and the Parson was forced to admit that the Major was blackmailing him in some way that I don't quite understand, but which involved an incident that had taken place during his time in Africa as a young missionary and which the Major had somehow found out about. (That's all a bit vague.) He now admitted that he had been lying when he had told the inquiry that the Major had never been out of his sight during the crucial period.

Monday

Dr. Titheradge now felt he had enough to confront the Major and force a confession from him. He tried to find him at the hotel and was told he had gone for a walk toward the Watters o

Doon up in the Killiecrankie Hills. He indeed found him by the Watters, and he seemed surprisingly affable. The two men walked together for about an hour chatting about this and that. They discovered that they had a shared interest in murder and in particular in the Whitechapel killings, which had taken place about thirty years earlier. In other words, the case of Jack the Ripper! Another of my interests! Dr. Titheradge was very interested to learn this because he had done a little work on the case himself. Then he brought up the subject of the investigation he was carrying out into the death of Mrs. Armytage. He told the Major what he had learned from Miss Latimer about the incident involving the broken-off engagement. He told him he knew the significance of the scorpion that was found in the old lady's hand: It was a Masonic symbol indicating revenge. And finally he accused the Major of planting it on his victim to indicate that he was revenging himself against her.

The Major made no response to this charge but simply reminded him that the Parson had provided him with an alibi by saying that he never lost the Major from his sight during the crucial period. Dr. Titheradge now revealed that the Parson had admitted that he had been blackmailed into lying about this. (As confirmation of this, incidentally, he committed suicide some years later. But I still don't quite understand this bit.)

To his surprise the Major, who had previously seemed so blunt and so hostile, now became oily and unctuous and, without admitting his guilt, tried to persuade him to keep his findings to himself on the grounds that otherwise there would be an unpleasant scandal that would harm everybody involved.

When the don remained obdurate, the Major said, *You are not merely a man of considerable acuity but also completely on the square. I congratulate you, my friend, on both counts.* He held out his hand, and when he took it, Dr. Titheradge felt the other man's middle finger rubbing against his knuckle. He said, *I should tell you that although I am privy to many of your ancient secrets, I'm not a Mason.* The Major, however, smiled as if he was not in the least discomfited by this. To the contrary, he brought the topic of conversation around—via Masonry and the Great Pyramid—to the Middle East and invited Dr. Titheradge to accompany him on an imminent trip to Egypt. He said he would be honored to pay the don's expenses and provide him with whatever entertainment or amusements he might take a fancy to in Cairo. Dr. Titheradge refused this obvious attempt at bribery, saying he had become so interested in the mystery of Mrs. Armytage's death that nothing could persuade him to leave Killiecrankie until he had resolved the matter.

The Major realized that his attempt to bribe Dr. Titheradge had failed, and now this bit gets really exciting. He and Dr. Titheradge had reached the Killiecrankie Glen by now and were walking along the top of the selfsame cliff from which Mrs. Armytage had fallen or been pushed—a very desolate and lonely place. It was dusk by now, and the moon had risen. The Major asked Dr. Titheradge how he knew so much about Freemasonry, and the don explained he had picked it up while investigating the Whitechapel murders because of the connections between it and Jack. Now the Major told Dr. Titheradge he had a theory about how Jack killed his victims. His idea was that he got the fallen ladies to turn their backs to him by telling them he wanted to "take them from behind" (!) and when they did so, he gripped them around the neck from behind, choked them into losing consciousness, and then cut their throats while still standing behind them so that the blood spurted forward and missed him. (I must say, I think that's rather an interesting idea. And he must have had very strong wrists.) Anyway, he offered to demonstrate his theory, but Dr. Titheradge got a bit suspicious and wouldn't let him.

Then the Major said that he himself had a personal connection with the case. He had known one of the police officers who had investigated the Whitechapel killings. This man told him that an object had been found near one of the victims and had actually given it to him. He had it with him and offered to show it to Dr. Titheradge. The don could not resist. The Major removed from his pocket a handkerchief, which he unwrapped. Dr. Titheradge took from him the object that was inside it and lit a match to examine it, turning away from the Major as he did so. He noticed out of the corner of his eye that the Major was putting on gloves. He just had time to see that what the Major had given him was a silver brooch in the shape of a scorpion, but at that instant he felt the Major's hands fasten around his neck and quickly tighten.

He heard the Major cry, *Always get your retaliation in first.* Then he lost consciousness. But then, when the Major took away one hand for a moment, he came around. He caught the glint of a knife in the moonlight, which the other man must have taken from his pocket.

Dr. Titheradge thought rapidly. Then, in a last desperate attempt to save himself, he rather ingeniously used an Oriental fighting trick that he had learned during his time in India. It was a way of turning the tables on an opponent by using his own weight against him. He leaned forward so that he let the Major support his weight and then kicked backward with one leg. He heard a cry of pain, and the Major's grip on him loosened. He had, not to mince words, nearly disqualified the man from the matrimonial stakes.

Instantly, Dr. Titheradge sprang away. He saw the Major holding himself in agony. He looked very bizarre, because he had put on a pair of huge leather gloves—angling gauntlets, in fact.

With a shudder, Dr. Titheradge realized that he had done this to protect his sleeves from the spurt of blood, and he remembered what he had said about the Ripper. Could this man even be the Ripper himself, he wondered?

The Major conceded defeat and now admitted that he had indeed murdered the old lady and had done so in exactly the way described by Dr. Titheradge. And he had put into her hands a silver scorpion so that she should know why he was killing her. He said he had also followed the guard and killed him by suffocation so that it would look like death from exposure. He said he could not face the disgrace of a trial. He begged the don to let him take the honorable way out, and Dr. Titheradge agreed. And so he watched while the Major threw himself over the cliff at exactly the place where he had done the same to his victim.

Tuesday

The final chapter had a whole lot of guff about Dr. Titheradge's love for Miss Latimer and how he decided not to impose himself on her in all her beauty and silent grief and a lot of sentimental rubbish of that kind, and so he went off back to Cambridge to try to forget her, blah, blah, blah.

Apart from the ending, I was really impressed by this book. He has found a lot of new facts about the case and, in my humble opinion, solved most of the mysteries that have puzzled scholars for more than sixty years.

Wednesday

I can't wait for him to come in again and give me a chance to ask him some questions. I wonder how he found out about Dr. Titheradge. And perhaps he'll have to revise his theory when I tell him about Great-uncle Hamish. And I might mention that drinking was never a problem for him.

Thursday
No sign of him.

Friday
Still hasn't come in.

Saturday
He didn't come in once again. In fact, not many people came in at all, except for one or two who just walked straight into the back office to see Jerry. I just don't know how he manages to make any money out of this place. Even given the pittance he pays me. Especially since the stuff he buys is such c--p. He just won't spend enough on it.

Sunday
Quietish sort of day.

Monday
No sign of him.

Tuesday
Still no sign of him.

Wednesday
I wonder if he will ever come in again?

Thursday
Fairly wet.

Friday
Showers and a little sun.

Saturday
Thought I saw him outside the shop, but when I ran out, he'd gone. If it was him.

DECEMBER

Wednesday

Odd coincidence. Looking through the stuff Jerry got at the auction last Friday (mostly rubbish as per usual, since he's so reluctant to part with a penny), I found another history book with some material in it on the Killiecrankie Mystery. It's Mr. Archibald Peddie's *Scotch Mysteries*, which was privately published in 1938. I looked it up, and it's pretty rare, though not much sought by collectors, which surprises me. It has various documents, such as autopsy reports, letters, eyewitnesses' accounts, genealogies, morgue photographs, etc. on famous murders. One chapter has what Mr. Peddie claims is an account written by the Major and the Parson of the events of the fatal night when Mrs. Armytage died, which they wrote at the request of the procurator fiscal. I just glanced through it. I'll try to find time to read it later. But the lighting conditions are so good just now that I don't, to be frank, have an awful lot of time for reading.

Thought Mr. Quaife might be interested, so when Jerry had priced it—far too high, of course, the greedy, ignorant twerp—I sneaked it into the private case behind *The Fair Maid of Perth*.

Thursday

Got a bit behind with the diary recently. Hasn't really been a lot to record. Been concentrating more on the observation records.

FEBRUARY

Wednesday

He came in today! As soon as I saw him, I hurried out from the office and told him how impressed I'd been by his book. It was an astonishing achievement to have discovered so much crucial new material on the case. He seemed quite overwhelmed and confused for a minute or two. I said his theory was brilliant. He'd proved beyond doubt who did it and how. And I asked him how he had found out about Dr. Titheradge's investigation. He looked somewhat taken aback at that and didn't answer. I suppose he doesn't want to divulge his sources. Anyway, we talked for a while. And then I showed him Mr. Peddie's book. He said he'd never seen or even heard of it! [*Scrawled in the margin:* **Liar!**]

I explained about not having had time to read it, but said that as far as I could see from glancing through it, the witness statements might confirm Dr. Titheradge's theory. He seemed at first quite keen on buying it, but when I told him the price—thirty quid—he went off the idea. I said I could probably get Jerry to come down to twenty, but he still wasn't interested. So I put it back in the private case to look at when I get time.

He started talking about how it was always possible for new evidence to turn up in any given case and then said that he was not very interested in the Killiecrankie Mystery now that he had "shot his bolt" on it. Then he talked about some article or book he is writing about what he called *murder mattresses*(!) and said: *Any account can always have a huge gap in it that one is not aware of except insofar as it has visible consequences. That is, other things might be odd because the explanation for them is missing. And of course a text may be missing, too. It would be wonderful if some other document emerged or was reinterpreted that gave the solution to the mystery. So the solution is in existence and findable if only we knew where and how to look.*

I found this absolutely fascinating. And of course it made me think about Great-uncle Hamish and what he always said about the young lady and the Theory that had been handed down in the family.

I told him there were lots of things I wanted to ask him about the case, and I mentioned about having an ancestor who had been involved in it and had some evidence about who was guilty. He looked at his watch and said he'd love to hear what I had to say—those were his exact words!—but he had to hurry off to give a lecture. Then to my astonishment he suggested we meet for a drink on Sunday! He said we might go to that pub with the funny name where the writers go at the corner of West End Park Street. I didn't tell him I hate pubs and never go into them. Mainly because of the ladies—if that's what they are!—that you tend to get there.

I'm really excited about this.

Sunday

I was at the pub a bit before the time agreed. Horatio arrived a bit late. (I call him that now. He asked me to.) He said something I didn't quite understand that sounded like: *Sorry, but I couldn't get away until I'd found out whether Calum and Roberta really were brother and sister.* Very odd. I didn't like to ask him what he was talking about, especially as he seemed to think I'd know. They must be friends of his and he must think I know them. Funny. I had my usual. He had a pint and a couple of chasers. We bought a round each. £3.40.

I must remember they do a very reasonably priced soda water there.

I told him how I thought his book was brilliant. It cleared up all the loose ends in the case. But I admitted I hadn't quite grasped the business of Mrs. Armytage getting rid of her first husband's original fiancée by some sort of trick and what this had to do with the Major, so he explained it. It seems that she "framed" her by dressing up and putting on a red wig to look like her and then went to the room of a footman at night, having previously arranged that her first husband would be watching. The fiancée made an unhappy marriage, and the Major was her son! Imagine that!

Horatio wanted to talk about the Major. He said it is typical of that type of person to appear so brusque and irritable in order to make people think he is completely straightforward. But the truth is he is secretive and devious. He went on about how it's just like that type to circle around and stab his victim in the back. He said, *He comes on so high-minded and uncompromising. But all he cares about is power, getting his own way. He always has to be in charge, no matter if he's leading the party into a blinding snowstorm along the edge of a cliff.* He said that the Major was Scottish. I said I didn't know that. *Oh yes,* he said. *He's a true Scot.* He kept repeating that in a rather meaningful way that I wasn't sure I cared for. He talked about how the Major was "one of nature's blackmailers." So I asked him about the business of him blackmailing the Parson, which I hadn't understood. He looked a bit surprised and said he thought it was obvious enough.

I asked him about where he got the information from about the scorpion that the old lady was found clutching and said I didn't remember Mr. Roughead mentioning it. He said he hadn't mentioned it. That was entirely his own material. He had read somewhere that the scorpion was associated with revenge—and particularly with the idea of revenge that destroys itself, because it was believed that the scorpion stings itself to death. The scorpion was also linked with s-x, because its sting was thought to be like the burning of insatiable lust. And also people once believed that syphilis was passed to human beings by the sting of a scorpion. And it all tied up nicely because syphilis was associated with revenge because ladies used to pass it to men to pay them back for things they had done to them. I must say, that's all very fascinating. Things like that really make you think.

Horatio said something awfully clever when he was discussing about revenge. He said, *To resent is human; to revenge, divine.* That was jolly good, I thought. He quite often says clever things like that. I must try to write them down.

We talked about other murders and he said Glasgow was a wonderful place for them. I agreed completely. There were so many famous ones just in the West End. Then he suggested we go and look at Blythswood Square. I thought that was quite a good idea because by that time he seemed a bit . . . Well, definitely a little bit at least.

So we walked there. Then we stood and looked at the very window that Madeleine Smith handed her lover, Pierre L'Angelier, his fatal dose of arsenic through. I think we were both a bit overcome. Then Horatio looked at his watch and said he had to hurry home for something at nine-thirty. He asked me if I'd like to meet him again next Sunday! So of course I said yes and we arranged to meet at the pub again.

Monday
Went out again with my four-and-a-half incher under my coat. It can be tricky hiding it when it's fully extended.

Tuesday
Nothing much.

Wednesday
Not a lot to report.

Friday
Dullish sort of a day.

Saturday
Quietish.

Sunday
We met at the pub and had a few drinks. (I had soda water, of course, as usual. But I had to buy him a whiskey. £2.30.) Then we went for a walk.

Horatio talked about murder and in particular the Prentice trial, which he said was the most fascinating for several years and which he was following avidly. He said it was marvelous that because of the judge having died, there has to be a new trial, so that we'd hear all the evidence again and maybe find out more about what had really happened. He said that as a murder it was very far from perfection. It scored barely one out of a possible four points. (Whatever that meant.) But that was an interesting remark about perfection. Then he mentioned that the Whitechapel mystery was a particular interest of his. He thought it was the most fascinating case in history and he referred to Jack as the inventor of the serial murder.

I was really pleased to hear him mention about the case. But before I had a chance to say anything about it, he had gone onto another topic. What a mind that man has! We must discuss Jack again. I think he might be surprised by how much I know about the case. And he'll be pretty impressed when I tell him my Theory.

I asked him about the business where Dr. Titheradge uses logic to work out that the old lady was murdered. He cried out, *Hah!* in that way he has. Then he said, *My friend, you have put your finger on the most interesting and important part of the whole book.* Then he said, as far as I could understand him, that Dr. Titheradge had devised a "mattress" of the case. (Mattresses again!) He said that it was his work as a logician that had got him interested in murder. As far as I can make out, it seems he is interested in a murder investigation as an exercise in logic. He said that what Dr. Titheradge had done was to assemble the known facts in a logical structure according to their degree of probability and whether they contradicted other facts, weighting each of them according to their verifiability. Then he had run through the resulting set of ramifying possibilities and had found the only path that was consistent and possible. I could hardly wait to get home to write it all up before I forgot the details. There's some pretty complex ideas involved, as he said himself.

Then he asked me back to his flat! I was really flattered at that. So we walked there, and, to be frank, I was pretty surprised that it's in the Woodlands area, which is so run-down, and by how small and ordinary it was. He just has a kitchen, a lounge, his bedroom, and what he calls his cogitorium, which is his study and is full of books. I suppose he can't have made much money from his book. Though there is his salary from the university. We had some tea. Horatio drank some whiskey. He asked if I ever watched something called *Biggert*. It's a TV program, apparently. I explained that I don't have a TV. He seemed very surprised. He said he'd watched the last series, which ended last week, and got a great deal out of it. A new series was just about to start. It was on at nine-thirty. He said you could learn a lot from it. And then he said something about how much he'd like to write to Biggert, or perhaps it was for Biggert. And we've arranged to watch it next week.

Monday
Not much to report.

Friday
Very quiet.

Sunday
We met at his place and then went for a walk, and Horatio talked some more about his work on logic and murder and said that the perfect murder is the Sidney Fire (I don't know who he was!) of Desire for everyone involved: reader, writer, detective, and murderer. (I don't know what he means by that, but it sounds an interesting idea. I've written it down just the way he said it, but I still don't follow it. I must try and find out who Sidney Fire was. Apparently he is or was a friend of someone Horatio seems to know called Gavin—or Galvin?—Oscars.) He said the Prentice trial showed the truth of that: Prentice was led into

it by Sidney Fire, who apparently made him believe that he had found the perfect murder. (Strange. I don't remember anyone called Sidney Fire being mentioned during the trial.)

Quite often I don't fully understand what he's getting at, but I don't like to stop him and ask him to explain because it annoys him. And I feel so stupid. I'm not an educated man as he is. I'm self-taught and proud of it, but I'm sure there are some gaps in my education. In fact, just today, I told Horatio how I had once followed a course run by the Adult Education Department at the university called "Great Thinkers of the Western World." I explained about how I'd only got to Plato. He looked quite interested, but he just said, *Was it alphabetical or chronological?* I told him about how I got interested in astronomy because of learning about the ancient Greeks. Often it's best just to write down the things he says when I get back and then I think about them and start to see what he was getting at.

Then we went back to his flat to watch *Biggert*. It was really interesting. It all takes place in and around Glasgow—mostly around this area in the West End, in fact. So it was fun trying to spot bits I recognized.

I must say, though, that it was quite difficult to follow what was happening.

It's about this beautiful young lady detective, called Esmeralda. She's gorgeous. Mid-twenties, long chestnut hair, lovely long legs. One of those pouting, arrogant faces that you just want to hit. You don't see nearly enough of her because, unfortunately, there's quite a lot about Biggert, the detective she works under. He has a strange face. He looks like a punch-drunk old boxer. Horatio said his face has a battered vulnerability. Even worse, there's also a tiresome young man called Craigie, who is another of Biggert's assistants. It was rather funny, though, because he was so tall, he kept towering over Biggert, who had to turn his head right up to look at him. He's even taller than Horatio. And thinner. Whereas Biggert is shorter than I am! But people refer to him as "Big Biggert," and they do it with a straight face.

It must have been filmed last Halloween, because the streets were full of children in their costumes and masks. They showed this man in a Halloween mask, so you don't know who it is. He was watching a lady in the street on Byres Road and then he followed her home. Then you saw him climbing in through the

window of her house. (I don't know how they got to film that!)
Then we saw Biggert—with his wife—at the Citizens' Theater.
He talked to McIlhargey, who is the theater reviewer on the local
paper. (They called it the *The Glasgow Tribune* but they got that
wrong, of course. It's the *The Glasgow Clarion*.) McIlhargey was
with a beautiful young lady called Angelina. He and Biggert
spoke to each other just before the play started. Biggert explained that his wife had got them a ticket to the press interview,
and all four of them arranged to dine together later at the
Vesuvio Restaurant.

The play started and we saw a bit of it. It was called *The Importance of Being Jack* and it was about the circle of people who were
friendly with Mr. Gladstone, Oscar Wilde, and the Prince of
Wales. (I didn't even know those three knew each other.) Then
we saw the lady back at the house lying in her own blood. Her
throat had been cut!

Then we went back to the theater and there was this moment
when one of the actors got killed in the middle of the play. I
hadn't heard about that. Mind you, I'm not surprised at anything that happens on that stage. I went once and some astonishing things took place. Quite disgusting. Lots of men standing
about in skimpy little briefs with their hands on their hips and
sort of pouting at the audience. I left at the interval. (I can't
bear to think about men like that. I just don't want to have anything to do with it. It disgusts me.) People talk about the waste
of public money! They don't know the half of it. It was a complete waste of three actresses! Not one of them took off a d----d
thing!

Anyway, the way it happened was there was this scene where
one of the unfortunate ladies was walking along at night solicit-
ing passersby. None of them were interested. (To be honest, I
wasn't surprised. She was no beauty.) She talked about her life
as an East End w---e to the audience—only she didn't really
know they were there, so it was as if she was talking to herself.
(Frankly, I thought her voice seemed rather deep!)

Then someone came on stage from the wings. He was dressed
as Jack is supposed to be with a coat with a fur collar and a hat
that hid his face completely. He sneaked up behind the lady and
then put his left hand over her eyes so that she didn't know what
was happening, and quickly cut the throat with the right. Blood

spurted out. Everyone in the audience loved it. But Biggert suddenly realized that the murder was real. He jumped onto the
stage in pursuit, but the masked figure escaped because Biggert
was obstructed by a stagehand called Jamie—either accidentally
or intentionally—dropping what you thought was a dead body
on him. In fact, it was this horrible dummy of a lady, and it fell
on him and the dress went over his head. (That's actually pretty
rude, when you come to think of it!) and he tripped and fell
over.

Just then, Craigie arrived at the theater to tell Biggert that the
body of the lady had been discovered in the West End. Biggert
and Craigie looked at the dead fallen lady and found out that it
was actually not a lady at all but a man who was an actor called
Cherryman! Typical of the b----y Citz! Craigie went off to investigate the other case.

Then we saw Biggert and McIlhargey and their ladies having
dinner at the restaurant. The owner, Cavalli, was a big, jolly,
friendly Italian. He had this beautiful young daughter, Fiammetta, who gazed soulfully at the party. It seemed like she fell in love
with McIlhargey, and Biggert teased him about this when Angelina wasn't looking.

Just at the end, there was a very good moment when Esmeralda was back at her flat (in Ruskin Terrace, I'm pretty sure)
having a bath, and Biggert came to tell her about some new lead
that had just come up. First, when he got out of the car, he
glanced through the bathroom window from outside. Then he
went to the front door and found it was unlocked. So he came
in and shouted that he was there, and she called to him to come
right in, so he came to the door of the bathroom and stood
there talking, and we could see inside the room, and she was
soaping herself, and you saw her chest quite far down.

Just then Horatio asked me if I thought that the logic of the
evidential apperception was in conflict with the motivization. Or
something like that. He wanted me to look at some b---ted diagram of what he called the "founding enigma" that he was trying
to draw up. Sometimes I think he lives in a world of his own.

Then he started talking about Sidney Fire and his friend,
Gavin Oscars, again. He seemed to have something on his mind.
He wandered a bit but at last he told me he was worried about
something he referred to as the Gavin Oscars Affair. He seemed

surprised that I hadn't heard anything about it. Mr. Oscars is apparently a brilliant man—a sort of philosopher, as far as I can make out—a world-famous Thinker a bit like Einstein or Freud. Only French. (He doesn't sound French. In fact, he sounds Scottish. A thought occurs to me: I wonder if he's really Scottish like so many Great Men in the past have been, only people thought they were English?) He didn't mention what it is that Mr. Oscars thinks about. He ran something called the Institute of Gavin Oscars Studies in Paris and he moved it to Glasgow a few years ago. Horatio became a member of it. It seems Gavin Oscars was lured to Glasgow by some of his admirers in the expectation of being treated with the respect he was entitled to, but he has been appallingly treated at the university and in particular by someone Horatio called his, Horatio's, "Enemy."

It seems that this person—who Horatio didn't say what his name was—orchestrated what Horatio called *a concerted plot to assassinate Mr. Oscars's character and reputation* about a year or two ago. He tried to get him thrown out by the university and even prosecuted for something or other. It was in all the papers. There was an awful stink about it. Someone actually died. A man called Dr. Bentley. Committed suicide, it seems. He was another philosopher. I asked if Horatio knew him and he said of course he did. Then he suddenly buttoned up, and it seemed that he didn't want to say any more about it.

I asked him what this Great Thinker, Gavin Oscars, thinks about. He said it was to do with desire and language and a lot of stuff like that. (I didn't fully understand the answer, I must confess.) Then I asked him if his Enemy is a thinker, too. Horatio said, *He doesn't think, he broods.* Then he said, *I admit that he's capable of making intelligent remarks, and the younger students are often taken in by a few linguistic tricks and mechanical paradoxes. But I long ago realized that all his best remarks were plagiarized. He must sleep with a dictionary of quotations under his pillow.* He really made a point of not mentioning this man's name, I noticed.

As I was leaving, Horatio invited me to come and pick him up next Sunday and we'll go for a walk and then watch *Biggert* again. I'm really glad to have made a friend. And how useful and interesting to have the chance to work with a man like him. What an opportunity to see how his mind works, a trained mind!

The thing about a program like *Biggert* is that you learn so much about the life of other people. For instance, theater folk.

Sunday

He had left the door unlocked, so I knocked and went in. Found him sitting in front of the TV having his tea. He was watching a program called *Gargunnock Braes*. He signaled to me to keep quiet and sit down, and so I watched it. It's about life in a small Scottish village. You saw the people living there going about their ordinary lives. It's typical of any Scottish village. The folk that live there spend all their time gossiping about each other and having little quarrels and misunderstandings. Now I found out who Roberta and Calum are. She is the postmistress in the village and she also runs the little general store where all the gossip is exchanged. (But Calum isn't her brother, as far as I can see.) It struck me as strange that a man of his intelligence and education should find anything of interest in it. He looked a bit embarrassed about it, in fact. As soon as it was over, he switched it off and jumped up.

Then we set off for a walk. While we were going down Hyndland Road, Horatio suddenly said something I didn't understand about remembering the soap. Then he said, *You're probably wondering why I watch* Gargunnock Braes. (Which I was.) *It's actually a complex text about appearance and the endless play of signs and so on.* He said something about "semi-optics." Then he started on about someone called Echo—now there's another funny name!—who is also a whodunnit-writer and as well as that is something called a semi-optician. I said I hoped he never examined my eyes because he'd only be half right, but Horatio didn't seem to see the joke. (Sometimes I think he doesn't have a very good sense of humor.) Anyway, he was going on about logic and deduction and mattresses and he said watching *Gargunnock Braes* was crucial to his work on the logical mattress (!) of murder. I found it very interesting, though to be absolutely frank I didn't understand all of it.

He said I should come a bit earlier next week and watch it if I was interested. I'm glad our Sunday evenings are becoming a permanent fixture.

Then back to his place for *Biggert*. The program was abso-

lutely brilliant once again. Biggert was interviewing the cast of
The Importance of Being Jack. The Prince of Wales, who turned out
to be a very nervous, shifty type who chain-smoked, told him
about the various personality conflicts involved in the show.
(They were trying it out in Glasgow before taking it, hopefully,
to the West End.) He told him about the hatred that there was
between Maturin and Spencer, the author and the director.
Spencer thought the play was terrible and wanted drastic
changes to it, which Maturin was refusing to make. Biggert then
talked to Sherlock Holmes, who said he had nothing to say and
claimed that he had noticed none of the rows and quarrels that
the Prince of Wales mentioned about. A likely story! He's obviously playing a very deep game. Then Biggert talked to the
young actor who had replaced the dead Cherryman in his main
role of Algernon Swinburne. He seemed very nervous and guilty
and admitted that the death of the older actor had given him
his big opportunity. For apart from Algernon Swinburne,
Cherryman had also played the landlord of the Ten Bells—and
both of them were big roles.

Then Biggert interviewed Primrose, the deputy stage manager
and prompter, and it emerged that he was bitter and twisted because he had always wanted to be a director and thought Spencer was totally incompetent.

Then there was this man who we didn't see his face, stealing
ladies' lingerie off a washing line. Then he got into some lady's
house. She came into her bedroom and found him doing something with her lingerie. I couldn't quite see what, but it looked
as if it might be very rude indeed. Anyway, he cut her throat too.

Then we saw Dr. Watson slinking about the lanes and alley-
ways of the West End at night. Horatio said he looked very suspicious indeed, but I told him he couldn't possibly think *Dr.
Watson* was up to anything bad.

Suddenly, there was Jamie, the stagehand from the theater,
driving a Bentley! He was with a scruffy-looking character we
didn't recognize. They were discussing how to operate a video
camera. It was very mysterious.

And then right at the end of the program we saw a young lady
undressing for bed. She knew there was this man outside the
house watching her and she was shamelessly teasing him with

her body, driving him into an ungovernable fury. We saw part of her right bosom. Then the man sneaked into the house and punished her just the way she deserved.

When it was over, I asked Horatio who he thought had killed Cherryman. He said he thought that Algernon Swinburne was the most likely one because instead of the tiny role of a London bobby he now took over two very big roles. I agreed with that.

Horatio seemed to be fascinated by Biggert and he said several times, *He's very good, isn't he?*

I said he is wonderful. Particularly because he has an uncanny ability to be near the scene of a murder, which is invaluable for a detective, though he was never quite near enough to actually prevent it from happening. Horatio didn't seem to be listening, because he got very excited about what he called his "silent maleness" and his "brooding, manlike strength" and said he was "an icon of masculinity."

When it ended, Horatio asked me to stay on for a while. But he was definitely a bit . . . And after about twenty minutes he just fell asleep, so I let myself out.

MARCH

Sunday
Horatio's for tea. Was already a bit . . . by the time I arrived.

While we were watching *Gargunnock Braes*, he suddenly asked me if I'd realized what a two-faced hypocrite Auld Rab is. Apparently if I'd been watching it as long as he has, I would have realized that he is the evil genius of the village. Despite appearances, he said, Auld Rab is actually a devious troublemaker who pretends to like people but really hates them and wishes them harm. I said it was hard to believe, given his cherubic old man's face with its apple cheeks, and I pointed out that everyone in the village liked him, and the young people went and asked his advice when they had problems, and the married ladies made casseroles and baked pies for him and left them outside his door, and so on. I said you always got somebody like that in a Scottish village, some older person who was loved and respected by the younger people and was a living repository of oral folk wisdom. I remember one of my teachers at school here in Glasgow telling us that. But Horatio just shook his head and said he was still unconvinced. So I said there was also the fact that he is a national figure. I know this because Jerry, who is a keen gardener, mentioned to me that Auld Rab has his own gardening program, in which he gives advice on how to bed plants and so on. And he appears on bird programs quite a lot, Jerry said. And that wouldn't be true if there was any suspicion about him of that kind.

I wonder if Horatio can be right?

We went for a walk, and I managed to keep us out of the pub.

Horatio started on about Gavin Oscars again. He mentioned about his Enemy and said he was another philosopher. As soon as he'd said it, he seemed to regret having revealed so much. But then he went on to tell me more about him. He specializes in Scottish philosophy of the Post-Enlightenment and its links with what he said were dark German reactionary ideas at the end of the nineteenth century and beginning of the twentieth. He has written a philosophy book called *Neitszher in Scotland.* (I didn't know Neitszher came to Scotland. I wonder where he stayed.) And he's also written a book called *Scottish Cant.* Well, there's plenty of that about. Horatio says he hates and fears the new Theory since he is a deep reactionary. I thought, What new Theory is this? But I didn't like to ask. Can it be anything to do with Jack?

Then he started saying his Enemy was complicit with what he professed to detest. He was fascinated by power. That was why he hated Mr. Oscars so much. He would have loved to have had dozens of adoring disciples the way Mr. Oscars had. Horatio said his Enemy was now writing a book about Hitler in relation to the history of German philosophy. He said his Enemy was obsessed by Hitler and kept referring to the way somebody called Carl Young (?) had called him "a truly mystic medicine man."

We got back in time to watch *Biggert.* What happened was that another lady rang up and reported to the police that a man was watching her house at night and said she thought he had even been following her.

Then we saw the director of the play, Spencer, going to visit somebody at the university in the zoological department. It turned out that since he had been in Glasgow, he had befriended the eccentric old Professor Arbuthnott at the university, who was the professor of reptilian zoology. Spencer turned out to be an amateur zoologist and to be fascinated by poisonous creatures. And Professor Arbuthnott had a laboratory full of scorpions and spiders, where Spencer spent hours at a time watching and feeding the things. Urrghhh! But it's funny— scorpions again!

Then we went back to the Citz. The first public perfor- mance of the play had just ended, and everyone was at the first-night party. Biggert was there with his wife, of course, and so were Esmeralda—looking very glamorous in a little black skirt—and Craigie. There was a tremendous row because McIlhargey had written a terrible review attacking Spencer's direction of the production. And he'd also been extremely rude about the performance of someone called Ellen Terry that we haven't seen yet. First of all Spencer started shouting at McIlhargey. Then when McIlhargey had stalked out, saying that everyone in the play was going to regret this incident, there was a fierce row between Spencer and Maturin in which Maturin accused Spencer of trying to wreck his play by delib- erately directing it badly.

The party was taking place on the stage. Suddenly the Prince of Wales, who was loafing about smoking a roll-your-own, asked where Jamie was. And Sherlock Holmes replied, *He said he was busy but he'd try to drop in.* At that moment we saw right up into the top bit above the stage, and something started moving. Then it hit the stage. It was Jamie's body! There was total panic. In the middle of it Biggert took command (in what Horatio rightly said was his typically masterful manner) and quieted the hysterical ladies. Then he examined the corpse and pointed out to Esmeralda and Craigie that there was no sign of the means of death.

It was really interesting, but I couldn't help noticing some- thing I'd sort of half noticed before—how many slips of the tongue Biggert makes. He would start to say something and then get it muddled and have to start again. Sometimes he didn't no- tice that he had said something all wrong. Horatio does that a bit when he's been . . .

Afterward I asked Horatio if he thought it was possible that Spencer murdered Cherryman in order to wreck the play be- cause Cherryman was so good that he was stealing his glory? Or that another actor or actress killed him because he—or she—was jealous of his success? Horatio said he wanted to keep an open mind at this stage.

Tuesday
A man who loves gardens—well, it's difficult to think of him as evil.

Wednesday
Mind you, Jerry loves his garden.

Sunday
Horatio's for tea and we watched *Gargunnock Braes*. I had to admit that he's right about Auld Rab. There was a scene when he had to break some news to Jenny about her little girl, Shona. We were watching him closely when he said, *Ye'll ha'e to be strang, Jenny lass. Awfu' strang, hinny. For I've ill tidings to tell ye. Noo, ye'll mind that ying Andro niver took his lorry to ha'e its brakes checked forby his auld feyther fell doon the stairs last Hogmanay and was in the hospital for weeks and weeks? Noo, ye ken yon corner by the wee school-hoos? It grieves me to tell yow, but the wee wan's gane tae her Makar, hinny.*

Horatio said, *Look, he's laughing!* And he was quite right. You could definitely see that he was trying to not laugh and making an attempt to hide it. *You see?* Horatio cried. *The old pervert! He's smiling with secret pleasure at the poor lady's grief!*

Than a bit later Horatio suddenly cried out *Ha!* He wouldn't tell me why but said, *All will be made known in good time, my dear fellow.*

Later, while we were on our walk, we talked about *Gargunnock Braes*. Horatio asked me if I'd worked out how Auld Rab can afford what the shameless old fraud (which is what he referred to him as) calls his "wee treats"—the hothouse, the orchids, his jaunts to the coast on the bus, the fillet steak he sometimes gives to his retriever, Rumpty, and his new big telescope. (An eight-incher, I think.) I said I hadn't. And then Horatio explained that Auld Rab is blackmailing almost everybody in the village. He said he had realized this tonight when he had seen the old rogue casting a glance of pure lechery at Jacqueline, Roberta's young daughter, when she mentioned that she had had an early night the previous evening. He had watched her going to bed! And he explained how he has worked out that Auld Rab has acquired information about people in the village by being a Peeping Tom under cover of his interest in ornithology. That's how he knows all about their s-x lives and other things like the minister's secret drinking.

I was a bit taken aback at this. I said it was only too easy to jump to conclusions. Just because a man was out at night with a telescope didn't make him a Peeping Tom. *Bird-watching at night!* Horatio exclaimed. As it happened, I pointed out, Auld Rab was particularly interested in night birds. Sometimes Horatio can be rather cruel.

Anyway, I said, I thought the police would surely be onto him. Particularly since it was being seen by millions of people. He didn't seem to understand my point.

Well, we left it at that because it was time to head for home to watch *Biggert.*

It was brilliant as always. Esmeralda was wearing a tight little skirt that barely covered her person above the knee. It must have been filmed on Guy Fawkes Night, because there were fireworks exploding all over the place.

We saw this man, who we still couldn't see his face, stalking his victims amid the bonfires and fireworks in the West End.

Then Biggert was talking about the pathologist's report on Jamie. To his amazement the pathologist told him that he died by the poison of a scorpion. Then we saw McIlhargey's girlfriend, Angelina, calling the police to say she thought a man had followed her home, and the policeman that took the call told her they'd had so many like that in the last few days that they couldn't help her. He just told her to keep her doors locked and not let anyone in she didn't know.

And we kept seeing this man walking about the streets at night who we still couldn't see his face, and we saw lots more ladies shamelessly flaunting their bodies at the windows of their houses.

And then we saw Angelina hearing someone ring at the door and looking through her peephole to see who it was. Then she opened the door with a smile and said, *Hello. This is quite a surprise.* But we didn't see who her visitor was.

Then we saw that Walter Sickert, the painter who was supposed to be mixed up with Jack and who certainly knew a lot about the Prince of Wales's private life, coming out of the pictures, and from the posters outside you could see it was a very rude film indeed.

Finally, right at the end, we saw the police finding Angelina murdered in her own home and calling in Biggert. That's a real shame because she was a lovely young lady and we won't be seeing any more of her. The last words were when the camera came in close on Biggert and he said, *I think we may have a serial killer on the loose in our lovely Glasgow toon.* Then some heavy, somber chords and the closing credits. It was very good.

Now, I was interested in this, because serial killing is something I think I can say I know about. Horatio got very excited, too. He said this whole business of the serial killer was very relevant to his work on logic and murder. He said he was trying to devise the perfect murder. That's a very interesting idea. (I wonder if I could come up with something that might interest him.) I asked if he thought McIlhargey had killed Angelina, because it must have been someone she knew or she wouldn't have opened the door to him. Horatio looked mysterious and said he hadn't ruled out that possibility but he was keeping an open mind.

As we were talking about serial killing and the perfect murder, I brought up the subject of Jack. I could see he was pretty surprised by how much I know about the case. We talked about how extraordinary it is that he was never caught at the time nor ever unmasked subsequently in spite of the massive attempts to identify him that have gone on for a century. (At least, as far as we know, he was never identified for sure.)

Horatio said it was all the more extraordinary that he was never caught because he killed repeatedly, and always the same type of victim within a small area inside a few months. I said that he was clearly an amazing man: cool-headed, brilliant, courageous. He agreed and said it was the most tantalizing enigma in criminal history.

We talked about some of the puzzles in the case. Horatio pointed out that Jack must have been covered in blood as he walked about the streets after committing the murders. He said, *You couldn't cut someone's throat without blood spurting out, even if you stood behind and reached around to do it. The blood would still go over your arm unless you were very lucky. That's why the Major in* The Right Lines *used gloves when he tried to kill Dr. Titheradge. So even if Jack had worn gloves, that still left the question of what he had done with them immediately afterward. No bloodstained gloves were ever found.*

I said that some of the authorities on the case had suggested that you could draw your arm away as you cut into the victim's throat so that the blood spurted past it. He wasn't convinced. I even offered to show him—a dry run, of course!—but he wasn't too keen.

He pointed out that even if this was right, there were the ritualistic mutilations that he performed on several of his victims and that must have got him covered in blood.

That got us onto the question of whether he had any medical knowledge. I could see Horatio was quite surprised that I was familiar with all the theories about this. Just to find out how much he knew, I mentioned about the theory that Jack was a butcher, which would explain how he had some anatomical knowledge and also how he could walk about in bloodstained clothes. Horatio pointed out that he could hardly have done that in the middle of the night, which was very acute.

I said there were other trades that involved walking about covered in blood or something that looked like it. (Heavy hint. But he didn't pick it up.)

Then Horatio started talking about his logical mattress and said that any plausible theory about the case must account for these puzzles we'd been discussing about. (Which my own Theory certainly does.) He went on about it for a bit and then said that the Whitechapel case was "the perfect murder mystery."

He said it was the fact that Jack killed victims who were chosen at random that made him hard to catch. By doing that he reduced his chances of being detected unless he was unlucky enough to be caught in the act. But I reminded him of the theory that there was a connection between him and his victims. The idea was they were blackmailing the royal family about the fact that the eldest son of the Prince of Wales, the Duke of Clarence, had had a child by Walter Sickert's model, Marie Kelly. She later became a fallen lady and was the last of Jack's victims. (She was the one he spent a whole night dissecting!) He sneered at this, which he called "the royal conspiracy theory" and said it was much more likely that, as he claimed in one of his letters to the police, he was simply "down on w---es."

We talked about it for a long time. I was quite impressed. He hasn't read as much about the case as me, but he spotted a lot of the flaws in the various theories. That's a first-rate mind for you. When Horatio said the Whitechapel case was the perfect murder mystery, he was absolutely right. Jack had no connection with his victims and just killed at random. So he had a very high chance of avoiding detection as long as he wasn't caught in the act.

I'm longing to tell him my brilliant Theory. But I think I'll try to lick it into shape a bit more first. And see if he can get to it himself, since he's supposed to be so clever. It'll be interesting to watch his trained mind arrive at it on its own—though I might need to point him along the right lines.

While we were talking about blackmail, Horatio said he had now realized what was going on in *Gargunnock Braes*. He was watching the repeat on Wednesday when he caught Auld Rab whispering something he couldn't catch to Maggy, Andro's wife, and has guessed that the "dirty old b----r" blackmails people into having s-x with him!

I said this was astonishing. But Horatio talked about how Auld Rab bears grudges forever and said he had noticed that anyone he has ever crossed comes to a sticky end. He reeled off a whole series of people living in the village who have died suddenly in the last couple of years. And each of them had had some sort of run-in with Auld Rab—usually kept pretty clandestine so that most people watching the program wouldn't have realized. He said Auld Rab was skilled at working out of sight, and he suspected, he said, that he was an accomplished back stabber.

Then he said that Auld Rab was what he called a child molester. He said that before he retired, he used to be the janitor in the village school—a post he held all his working life—and he is sure the old rogue must have molested every man and every lady in the village who was now between the ages of fifteen and fifty-five. He said that explains why they treat him with what looks like affection and respect but is actually fear and distaste. I was absolutely stunned. He looks such a quiet old chap.

Sunday

I was over at his place and we were in the middle of watching *Gargunnock Braes* when Horatio suddenly shouted, *That's it!* It was when Roberta answered the phone and she said to Auld Rab, who was visiting her, *It's my lover. I mean my brother.* Horatio cried out, *Did you hear what she said? She said her brother, Calum, was her lover?* I said it was just a slip of the tongue.

Horatio said, *No, it's deliberate. She's sending a message. She's trying to signal the truth to the viewers. She's trying to convey that she has been having an affair with her brother.* I was skeptical at first, but then he explained that she only found out a few programs ago—before I started watching it—that Calum was actually her brother. Then he said he had an idea about why Roberta was trying to signal this.

He explained that Roberta and Calum were summoned by Senga some months ago to come and see her one afternoon. She's the wife of the minister and is a wise old lady with beautiful white hair who everybody in the village confides in. (Her husband is a mild old man but far too unworldly for anybody to tell him their problems—especially if they have anything to do with s-x. They're too afraid of shocking him.) Senga told them she had something astonishing to tell them. Something she thought they ought to know, even though their parents had never chosen to reveal it to them. Then she explained that Roberta and Calum are brother and sister! In fact, they are twins! They were born to someone in the village who she refused to name. This young lady was unmarried when her misfortune occurred, and both children were given to be adopted by Donalda and Moira. Senga said, *Try to understand and forgive this poor frightened young woman. Think of the pain she has suffered in giving her wee babies away and then seeing them grow up into a fine young man and woman and know that they will never love her as a mother. Always watching from afar, always yearning to give them a mother's love.* By the end all three were sobbing. It was really stupid. But as Horatio said, Senga made it clear that their real mother was someone in the village even though she refused to say who. And despite their pleas, she refused to reveal who their father was, either.

He started on about how slips of the tongue were attempts to communicate that are neither intended nor unintended. And then he began talking about some idea of Gavin Oscars who apparently believes that slips like that are "deliberate accidents." Then he said it was just like the way that a murderer always confesses in some way or other! While I was trying to digest that, he announced that murder itself is a form of confession! Apparently a murderer always wants to be caught! And that's why Jack sent letters to the police. Well, that all seemed very bizarre to me.

So to change the subject and get us back onto firmer ground, I mentioned about the theory that Jack was a doctor who worked in the locality. That gave him the medical knowledge, it let him walk about at night, it allowed him to have at least splashes of blood on him, and it meant he was trusted by both the police and the fallen ladies. Horatio knew all about this and was very scathing about it. He said it had lots of holes in it. One of the most crushing objections is that the doctor is never the murderer unless he is also a drug addict, and nobody who was addicted to drugs could have carried out such a distinguished series of murders.

Frankly, I was impressed.

Then I said, *So if he wasn't a butcher or a doctor, I wonder who else would have some anatomical training and be able to walk about the East End splashed with blood.* I must admit that I was teasing him a bit, just to see whether he'd spot the solution himself. He didn't. I can't wait to tell him. But not just yet.

We discussed about various other theories that have been put forward, and I told him straight out that I was convinced that Queen Victoria was not involved in the Whitechapel killings and had known nothing about them at the time. Or only very little. He agreed entirely.

Went for a walk. Still on the subject of Jack. Horatio said something very interesting: *The first murder must be the difficult one and after that it becomes easier and more enjoyable each time.*

Then just as we were going down that long dark lane off Turnberry Road that goes along the back of the gardens, he said, *Talking of murder, this would be a wonderful place for one.* He was quite right. Then he said that it was used by ladies of the night. They bring their customers here because it is so dark. *How does he know?*

Got back in time to watch *Biggert*. The police had started calling the guy the "Scorpion Killer"—apparently because he
"stings from behind." And also they thought the same man who
was doing ladies in the West End poisoned Jamie. They didn't
seem to be any closer to catching him. He was far too clever for
them.

There was a lot of stuff showing Oscar Wilde hanging about
in pubs. (Presumably he was looking for men to do disgusting
things with.) And we saw a lot of the Prince of Wales hanging
about shady places, too. (I dare say *he* was looking for ladies.)
And we saw various things going on in the laboratory of Professor Arbuthnott. There was this young man who works there
called McGinnity who is a taxidummyist for the university, which
means that he makes dummies by stuffing the animals when
they die and need to be kept for some reason. We saw some
more ladies in the windows of houses in the West End. Then we
saw McGinnity talking to Cavalli about something neither of us
could quite grasp.

It's quite a thought that Glasgow has a brilliant serial killer on
the loose to rival England's Jack, who has collected all the glory
up to now.

Monday

Nothing in *The Clarion* about "the Scorpion." Very strange.
Are they trying to hush it up?

Was at the shop until late and when I left, I took the four-and-
a-half-incher from the private case (where it had squashed *Count
Robert of Paris* a bit) and did some work up until nearly midnight.

Thursday

When I was over at his place last Sunday, Horatio said something really nice. Made me feel really flattered.

We were talking about how clever Jack must have been,
when Horatio said: *I don't think you need to be brilliant, but undoubtedly intelligence is crucial. Someone with superior intelligence
could commit a successful murder. Particularly someone with a trained
mind. There is also the fact that the police are always stupid. Look at
their blunders during the pursuit of the Yorkshire Ripper when they in-*

terviewed the murderer a number of times and he kept coming up in their computers.

And I said, *That's right. Think of Lestrade.* He said, *Yes. Even Watson isn't as stupid as him.* And I said, *As you said the other day, the cleverest detectives are never policemen: the great Sherlock Holmes, Hercule Poirot, Lord Peter Wimsey, Miss Marple.* And then I couldn't help teasing him a bit, so I said, *Except for Maigret. You said the other day that he was pretty shrewd.*

He said rather curtly, *A rare exception.*

Then he said something like, *Now that we've changed the topic* (Had we?) *my view is that you don't need to be highly educated to devise the perfect murder. Just very intelligent and rational. Look at Christie.*

Mr. Christie! One of my favorites! *Christie was certainly very clever,* I said. *And got away with it over and over again.*

He agreed.

You can learn a lot from Mr. Christie. What a mind. He got another man hanged for the murders he'd done! He was in pursuit of perfection. Of course, he got caught in the end. Hanged, in fact. Horatio is absolutely right that a person doesn't need to be highly educated to devise the perfect murder. He just needs to be extremely intelligent and very cool.

[*Added later.* **Seems I got a bit muddled here**.]

Then he mentioned suddenly about how he found my mind "fascinating" and "highly useful" to him as a philosopher. He said I had a mind like a razor. Then he laughed and muttered something like *a tablet razor.* Or maybe it was *a tubular razor.* Anyway, it sounded really flattering. So maybe he does respect my mind more than he sometimes gives the impression of doing.

That conversation—about Mr. Christie and everything—has made me realize how much we agree about things. So I've decided to tell him my Theory.

APRIL

Sunday

Told him the whole thing while we were having our walk. As soon as I mentioned it, he exclaimed, *That's utterly fascinating.*

You've got hold of something quite brilliant there! I felt really encouraged. But once I'd started on it and gone into it in depth, he went very quiet. And when he'd heard the whole of it in detail, he was very negative. And really quite nasty. He let me lay out the complete Theory about Jack having been an artist without saying anything, and then when I'd finished, he ripped into it and tried to tear it to shreds. Said it didn't match his b---ming mattress at all. Dismissed my claim that it solves the problem of whether Jack had medical knowledge. Said it would not have been "deep" enough. (He was very pleased with that joke, which I thought was very feeble.)

Pooh-poohed my idea about how it meant he was able to walk about in a red-stained smock and beret. And he said no lady of the night (only he used a much ruder expression) would have gone into a dark alley with a man wearing a red-smeared smock while the panic was on. I said of course the smock was only splashed with red *after* he had done it, but he said he was still unconvinced that any w---e would have gone into an alley with a man wearing a smock.

I'm tempted, frankly, to show him I'm right.

This has been one of the worst days of my life. I really felt entitled to a bit of respect. But his whole attitude seemed to be that my ideas were just stupid. Just because I never went to university. As if you have to be a logician to be clever!

Had another shock when we got back. Seems I've been totally wrong about *Biggert*. What happened was, we were watching it when I said something about Biggert making even more slips of the tongue than usual. And Horatio said, *That just shows how b----y good MacMangan is. People do slur their speech and make silly slips of the tongue. And so the slips give an air of verisimilitude.*

I said, *MacMangan? What are you talking about?* (Thank heavens I didn't say anything to give myself away! I don't think he realized.)

And Horatio said, *The actor who plays Biggert.*

Actor! It turns out the program is all invented! So there's no "Scorpion Killer," and Glasgow doesn't have a talented practitioner to rival Jack! Esmeralda doesn't really live in Ruskin Terrace! All that time I've wasted! D--n, d--n, d--n!

It was pretty dull, actually. We saw the Prince of Wales going into a sauna called Fingers.

Then there was a scene in which someone who you still didn't see his face stole ladies' lingerie from a launderette.

And then McIlhargey took this very beautiful young lady, who was the Countess of Warwick, to dinner at the restaurant run by Cavalli, and once again we saw Fiammetta gazing at them. Horatio said she was clearly pining for McIlhargey and he had a shrewd suspicion that she had killed Angelina out of jealousy. He said if the Countess of Warwick was killed, he'd be pretty sure his hunch was correct.

Monday

What I can't understand is why anybody would want to watch it when it's all invented!

Tuesday

No wonder I never managed to catch a glimpse of her! That old man who lives there must have been surprised. I thought he must be her dad.

Sunday

Over at his place. Watched *Gargunnock Braes*. Nothing much happened. Afterward I asked him if it was fiction too, and he laughed. Then he started on about Jack as one of the great English artists. You'd honestly think there was nobody else who'd ever done anything like that. Has he forgotten all those great Scots? Burke and Hare. Dr. Pritchard. Peter Manuel. And people forget that though he practiced in London, Dennis Nilsen wasn't English. He was Scottish.

Anyway, we don't know that Jack was English. Chances are he was a Pole or a Russian. He might even have been Scottish. Now, there's a thought. I wanted to point that out to him, but I couldn't get a word in edgeways.

He was going on and on about something he claimed I'd said—or he'd thought I'd said—the other day. Seems he had misunderstood my use of the word *artist* the first time I said it and that had given him a "brilliant" idea. Frankly I wasn't paying a lot of attention at that point.

It was something about Jack as the culmination of the great romantic artists, but a frustrated artist. Art for art's sake. The purity of killing solely for the sake of killing. And then Jack as the counterpart of Oscar Wilde. He had no motive except to commit an elegant murder. He was trying to perfect murder as an art form! If he had no connection with his victims, then the murders were too easy. So he made the "game" more interesting by sending messages that gave the police a better chance of catching him. Art has to be difficult to make it worthwhile, and so does murder. And not just difficult but elegant and economical. Then he started talking about something he called a points system. He said, *One point for knowing the victim well. Another point for disguising the murder as suicide or accident. Another for an irrefutable alibi. And another for communicating with the police. We don't know about his alibi, but otherwise Jack scores, at most, only two out of three. Say ninety percent for the first and another ninety for the third. A hundred and eighty out of a possible three hundred. Sixty percent overall. Not that brilliant.*

Sounded pretty nonsensical, to be absolutely frank. I just heard him say for about the third time that I'd said something more intelligent than I'd meant to say when I sort of switched off. I just looked at him sitting there in his silly getup with his glass of whiskey in his hand, holding forth. And I just wondered if that was what he was like when he was teaching. Without the whiskey, I mean. At least, I suppose without the whiskey.

I was so fed up with him going on and on about Jack (plus my disappointment about "the Scorpion") that I interrupted him in full flight. He *did* look surprised. I said he almost gave the impression that he had never heard of Bible John, often called the Scottish Jack the Ripper. (I was being really sarcastic.) And of course he had to admit that he hadn't heard of him. So I told him about how he killed three ladies in Glasgow in 1968 and 1969 and has never been caught. He picked the ladies up at the same dance hall in the Barrowland in the East End and told them Bible stories while they danced. Then he took them to somewhere nearby and started doing things with them but then strangled them with their own tights. I said his coolness was amazing. He went back to the same place to find his victims twice more after the first time. And on the last occasion he shared a taxi home with the sister of one of them, and talked to her for a long time. What a risk he was taking! (That's how we know about the Bible stories.) He calmly dropped the sister off, paid the taxi, and took the victim off and did it to her. Horatio got very interested indeed. I said there was something else. All the victims were in a particular condition. Horatio didn't understand me at first. I practically had to spell it out for him. I said John seemed to have a particular interest in blood. He still didn't get it. So I had to say I meant ladies' blood. Then at last he saw what I meant.

Of course the whole city became panic-stricken while these things were happening. I said it was just like the way Jack could somehow persuade the ladies to go into dark back courts with him at the height of the Whitechapel panic. Bible John was able to pick his victims at the same dance hall a second time and then a third one. Both he and Jack must have had the same quality of being very charming. I said there were a lot of resemblances between the two. And John was just as daring and cool as Jack. Horatio said he was just a pathetic plagiarist. He just ripped Jack off, he said. He said he should have been called Jack the Rip-off! I was getting really quite annoyed. I thought he had a point, but I wasn't prepared to let him see it.

Then he made some clever-clever remark about how strange it was he wasn't caught, since it should have been easy to find a Scot who was charming and paid for taxis. I was very calm. I just pointed out that—as I'd been reflecting for some time—we don't know that Jack himself wasn't Scottish. He laughed. Just let him wait and see!

Watched *Biggert*. We saw some man who we couldn't see his face, and he was in a lingerie shop fondling the underwear. A female assistant looked at him and then suddenly panicked. The man ran out. Biggert interviewed her, and she kept going on about how she suddenly saw a look of pure evil on his face. She was so hysterical she couldn't describe him at all. Just kept saying, *Evil. Such evil.*

And then we saw Oscar Wilde playing video games in a pub. And he got into conversation with a rough-looking character called M'Lay. Horatio pointed out that he was the man that Jamie was with when he was driving a Bentley shortly before he was killed.

Then we both got a real shock. What happened was we saw the actors at the Citz rehearsing *The Importance of Being Jack* again, and someone said that Ellen Terry was about to appear, and then on she came. To our astonishment, it was none other than Roberta! She was in late Victorian clothes and she looked so glamorous and exotic that you could hardly believe she was really only a village postmistress. She was claiming to be a famous actress and one of the Prince of Wales's girlfriends. Horatio was as surprised as I was. He said this confirmed his theory about what was really happening in the *Braes*.

I must admit, Biggert is very good because you can see that he's really acting. He really takes his time to register when he hears something surprising. And he often speaks very slowly and carefully when it's a complicated bit so that you can understand every word. Now I can see how he even slurs his words and makes slips of the tongue and calls other characters by the wrong name just the way people do in real life. Horatio says his technique is masterly. On the other hand, the guy who plays his young assistant isn't so good because he just behaves the way any policeman would under those circumstances. (Though Horatio seems to like him.) Esmeralda is wonderful, though. I hope we get to see more of her. A lot more.

Monday
I have to admit, Horatio has a point about Bible John. I'm afraid he was just a poor man's Jack the Ripper. And, to be frank, one with some rather perverted tastes, too. I'm almost ashamed he was Scottish.

Tuesday
Maybe he was English!

Wednesday
This business of Jack being Scottish has been much on my mind. I've also been thinking about what Great-uncle Hamish said about the old lady's neck. After all, as Horatio himself said, there can always be some missing fact that turns up later and gives a completely new interpretation of events. So maybe this is true of the Killiecrankie Mystery. I don't see why it shouldn't be. And if Jack *was* Scottish, then why shouldn't

there be a connection with the most famous murder in Scottish history? Especially since it occurred only a few years after he was practicing!

If it's true that instead of her neck being broken, her throat was cut from ear to ear, then there's a definite link for starters.

It's a real problem that I can't quite see how the silent young lady fits in. It's really frustrating. Great-uncle Hamish was so sure about her.

I must say, the Major interests me more and more. I wonder if he is the key to more than just the Killiecrankie Mystery. He has his fingers in so many pies: Freemasonry, the connection with Jack, the scorpion, and the way he uses Jack's modus operandi. Bluntly, what I'm wondering is this: Was the Major really Jack? Horatio has come up with a lot of evidence that points that way. But if Great-uncle Hamish was right, the Major didn't kill the old lady. It's all very puzzling.

I wonder if Horatio has found out more about the Major than he has admitted.

Thursday
Coming back to that idea I had. Been thinking about it a lot. Would certainly show Horatio he had seriously underestimated my intelligence.

Started doing some fieldwork. Planning is crucial. Been thinking a lot about the site.

Friday
Been doing another recce. That long grassy lane off Turnberry Road is looking very good.

Saturday
Sunday.

Sunday Afternoon

I feel now I can look at him in the eye as an equal. I've earned his respect.

Sunday Evening

I got a very nasty shock when I arrived. He greeted me with the words *There's been a murder! And I know all about it! I've figured it out.* I sat down rather quickly, I might say. Luckily he was too excited to notice that I was shaking like a leaf.

Then he explained it all to me. I'd missed the *Braes* because of being held up. Astonishing! He is quite extraordinary. It must be his trained Cambridge mind, as he says. He itemized the reasons for his theory that a murder has been committed. What a relief!

He said he had worked out what has been going on with Roberta. When she admitted a few weeks ago that her brother was actually also her lover, she was signaling that she was in danger of being murdered and trying to save herself. He reckons that Auld Rab has been blackmailing her. Because he had been spying on them at night under the cover of his bird-watching, he had found out about her affair with Calum, which had started innocently enough long before they found out they were brother and sister. (I didn't say anything, but I thought to myself, *Innocently! When they are both married and have families! How typically English! What a degenerate people they are!*) Horatio said Auld Rab was threatening to expose them both unless she provided certain services for him. (At first I didn't realize what he meant until he put it even more bluntly. Then I was really embarrassed.) She was threatening to expose him as a blackmailer. Well, I could go along with all of that.

But then he went on to argue that Auld Rab had actually murdered her because she was about to expose him. In fact, her so-called slip of the tongue was an attempt to confess to the affair and so make blackmail impossible.

When he'd finished explaining all this, I said I wasn't completely convinced. (I think he was a bit taken aback at that!) I asked him for his evidence, and he said that it was the fact that Roberta had disappeared. We haven't seen her since her confession.

Well, that was true. Though only in a sense. In fact, as we both know, she's taken on a false name and gone to work at the Citz.

I didn't say that, though. I just said that his evidence didn't seem to be a clincher, and he said we'd keep the subject under review. He reminded me of something that Sherlock Holmes once said: *When you have eliminated the plausible explanation, the implausible one is all that remains.* Well, that's true enough.

I'd missed the program because I was so late, so we went for our walk straight away. Of course, I was longing to tell him about my own fieldwork. But I have to choose my moment carefully.

Unfortunately, then we had an argument about Jack. I suppose I was a bit excited and that was why I wasn't prepared to let him lay down the law. He sneered once again at my Theory about how Jack had learned enough anatomy at art school to be able to deal with and then dissect his victims so quickly and expertly, and said he was quite sure he must have had at least some medical training. I was longing to tell him how wrong he was. I wanted to say, *But I know I'm right. I know you don't need much anatomical knowledge in order to render someone unconscious and then cut their throat. And open their stomach.*

Then I made some remark about him being the perfect murderer and he jumped down my throat. So I said, *I thought you and I had agreed that Jack committed the perfect murder several times by randomly killing fallen ladies who had no connection with him.*

Horatio said, *You've completely misunderstood me. (But don't blame yourself for that. There are probably faults on both sides.) Anyone could commit a successful murder by killing someone at random. That's not what I mean by the perfect murder. The challenge is to kill someone to whom one is connected so that one is the most obvious suspect. Think of the Croydon poisoner who murdered her three closest relatives and got away with it. Now, that really was an achievement!*

Well, that was a bit of a stunner! *Now* he tells me! Had to have a connection! That gave me plenty to think about. I nearly blurted out that he'd been wasting my time. But I suppose it wasn't really his fault.

Watched *Biggert*, though to be frank, I wasn't able to concentrate on it very hard after what Horatio had said. Anyway, Roberta was offered a role in a television show called *Tillieknock Nuik*. And because of all the horrible things that had been happening at the Citz, the quarrels and the murders and such, she decided she wanted to take it. That would mean leaving *The Im-*

portance of Being Jack. There was a huge row with Maturin and
Spencer about this because Spencer wanted her to go so that he
could get someone he thought was better than her. But
Maturin—who Horatio says is in love with her—wanted her to
stay because he thought she was so good that the whole play
would collapse without her. More about Cavalli, who seems to
know McGinnity, the taxidummyist. But quite honestly I didn't
make a lot of effort to follow it all, though Horatio sat there
staring at the screen with his mouth hanging slightly open. Especially every time b---sed Biggert was on.

Anyway, in the end Roberta did succeed in leaving the production. One of the other actresses—the Countess of Warwick—
expected to be promoted to the part, which was a lot bigger
than hers, but Spencer insisted on bringing in a new actress to
play Ellen Terry. (Horatio commented that she is almost certainly his mistress.)

We saw Mr. Gladstone, who was clearly up to no good,
skulking about the West End after hours and without his beard.
We know about his after-hours interests. And his famous "bag."
Three guesses as to what he was up to!

By the time I left, Horatio was too far gone to see me to the
door.

Monday

I've been thinking about my Theory. It's clear to me now that
Jack *did* indeed know his victims. He had used them as his models! That's why they trusted him enough to go up a dark alleyway
with him even at the height of the panic. My Theory can certainly accommodate that possibility.

So Jack *did* commit the perfect murder—and did it five
times!

I must think about the implications of this for any future
fieldwork.

Tuesday

Horatio has a good point, I suppose, when he said on Sunday
that if an artist had used even one of the dead ladies as a model,
the police would have discovered the link. (And he also said that
apart from Marie Kelly they were too old and ugly, which is another good point.) But perhaps the police *did* know about this?

Perhaps they knew who Jack was but protected him? The old theory that he was a Freemason might be the answer. The police force was full of Freemasons. They would have wanted to cover up anything that linked Jack to them.

I must do some work on this.

Wednesday
BrannyBrekkers has started a series on reptiles and things like that. I must try and collect them.

Sunday
When I arrived, he was well gone. When we left the house for our walk, he insisted on going to that pub for writers that I've been trying to keep him out of, and sure enough, when we went in, there were McConville and McAlweenie sitting there, two of the most notorious literary boozers in Glasgow—which is saying quite a lot. I could see this costing me a week's spending money if I wasn't pretty careful. They nodded at him in a not very friendly way. I don't think either of them recognized me, though they both come in the shop quite often. Horatio went straight up to them and cried out, *How is the life literary, my fellow scribes?* Their faces! I think they would have told him to go away in no uncertain terms only he offered straight away to buy them a round. They didn't look too pleased to have to talk to him. It turned out they both knew him because they'd read their stuff up at the Uni and he'd come along and met them.

That McConville's language is quite dreadful. I'm told his writing is just the same. A stream of filth. I'm glad to say I've never read any of his books. I understand they're stories, and I never read story books.

They started talking about the Gavin Oscars business that Horatio had mentioned to me about and that it seems everyone at the Uni is interested in.

McConville said Mr. Oscars was a total fraud: *It's a load of s--te, all that stuff that c--t does. All that theoretical s--te.*

He said it was deeply inimical to the Scottish commonsense tradition. It was being foisted on Scottish philosophy by English woofters and French frog-f--kers.

Horatio disagreed violently. He said, *It's very important work on the boundaries of philosophy, psychoanalysis, and language. It has far-reaching implications. It's ironic that it was a philosopher—so-called, at least—who attacked Gavin Oscars most viciously. And in a two-faced, back-stabbing manner.*

I pricked up my ears at that, because I knew he was referring to his Enemy and I was hoping to find out the name at last.

McConville said, *What the f--k are you talking about?*

Horatio said, *I'm referring to the fact that he took advantage of his position in the Senate as a professor to attack him under privilege.*

He must of forgotten that he had told me he was a philosopher, because now he had revealed to me that he was a professor.

McConville said, *That's s---e! That man's brilliant. He's a f--king genius. He's just what this f--king country needs. He's not afraid to call a load of s--te a load of s--te. What he said about Gavin Oscars was f--king right. He said Gavin Oscars had founded an empire of nonsense and crowned himself king.*

Unfortunately he didn't mention his name.

Then McConville said, *Talking of irony, I'll tell you what's ironic. It's ironic that it was someone in the English department who was Gavin Oscars's biggest defender. What the f--k does a c--t like that know about philosophy?*

Horatio looked pretty annoyed at that and he got up and went to the bar to get another round, even though he'd just bought one. (Thank heavens.)

While he was away, I said to McConville, *Who's the professor?*

He said, *Speculand.*

So that's his name! [*Added later.* **Got muddled here, unfortunately. Professor Speculand is the professor of English!**]

Then McAlweenie said, *How do you know the Don with the Luminous Nose?*

I thought that was quite funny. And he does have a rather red nose, now that I think about it. Hardly surprising.

Before I could answer, McConville said, *Do you know how much f--king money that c--t made out of that book of his about the Killiecrankie Mystery?*

I said, *No. How much?*

He said, *I don't f--king know. I was f--king asking you. You're supposed to be his f----g friend. Hasn't he told you?*

McAlweenie said, *It was one f--king h--l of a lot. I've seen the f--king thing in all the f--king bookshops.*

What do you think? I asked. *A thousand?*

After all, they're the writers. They should know.

McConville whistled and McAlweenie said, *Don't be such a f--king c--t. Tens of thousands.*

Well, that was a surprise. I'd never thought of it before. No wonder he can afford to throw his money around in taverns.

Then McAlweenie said, *That's a f--king Scottish crime he's based that f--king book on. Another piece of f--king Scotland that's been colonized and appropriated. He's f--king stolen a slice of Scottish f--king history! Are those English c--ts going to leave us anything of our own?*

He had a point, I must say. We couldn't say any more, though, because at that moment he came back with the drinks.

He could have stayed there all b---ming night. I could see another round coming up, and it didn't look to me as if McAlweenie and McConville had any intention of buying it. In the end I only got him out of there when I whispered in his ear that it was time for *Biggert.* I might say I had some difficulty getting him up the stairs.

When we got back to his flat, he was very excited and started saying that if he could commit the perfect murder, he'd do it. He said the perfect murder needs the perfect victim, and he had just the right candidate. I asked him what he meant. He said he'd explain all that to me sometime soon. He thought I wasn't quite ready for it yet. He says *I'm* not ready! I could give *him* some surprises!

We watched *Biggert.* It was Christmas Eve and we saw all these men dressed as Father Christmas. One of them was following a young lady through the West End. She kept glancing back and then hurrying on, and every time this Father Christmas was right behind her.

Then we saw Mr. Gladstone being caught by the police trying to peddle drugs to an undercover detective in a gentleman's t----t. They brought him in for interrogation, and Biggert said to the girl, *This is it, young Esmeralda! I think the case is beginning to crack!* He told her to stay outside the interview room for the first ten minutes. Then he went in and told the uniformed officer to get the h--l out.

Then there was something really very disgusting. McIlhargey and the Countess of Warwick were back in his flat and they were kissing and touching each other.

Then we saw the interview room again, and Biggert called Esmeralda in and said he'd dusted Mr. Gladstone down a bit, as he put it. And now he was anxious to tell him everything from the time he first wet his pants to his last c--p. (That was really rude but quite funny. And Horatio really loved this bit, too.) Biggert was really nice now and stuck a cigarette in poor Mr. Gladstone's mouth while Esmeralda cleaned up his face a bit.

Then McIlhargey and the Countess of Warwick were lying on a bed and doing things. (I was really embarrassed with Horatio there.) But luckily they hadn't done much when she suddenly screamed and we saw this scorpion running across the pillow. McIlhargey cried out in pain as it stung him.

Then Biggert was interviewing Mr. Gladstone, who started telling him all the dirt that had been going on behind the scenes at the Citz. He told him that Cherryman was having an affair with someone, but he wouldn't say who it was. He said he was too scared to say any more. After all, two people had died already. At that moment Craigie came in and said, *Make that three.* McIlhargey had just died in terrible agony. When he heard this, Mr. Gladstone smiled. (But after all, McIlhargey had been pretty rude about his performance, too.)

Meanwhile we saw Father Christmas catching one of his victims in a dark alley and doing it to her.

Horatio suddenly sat up in his chair. *Look at that!* he cried. *That's Athole Lane!* And he was absolutely right! It was the lane into Athole Gardens, which we have occasionally walked down on Sunday evenings.

Then Biggert and the others discussed the murder of McIlhargey and decided that Fiammetta, who they agreed was in love with McIlhargey, must have intended to kill the Countess of Warwick but killed him by accident. They decided that she might even have been the person who killed Angelina and that she might even be "the Scorpion."

Then they got the news of the latest murder in the West End, and the episode ended with Biggert saying, *What we still don't know is whether we're dealing with two series of killings or one.*

I stayed on for a bit and made myself some tea. The program

has lost a lot of its charm for me now that I know it's just made up. Horatio opened another bottle. We discussed about whether Fiammetta could be the killer. Horatio said he was reserving judgment, but he said he had some quite interesting ideas he would tell me about later. Then he brought up that business of the other week that he'd read about in the papers. He said it was odd how it had happened in the lane off Turnberry Road. And the *modus operandi* being what it was.

Oh, and that reminds me. I've told him not to come in the shop. Or if he does, not to talk to me as if he knows me. (I don't want Gargantua—that's what he calls Jerry!—listening to us and knowing all about my private life.)

Anyway, after that he fell asleep on the sofa.

I just had a little tiny look around the flat. To be quite honest, I'd been made a bit curious by what McConville and McAlweenie had said. I noticed a new hi-fi and a new computer. Signs of affluence. Then I let myself out and came home. Much to think about.

Sunday
What a day this has been! Probably the most exciting and gratifying in my entire existence to date!

He was very full of himself when I arrived. I knew there was some bit of news he was longing to tell me. And then while we were watching *Gargunnock Braes* he kept humming and muttering to himself and grinning. I asked him what he was up to and he said, *Just wait, my friend. All will be made known in due course.* Then he suddenly shouted, *That's the proof I need!*

What happened was that Calum was talking to Senga, the minister's old wife, about Calum's wife wanting a trial separation from him and planning to go to Perth for a few months, taking their daughter, Maureen, with her. Calum was getting very upset at the thought of losing the affection of his young daughter, and at one point, when Senga gently suggested it might be best for the little girl, he cried out, *Jacqueline is my child! I mean, Roberta is my child.* And then (as Horatio said later) a look of real horror appeared on Senga's face and she almost blurted out, *You mean, Maureen's your child. Roberta is your sister.*

At that Horatio clapped his hands and shouted, *You see? Calum has just spoken the truth. Jacqueline really is his child. His child by Roberta. Their incestuous love child! I understand it all now! Auld Rab was blackmailing her about this as well. Now he's blackmailing Calum about it.*

I said, *But Calum also said Roberta is his child. Do you think that can be true, too?*

Horatio said rather irritably, *Of course not. They're brother and sister—they're twins, for G-d's sake! That was just a slip of the tongue.*

I said, *All right. But there's another explanation. Perhaps Calum himself murdered her to stop her telling his wife about their affair? Or his wife found out about it and killed her? That's the real reason why she wants to separate from him.*

Horatio said very curtly, *The hypothesis is unlikely, but produce your evidence and I'm prepared to consider it. That's what I always say to my students.*

Then he went on to say that this was the "clincher." Everything fell into place. Having murdered Roberta, Auld Rab was now blackmailing Calum. I asked what he was trying to gain, since Calum earns very little, but Horatio just looked mysterious and put his finger alongside his nose in that irritating way he has.

I said that although I was keeping an open mind about it, I still wasn't entirely convinced that Roberta had been murdered, because it hadn't been made explicit. Horatio got very excited at that and said, *Exactly. It's the perfect murder—one that nobody notices or realizes is a murder!*

And then he said that blackmail is the perfect motive because it will always be better hidden than the crime itself, since both blackmailer and victim want to cover it up.

He's absolutely right about that. And I must think about the light that might throw on Jack's motive.

And so I said, *Like the Parson in the Killiecrankie case, where we still don't know what the Major had on him.*

And he looked a bit embarrassed and said, *Well, we do, actually.* Then he explained that the Major had found out that the Parson had certain inclinations. I didn't understand, so he said that there had been some sort of scandal out in Africa involving a native youth. I still didn't get it at first until he said the Parson had had a particularly close relationship with this boy. Then I got the point immediately and told him to say no more. (I saw now that, naturally, he didn't want to make it too explicit in his book about the case.)

Anyway, I thought that business of the *Braes* must have been why he was excited. But it turned out that that wasn't it at all. Because then he said he had something very important to tell me. He had arranged to go and consult with Biggert that very evening. Once again I was astounded at the intellectual audacity of the man. After all, Biggert is Glasgow's best-known detective! *Don't be absurd!* I exclaimed. *He'll be far too busy!*

I rather fancy he'll agree to see me, Horatio said. *It could be very valuable. He has quite a good mind.*

Then he said, did I want to come too? *Did I want to come!*

I guessed he wanted to ask him about the murder of Roberta. Perhaps he was going to suggest that he and Biggert should team up to investigate it? Whatever my reservations about Horatio's evidence, I had to admit that this would be quite a combination: Horatio's trained mind and Biggert's knowledge of the field. He said he had already telephoned and spoken to Biggert, who had told him they were filming an episode that very day at the BBC and suggested that he should come over, so we agreed to set out straight away. As we were leaving, Horatio made a big thing about finding his hat, which he couldn't locate for a few minutes. He said, *I can't think without my hat.*

When we arrived, we were taken to Biggert's dressing room. He was there waiting for us. Or at least for Horatio. He's even smaller than you realize when you see him on TV. I noticed he wears built-up shoes, which still leave him about an inch shorter than me. When you see him close up and without his makeup on, you can see the broken veins all over his face. Especially his nose. And he smokes all the time, which he never does on TV.

I noticed that he seemed somewhat flushed. Horatio shook hands and introduced himself. He asked him how he should be addressed and he said, *Just call me Detective Chief Inspector Biggert, petal.*

Horatio introduced me, and he just nodded. Then Horatio told him how much he loved the program and, frankly, I thought he went over the top a bit.

Biggert took these remarks very seriously, and when Horatio

had finished praising it, he asked, *Do you like everything about the show?*

Everything, Horatio said.

Even the f--king script? Biggert asked.

Well, I am a bit puzzled by some of it, Horatio said. *What is M'Lay up to? And what's Dr. Watson doing out at night like that? And what's Fiammetta's involvement with everyone else?*

Biggert said, *Search me, pal. Nobody ever understands these f--king plots. Not even the f--king writer. Most of this stuff about minor characters he brings in turns out to be nothing but red herrings.*

Horatio asked, *Are the murders by the Peeping Tom killer linked to the murders of the Citz actors?*

Biggert answered, *Now you're asking, petal. I've read the f--king script three times and I still don't understand it. I reckon the writer has got tired and run out of ideas. That's why he's trying to take the show in a whole new direction. Crazy. Just crazy.*

I wondered if he was referring to a future series, so I asked him how many more there'd be.

He got very excited and turned to speak to me for the first time and said, *As many as I f--king well want. And what c--t's been trying to tell you any f--king different? Eh?*

Horatio shot me such a glare.

Then—rather to my surprise but I suppose it was because he wanted to change the subject—Horatio started telling him he had written a book he thought Biggert might be interested in.

Biggert got very excited: *You're a writer! That's what you said on the phone, right? A writer's just what the f--k we need. We've got script difficulties right now. Right today.*

He seemed to forget what he was talking about, because he just started puffing on his cigarette and looking down at the floor. Horatio told him his book was on the Killiecrankie Mystery.

Biggert perked up a bit at that and said he'd heard of the case, though he didn't seem to know much about it and hadn't read either Mr. Roughead's account or Horatio's book. He didn't even know who the victim had been. In fact, he struck me as a fairly ignorant sort of person, to be blunt.

Horatio started talking about the possibility of a TV series based on it. Biggert got very excited, and it seemed to me that

that was obviously why he had agreed to see him! Horatio told him what had happened and described the people who had been involved.

Biggert said, *What director do you have in mind? I'm not having that leather queen who's doing this show, Perkins, f--ting around like a kid with a camcorder. I can tell you right now, I'm not working with her! That screaming fairy! Who does she think she is? Just where does she think she gets off?*

Horatio said, *You can choose the director, as far as I'm concerned.*

Biggert said, *Great. Now, do I have a mustache? I grow a lovely mustache, only I haven't had a chance since I've been doing this show. That's my one regret about the part.*

Horatio said, *I'm afraid for this you'd have to be clean-shaven.*

Biggert said, *But I'm a military man, aren't I?*

Horatio looked surprised and said, *No, you're Clarence Titheradge. The don.*

Biggert looked really angry and he nearly shouted, *What? Clarence f--king Titheradge! You want me to play some English p--fter w--king about the heather in a f--king deerstalker?*

He seemed to have forgotten that Horatio is English.

Horatio looked a bit upset, but he said, *That's the whole point. We'd be casting you against type.*

No, Biggert said, *I just can't get off on that.*

But Horatio said, *I see you with your strong Scottish maleness playing an English don in a way that would be very intriguing. You're an actor of great presence—that goes without saying—but also an actor of great technical skill, which is something that people don't often notice about you.*

Biggert said, *True enough, pal.* Then he said, *Listen, would this English ponce have a beard? A wee goatee?*

He might, Horatio said. *We could very possibly work something out.* Then he said, *You see, you'd be right for this because you'd bring out that darker element of danger and violence in the character. You can see it in the scenes where he uses interrogation methods of a very effective kind to make the witnesses talk. Just as Biggert employs methods that are essentially psychological.*

Biggert said, *Aye, psycho all f--king right. You can say that again, petal. And sometimes my methods are palmological and sometimes I use a bit of the old fistological technique.*

Horatio: *Phystological?*

And Biggert answered, *Aye, and kneeological too.*

Horatio looked as if he hadn't understood him. There are times when he's a real outsider, not being a Glaswegian. He misses our dark, bitter humor.

He said, *It would be quite fascinating to see you make that character—tall, elegant, fastidious, upper-class—come alive in a quite different form. You need a challenge. As I see you, you're a perfectionist.*

Biggert said, *Aye, that's my f--king problem, darling. I'm a f--king perfectionist. That's why I might need a dozen takes before I'm really happy with a scene. And then these little c---s go crying to the bosses up in their f--king penthouse and start complaining about costs. Who the f--k cares a s--te about costs when you're making art? And it is art. That's why four million f--king viewers watch every f--king episode. That's a h--l of a responsibility, pal. People look to the show to tell them about things. Sometimes the wrong things.*

He broke off for a moment and then said, *Take that killing the other day right up the road here. Turnberry Road. That poor wee girl. I don't care a f--k if she was a w---e. (Christ, we're all f--king w---es one way or another.) Some c--t takes her up the lane and cuts her f--king throat. In my book, that's sick. I don't care what anyone says. I hear the papers are saying he got the idea from watching the show. If I thought there was some sick pervert out there imitating the show, I'd be horrified.*

I said quite coldly, *I shouldn't lose any sleep over that.*

He turned to me with his little blue eyes glittering and his face bright red: *What the f--k do you mean, pal?*

I said, *I'm sure he was capable of thinking up a way of killing a lady of the night without having to watch your show.*

Without taking his eyes off me, just like he does on TV, he said to Horatio in that soft way he's got at times, *Hey, your chum has a problem.*

I just stared back at him. I was thinking, *You pathetic little twerp.* And I think he could read it in my eyes. Finally he looked away.

Then, looking at Horatio just as if I didn't exist, he said, *I've heard the cops have got some information about the murder they're keeping secret. I reckon that's something that ties it in with the show.*

Really! The presumption of the man!

Then he began rambling. He said something about how the high-ups at the BBC were all a bunch of English s--tes and they'd got it in for him. And this might be just the excuse they were looking for.

Horatio started saying encouraging things about how good the series was. But Biggert got very upset and popped out for a moment into a little room at the back, which I assumed was the toilet.

When he came in, he wiped his mouth and said, *They're trying to kill me, you know.*

Frankly, I thought he'd gone mad. But Horatio didn't seem to notice.

Biggert went on: *They think they don't need me. They think some little c--t fresh out of drama school that doesn't know his c--t from his a-shole can do this job as well as me. But Biggert without Biggert would be like Hamlet without the f--king prince.*

I couldn't stand this any longer. Maybe it was a bit tactless of me, but it looked as if Horatio wasn't going to mention anything about Roberta, so I decided to bring it up myself. I told him we had come to ask his advice about it.

He took a long time to get the point. (He's stupid as well as ignorant.) He stared at me and then said to Horatio, *Is your friend all right?*

Horatio looked at me very angrily.

I said, *Is there a problem?*

Biggert came toward me and thrust his face right up against mine and said, *Aye, there's a problem. You're the f--king problem, pal.*

Then he went and threw open the door and stood there looking at me and said, *Out. Go on. Hop it.*

But there was somebody standing just outside the door as he opened it. And to my inexpressible delight it was none other than Esmeralda! She was as lovely in the flesh as on screen. Lovelier. She had her face bare of makeup and her hair was wet and tied up in a sort of turban. She had a towel wrapped around her—perhaps it was all she was wearing!—and it was very low over her bosom. Her beautiful face was flushed and without glancing at me or Horatio she said,

Listen, c--t face. Get this into your thick skull. I get that speech.

Not you. I get it. For one thing, if I say it, then it might have a chance of getting said properly. Not slurred and mumbled and mangled. For another, it was written for me and it doesn't make sense if you say it.

Biggert looked at her with those little blue eyes of his and he said very slowly, *I've tellt you, there's gonnae be a script change. I'm the decoy, no you. End of discussion.*

She said, *Oh yeah? Are you planning to put on a skirt and falsies? Is that how you get off? Or maybe you reckon Jools would be turned on by seeing your legs in a pair of stockings?*

His face went quite pale and he came toward her with such an expression. He looked just like he does on TV when he has a suspect to interrogate and he locks the door behind him and tells the uniformed constable to b----r off. She stepped behind me so that I was between her and Biggert. Then she looked right at me and said, *Listen. This is the speech this stupid p---k wants to steal.*

Then she went into this amazing takeoff of Biggert, complete with all his usual stumbles and slurrings and slips of the tongue: **If anyone can be spared out of the two of us, it's me. G-d knows, I'd gladly give my life to catch the most fiendishly cunning criminal this city has ever seen. But you, you're too precious to be spared. You're the greatest detective this poor wee country has ever known. I used to read about you in the papers when I was just a wee lassie.**

Biggert said, *I've tellt you, you b---h, it's gonnae be rewrote.* I say, **You're young. You've your whole life before you. Fresh young womanhood. I couldn't bear to see you risk that, young Esmeralda.** *You ken that fine, you clarty wee c--t.*

Esmeralda exclaimed, *You've rewritten it! Look, this show doesn't exist for you to rewrite the scripts and f--k a-s and sack people if they won't suck your d--k because you're so old and ugly.*

To my horror he raised his hand and threw himself toward her. She grabbed my arm and pushed me toward Biggert so that I bumped into him and meanwhile she dodged around the door and ran out of the room pulling the door shut behind her. He was going so fast, he sort of collided with the door so that his fist banged against it and then he stood there hitting it and shouting, *You b---h. You dirty f--king little b---h.*

He stood there for a moment with his fist pressed against the door looking really stupid, and then he turned around and, completely ignoring yours truly, said to Horatio, *Christ, does this show need a f--king kick up the a-s! Starting with that b---h. There's some unbelievably stupid things happening in the final episode, unless I can stop them.*

Horatio said, *But the stuff about the serial killer's good.*

Biggert said, *Aye. Lots of suspense and blood and at least one f--king corpse at the end of each f--king episode. But the final episode is unbelievably stupid. See, what's going to happen is I decide to use a decoy to lure the killer into a trap. Okay, fair enough. But the tit that wrote the script's got f--king Esmeralda volunteering for the job! Now, where's the dramatic suspense in that? Who cares a f--k about that little b---h getting topped? Frankly, the viewers have had enough of her.*

He sat down and lit another cigarette and said, *And it gets worse. Right at the end I get shot rescuing her. So the final show of the series is going to end with me lying there, badly wounded, and the f--king bosses will be sitting upstairs in their penthouse reading the ratings and the age-profile and deciding if I live or die! And I can see the way their minds work. They've given that c--t Craigie an extra stripe already.*

He stopped and literally chewed the end of his cigarette. It was quite disgusting.

Horatio said, *What do you mean? Surely you don't mean . . .* He broke off, looking really horrified.

Biggert said, *Aye, that's exactly what I do mean. The way they're planning it, I f--king die and he takes over as DCI in the new series. Save on my salary and bring in younger viewers. They're going to start shooting it straight after this. But the c—ts haven't offered me a contract yet. They're making me sweat. And the little s--t's not even committed to the series. He's moonlighting. When did you ever catch me doing that? I've given my life to this show. Have you ever seen me in anything else? Of course you f--king haven't. Whereas that little c--t's anybody's. Any f--king show that fancies his a-s can get it. All right, I say, if he's not committed, get him off the show. I've said for the last seven or eight years it needs a change of face. The public's sick and tired of him and that c--t, Esmeralda. They're dragging us down in the ratings. That's why we're falling. Can't they see that? My assistant's the worst. The b---h can't act, though she thinks she's Larry f--king Olivier. She's more like Larry the f--king Lamb! I want her out of the show. Frankly, I want the b---h dead. No question.*

I thought he was talking about Esmeralda and I was quite angry. But then I realized he meant Craigie.

Biggert went on: *Now's the chance for a clean sweep. And I've got some ideas. Keep the decoy idea, yes. But the way I see it is that I insist on being the decoy.*

Horatio said in surprise, *You?*

Biggert said, *Aye, I've done drag. I look quite nice in a frock. This is how I see it. Now, you're a writer. Tell me if I'm right. It's me that offers to be the decoy. How's that for tension, eh? Biggert's going to put on drag and undress real slow in front of a lighted window in a house in the West End. That'll get to the viewers all right. So first there's this great scene with my chief constable where he pleads with me to give the idea up. And I say, Christ, I don't care how often I have to do a strip if it's going to catch this sick pervert.*

He got up and walked into the middle of the room and said, *Right, now I'm doing my strip.*

To my horror he started undoing his shirt and then taking it off really slowly, turning around in little circles and smiling at us in this really disgusting way. He looked incredibly stupid.

Then he said, *I'm in the middle of doing my strip—in fact, I'm down to my bra and knickers—when suddenly the penny drops. I realize the killer has taken me for a ride.*

As he spoke, a look of what he must of thought was dawning enlightenment appeared on his stupid round face.

Then he went on: *I shout into my hidden mike, We've been set up! Get all available men to Esmeralda's flat! Then I get moving.*

He pulled on his shirt—thank goodness he hadn't removed his trousers—and then turned as if to hurry out of the door. He mimed opening it and going through it and then did a little run on the spot, still turning his head to look at Horatio: *I hurry to that c--t's flat in Ruskin Terrace. I burst in.* He pretended to fling himself through a door then crouched like a hunting animal, looking round him by moving his head very slowly with his scraggy neck stuck out so that he looked exactly like a tortoise. Then in a sort of breathless whisper he said, *First thing I see, she's lying on the floor. Covered in blood. Quite dead. No doubt about that. Her f--king throat's slashed from ear to f--king ear. I'm upset. But I don't panic. I know the killer might still be here. Treading cautiously, I go into the next room.* He crept across the floor, keeping his eyes on Horatio, and then whispered, *There's the killer wiping his big curved knife clean. He's got his back to me. He hasn't heard me. He turns around. It's f--king Craigie! What a shock for the viewers! But I've guessed that, see. I realized he would seize his chance and go to the c--t's flat because he knew I'd be tied up being the decoy along with most of the police in Glasgow. I go to grab him. He comes at me with the knife. I take it from him. He pulls out a gun. I have to defend myself. I stab at him with the knife. Goes straight through the c--t's heart.*

He turned to us panting and, pulling out a handkerchief, wiped the sweat from his brow and said, *Well, what do you think?*

Horatio said, *It has a lot of potential.*

Then to my amazement Biggert said, *Would you like to write it?*

Horatio got very excited at that and said he'd love to.

Biggert said, *I can't commission you myself, but if you're prepared to work on spec and you do a good job, I can pull strings to make sure you get a proper contract. But I want Craigie dead. Okay, pal? Do you think you can do it for me?*

Horatio said, *I can do my best.*

Biggert nodded and said, *Then I get a new assistant for the next series. I've got a lot of ideas about this guy that I need to develop with a writer.*

Horatio asked, *How do you see the character?*

Biggert said, *Small.*

Horatio said, *Yes, but give me some more help.*

Biggert said, *About five foot three.*

Horatio said they could discuss the details later. Then Biggert was called onto the set to start filming, and so we had to leave.

We went out of the BBC into Hamilton Drive. Horatio was too excited to notice where we where going, so I led us up Ruskin Lane—that long, dark path between the backs of gardens that leads from the BBC to Ruskin Terrace. I wanted to just have a look at Esmeralda's place. Then we went for our usual brisk walk and talked about what had just happened.

After a bit I said, *I don't think Biggert was any help with Gargunnock Braes.*

And Horatio said, *I'm skeptical about that myself.*

Following a train of thought of my own, I said to him, *Is Biggert married?*

He said, *You know he is. He's always ringing his wife to say he's go-*

ing to be back late. And she always says, 'I'll be sure to keep your tea warm, Guthrie.' And when he gets home in the small hours, he takes it out of the oven, and it's always stuck to the plate.

Then I said I thought he was much less impressive in the flesh than on screen. Horatio disagreed very strongly and talked a great deal about his brooding masculine strength. I thought I'd better not say any more.

As we were approaching his flat, I saw McConville and McAlweenie disappearing, as per usual, into the Celtic Twilight. Luckily Horatio didn't notice them, or he might have wanted to go in and boast about meeting Biggert. When we got back, he was still so excited, he opened a bottle of champagne to celebrate.

Then we watched *Biggert*. There was a brilliant scene where Biggert visited Professor Arbuthnott, who told him all about scorpions and showed him how you should deal with one if it attacks you. He told him he had lost several recently and mentioned the fact that he was visited several times by Spencer, who was very knowledgeable about scorpions. Biggert noticed McGinnity, the taxidummyist, skulking about in the background and later on told Craigie to do a check on him and see if he had any "form."

Then we saw Dr. Watson out at night in the back lanes of the West End again. Now we could see what he was doing: He had a big net and he was chasing moths! His hobby was leper-optics. (Optics again!) That means he collects butterflies and things like that. As Horatio said, he must specialize in nocturnal moths. He was going down that long, badly lit path behind Great Western Road called Bellhaven Terrace Lane when he almost ran into the Prince of Wales running at full speed. Then he went on a bit and stumbled across the dead body of another young lady.

Then Biggert and Esmeralda interviewed Fiammetta about the murder of McIlhargey, and she gave away nothing. Just as they gave up trying to get anything out of her, Craigie came in and said he'd found out that McGinnity had done bird for drugs and GBH.

Afterward Horatio started talking about how he was thinking about his next book. He was interested in doing another murder, he said. He was fascinated by the Prentice case. Especially by the idea that Ireland was tripped up by Prentice not by being outwitted by him but because he underestimated his stupidity. He said that the thing that can catch out a clever person is the unpredictable stupidity of someone much less clever. I must say, I found that particularly thought-provoking.

Then he suddenly asked me if I thought Bible John was still alive. After all, he pointed out, if the descriptions of him at the time had overestimated his age by only a few years, then he would be about the age we were. Then he started talking about how many points he'd give him: Zero for not knowing his victims. Zero for failing to disguise the murders as something else. Zero for not communicating with the police.

I pointed out that he should get something for the daring way he kept returning to the same place to select his victims. So Horatio said very grudgingly, *All right, make it twenty percent ex gratia for flair.*

Frankly, I hold no brief for John. I think he was just a plagiarizer. But I thought Horatio was revealing his anti-Scots prejudice.

Because he was a little under the influence, Horatio started telling me about the Gavin Oscars business again. He told me how upset he had been at the concerted attempt at character assassination against him. A man of such astonishing profundity of thought. For a long time the identity of the person responsible for organizing the plot against him had remained unknown. But he said that he now knew it had been organized by the man he called his Enemy, though at first he was taken in by him. As an Englishman he said that he expected devious, untrustworthy people to be charming and believable. So when he found that his Enemy was so aggressive and brusque toward everybody, he assumed he was at least honest.

Then he started on about how he had "rather ingeniously" used logic to work out that the secret assassin was indeed his Enemy. For he had managed to find out that after opposing Mr. Oscars unsuccessfully out in the open in Senate, his Enemy had deviously circled around and back-stabbed his victim. He had dropped his open opposition and even encouraged the university to let him have his head. Meanwhile he started infiltrating spies into the Institute, using bribes and blackmail to get people to do what he wanted. His policy was to give the Institute enough rope to let it hang itself.

This plot had succeeded, Horatio said, for one of his colleagues in the Department of Philosophy, Dr. Bentley, had been unmasked as a traitor by Gavin Oscars and had then committed suicide. In fact, there was good reason to suppose that Dr. Bentley had not been a traitor but had been "framed" by Horatio's Enemy. This had all happened back about the time he had started writing his whodunnit about the Killiecrankie Mystery. With the evidence he had collected, Horatio went to confront his Enemy in order to try to stop him making any more trouble for Mr. Oscars. This man was furious and accused him of butting in where he had no business. And then, in an attempt to scare him away from investigating the case, this man hinted that he had evidence that would enable him to accuse Horatio of something quite serious. Horatio was very vague about what exactly this was.

At just about that moment a book by someone called G.K.O. (odd sort of name!) was published. This was full of lies about Gavin Oscars, but Horatio's Enemy seized on it and launched an attack in the Senate with a series of charges about Mr. Oscars and his Institute that were based on what his spies had told him. And he also persuaded some other professors to take part.

One of them was the notoriously right-wing and venomous Dugdale—some kind of biochemist but best known to the public as the inventor of the "electronic cat." (Apparently this is a robot in the form of a cat with a computer chip for a brain that is intended for people who want to keep a pet but can't be bothered with looking after it. You touch it and it starts to purr, apparently.) Dugdale was easily persuaded into joining an alliance against the Institute because he saw an opportunity to gain himself some publicity by attacking a target that could be easily caricatured.

Horatio confronted his Enemy and told him that he had found out—and could prove—that he had been blackmailing Dr. Bentley over the fact that he had formed an improper relationship with a student. I didn't understand what Horatio meant at first until he spelt it out: He had had s-x with a student! And so his Enemy, by threatening to report this to the authorities, had forced him to become his spy and agent provocateur and had used him in order to provoke and seduce the Institute into going too far. Dr. Bentley had gone along with this until he had been detected by Gavin Oscars. And then, because he was in such an impossible position, he had committed suicide.

When Horatio had revealed what he had learned, to his surprise his Enemy became oily and unctuous. He tried to bribe Horatio into keeping quiet first by giving him a Masonic handshake and then by inviting him to go, expenses paid by the university, to a conference in Cairo, Illinois. And he hinted that he would get him a sabbatical and a lighter teaching load and even secure his promotion to senior lecturer.

Horatio refused to be bribed. So then his Enemy begged him to keep his findings to himself on the grounds that otherwise there would be an unpleasant scandal that would harm everybody. But Horatio refused all these blandishments and offers.

When his Enemy realized that Horatio was not to be bought, he tried to frighten him by reminding him of the evidence he claimed to have of something that he could be blackmailed about. But Horatio turned the tables on him, so his Enemy realized that he had failed and made a full confession and promised to resign. (I didn't quite understand that bit.) But he has failed to keep his word, Horatio told me. That's because when Horatio published *The Right Lines*, shortly after that, his Enemy, for some extraordinary and paranoid reason, interpreted it as an attack on himself! And he also got very upset and envious at the fact that it made Horatio quite a lot of money. (That's the first time he's admitted that!) They had a tremendous row, and relations between them have remained terrible.

Went home. Thought about what Horatio had said. Not all of it was clear. But I was very struck by the conduct of his Enemy. What an appalling story. Envying his success with his book to the point of wanting to destroy him. How can someone be so spiteful?

But who would have thought that this day, which opened so

mundanely, would be the one on which I met *her*. What a day! How many new vistas have suddenly opened before me today!

Monday

Spent a lot of time thinking about it. Am determined to go ahead. It's a way of expressing my gratitude to him. And he'll respect me the more.

Wednesday

Got the BrannyBrekkers. Good old Muhammad lets me look in the packet before I buy so as to make sure I get the one I want. Last time they did a series, I ended up with four giraffes and no camel!

Easter Sunday

Very frustrating day.

Got to Horatio's about an hour late and rather out of breath. He was a bit annoyed and fairly far gone. Said he'd thought I wasn't coming just on account of its being Easter Sunday. I said of course that made no difference. I told him some story about how I'd been held up leaving my place. Honestly, I really began to regret the trouble I'd gone to on his behalf. I'd missed *Gargunnock Braes*, of course. I asked Horatio what had happened. He wouldn't tell me much about it, but he started going on and on about Auld Rab and his various villainies. He called him a "lecherous old goat" and said he'd had every lady and every child in the village. Then he started saying that he wasn't only interested in ladies and children. I tried to stop him, but he made some very nasty allegations about Auld Rab's private life. Basically, he said he is interesting in doing s-x with other men! And he then said he is now convinced that Auld Rab is blackmailing Calum for s-x! I couldn't believe that! Sometimes he gets the most lurid ideas.

Incidentally, Roberta hasn't been seen since that episode when she admitted she was having an affair with Calum. Horatio brought this up again and said he was more than ever convinced that this means he is right to think she has been murdered.

For our walk he insisted on going toward Hyndland, though I tried to persuade him we should go in another direction. (He was still pretty steamed up. And so was I, to be absolutely frank.) As we went along the top of Byres Road, I noticed the flashing sirens of a number of police cars and a small crowd lower down the hill around Athole Gardens.

Frankly, I was too tense to notice much of what he said.

And I didn't really take in a lot of *Biggert*, either. There was a scene where we saw the Prince of Wales going into Fingers, the sauna, and then lying there virtually naked—only with a towel over his "bits," thank heaven!—being massaged by some mysterious hands.

Then we saw Oscar Wilde with M'Lay looking at cars parked in a street. They seemed to be stealing them, but Horatio said he thought that what they were up to would turn out to be more unusual than that.

MAY

Sunday

I had a lucky escape, as it turned out. How ironic.

When I got to his place, I found he was in a terrible state. Turns out Professor Speculand is one of his closest friends and allies in the university!

He said he didn't know if it was the Institute or its enemies who had gone so far as to try to kill someone. Professor Speculand had been one of Mr. Oscars's right-hand men, but recently there had been some sort of coolness between them. Professor Speculand had now resigned from the Institute and believed that Gavin Oscars's wife had organized the attack on him. Horatio went on and on about the things that have been happening: Dr. Bentley's death and Mr. Oscars's being disgraced and now this latest "outrage," as he called it. He didn't want to go for a walk. Said he didn't feel safe outside! He didn't even want to watch TV, but I insisted. Thought it would take his mind off it.

In fact it was a good thing I did because when we watched *Gargunnock Braes*, Horatio cheered up quite a bit. It turns out he was quite right! Roberta reappeared this week for the first time for ages, but the point was IT WASN'T HER! It was someone who looked like her, but it certainly wasn't the same lady! Amazingly, everyone appeared to be taken in. Or at least, they pretended to be. As Horatio said, Auld Rab has not merely killed the poor lady but got someone to impersonate her.

I see how the mistake happened. When we were all in the Twilight, they had just been talking about Professor Speculand, so when I asked McConville who "the professor" was, not realizing that Professor Speculand was also a professor (though of English, not philosophy), he thought I meant him rather than Horatio's Enemy. Bloody McConville! It's all his fault.

So I still don't know who the professor of philosophy is!

We watched *Biggert* and not a lot happened. He found out that the Countess of Warwick was in love with Cherryman but that he did not return her affection, which is odd because she is very beautiful.

And then we saw Dr. Watson—who seemed so ordinary with his interest in nocturnal moths—doing something rather unusual with some ladies' lingerie. Horatio says that makes him a prime candidate to be "the Scorpion." But I still can't believe it of *him*.

Sunday

I got a nasty shock today!

But at least Horatio was a bit more cheerful this week and less boring. He told me a funny story about Dugdale—one of the enemies of the Institute. One of the technicians in his laboratory has just been killed in a bizarre accident. On Dugdale's instructions he was trying to get the electronic cat to lap milk. Some sort of short circuit occurred, and the cat became "live." It went berserk and sank its teeth into his arm. He couldn't get it off and the voltage killed him. Horatio said that there was a really juicy bit of scandal attached to it in that the technician's wife was rumored to have been having an affair with Dugdale. He said something rather similar once happened involving Dugdale thirty years ago or more when he was in the U.S.A. He thinks this has neutralized him as a threat to Gavin Oscars.

Then it was that we turned on the *Braes*. Straight away we saw this man arriving in the village with a moving van who we hadn't seen before. He's called Murdo. *And it was the actor who plays Biggert's assistant, Craigie.* So the *Braes* is all made up, too! They're all actors! (Now I realized what Biggert was referring to when he said Craigie was moonlighting.) I was really disgusted. Frankly, it seems you can't believe anything you see on television.

Murdo is Donalda's son—and so the brother (or, rather, foster brother) of Roberta—who has been away studying and then practicing in England for years and has now come to work in the village as a vet. The write-up in the paper says he's "a macho character who has a devastating effect on the women of the village." He didn't look particularly macho to me, but Horatio got very excited about his "dark masculinity." When he first appeared and greeted the lady who calls herself Roberta, he didn't look at all surprised to see that she was a different person from the one he must have seen last time he set eyes on her. I'm a bit puzzled by that, but Horatio says he has a theory about what is really going on. I must say, though, that Murdo didn't bat an eyelid when he saw her, and that really is acting of a high order.

I brought the subject around to money, since he was fairly well oiled by now. He said he had done so well from the first book that he was tempted to write another one—even a series! He said he'd use the idea of a detective investigating famous unsolved crimes. There were some fascinating cases: The Croydon poisonings. The Wallace case. And others. Especially in Glasgow.

There was an awkward moment later on during our walk. He had been banging on again about what a good place Glasgow was for murder, but then he started comparing it unfavorably with other places he'd lived in down south, like London and Cambridge. But I told him straight out I thought Glasgow was the finest city in the world and its citizens the most generous-spirited people on G-d's earth. That silenced him.

Watched *Biggert*. Lots about the Citz cast. But something puzzling. We saw this new character, Trevor, with M'Lay. Horatio pulled his chair forward to get a better look at him and commented that he looked as if he might be an athlete. He was certainly fit and well built, but I said I thought he looked a bit too wet to be a footballer or anything like that. He and M'Lay were setting up video cameras in some place that neither of us recognized.

Then we saw Fiona, from Professor Arbuthnott's laboratory, getting out of a Rolls-Royce driven by Oscar Wilde. We couldn't work out how he came to be driving one of those. I pointed out that it was like the way Jamie was riding around in a Bentley.

Afterward Horatio was a little animated, as per usual. He started talking about philosophy. He said that somebody called High Digger was the profoundest thinker of the twentieth century. I pointed out that only two or three weeks ago he had said that Gavin Oscars was the profoundest thinker of the twentieth century. So I said quite impatiently, *Make up your mind. Which of the two was really the profounder?* He said. *You must have misunderstood me. High Digger was profounder even than Gavin Oscars.* So, quick as a flash, I riposted, *All right, but how much profounder?* That took him by surprise. He said, *Have you read High Digger?* I thought I'd risk a bit of an overstatement so I said, *Yes. And I agree with every word.* He looked astonished but didn't answer. He just opened another. I didn't stay long.

Monday

Spent hours turning it over and over in my mind. Should I make one last attempt to retrieve what I've lost? I must think hard about the risks I'd be running. And one thing's for sure: This time there must be no mistakes. Ice-cool and everything worked out in advance. That's the only way.

Tuesday

He just doesn't respect me. He sneers at some of my best ideas. I just want to show him what I'm capable of.

I know I'm right about Jack and he's wrong. Jack *did* have a connection with those ladies. And he used that method of the Major's—whether or not he *was* the Major.

I have to show him. I can't see any other way. But I'm not too happy about it. It has to involve a risk. That's the whole point.

A connection. There's no getting away from that. The only question is, how close a connection? Close enough to prove the point but not too b---ming close!

Wednesday
I must get the right person this time. Still don't know the name, though.

Thursday
Been racking my brains to think how to find out.

Friday
Had a brilliant idea. Rang the Uni and asked to speak to "the professor of philosophy." Simple as that!
Been doing a recce. Everything's ready. What I'll do is, I'll put my equipment in the private case.

Saturday

JUNE

Sunday
I can't believe it! I seem to be the most unlucky person in the world!
Horatio was very subdued when I arrived. I couldn't get him to talk about anything else. Not that he wanted to say much. He'd got his usual bottle half drunk by the time I arrived. He wouldn't leave the house when I suggested a brisk walk. And he wouldn't watch *Gargunnock Braes,* even when I turned the TV on and watched it myself. But he must of been listening because he got very upset when Calum said good-bye to his mother and went off to England. *That's it,* he said. *He's had his chips.* Then he

started counting up all the people who have gone away or died or just not been seen for some time. He said, *What's happened to Cameron? And where's Margaret? She was supposed to be in Edinburgh for a week, but that was months ago! And Dougal! We haven't seen him for weeks, either. They've all been murdered, haven't they?*

I tried to reason with him, but he's become convinced there's a serial murderer on the loose in the village. After that he just sat there with his bottle beside him staring at the wall. You can't help some people.

I didn't stay for *Biggert.* He would of spoiled it. I could see that my evening was in ruins. I left early and came home.

You'd think, being a philosopher, he would be a bit more philosophical about it!

Monday
Frankly, it's all really very unfortunate. It seems that Professor Moncrieff was just about the closest friend Horatio had in the department. Not only is he upset about that but he's also become somewhat paranoid about his own safety.

Still, I think I've proved my point about the connection. And about the gloves, which worked perfectly. Not a drop went where it shouldn't. (Pity I dropped one of them on the way home. I hope it wasn't too near.) It certainly wasn't random, even though I never had met him personally until last Saturday. But he's connected to me through Horatio, and so far nobody has worked that out. And my bet is that nobody ever will.

The police seem pretty much at a loss, judging from the papers. Apparently the city is in a state of panic. Can't say I've noticed.

Tuesday
Police still baffled, according to the papers. They don't give much information. Nothing above gloves, for example.

Wednesday
How was I supposed to know there were two professors of philosophy?

Thursday

At least I now know for sure that his Enemy must be the other one, Professor Angus MacMaster. It said in the paper he was the "remaining professor in the department."

Sunday

Got a very nasty shock just as I arrived. Horatio greeted me by saying he knew who the serial murderer is. I sat down quickly and then he said he'd worked out that it was Auld Rab! He's been murdering people for years, he said, and the village cemetery must be full of his victims. He probably started murdering in order to conceal his child-molesting activities. And of course he murdered his wife years ago.

Well, frankly I've got enough on my plate without worrying about that.

Though my mind wasn't really on it, we watched the *Braes*. Had rather a sharp disagreement about it. What happened was that Auld Rab found a pie that someone in the village had left outside his door, as they often do. He gave a piece of it to his dog, Rumpty, who was sick. Just to annoy Horatio, I said, *How can you think such terrible things of a man who is so fond of his dog that he gives it half of his own dinner?* And Horatio said he wasn't being generous, he was testing the pie for poison! I said that leaving a poisoned pie outside his door would be the perfect murder method. Nobody would know who had done it. And anyway, the victim would eat up the evidence. But Horatio was in a difficult mood and he said, *No. Poison is a very inelegant method. I'm writing about that in my monograph on mattresses. Sayers and Christie could get away with it, but, frankly, poison's not acceptable these days. It's a question of taste.* What's he talking about? Mr. Christie suffocated his ladies. And who did this Mr. Sayers kill? I've never heard of him.

But the *Braes* got very interesting right at the end. Senga, the minister's wife, summoned the lady who calls herself Roberta to come and see her at the same time as Calum and without letting anyone else know where they were going. When they arrived, she told them that she had decided that it was only right that they should know at last who their mother is. She told them to prepare themselves for a shock. Then the show ended.

Horatio said, *Who do you think it is?* I said I was keeping an open mind but it wouldn't entirely surprise me if it turned out to be Andro's wife, Maggy. Horatio pointed out rather offensively that she was younger than the twins, so it couldn't really be her. I had to admit I'd forgotten that. Then he said, *What do you think Auld Rab would look like in a dress?* I said, *Horrible. What are you driving at?* He said it was just a wild hypothesis, but he'd wondered if Auld Rab was really a lady. Frankly, it seems to me that sometimes he's too clever by half.

Apart from the *Braes*, he was full of this business of the police putting out a statement saying the *modus operandi* of this latest incident involving Professor Moncrieff is identical to the business of that man in the English department, Professor Speculand. Fair enough. And that demonstrates my point about the connection. But they also claim there's a link with the death of Dr. Bentley, which they now believe was not suicide but murder. Very odd. But they don't say anything about Turnberry Lane. And still no mention of either the scorpion or the glove. It strikes me that if anyone who knows about them happened to read that book of his, they'd spot several connections that could be rather embarrassing for Horatio—especially considering that some of the people involved are people he knows in the philosophy or English departments.

The police seem to think that it is incredible that the violent death of a second member of the philosophy department, Dr. Bentley, a year or so before should not be linked to these two recent incidents. They're going to exhume Dr. Bentley and do an autopsy.

Horatio was altogether in a very odd mood. I suppose it's the Professor Moncrieff business still. We were watching the *Braes* and there was a scene when Calum mentioned that his job was going to take him away for a few months. Horatio shouted, *That's what you think, mate! The truth is, you're for the chop!* He was convinced that Auld Rab is about to kill him as well. Then he started on about how worried he was about Murdo being blackmailed next. And then maybe even murdered. Although I pointed out that he is a vet and as such knows what's what, Horatio got very upset. But he kept saying, *As long as he keeps his head and plays his cards right, Murdo will sort things out. He'll get to the bottom of things.* I asked him what he meant, and he explained this theory he has been working on. Basically, his hypothesis is that Murdo is actually a detective and that he has come to the village disguised as a vet and pretending to be Donalda's son because he is really investigating the murder of his adopted sister and her substitution by the lady who calls herself Roberta.

I suppose it's possible. I was quite impressed when I first heard the idea, but on reflection I must say I can't go along with it. He certainly looks like a vet and he seems to be practicing quite effectively. Nobody's goldfish has died or anything like that. I'm keeping an open mind on the issue.

We went for our walk. It was a beautiful night, and Horatio suddenly looked up at the sky and said, *Isn't that Ursa Major over there?* and I said, *Yes, I expect so.* Then he said, *No, it isn't. I'm looking in completely the wrong direction. It's Cassiopeia.* And he made an unkind remark about my astronomical knowledge. But to be absolutely truthful, when it comes to the stars, I'm more interested in the poetry of the whole effect than in any single star. On the other hand, Horatio has the academic's obsession with pointless detail. After all, when you come right down to it, one constellation is pretty much like another. But then he went on to make some quite uncalled-for remarks along the lines of, He sometimes wondered what I did with my telescope. And he wasn't sure where I was in the habit of pointing it.

Then he mentioned about Professor Dugdale and said they've found that someone reprogrammed the cat and de-earthed it before the technician tried to get it to lap milk. So it seems that someone was trying to kill him. And since Dugdale was having an affair with the man's wife, the finger of suspicion was pointing at him. I must say, my heart often sinks when I think of some of the failings of my fellow citizens.

After our walk, we watched *Biggert.*

It was Burns Night, so the police station was full of people wearing silly hats and singing and reciting Burns's poetry and getting drunk. They hardly did any work at all.

We saw a lot of the actors from the Citz. But it was quite difficult to follow, having missed the last one. For example, there was this scene where we saw the Prince of Wales being massaged in the sauna again. This time we saw that the person massaging him was Trevor, who we had previously seen setting up video cameras with M'Lay. It was very odd. Trevor smiled at him and then went and closed the door. That was the end of the scene. I asked Horatio what he thought it meant, but he didn't seem to want to answer. He just looked very knowing in that infuriating way he has with him.

Thursday

According to the papers, the autopsy on Dr. Bentley has discovered he had had a mysterious operation for which no medical reason could be found. Very odd. Other than that they can't find any evidence to contradict the idea that he cut his own throat. But apparently they're still very suspicious.

Sunday

Not a terribly good day. Went around to Horatio's and watched the *Braes.*

Bit of a bombshell. Turns out we were both wrong. Senga announced that it was she herself who was the mother of the twins! Could have knocked me over with a feather! She's a minister's wife! Horatio had to admit that he was taken aback, too. There was a big, tearful scene with all three of them falling into each other's arms and hugging and kissing and sobbing. Pretty disgusting, in fact. She told them about how, as an innocent young girl, she had been seduced and then abandoned by this older man. But she refused to tell them who he was. Horatio cheered up a bit after that because there was a scene when Auld Rab was sobbing because Rumpty had died. Horatio said, *See? I was right. That pie was poisoned.* Then he said the old man wasn't crying from grief over the dog but out of terror because someone had nearly killed him.

Apart from that, he didn't want to talk about anything except what's been happening in his department. (I suspect he's really worried that with Professor Moncrieff gone he'll have to teach Scottish commonsense philosophy, which he once said he "hates." To be blunt, it doesn't completely surprise me that he has a thing against common sense, since he doesn't have an awful lot of it himself!) And he said several times, *Bellhaven Terrace Lane! Why there?* But I got him back to the Killiecrankie Mystery at last, and finally I told him that the driver of the train had been my great-uncle Hamish. (He married my grannie's elder sister.) He didn't seem particularly impressed. (I also mentioned about how Great-uncle Hamish was a lifelong teetotaler, so the part of his book where he implies that he'd had a few drinks that night was definitely wrong.) I explained that my great-uncle knew something important about what really happened, which had been passed down in the family. This was it. When he had gone to look for the old lady, he had followed the party's footsteps back along the edge of the cliff. To his amazement he found that the silent young lady's footsteps led from the edge of the cliff and that there was evidence of a struggle just there. He concluded from this that the young lady, Miss Latimer, led Mrs. Armytage to the edge, pushed her over, and then came forward to tell the others that she was lagging behind. He also thought Miss Latimer had been wearing the scorpion charm as a brooch and that the old lady must of torn it off during the struggle. When he got back to the rest of the party, he looked at her carefully and noticed that she had what seemed to be scratches on her face. He kept quiet about it in order not to get the young lady into trouble, because he was sorry for her. He always said he would have come forward with his evidence if anyone else had been charged with murder, but nobody was.

Well, when I'd explained all this, he was perfectly quiet for a few moments. Then he said that it didn't sound convincing because Miss Latimer had no motive. She didn't stand to inherit anything. I said she might have wrongly believed she was mentioned in the old lady's will. Or she might have had a motive that had never come out. Maybe she was even blackmailing the old lady about something.

He ignored all those perfectly reasonable suggestions. And then he said he thought Great-uncle Hamish was lying! And as if that wasn't enough, he then gave that irritating smile of his and said that he suspected that Great-uncle Hamish himself murdered the old lady!

I didn't think that was very funny and I told him so.

But instead of apologizing, he actually went on to suggest that Great-uncle Hamish was drunk while he was driving the train and that was why it had turned onto the wrong track and got stuck in the snow. I said it wasn't on the wrong track! But he just ignored me and went on to say that Great-uncle Hamish was still drunk when he went to look for the old lady and in his drunken rage he then tried to r--e her. She fled from him and fell over the edge of the cliff! And then in a very pointed way he said that things like that run in families.

I know exactly why he was so put out. My evidence—which is irrefutable because it's based on an eyewitness account—completely discredits his theory that the Major was the killer.

He is so petty! Frankly, if he hadn't written that history of the Killiecrankie case, I wouldn't have any respect for him. But I have to admit, that was a piece of real scholarship.

We went out for our walk. He got back to the b----y *Braes* again and started speculating on who Auld Rab was going to murder next. I was still feeling very annoyed indeed, so I said, *How do we know for sure it's Auld Rab? How do we know it's not Murdo who's killing people?* I turned the tables on him and he didn't like it one bit. He said that was nonsense, because the murders started before he ever arrived in the village. But I said, *It's quite possible he was in the village secretly and carrying out the murders without anyone even knowing he was there.*

He just sneered in that way he has. Especially when he can't think of a good answer.

I was so annoyed, I almost didn't stay for *Biggert,* but I'm glad I did because it was very good. What happened was that Biggert got a warning that something was going to happen at the play that night, so he planted officers in the audience and all around the theater and he went to see the play himself.

Nothing happened until the very end of the play. In the last scene all the major figures—the Prince of Wales, Oscar Wilde, Mr. Gladstone, who arrived with one of his famous bags, Sherlock Holmes, Dr. Watson (who also had a Gladstone bag with him), Roberta and the Countess of Warwick were all gathered together in Sherlock Holmes's rooms, and by this time the audience knew that one of them had to be the Ripper.

Sherlock Holmes told them he had called them together to tell them he had solved the case. He started to give a lecture on the Ripper's crimes. He described each of them and the *modus operandi.* (As Horatio and I agreed, a lot of this was quite seriously mistaken.) In the middle he had something quite large brought on stage by his manservant. We couldn't see what it was because it was concealed under a sheet.

Eventually Sherlock Holmes whipped the covering off it, and

we saw that it was a very lifelike dummy of a lady standing up. (It's the thing that Jamie, the stagehand, dropped on Biggert just after Cherryman was murdered.)

Then Sherlock Holmes used the dummy to demonstrate how the Ripper killed his victims and to prove that he used a particular kind of knife with a curved blade. (Horatio got quite excited about this idea, but he said he thinks it's essentially flawed.) Sherlock Holmes showed how they turned their backs and raised their skirts (I don't quite know why) and he threw their dresses over their heads and once they were pinned like that, he strangled them. Then when they were unconscious, he cut their throats. Then Dr. Watson—who, frankly, seems a bit slow sometimes—said he didn't understand how this worked in terms of female garments—which is a piece of cheek, since we know all about his little hobby! (The truth is, he probably knows more about ladies' lingerie than anyone in Glasgow!) And the Prince of Wales said that what seemed to work on a dummy would not work on a real female. And he sort of sniggered knowingly. (We know what a ladies' man he is!) So Sherlock Holmes removed the dummy's dress and asked for a volunteer to put it on and impersonate the victim. There was some comic business with the Prince of Wales volunteering. (Horatio said that none of them could wait to get into a frock!) Finally, Oscar Wilde put the dress on. Sherlock Holmes threw the dress over his head and demonstrated how the Ripper pinned his victim and showed that the victim could not escape. Then he went into a brilliant lecture that proved that Oscar Wilde must be the Ripper. All the time Oscar Wilde was standing there with the dress over his head. He realized the game was up. Then suddenly his hands started moving under the dress (this looked a bit disgusting) and then he cut his way free from it, and when he had thrown it aside, everyone could see that he had used a knife with a curved blade. The Countess of Warwick screamed and collapsed into the Prince of Wales's arms, while Roberta looked furious at this. Now Oscar Wilde admitted that he was the killer. To my amazement he came out with a whole lot of stuff about being an artist who was looking for perfection and a way of elevating mere humble reality into a work of art, and how the ultimate work of art was the perfect murder! He talked about murder for murder's sake and the idea of a murder committed for no other motive than to kill with style and elegance and daring in such a way as to make the police look stupid. It was almost exactly what Horatio had been grinding on about. Of course, he turned around and smirked and grinned at me fit to bust while this was going on.

Then Oscar Wilde said he was going to kill the Prince of Wales as his final, glorious act of murder. But Sherlock Holmes just said very calmly, *I think not. Watson, have you your service revolver?* Doctor Watson brought it out of his Gladstone bag and pointed it at Oscar Wilde. So Oscar Wilde was forced to throw down his knife and was led away by Sherlock Holmes's man-servant, who was actually Walter Sickert—I happened to notice.

The Countess of Warwick insisted that the weapons be put away, so Doctor Watson put his gun in his Gladstone bag and Sherlock Holmes wrapped up the knife and placed it in *his* Gladstone bag, saying it would be the centerpiece of his collection. Then a fierce quarrel broke out between Roberta and the Countess of Warwick over the Prince of Wales. In fury, Roberta seized the knife from Sherlock Holmes's Gladstone bag, and before anyone could stop her, she rushed at the Countess of Warwick and cut her throat. It was really interesting. Blood spurted from the Countess of Warwick and she collapsed. (I was waiting for Biggert to jump on the stage and arrest Roberta. But luckily for me I didn't say anything out loud.)

Within about a minute the Countess of Warwick had died. Now Roberta stood there brandishing the knife and threatening to kill the Prince of Wales. (I was a bit surprised by that, since I thought she was supposed to be in love with him, but Horatio said it was "the action of a jealous woman.") Sherlock Holmes reached into Dr. Watson's Gladstone bag for the revolver but instead pulled out a live scorpion, which clung to him until he flung it onto the stage. Pandemonium. The cast frozen with horror. Some of the audience started screaming. Instantly Biggert leaped onto the stage and dealt with it in the way old Professor Arbuthnott had shown him. (It was a stroke of luck the old fellow had showed him how!)

At that moment there was a cry of agony from offstage.

Biggert rushed into the wings, and there was Maturin, the author of the play, lying on the ground in agony. Biggert searched him and found that he had a number of scorpions in his pocket—and that one of them was stinging him. There was nothing he could do, and Maturin also died.

Then the three detectives discussed the incident, and Craigie explained what must have happened: Maturin wanted to kill Sherlock Holmes and so he planted a scorpion in Dr. Watson's Gladstone bag. But his plan went horribly wrong and he died by his own device. When he had finished, however, Biggert looked skeptical and said that Maturin had no motive.

I must say, I was a bit surprised to notice that Craigie was wearing a deerstalker. He must of copied it from Sherlock Holmes.

It was a really good episode. Anyway, after that I was just about to leave when Horatio suddenly gave that smile he has and said, *Oh, I've had some more good news about* The Right Lines *that I'm sure you'll be interested in. The So-and-So Book Club of America has just paid fifty thousand dollars for the rights. Not bad, eh?*

I don't know what my face must have looked like. Then he said, *Of course, I don't get all of that. My agent takes quite a big cut.*

Quite a big cut! I suppose that only leaves him about forty thousand! I just nodded and said *Very good.* And then I politely said good night and walked out.

Monday

I was pretty shaken after Sunday evening. I was really upset by the way he'd jeered at my theory. And he'd taken my idea that Murdo was the murderer very badly. The more I thought about how Miss Latimer could have done it, the more convinced I became that it really was the truth. I thought I'd do a little research on the case and see if I could show Horatio up. I remembered that history book I'd put in the private case—Mr. Peddie's *Scotch Mysteries*—and got it out. I'll start it as soon as I have a spare moment.

Tuesday

Devastated to discover the depths of the man's dishonesty. He's thieved masses of material from that history book! He's plagiarized all the stuff about Mrs. Armytage stealing another lady's fiancé! And the idea about the Major giving her a scorpion to signify revenge is pinched from the story the Major told in that book. And he had the brass nerve to tell me he had never heard of the book! Frankly, I suspect that even his so-called brilliant solution about the Major doubling back in a big circle is stolen from somewhere.

Not quite sure how to play this. I think I'll give him the chance to come clean first when I see him on Sunday.

Wednesday

McAlweenie's right. The English stole Scotland's oil. Now they're exploiting one of our other natural resources: crime. Scotland has some of the finest murders in the annals of criminology. It seems a shame that the English are trying to get their hands on the profits from that as well!

JULY

Sunday

Confronted him with the book and showed him the relevant passages. He denied once again that he had ever read it. He said he had read a lot of material while researching his book and it was possible he had read someone's summary of this work—or even that he had skimmed through it himself but forgotten that he had done so! That was rather a serious concession!

Then he said that even if he had used it—quite unconsciously—he had not breached anyone's copyright, since the material was in the public domain! (What a devious, slippery rat he can be!) I had to point out to him that it wasn't a matter of legal copyright. It was a matter of plagiarizing from reality. He had taken material from actual history and then distorted it for his own purposes. And then to my amazement, he said, *Well, so what if I did? I was writing a novel, not a work of scholarly history!*

A storybook!

So the whole thing is just made up! There was no don called Clarence Titheradge! He never came to Scotland and fell in love with Miss Latimer and investigated the Mystery.

When he said that, I just stared at him with my jaw dropping. Then with great dignity I just turned and walked out.

I just don't know what to think. The scales have fallen from my eyes.

Monday Morning

Another thing that horrifies me is that there is nothing in Mr. Peddie's book about lots of the "new material" that Horatio claimed to have discovered. There's nothing about either the Major or the Parson committing suicide. Nor about the guard dying in the attempt to summon help, much less turning out to have been murdered by the Major. Nor is there anything about Miss Latimer's brother and fiancé being killed in the Great War. He made all that up! What a hypocrite the man is! He goes on and on about how a murder needs to be based on the principles of elegance and economy and yet he himself has killed all those people just for the sake of his plot!

Monday Afternoon

I rang him up, and as soon as he answered, I gave it to him straight: *You're not only a plagiarist and a liar but also a hypocrite. You talk about taste and elegance and economy, but look how many people you killed in your book: You murdered the old lady, you made the Major and the Parson commit suicide, you killed the guard and Miss Latimer's fiancé and brother! You're worse than Auld Rab!*
Then I slammed down the phone.

Monday Evening

I wonder if he'll apologize. He's totally in the wrong. But will his pride let him admit it to himself, let alone to me?

Tuesday

Rather to my surprise, I must say, I found a letter from him. It was on his department's headed notepaper. Very grand. But no "Dear Sholto" or even the date or anything. It just said:

> I'm sorry I killed so many people. I admit that it was some-what tasteless—and certainly very inelegant. I suppose I was obsessed with the idea of the perfect murder. But what can I do now?
>
> HORATIO QUAIFE

That's a fairly reasonable apology. I'll go around on Sunday as usual. It's obvious that he values our friendship very highly. More highly, I suspect, than I do.

Wednesday

Even after getting his apology, this episode has made me wonder what his new mystery book is about. What liberties with the truth he might be taking in the name of "fiction."

Thursday Afternoon

Reading over what I wrote only a few months ago, I am amazed at the skill and ingenuity with which an essentially very stupid—and more than just stupid—man managed to take me in. I can't imagine how I fell for it. I was dazzled by a few linguistic tricks and mechanical paradoxes. And by jokes and epigrams looted from other writers. I realize now that he has stolen every intelligent remark he's ever made. He must sleep with a dictionary of quotations under his pillow.

Thursday Evening

I can't stop thinking about Mr. Peddie's book. I suspect very strongly that when Horatio plagiarized from it, *he misunderstood it!* He's not just a plagiarist but an incompetent one! The solution to the mystery is somewhere in that book, but he was too stupid to spot it.

Friday Morning

Stayed up till early this morning rereading Mr. Peddie's book very slowly and carefully and making notes. The account he prints there confirms practically everything Great-uncle Hamish said. And most of my own hypotheses, too. And it's completely authentic, because it was written by the two crucial witnesses, the Major and the Parson. Two gentlemen of the utmost respectability, who had no reason to lie—once one discounts Horatio's absurd ideas about the Major. (And his nasty-minded allegations about the Parson's private life.) Indeed, on the contrary, the two men were so anxious to tell the whole truth that they collaborated on the account, adding passages if it seemed to one of them that the other had forgotten something important that could throw light on what happened.

Mrs. Armytage's throat was obviously severed, because it virtually spells it out in the book when it says, *There were injuries to the deceased's neck that were not wholly explicable by her presumed fall over the cliff.*

There is no reference to the fact that the old lady was found clutching a silver brooch in the form of a scorpion. But the Major describes how he told a story that makes it clear that the scorpion is, as Horatio wrote in his nasty exercise in plagiarism, a symbol indicating revenge. I wonder if it's Masonic, as he stated.

Friday Evening
I've been thinking about links between Killiecrankie and Jack. I believe I'm close to a breakthrough.

Friday Night
I've got it! I've done it! It's when the old lady says the fiancé was *a talented amateur artist and member of the British Society of Painters.* That's the clincher! I honestly believe I've solved two of the greatest mysteries in British criminal history! Even Horatio will have to admit I've done something pretty extraordinary. I'm too excited to write any more now. I wonder if I can find out anything about that society.

I still don't see, though, what the young lady's motive was for killing the old one.

Saturday
I've discovered the British Society of Painters was full of Freemasons!

Brilliant! Absolutely, b---ming brilliant! The first husband of Mrs. Armytage, Sir Rudolph, was an artist and a member of the British Society of Painters. He fits the bill precisely: a painter, a Freemason, Scottish, went mad and was put in an asylum. There can be no doubt about it at all. I'll bet anything he had a studio in the East End to be near the hospitals for watching anatomical dissections. That's why he was able to go to ground so quickly in the middle of the night. *He was Jack!!*

There's just a few loose ends to be tied up and then I can go to the world's press.

Sunday

Went over to Horatio's. Found his nibs very pleased with himself. Sat there cradling his glass and smirking like the Cheshire Cat when I arrived. I wouldn't give him the pleasure of asking what had happened, so eventually he had to tell me. He's had a large advance for *The Right Lines* from the U.S. for the paperback rights. He said, *There's money in crime, it seems.*

There certainly is, mate, I said to myself. *Steal someone else's idea and make a fortune!*

Watched the *Braes*. There was a scene when Auld Rab was talking to Maggy and she was telling him about how Andro hadn't got over the accident that killed Jenny's little girl. She was saying she thought their marriage might be destroyed by his failure to come to terms with what had happened even though it wasn't his fault. We saw a close-up of Auld Rab, and his eyes seemed to be twinkling with mirth. At that moment Horatio said he was ninety-nine percent sure that Auld Rab fixed the brakes of Andro's lorry. I suspect he may be right, but I didn't want to give him the pleasure of knowing it, so I just grunted noncommittally. Then he started going on about had I noticed how thin Auld Rab was getting. I said he was eaten up with malevolence and that was bound to affect his weight, but Horatio insisted that someone is poisoning him. I said nothing, but I only hope he's right. He went on again about how much he hated poison and it should never be used. He's got a real obsession about it. But then, frankly, he's the obsessional type.

As we were leaving the flat, he made that remark for the umpteenth time about how he can't think without his bl-ssed deerstalker. The truth is, he can't think with or without the wretched thing!

During our walk he said he was going to "turn his attention" to the so-called Scorpion Killings. He obviously thinks he has only to direct his "trained mind" to the matter for a short time and all will become clear. We'll see.

Got back and watched *Biggert*.

Nothing much happened except that Biggert went to the flat of the deceased playwright Maturin and opened a cupboard and it was full of whips and masks and chains. (Heaven alone knows why! Was he running an ironmongery business in his spare time?) Then Biggert went to Oscar Wilde's lodgings to arrest him for stealing cars but found that he had disappeared.

We discussed about *Biggert*. Then he suddenly asked me if I could recommend a book about the Bible John case. I said I didn't know of one. (I'm not that stupid! Planning some more plagiarisms, eh?) Afterward, he dozed off with his bottle lying beside his chair. A very edifying sight, I don't think. I decided I'd have a little look around. I went into his "study" (which he insists on calling his "cogitorium") and noticed a pile of magazines stuck under a stack of books so I couldn't move them. They didn't look very interesting. They seemed to be mostly academic journals such as one called *Diarrhea* (I think it was) that was on a shelf and that I looked through. Unbelievably boring. Saw a piece in it by that Professor Speculand. Looked completely unreadable. And there were some other magazines in the stack that I assume were the same, though the spines—which were all I could see—were a lot brighter colors. They were mostly on philosophy and education, as far as I could judge from the titles: *Land of Cockagne*. (Literature?) *Up and Coming*. (Education?) *Whoppers*. (Moral philosophy and lying? Well, he's an expert on that!)

Found his diary! Thought it would be very interesting, but it turned out to be unbelievably dull. I copied out one or two entries:

> ML came for his first private tutorial. First we discussed Wittgenstein vigorously for half an hour with neither of us coming to any final conclusion. Then we did Kant with me taking the lead. This was one of the best discussions I've ever had and it lasted a long, long time. Eventually I brought the discussion to a dramatic conclusion. We were both exhausted afterward. When we had recovered, I suggested we try it the other way around. He was reluctant at first but eventually consented. He performed excellently and I was able to tell him he had the potential to be a fine philosopher. I wonder if he is ready for Husserl.

Oh my God, I thought to myself. Philosophy again. Does he think about nothing else? There was clearly nothing here I could use against him. There were pages of this sort of stuff describing tutorials and sometimes group seminars, mostly on Kant and Wittgenstein but with an occasional "go"—as he called it—at Hegel. I'm a bit surprised, quite frankly, to see how conscientiously he takes his teaching.

Checked to see how he was. Lying there with his mouth hanging open snoring. Then I let myself out.

Monday

Now it's all becoming clear. The silent young lady must have been blackmailing the old lady. Obviously, if knowledge of the dark secret in her family had become public, it would have destroyed Mrs. Armytage and all her descendants and relatives. So she was paying Miss Latimer to keep quiet. In that case I wonder why she killed the old lady?

Tuesday

I've got it! Suddenly it all came clear. It's amazing how that happens sometimes. You're staring at a problem for hours and then suddenly you see the solution. Because the young lady was blackmailing her, the old lady decided *she* would try to kill *her.* So she lured her to the edge of the cliff (which explains how they got there), but then it all went wrong. She tried to catch Miss Latimer by surprise, but she fought back. There was a furious struggle, and the old lady was pushed to her death.

But then how did her neck get slashed?

And what about the scorpion? That suggests revenge. And maybe something to do with disease. Where do they come in?

The papers are reporting that the police have now decided that the murders of Professor Moncrieff and of Dr. Bentley (!?) and the attack on Professor Speculand were carried out by the same person who dealt with the fallen lady in Turnberry Lane. They say that, except in the case of Dr. Bentley, there are striking similarities in the *modus operandi.* Well, well.

Wednesday

The last bits of the jigsaw are falling into place! I suddenly realized that Sir Rudolph must of caught syphilis from a lady of the night in the East End! That's why he started to kill w---es! He wanted to get revenge on them. Or maybe he even wanted to kill the one who had infected him. Perhaps he went mad because of the disease. And now that I think of it, he probably passed it on to his wife and children! That's the answer! Miss Latimer knew all about this and that's something else she was blackmailing the old lady about!

Did he stop practicing because he achieved what he set out to do? Or did his family find out that he was Jack and incarcerate him? What am I thinking of! Of course, we know for sure from the account in Mr. Peddie's book that Sir Rudolph died in a madhouse! There's the answer!

Thursday

Odd incident. A man came into the shop today with tattoos all over his hands and wearing a leather jacket covered in studs and said he was "into fantasy" and wanted some material. I said *Do you mean fairies and that kind of thing?* He sort of glared and said, Yes, he supposed he did. So I showed him the Tolkien section. He looked very put out and said it wasn't what he meant. Then Jerry, who had been watching, sort of nodded to him and they went into the back of the shop. Didn't look the type to be interested in elves and fairies. And then I noticed this other man watching them. I'm sure he's been in before. Doesn't look like most of our customers, who are mainly long-haired, scruffy types from the Uni. He had short hair and he was quite smartly dressed.

Friday

I wonder who Miss Latimer was. What was her connection with Mrs. Armytage?

She seems to have been adopted as something more than a mere companion but less than a relative, which implies that she had some kind of link with the family. And why was she mute? I just don't believe that stuff b---ming Horatio wrote about her brother and fiancé being killed in the same battle.

Saturday

I've got it! The young lady's mother was *his* mistress! That explains why she was not recognized as a legitimate member of the family but was looked after by Mrs. Armytage.

There are times when I'm absolutely b----y brilliant!

Sunday

The *Braes* at Horatio's. He was still up to his old game. He said he believed Auld Rab has started blackmailing Murdo into doing disgusting things with him. (He didn't put it like that.) I can't see any evidence for that at all. Sometimes—dare I say it—Horatio's "logical mind" lets him down rather badly.

Just as it ended, he started talking about how some film company was trying to buy an option on *The Right Lines.* Then he said he was hoping that it would be made into a movie and then his new book would do well as a result. His greed and boasting are becoming intolerable. But it occurs to me that he has said suspiciously little about the book he's started writing. I asked him about it, but he shut up like a clam.

Set off for our walk. Horatio mentioned about that professor and said he "died by his own venom." The one who invented the cat that killed a technician. He was poisoned by a red sand scorpion in his laboratory. Said something about how he was probably killed in revenge for having murdered the man. Dugdale, I mean. Murdered by the technician's girlfriend or something. Or by one of his wife's other lovers! How sordid it all sounded. I just didn't want to hear any more about it.

Then he started on yet again about how he was going to solve what he called "these horrible murders" and said that his trained and logical Cambridge mind should be able to give the police quite a lot of help. He had started constructing a mattress of possibilities. He said there were three instances to consider: the fallen lady in Turnberry Lane, the attack on Professor Speculand, and the case of Professor Moncrieff. (He said he was certain that Dr. Bentley had not been murdered by the Scorpion. How does he know?) Then there was a lot of incomprehensible jargon about logic and probability. The upshot seemed to be that he himself was the most probable next victim and Professor MacMaster the most probable murderer! Or the other way around! When he said that, he laughed. He has a somewhat warped sense of humor.

As we went into Westbourne Gardens, he was going on about how much he fancies one of those lovely big houses there. He said he's made so much money from his book that he can easily afford one. He casually mentioned that the movie company had made "a substantial offer" for the rights. He's got his eye on the one on the corner with Lorraine Road. He'll have four floors (plus a basement for his gym and whirlpool bath!) with his "writer's den" in the attic, which looks out over the whole of Glasgow. He thinks he can get it "for a snip," and then he said what the figure was and I worked out that it was only about thirty times my annual income!

I suppose he thinks his new book is going to make him even richer. Sometimes he disgusts me.

Back for *Biggert*. Dr. Watson was caught stealing lingerie from a shop. When Biggert heard this, he got really excited and predicted to Esmeralda that the case would pretty soon be wrapped up.

Then we saw the actors rehearsing at the Citz. Because Oscar Wilde had disappeared, they had to replace him, so they had to rehearse the scene with a new actor. It was tricky because Sherlock Holmes and Mr. Gladstone had to be sure to switch Gladstone bags because the fake knife was in Mr. Gladstone's bag. So when Ellen Terry reached into it to pull out the knife and rush at the Countess of Warwick and cut her throat, she had to get the right bag or she'd pull out the real knife that Oscar Wilde had used to cut himself free! Smarty-pants Horatio said, *Of course, at some point she'll get the wrong knife.*

Then we saw Biggert with the female shop assistant who had been so terrified of the lingerie thief when he looked at her. She was now looking at Dr. Watson standing in a lineup and she said he was the man who frightened her. Biggert said to Craigie: *I think we've got "the Scorpion."*

Horatio said, *No, you b---y well haven't!* And next minute, I have to admit, we saw the mysterious man stalking another young lady in the back lanes of the West End. (Kinnoul Lane, I think.)

Monday

I was thinking hard about it, and then, suddenly, it came to me in a flash. Miss Latimer's mother had been Jack's model. She was one of the East End w----s who posed for him. Why didn't I realize that before!

That's why Miss Latimer was mute! Of course! She was struck dumb with shock when she discovered what her father was doing! It all fits together! Brilliant! Brilliant!

I wonder if she saw him return late one night covered in blood and then heard the next day that there had been another killing? Or perhaps he brought home a corpse and his daughter found him with it?

I'm so close. I just need that last bit of evidence to lock into place.

Tuesday
Papers still full of this business about that professor being found dying in his lab. Now they're saying the Scorpion did it!

Wednesday
I've got it! It's all fallen into place in the most convincing way! And through a remarkable coincidence! I was sorting out new stock that Jerry had brought back from auction(where he occasionally deigns to go) when I found a rather battered old story-book. It's called *The Throat Surgeon* and it was published in 1958 by a writer called Lavinia Armitage. The name struck me immediately.

I glanced through it and found a scene when the heroine, who is a young nurse, has to go into the hospital morgue late one night for some reason. There she finds a surgeon who she has felt strangely attracted to, although he also frightens her. He is alone, bent over something with only a small lamp for illumination, and he doesn't realize she is watching him. This man *is Scottish and an amateur painter and because of his brutality as a surgeon he is known to his colleagues as Jock the Ripper*! The young nurse watches in surprise as he does something to a recently deceased corpse. She creeps a little closer and sees with horror that he is practicing throat cutting!

What could be clearer? The storybook was obviously written by Miss Latimer in old age and describes her discovery that her own father was Jack the Ripper! She knew this because her mother was one of his models *and one night she saw him murder her*! This was something she had been haunted by all her life, and she finally found a way to work it out of her system by writing this storybook.

Not only that but the story is full of phrases from Jack's letters! And the nurse is called Marie Kelly! Just like Jack's last victim! And also like her, "she had been christened Mary Jane but had always called herself Marie Jeanette"! Maybe Lavinia Armitage—alias Marcia Latimer—was Marie Kelly's daughter and watched her father kill and dissect her!

I'm so excited, I'm going to call on Horatio first thing tomorrow at the university. I can't wait to see his face! He'll eat his heart out!

Thursday
The patronizing, supercilious something!

I turned up and he had a student in his office. When I opened the door, he looked horrified to see me. He told the young man to leave and then asked me, rather rudely, what I had come there for. At least he asked me to sit down. I was surprised by how poky his office is. They can't think much of him there.

Anyway, I told him the whole Theory. When I ended, he said in that prissy way he has, *Let's take it point by point, shall we?* Then he went through the whole thing raising one footling objection after another. And he was quite unnecessarily offensive. For example, he sneered at the idea of Rudolph having been Jack by saying he was more likely to have been a reindeer than the Ripper and asking if he had a red nose.

But some of his points had some value. For example, he said he didn't believe that Jack's daughter had written the storybook about the nurse. (He called it a bodice ripper, though I pointed out that it was more of a bosom ripper.) If she had, then she would have made him an artist and not a surgeon. I tried to argue that the surgeon in the book was an amateur artist, but I had to admit that he had a point. And one way or another, he virtually pulled the whole thing apart until I was left with practically nothing. There's a cold, mean streak in him. He was really enjoying himself. Finally I crawled away feeling really flat and stupid.

But the thing is, I saw his Enemy at last. When I was looking for his office, I went into the corridor marked "Philosophy Department," and this tall, burly man was standing in the door giving instructions to the secretary. He had a big hooked nose and deep, staring eyes and he looked as if he had a very short temper. I had the odd feeling that I'd met him before somewhere, though I have no memory of it. I'm pretty sure he's never been in the shop. He had a very strong Scottish accent. I thought it was him and I heard the secretary say, *Yes, Professor MacMaster.*

Been thinking about how surprised and guilty Horatio looked when I went into his office and found him with that student. I must admit, it has occurred to me from time to time that members of the gentle s-x do not feature in Horatio's life as prominently as they do in mine. Just a thought.

Friday

Suddenly realized something about Professor MacMaster! He's exactly like the Major! The same nose, the same reddish face, the same grating voice! No wonder he was so angry with Horatio over the storybook. I bet it was that and not the fact that it made him a lot of money! Or not just that, anyway.

Saturday

I've been wondering about his new book and whether he has had the audacity to put *me* in it. And whether he has plagiarized ideas from me. I wonder if there's any way I could get a proper look at it.

I must try to have another peek around his place tomorrow and see if I can get a good look at it.

Sunday

I can't believe it! I just can't believe it! The duplicity of the man! The sneaky, shabby cunning! And the nasty, slimy lustfulness!

And I only found out about it by the merest chance. After we'd watched *Biggert,* he'd had so much, he actually fell asleep while I was there. I started trying to have a look at a big box file lying on the table. It had a thick bound manuscript inside it, which I assumed was the new book. Suddenly the phone rang in the study, and then I heard someone's voice leaving a message on the answering machine. It was so loud, I could hear it in the lounge. I went through to listen, and to my astonishment I recognized the voice. It was Auld Rab! And he sounded very angry indeed. I've never heard him sound like that. I saw straightaway the depths of lust and determination in the man that he manages to hide while he's in front of the cameras. He sounded dreadful. Husky and weak. But still very angry. This is what he said:

I hope you're happy f--king the horny little b---h. Everyone knows she's anybody's for the price of a good dinner or a decent part. I suppose you know she was f----g me until a better offer came along? She only got onto Biggert by f--king that c--t MacMangan. Then she dropped him for that little piece of s--te, Perkins. And now she's f--king you because she thinks you're the man of the future. How desperate can you get? Well, maybe the little b---h is right because I certainly don't have a future. And I suspect she doesn't either. After all, old pal, we did know each other awfully well.

I was so shocked, I just stood there. The meaning of this was quite clear. He's been seeing Esmeralda! I thought I was going to faint. And then I felt such anger. He's been conducting a secret affair with her. Betraying me with her. What a devious little creep the man is. When I think of all I've done for him. (Or at least, tried to do. It wasn't my fault if things went a little awry.)

I stood there just panting for breath. And then I went back into the lounge and looked at him sprawling in his chair, his mouth hanging open, wheezing and snortling with one hand dangling a couple of inches from the whiskey bottle. And I thought, *If she could just see you now. If Esmeralda could just walk in that door now and see you for what you are: a pathetic, drunken, pretentious little twerp.*

I've got to show him up for what he is. I've got to do something decisive. I wonder where he meets her. I'll try to follow him.

Anyway, before that, we'd watched the *Braes*. Horatio showed himself as stupid and as stubborn as usual. He went on again about his theory that Murdo is an undercover policeman who has been sent into the village disguised as a vet in order to find out who is committing all the murders. I could have poured ridicule on it just the way he did to my Theory, but I didn't bother. The truth is, you can see Murdo's a vet and not a policeman because of the wholly professional way he handles a cow. That's something you can't fake. I didn't make this point because naturally he would have brushed it aside the way he always does.

While we were having our walk, he was talking about the Scorpion case again. It was interesting to watch this so-called trained mind at work on the problem. For all its much-vaunted logic it was getting nowhere fast.

We got back in time for *Biggert*. I sat there trying not to hear his inane comments on it. Once again "the Scorpion" was haunting the lanes around here late at night. Then he attacked a lady, but this time she escaped from him. What happened was he sneaked up behind her and then put his left hand over her eyes while he brought this big curved knife out of his pocket with his other hand. But she somehow managed to kick backward in a way that must of been very nasty and painful for him. And then she ran off, just quickly looking back at him while he was clutching himself in agony. Horatio pointed out that she would be able to identify him.

Then there was something I didn't understand at all. (Though of course I didn't say so.) It was Cavalli, the man who owns the restaurant and is Fiammetta's father. He was with McGinnity, the taxidummyist, of all people. Heaven knows what the connection is between those two.

Then we saw the play being acted on the stage of the Citz with Biggert sitting in the audience again. When the play was reaching its climax in the last scene, this time there was something really brilliant. When Sherlock Holmes whipped the sheet off the dummy, it wasn't the dummy at all. It was Oscar Wilde! He was dead and he had been stuffed—properly stuffed like a stag's head!—and he had a green carnation sticking out of his mouth! Not only that, but he was wearing nothing but a few scanty items of exotic ladies' lingerie! I had a good laugh at that!

The cast were so surprised that they stopped acting and the play came to an abrupt end.

At that moment Biggert came jumping up out of the audience and arrested Sherlock Holmes for the murder of Maturin. Sherlock Holmes of all people! I couldn't believe it! I thought he must of been framed, but apparently not, because he broke down and admitted it, standing on the stage in front of hundreds of people. We saw Dr. Watson looking at him in horror. How that man must of felt betrayed!

Then right after that we saw Biggert explaining to Craigie and Esmeralda about how Sherlock Holmes had killed Maturin and he said, *The species of scorpion that stung Holmes was poisonous, as I said at the time, but that particular specimen wasn't dangerous. Its poison had been removed.* Apparently Sherlock Holmes was only faking an attempt on his own life. He wanted to kill Maturin and at the same time frame him as the murderer by using the same scorpion method that killed Jamie!

Then we saw Esmeralda interviewing the lady who managed to get away from "the Scorpion," who was called Mrs. McCrum. She was describing how the attacker tried to kill her and explaining that she'd taken a course in one of the Oriental martial arts, which is why she'd been able to defend herself, and suddenly the camera went in close on Esmeralda and she looked as if she'd just heard something important.

Then Biggert and Craigie went to visit Fiammetta at her flat. When she opened the door, her face was covered in bruises. Biggert didn't look at all surprised. He just said in that way he has, *Do you want to tell me about it?* She nodded. They came in and sat down in the flat, which had been wrecked. All the furniture was turned upside-down and slashed, and the ornaments were broken, and the curtains had been ripped down. And then Fiammetta told them how her father had found out about her love life and had come around and beaten her up and smashed the place. She said she would now get her revenge on him. So she explained that he was running a sophisticated drug operation. Biggert nodded as if he'd known all along. It had an ingenious distribution network. It started with Fiona, who was responsible for processing the drugs using the equipment in Professor Arbuthnott's laboratory. (But the old professor was starting to get suspicious, and she was afraid the gang were planning to kill him.) Then McGinnity was involved. What he did was to take the deer that Cavalli bought to supply venison to his restaurant. He stuffed them, since he was a taxidummyist, and while he was doing so, hid the drugs in them. Then M'Lay and Oscar Wilde stole expensive cars like Jaguars and Rolls-Royces, changed the license plates, strapped the deer to the roofs to look as if they had been deerstalking in the Highlands, and drove them down South. M'Lay drove, wearing a chauffeur's uniform, and Mr. Wilde lolled in the back smoking a cigar and looking really aristocratic. But they never had any trouble, because the police would never stop a posh car like that. And there was something else she explained. Trevor and M'Lay were responsible for taking photographs in the sauna where Trevor worked. I didn't quite understand this bit, but it seemed that they were able to use the photographs to blackmail people like the Prince of Wales into cooperating. (I suppose people don't want anyone to see them in the nude. I certainly wouldn't.)

Biggert said it was "a neat wee scam." Then Fiammetta told him and Craigie why everything had started to go wrong. The problem was that people employed at one point in the operation found out what was going on in the rest of it, and when they realized what big sums of money were involved, they got greedy. That's why Jamie had to be killed. And more recently, Mr. Wilde thought for a long time that he was just helping to sell stolen cars, and when he found out about the drugs inside the stuffed deer, he wanted to be cut in on the profits from that racket, too. Fiammetta said, *Well, he got his cut. Right in his stupid throat.*

Biggert told Craigie to go and arrest everyone involved, and he hurried out. When he was left alone with Fiammetta, he said, *You mentioned your dad finding out about your love life. Do you want to tell me about that?* She shook her head. Then he said, *Come on, hen. I've sent the young lad away. Nothing can shock me after thirty years of coppering.*

She lit a cigarette and looked really upset. Then she said she had killed McIlhargey. But it wasn't because she loved him and was jealous of his relationships with other ladies. It was because she was in love with the Countess of Warwick. (Well, I didn't know where to look when she said that.) And then she explained that she had good reasons for hating McIlhargey. They had the same taste in ladies, because months earlier she had fallen in love with Angelina. And she had blamed McIlhargey for her death. So when she realized that the Countess of Warwick was also in love with him, she had persuaded Fiona to supply her with one of the scorpions from the laboratory and had smuggled it into his bed. Then she broke down and started sobbing. Looking really upset, Biggert arrested her.

There was a quick jump, and we saw this shot of old Professor Arbuthnott dead in his lab with a tarantula sitting on him. It had obviously just bitten him.

Then Esmeralda was saying to Biggert and Craigie, *We don't know if "the Scorpion" was the person who killed Cherryman or not. But we know two things about him. One is that Angelina knew him or she would not have opened her door to him. And now I can tell you a second thing. He was at the Citz the night Cherryman was killed!* The other two looked amazed, and she explained that she had realized that what Mrs. McCrum had described as "the Scorpion's" *modus operandi* was precisely the method used by whoever murdered Cherryman. They both looked very embarrassed at that. She's a bright girl, that Esmeralda. Deserves far better than some pretentious middle-aged academic.

Then Horatio said that this meant that Biggert was a suspect, since he was in the audience on the night Cherryman was murdered. (He's really got it in for Biggert now. What a turnaround! I wonder why.) And quick as a flash I pointed out that Craigie was there too. He arrived with news of the first murder just before Cherryman was killed. He was watching the performance from the back of the audience. Well, Horatio couldn't deny it and he looked pretty put out at that!

Monday
Have to know the truth about him and Esmeralda, however much it hurts.

I waited around the corner from his place. When he came out a couple of hours later, I followed him. He went into several bookshops and then Marks and Spencer's. Then he went home. I wonder if he knew I was following him?

Tuesday
I waited again. Never came out.

Wednesday
Again. No result.

Thursday
This time he came out and walked up to the university. I hung around looking inconspicuous. When he came out a few hours later, he just went home.

What the h--k is he playing at?

Friday
He just went to the university library, where he spent a good

three hours. Has he guessed I'm following him? What *was* he doing there?

That b----y Jerry! No idea how to behave! A customer came in and asked him what we had on murder. Did Jerry say, *Would you care to consult my colleague, Mr. MacTweed, who has a specialist knowledge of the subject?* Like h-ck he did! He just nodded toward me and said, *Ask him.*

Saturday

At last! I waited for a few hours and he came out. And this time—just as I expected—he sneaked off to the BBC! That clinches it! I waited outside for three hours and then gave up when neither of them had come out. What is he doing in there with her? Are they doing disgusting things in her dressing room?

AUGUST

Sunday

Arrived at his place. He greeted me cool as a cucumber. I didn't let him see how angry I was.

Watched the *Braes*. Horatio driveling on about how worried he was that Murdo might get killed by Auld Rab before he can gather enough evidence to arrest him. I said he must have enough evidence by now, given the number of people the old rascal has killed. So that proves he can't be a policeman. Horatio got very indignant at that and said that Murdo was letting him have enough rope to hang himself. Any moment now he'd go too far, and then Murdo would have him just where he wants him. I said he'd better hurry or there wouldn't be anyone left alive in the village.

We went for a walk. Didn't talk much. I didn't trust myself and he seemed to have plenty on his mind.

Got back in time to watch *Biggert*. It was supposed to be the episode they were filming the day we visited the studio. As I was sitting down in front of the TV, Horatio said, *It won't be on, you know.* I pointed out that it was scheduled and asked him what he was talking about. He just put on that look he has that makes you want to slap him across his stupid face and said, *My lips are sealed.* (I wish they b--ming well were! Permanently!)

As it turned out, he was right. Because suddenly we got an announcement that there would be no show because it's been suspended. What a disappointment! When he saw how upset I was, he laughed in that dreadful way he has. It's really irritating. He sort of holds his mouth open and giggles from the back of his throat as if he was gargling, and then toward the end his giggle rises to a high-pitched squeal. It makes you want to . . . Well.

Apparently, Horatio said, there was a story in the paper about how the police think the Scorpion—the real one who is at work in Glasgow—is copying the one in the show! How absurd! These people have such an inflated idea of their own importance!

Horatio was very pleased with himself, but wouldn't say how he knew. Sat there smirking.

I couldn't bear it any longer so I said I was feeling sick— which was nothing less than the truth. So while he was sprawling in front of the TV, I went into the kitchen to make myself a cup of tea. While the kettle was boiling, I nipped into the study in order to have a peek at the manuscript. I hadn't seen it in the lounge, so I'd guessed that's where it was. And there it was on the desk still in the same box. But while I was in there, I noticed something very puzzling. I saw a clipping lying on his desk that had been cut from *The Clarion*. It had a headline saying, "Health bombshell for 'Scotland's grandad,' " I copied it down so that I could think about it later.

Close friends confirmed yesterday that TV actor Frazer Pittendrigh is seriously ill. The mystery illness has caused progressive weight loss over the last few months, which fans of the show have noticed. Extrovert bachelor Pittendrigh, 66, who has for nearly twenty years played the central figure of Auld Rab in *Gargunnock Braes*, Scotland's favorite TV soap, was said last night to be resting with friends in the country. Auld Rab, whose preretirement position as 'jannie' to the village school has won him the affectionate nickname of 'Scotland's grandad,' has been known and loved by generations of Scottish schoolchildren, both in the fictional world of *Gargunnock Braes* and in real life. Until a dramatic and well-publicized breakup five years ago, Fraser Pittendrigh shared a flat in Glasgow's fashionable Westbourne Gardens with fellow actor Scott MacMangan, who himself plays craggy D.C.I. Biggert in Scotland's most popular television export. MacMangan, contacted last night, refused to

make any comment on the dramatic news about his former
friend or to answer questions about his own health.

I wonder if someone has poisoned him? One of the parents in
the village, maybe. Did he eat one of those pies after all? There
was no hint of any of the things Horatio and I have spotted, I
noticed.

And I wonder why he cut it out?

Anyway, then I looked at the manuscript. The title was on the
cover. My heart missed a beat because it suggested that it was
about Jack. But although I only had time to flick through it, it
doesn't seem to be. And it looks like a storybook!

So when I was back in the lounge, I waited for him to wake
up and then I asked him about the new book. He said, *Oh that?*
It's my little monograph "The Detective Novel as Philosophy." (And
then something about b---ming mattresses.) *I've told you about it.*
I try to formalize the structure of the whodunnit into a combinatorial se-
ries of logical propositions using a computer program. So it's a mixture
of a book about the whodunnit and a logic textbook.

He's lying. What's he up to?

Monday
I waited outside and then followed him again. Nothing.

Tuesday
This time I went and waited outside the BBC. After four hours
she came out at last. Unfortunately, she got straight into a taxi
at the corner, so I lost her.

Wednesday
I waited outside the BBC again. At last she came out. I followed her for nearly an hour. She went shopping in Byres Road.
I had to hang around outside dress shops for ages. Then she
suddenly hailed a taxi, so I lost her again. I think she might just
possibly have noticed me.

Thursday
I waited again. Two hours this time. When she came out, I
had a plan worked out, which I put into operation. So that she
wouldn't notice me, I walked on ahead into Ruskin Lane on the

assumption she was going to Ruskin Terrace. Then I waited for her to come around the corner. She didn't! So she must have gone somewhere else. D--n! D--n! D--n!

Sunday

I'm so angry, I hardly know where to begin. I feel so betrayed. So humiliated. He's tried to take everything from me.

This is what happened. First of all we watched the *Braes* and there was this scene when Auld Rab was with Senga. Right at the end she put her hand on his arm and told him to take better care of himself. (She must of noticed how thin he's getting.) It came to us both at exactly the same moment: Auld Rab had an affair with her years ago and is the father of the twins! We gazed at each other in amazement as the implications of this sunk in. He had seduced, blackmailed, and then murdered his own daughter! The sooner someone succeeds in murdering him, the better for all concerned.

Anyway, the *Braes* had just ended when he got a phone call. He went into the study to answer it and then came back and told me it was from the BBC and that he had to go to a meeting there straight away. Then he said it was about time he told me something he had been asked to keep secret. But it would soon be public knowledge. He said that he and Biggert had stayed in touch after that time we went to meet him because they had gone on discussing making a TV series out of Horatio's whodunnit. But Biggert had also wanted to talk about his revising the present series of *Biggert* and perhaps writing a new series.

Now he explained how he knew the final episode of the show would not be screened. About a week before it was due to be broadcast, Biggert rang and told him this extraordinary story. The police had just contacted the BBC and requested to see the final episode. Then they had asked for it to be suspended. It was because they have this incredibly stupid idea that the Scorpion—the real one—is imitating the series. The final episode was about the use of a decoy to try to trap "the Scorpion." And the police are actually planning to use a very similar trap. They were afraid that the episode would warn him off. Then they had asked the BBC if a new final sequence could be written and filmed at very short notice in order to help to entrap him. They would pay for this to be done! The BBC had agreed to do this.

None of the regular writers on the show were free to drop everything and produce a new final twenty minutes to replace the original ending. So Biggert had persuaded the producer to talk to Horatio. Horatio had gone to see him, they had talked about ideas, and he had been commissioned to do the rewrite. Then he said he had also talked to one or two of the rest of the cast about how the final episode might turn out. There was quite a conflict between possible different endings, he said. When he had got to that point, he looked at his watch and said he had to go and he'd tell me the rest next time.

Well, I was staggered by that. And particularly by his deviousness in hiding all this from me. So he's been trotting off to see Biggert at regular intervals and in secret, has he? Biggert *and others*. That's very interesting. Very interesting indeed.

As for the police! Well, they must be astonishingly stupid is all I can think. Trapping the Scorpion with a TV show! What *do* they imagine! I feel quite indignant at the waste of taxpayers' money.

Anyway, that's only the half of it. What happened then was he put on his coat and that silly deerstalker of his and told me to finish my tea before I let myself out. Then he hurried off. Well, now I had my chance. As soon as he'd gone, I bolted the front door and went to find the box file. It was on his desk. I opened it up and took out the manuscript.

I can't bear to think about it! Lies! Plagiarisms! Filth!

It was *me* that told him about Bible John. He'd never even heard of the case before I put him onto it! He's robbed Scotland of another piece of its heritage!

He's even plagiarized from himself! Clarence Titheradge Lovebone, the great-nephew of Clarence Titheradge!

And MacSporran! Oh, very funny! And the name of the bookshop. Not very clever, I don't think. And astrology! *Astrology!* Does he think I'm stupid? And the hint that it's a cover for going out and doing disgusting things at night!

I'll sue him for "child-molester eyes." And for that coat "creaking with grease." And for the "grubby lambs' tails." And so on. And so on.

He's plagiarized my solution! My beautiful Theory! He said he didn't believe it, but he's stolen it!

He won't get away with it.

By nearly midnight I'd only read about half the manuscript and I didn't dare stay any longer in case he came back and found me still there. But I dread to think what might be in the rest of it.

Monday

The devious, two-faced b-----d!

It's my life. He's stolen it! This is more than mere plagiarism! He's trying to turn me into a product of his own imagination. He's trying to imagine me out of existence!

Tuesday

I'm so angry, I can hardly concentrate. I've got to do something to get back at him. To show him I'm not just a character in his book. He's taken everything from me: my Theory, Esmeralda, my self-respect, my family history. Even my whiskers!

Wednesday Morning

Had a brilliant idea! It would be poetic justice. He stole from me and it's only right that his stealing should be appropriately punished. I was thinking about the glove I dropped. I don't know whether the police ever found it. But there's the Scorpion as well. And since the police know that the victims of the attacks/murders are members of the Philosophy Department—or, in the case of Professor Speculand of the English Department—he must be a possible suspect. So I just need something taken from the new book.

Wednesday Evening

The trouble is, my idea won't work until someone else has read that horrible book. And so far I don't believe anyone else has. I remember that he mentioned that he was about to send it to his agent.

Thursday Morning

If only I knew he'd sent off that manuscript! I must find out.

Thursday Evening

I couldn't bear the suspense any longer. I rang and made small talk for a bit and let him sound off about how well he's doing at the BBC and how much they all think of him up there, and then eventually—really casually—I got the conversation around to his new book and he went on about it for a bit—still claiming it was a work of scholarship—and then at last he said he had posted it to his agent.

It's a lovely new moon tonight. This time I must get everything right.

Friday

Evening paper full of it. No details given, though. I wonder how long it will take the police to work it out? When will they arrest him?

He'd written far more books than Horatio, I'm interested to see from the obitchuaries. I'll bet Horatio was really envious of *him* and not the other way around. And it was Kant, not "cant." Silly me. And I spelled Neitscher wrong.

I remember what he said once about someone being unpredictable if someone else was very clever. I suppose he thinks I'm not as clever as him. Well, we'll see.

Saturday

Still nothing in the papers. If I don't hear anything before then, I'll go around tomorrow as usual.

Can't they *read*?

Sunday

Got to the flat. Knocked, and there was no answer. I was just thinking they must of come for him when he called out from inside. He wouldn't let me in until I had identified myself! I found him practically shaking with terror. He'd had quite a lot, too.

It turned out that he wasn't just frightened because this was yet another member of his department. He said he himself was bound to be a suspect! (Here was an unexpected bonus!) I asked him why, and he got very upset and rambled and stammered and poured himself another whiskey. Then finally he told me that Professor MacMaster had had some "dirt"—as he called it—which he had been blackmailing him with.

When he said this, I remembered that I was a bit puzzled when he was telling me ages ago that his Enemy tried to blackmail him. And then I thought about the Major trying to blackmail Dr. Titheradge. He said it was completely false. Professor MacMaster had fabricated a statement by someone alleging something against him. But he said that if the police found it among his papers, they might assume it was true and that it was a motive for Horatio to have killed him.

I wonder what it might be that Professor MacMaster had on him. Did he find out about the plagiarism from Mr. Peddie's book, I wonder? Or could it have been something even more serious?

I asked him if he could get into Professor MacMaster's office and try to find and remove the files on him. I was hoping he'd attempt such a stupid trick and then I could tip off the police and he'd be caught. That would look very incriminating. But unfortunately he said he was sure they would have taken measures already to secure the files.

He was too frightened to want to watch the *Braes* and he shuddered when I asked him about going for a brisk walk. But he was anxious to turn on the news to see if there was anything new to do with this business about Professor MacMaster. There was. The police have announced that they have found voluminous files of Professor MacMaster's on a number of people: colleagues in the university, students, local politicians. Horatio said he wasn't surprised, because he had always suspected that MacMaster was blackmailing lots of people. He said he was sure the police have started searching through the files looking for suspects. He seemed very upset at the idea. He obviously didn't want company, so I left him fairly early and went out on my own to do a little work with my four-and-a-half-incher.

Monday

Papers obsessed with this business. At least they're now saying
that the Scorpion left a message written in blood at the scene.
They don't say what the message was. And apparently he misspelled a certain word. This naturally arouses my curiousity.

Tuesday

Bought the local rag for once. Still no arrest. I suppose none
of them ever read books. Not even detective stories. What an illiterate bunch! I'm tempted to write to them. Score a few more
points!

The police say they have discovered from Professor MacMaster's
files that he was blackmailing Dr. Bentley, because he had found
out he was in the habit of doing disgusting things with other
men—including his students! I know he and Horatio were close
friends. I can't say this makes me any happier.

Wednesday

I remember that Horatio told me that that Dr. Bentley was being blackmailed by Professor MacMaster over his relations with
a student. But it now occurs to me that he led me to believe the
student was a girl, not a boy! That seems to me to be highly significant.

Thursday

According to the papers, the police have started to doubt that
the business of the fallen lady in the lane off Turnberry Road was
carried out by the same person as the cases of Dr. Bentley (?), Professor Speculand, Professor Moncrieff, and Professor MacMaster!
Well, well. Still, looking at it from my point of view, that suggests
that the net is closing in on him.

Saturday Evening

He actually phoned and asked me to come over! On a Saturday!

When I got there, I found him very upset. He told me he had
just been interrogated by the police! I had a real struggle to
hide my feelings when I heard that. But it turned out that it
wasn't quite what I'd thought. What happened was that the police have been going through Professor MacMaster's files and

yesterday they came across documents pertaining to Horatio. He said they showed that Professor MacMaster had been black-mailing him, which he had mentioned to me recently. But now he seemed to want to tell me what was in them. At first, though, he wouldn't say much. Then he said Professor MacMaster had concocted evidence that he had had an improper relationship with a student. And then at last he admitted that it was a male student. That gave me food for thought. He said it was completely untrue. Professor MacMaster had got the young man to write a statement saying that Horatio had seduced—if that's the right word!—him by promising to help his academic career in a most improper way. Horatio insisted he had not touched him.

The student's name was Magnus Lorimer. Horatio told me that he had first noticed him as someone who seemed very quiet, and mysterious. It seemed to him that he knew a great deal more than he revealed and that he was under some sort of constraint. So he had set out to befriend him simply because he suspected that he knew something about the attempt at character assassination against Gavin Oscars. He had had to spend a great deal of time winning his trust. Eventually the young man told him that what he had suspected was true: that Professor MacMaster had brought pressure on him to become a sort of spy. In return, he had promised to give him some part-time teaching and had even hinted that he would use his influence to ensure that his doctoral thesis was accepted and that he was given a permanent post. Lorimer had confirmed to Horatio that Professor MacMaster was infiltrating spies into the Institute, who were reporting back to him. And that he was using *agents provocateurs* to encourage the Institute into committing various excesses as part of his policy of giving it enough rope to hang itself.

Horatio had become convinced that Dr. Bentley had been another person being blackmailed by Professor MacMaster into helping him to discredit the Institute. He had attempted to persuade Dr. Bentley to confess the truth to him. But Dr. Bentley had resisted right up to the moment he died. (I said that the fact that he had committed suicide was, in effect, an admission that he had betrayed Gavin Oscars and the Institute. Horatio just nodded.)

Horatio admitted that he had not told me the whole truth

previously in giving a description of his climactic encounter with the evil genius who was behind all of this. He had apprised me on that occasion that he had turned the tables on Professor MacMaster who, having failed to blackmail him, then made a full confession and promised to resign.

The truth was really this:

After getting a confession from Lorimer and talking to Dr. Bentley and seeing how frightened and uncomfortable the man was, Horatio felt he had enough evidence. He had finally decided to confront Professor MacMaster when he heard the news of Dr. Bentley's death. He had therefore met Professor MacMaster and told him what he had learned of his blackmailing activities from Lorimer. Professor MacMaster, to his surprise, became very unctuous and told him that the fact that Dr. Bentley himself had accused him, Professor MacMaster, of being an enemy of the Institute shortly before he killed himself made it clear that Horatio's allegation was absurd. Horatio turned the tables on him and told him what he suspected in the case of Dr. Bentley: that Professor MacMaster had been blackmailing him into playing an elaborate charade and that he had denounced Professor MacMaster simply in order to make himself seem the more loyal to Gavin Oscars. The pressure of this charade had driven him to take his own life. Then Professor MacMaster became even more oily and, without admitting his guilt, tried to bribe Horatio to keep his findings to himself. He offered him a trip to a conference in Cairo, Illinois, at the department's expense. But Horatio insisted he was determined to clear up the scandal and exonerate Gavin Oscars and other victims of Professor MacMaster's character assassination.

Seeing that he was not to be moved, Professor MacMaster now went in for the kill. He told him he had known for some time that Horatio was up to no good with Lorimer. Acting quite legitimately in his capacity as head of department, he had spoken to Lorimer and persuaded him to hand over some letters from Horatio and to make a written statement giving his version of events. He now showed this document to Horatio. It was, according to Horatio, a pack of lies. In it Lorimer claimed that Horatio had propositioned him and seduced him with bribes and threats. He had lured him to his flat several times on the pretext of wanting to give him extra tutorials, but once there, he had blackmailed him into doing disgusting things. Horatio told me how easily his well-meaning efforts to persuade the young man to help him expose Professor MacMaster's plot against the Institute could be misrepresented as attempts to seduce him. He said he had also written one or two somewhat ill-advised and carelessly worded letters to Lorimer and that the language he had used was open to a malicious interpretation.

So Horatio had had to keep silent about Professor MacMaster's activities. And in fact he had actually had to collaborate with him in what he admitted had been one or two rather disgraceful actions.

He said that all of this must seem highly incriminating to the police and they might even think it was a motive for murder. However, a major factor in his favor was that Professor MacMaster had similar files on several dozen other people. So there were lots of people with motives for killing him that were at least as good as his.

I asked if the police were interviewing all of them. He said he thought they were, but that they had probably put him near the top of their list of suspects because they knew that there had been bad blood between them, and, of course, because he was at the university and involved in one way or another with Dr. Bentley and Professor Moncrieff and Professor Speculand.

I knew he was lying. The scales had fallen from my eyes and I saw his feet of clay. I knew that Professor MacMaster had been right. He had been doing disgusting things with that student. He was one of those men.

In the middle of my horror and disgust the thought came to me: At least this means he has not been seeing Esmeralda. But in that case, who had Auld Rab been referring to? Who was the mysterious person he was seeing at the BBC? From the way he had turned against Biggert, it couldn't be him. Who could it be?

Then I thought of all the times I had been alone with him in his flat and I nearly fainted with horror and relief. He must of been sitting there looking at me in that way.

I now saw so much in a completely new light. All that stuff about Freemasons and strange handshakes. It was clear to me that this was all about men of that kind recognizing each other. His book was full of it.

Trying not to let him see how horrified and disgusted I was,

I left his flat and went back to my place. I found his horrible book and reread that scene where the Major tries to kill Dr. Titheradge. The secret handshakes that are supposed to be from Freemasonry! The way he talks about Jack pretending to take ladies "from behind"! And the way he tries to get Dr. Titheradge to let him demonstrate on him! How could I have been so naive!

A horrible idea suddenly came to me about Jack! No! No! I can't bear to think about it.

Saturday Night

I'm so angry when I think about it. Deceiving me all that time. The only thing that stops me beating him to death and killing myself is that people might think we were a couple of perverts like that playwright and his "lover" down in London. He's already done my reputation enough harm if anyone else finds out about him. Thank heavens nobody knows we're friends. Thank heavens I told him never to speak to me when he comes in the shop!

I simply can't believe it about Jack. And there's no evidence to suggest that his relations with the gentle s-x were anything but perfectly normal.

Sunday

Despite my misgivings, I took my courage in my hands and went over to his place as usual. He started telling me about the final sequence he's writing for *Biggert*. When it was time for the *Braes*, he turned on the TV, but he had so much to say he turned the sound right down and we just glanced at the screen now and then.

He said the BBC are going to broadcast the last half hour live! This is because the police believe that the Scorpion, because of what they absurdly think is his obsession with *Biggert*, is planning to kill Esmeralda! They've apparently come to that wonderfully intelligent view because she has told them she has noticed someone following her out of the BBC building! So the police intend to use her as a decoy to lure the Scorpion into the trap! They expect that he won't be able to resist coming to watch the live broadcast, so they plan to swamp the area with plainclothes detectives. They apparently think he is stupid enough to attempt to

kill her during the broadcast! But Horatio said they have devised
what he called "a fall-back position." (I can see he's been at his
mattress again!) If the Scorpion watches the show on TV at
home, then something in it is intended to lure him into a trap.
It seems they intend to plant in his mind an idea that will inspire
him to an attempt to kill Esmeralda at a later date. He wouldn't
tell me what the trap was. And he became very mysterious and
knowing, but I kept on at him until eventually he admitted that
he wasn't even sure yet because the rewrites were still under discussion and would probably go on up to the last minute. And he
said there was some information the police were holding back
that they intend to release at a crucial moment. (Ah hah! I
thought to himself.) He said he had no idea what it was. Because
of the lack of time and the need for secrecy, he said, the actors
will be told what is in the script just before the shoot. But he did
say that Biggert would be absolutely furious when he found out
that the police have insisted on a change from the original ending in which Esmeralda got killed. He said Biggert had been
pushing hard for "the Scorpion" to turn out to be Craigie, since
that would get him out of the next series! And it wasn't that far-
fetched, Horatio said, because "the Scorpion" had to be someone who was known to Angelina and had been at the Citz the
night Cherryman was killed.

At that moment I happened to look at the TV. Murdo's head
was filling the screen. *And he was wearing a deerstalker!* My mind
was racing. Suddenly it came to me: Horatio was having an
"affair"—as men like that call it—with Craigie! That was why he
turned against Biggert! Craigie and Biggert hate each other. Everything fitted together now. Craigie is young and tall and good-
looking and therefore attractive to men like that—at least, I
assume he is. I suddenly realized that that was why Horatio
watched the two TV series—because Craigie was in both of
them! How naive I've been!

Somehow I managed to switch back to what Horatio was telling me.

In the new version, he was explaining, Esmeralda will be left
alive at the end so that the Scorpion—did he mean the real
one? I was getting somewhat confused!—will be lured into trying
to kill her later. Then he looked very mysterious and said that

that wasn't the only thing that was likely to annoy Biggert in the final script and that the way things were going at the moment, he might be in for a very nasty surprise indeed.

Well, that whetted my curiousity to see the script. Based on what I now knew, I suspected he had built up Craigie's role as much as possible and played down Biggert's and Esmeralda's.

I was wondering how I could sneak a look at the script. Then, lo and behold! he started telling me all about it in great detail! He's so b---ming pleased with himself, he couldn't resist taking me through the whole thing scene by b---ming scene! That was his biggest mistake ever!

He's only had to write a few new scenes and the BBC will record several of them this week so that they have them ready before Sunday. And they've already taped all the scenes involving the Citizens' actors so they'll slot them in between the live scenes to give them time for the technical things to be done. So there's just four scenes at the end that will be done live.

To start with, he showed me how, in the first scene where Esmeralda was at home in the evening watching *Tillieknock Nuik*, he had made "brilliant" use of the idea of a slip of the tongue. She was looking at where Roberta was telling her mother about her feelings for her husband, Jock, and she said something rather odd and then corrected herself. She said, *I've never loved anyone the way I love that woman. I mean, that man.* Horatio had written that at these words Esmeralda sort of perked up and got out her police notebook and wrote something. Suddenly she heard a noise outside. She crept to the window and looked out. She could see that someone was out in the garden trying to look into the flat, but she couldn't see who it was. She moved cautiously toward the telephone and picked it up. And Horatio said something about how he wanted to plant the idea in the audience's mind of this "sad little psychopath" staring in at Esmeralda voyeuristically.

In the next scene Biggert was interviewing Trevor, the man who works in the sauna, who had been arrested with Cavalli's drugs gang. And now at last he learned why Cherryman was not interested in the beautiful Countess of Warwick, who was passionately in love with him: Trevor told him that Cherryman liked other men! He had often come to the sauna for a massage. (I'm beginning to suspect that there's more to this massage busi-

ness than I'd realized!) And there was this close-up on Biggert's
face, Horatio said, expressing amazement and interest. (An expression on *Biggert's* face?!) Then he asked me if I thought that
revelation about Cherryman "worked." I just said to him, *No
comment.* But if he's happy with that sort of filth, that's his
choice.

Then there was a scene where Esmeralda told Biggert and
Craigie that she thought "the Scorpion" had not only been
watching her from outside her flat but had been following her
for several days beforehand. She said she had seen him as she
went in and out of shops and had once had to jump into a taxi
to get away from him. (I had a nasty moment there! I thought
she was going to describe him.) Biggert said he was afraid "that
sick weirdo" had decided to kill her. He got awfully upset about
this, and there was a whole lot of stuff about how she was like a
"wee daughter" to him and he "wouldnae let any harm come to
her for the world." (Horatio said he'd love to see Biggert's face
when he reads this bit! And he sort of smirked to himself.) Then
Biggert said he was going to turn the tables on this "pathetic
wee pervert" by using Esmeralda to trap him. (What's Biggert
got against little men? He's no taller than I am! That's Horatio's
work.)

Next there was a scene at the Citz where they were rehearsing
the moment when Oscar Wilde is unmasked as Jack, and Ellen
Terry cuts the throat of the Countess of Warwick.

Horatio explained how they were doing it in great haste because they had to perform it that evening with a partly new cast.
Since both Oscar Wilde and Sherlock Holmes were no longer
available, they were doing it with the Prince of Wales playing Oscar Wilde and Dr. Watson playing the Prince of Wales and Mr.
Gladstone replacing Sherlock Holmes and Algernon Swinburne
replacing Mr. Gladstone and Aubrey Beardsley replacing Dr. Watson. Horatio sniggered and said, *Because of the way they've all
switched roles, they get really mixed up.* And the way he'd written it,
they kept confusing Mr. Gladstone (now played by Algernon
Swinburne)'s Gladstone bag with Sherlock Holmes (now played
by Mr. Gladstone)'s Gladstone bag and Dr. Watson (now played by
Aubrey Beardsley)'s Gladstone bag. And it kept going wrong. At
one point Aubrey Beardsley (who was now playing Dr. Watson)
brought out the knife instead of the gun and pointed it at the

Prince of Wales (who was now playing Oscar Wilde). And then at the end of the scene Ellen Terry rushed at the Countess of Warwick and tried to cut her throat with the gun. And instead of helping to sort things out, Primrose was giving them directions from his prompt corner that were making them all more and more confused.

In the next scene Biggert was telling Esmeralda and Craigie how he was going to set a trap for "the Scorpion" by having somebody lure him into Esmeralda's flat. And then he announced that he himself was going to be the decoy! They both tried to argue him out of it, but he was adamant. And he told them that secrecy was essential and only the three of them would know that he would be doing it. All the other police involved in the operation would be led to believe that Esmeralda was the decoy. Then he told Craigie he would be in charge of coordinating the operation from police headquarters.

In the next scene Biggert was interviewing Fiammetta. He was trying to find out who the person was that Cherryman was having an affair with. He couldn't get her to tell him. But she did tell him that Roberta was deeply jealous of Cherryman because the Countess of Warwick was madly in love with him—though he did not return her affection since, to put it bluntly, his inclinations tended toward a rather different direction. So I said, *You mean, Roberta was in love with Cherryman even though he was a man of that type?* And Horatio just smirked and told me to wait and see.

Then we saw Craigie and Esmeralda making the preparations for the "stake-out" of Esmeralda's flat. They were talking about how brave Biggert was to expose himself in that way. At that moment he came in and announced that during the "op" they would not use radios in case "the Scorpion" was listening in. Then he told them that Fiammetta had told him that Roberta had been madly jealous of Cherryman. At that moment Esmeralda remembered that Roberta had made a revealing slip of the tongue during the episode of *Tillieknock Nuik* she had been watching. She told the two men what Roberta had said and suggested that this implied that she was like those men with particular tendencies. That, to put it frankly, she was in love with the Countess of Warwick. That was why she had been jealous of Cherryman! So Biggert told her to go to the BBC to interview

Roberta. When she had left, he told Craigie that he had done this so that she would be safely out of harm's way.

In the next scene Esmeralda was at the BBC and talking to Roberta. She was trying to get her to talk about her emotional relationships with different members of the Citz cast. I said to Horatio, *Shouldn't she ask her why she ran away from* Gargunnock Braes? *Isn't that relevant?* But he just shook his head. He obviously didn't want any help from me. Just applause.

Then we saw Biggert dressed up in ladies' clothes and acting as the decoy at Esmeralda's flat. He was parading up and down in front of the lighted window, and then Horatio pointed out where the directions in the script said, *He starts to take his clothes off slowly and seductively!* I looked at him, speechless with amazement. He was just smiling.

Then Esmeralda was interviewing Roberta again. And now at last she broke down and confessed that she was the person who murdered Cherryman. She described how she had dressed up as a man and walked onstage and killed him because the Countess of Warwick, who she was in love with, was obsessed with him. Then said she now hated the Countess of Warwick because she had spurned her. And she smiled nastily and added mysteriously, *But I won't hate her for long.* I asked Horatio what she meant by that and he said, *Wait and see. It's just over the page.*

When Roberta had finished her confession, Esmeralda ordered her to be taken away and then stayed on by herself to phone headquarters.

Horatio said that up to this point, all the scenes have either been taped or will be taped before Sunday. The next scene was the first one that was going to be done live. Then he said, *And it's a real shocker.* And it was. It described Biggert walking out of Esmeralda's flat and going down the street in his female garments! He looked from a distance just like any middle-aged lady, so none of the police officers who were surreptitiously watching the flat recognized him—especially since none of them even knew he was acting as the decoy. As Biggert went past, one of the plainclothes officers was in a phone box, and he looked at him curiously. Then Biggert hurried up Ruskin Lane toward the BBC.

I was puzzled, so Horatio said, *Don't you get it? He's "the Scorpion."* Then he waited for me to tell him how clever he was, but

I didn't say anything. Frankly, I thought it was pretty stupid. Biggert simply isn't clever enough to have done what "the Scorpion" has managed to do. By no stretch of the imagination.

Then he said, *Do you remember that scene early on in the series when Biggert was looking through the window into Esmeralda's bathroom as he approached her flat?* I said I certainly did. And he said, *That was what gave me the idea that he was the killer. And that scene anticipates this revelation nicely, doesn't it?*

Then he insisted on explaining to me how clever Biggert was being—which means, how clever he had been himself! He said that Biggert knew that Esmeralda was undefended at the BBC while the police were watching Ruskin Terrace because he had sent her there himself. And the fact that he had ordered the police not to use radios in case "the Scorpion" was listening in allowed him to get out, deal with Esmeralda, and get back without being detected by any of his colleagues. Horatio said, *It's close to being the perfect murder. A hundred percent for the alibi. Another hundred for knowing the victim well. And I think he deserves at least an eighty for communicating with the police. Nothing, admittedly, for disguising the murder as suicide or accident. I make that seventy percent overall. Not bad.* Then he smirked unbearably.

Just to stop that smirk, I asked about the next scene. This one, also to be broadcast live, showed Craigie organizing the whole operation at police headquarters. At that moment the police officer in the public phone box called in and spoke to Craigie. He described the "lady" who had just left the house and commented on "her" horrible little bandy legs and "great jutting a-s."

And Craigie said, *What did you say her a-s was like?* and the detective answered *I said it sort of juts out. It's the most horrible a-s I've ever seen.* And then Craigie cried out. *I know that a-s!* (I'll bet he does, I thought.) *It's Quasimodo's!* (Apparently that's his nickname for Biggert. Heaven only knows why.) He quickly dialed Esmeralda's flat and there was no answer. He guessed immediately what Biggert was up to and rushed from headquarters, telling his subordinates he was going to defend Esmeralda at the BBC.

In the next scene, on tape of course, the last act was starting at the Citz and the actors, who were already totally confused, were being made even more muddled because Primrose was misdirecting them from the prompter's box.

The next scene, to be broadcast live, showed Biggert getting into the BBC building by climbing through a window on the ground floor at the side. And then Horatio, practically hugging himself at his own ingenuity, explained that this was going to be the police's real trap. They thought there was only a very remote possibility that the killer would attempt to kill Esmeralda during the actual shooting. What they hoped was that when it was announced that filming of the next series had started, he would assume that she would be alone and undefended in the same dressing room at the BBC and would climb in through the same window that Biggert had used. But the police would be lying in wait to catch him.

Then Horatio explained that because the BBC are filming the final sequence live, they have to shoot it in two places, which are very near each other so that the actors can get from one shoot to another quickly. So when Craigie rushes from police headquarters, he will in fact run from Ruskin Terrace along the lane to the BBC. Along that dark lane we've often walked down on Sunday evenings!

And while he's rushing along the lane, viewers will be watching the tape of the climactic scene at the Citz. Right at the end of the play, Primrose is going to prompt the actors into delivering the wrong lines so that when Ellen Terry and the Countess of Warwick start to quarrel, Ellen Terry will reach into Mr. Gladstone (now played by Algernon Swinburne)'s Gladstone bag for the fake knife, since this Gladstone bag should have been switched with Sherlock Holmes (now played by Mr. Gladstone)'s Gladstone bag, which has the real knife, but of course it'll be the wrong Gladstone bag because Primrose will be confusing the actors from the prompter's box and saying things like, *No, Gladstone, it's not your Gladstone bag you pick up. It's Sherlock Holmes's Gladstone bag!* So Ellen Terry will pull out the real knife that Oscar Wilde used to cut himself free rather than the fake knife that she is supposed to attack the Countess of Warwick with. She'll rush at the Countess of Warwick and stab her throat with it and real blood will spurt out. (I mean, real fake blood. Or, rather, fake real blood.) So the Countess of Warwick will really die acting. Or, rather, really act dying.

The next scene, live of course, showed Craigie arriving at the BBC, rushing to the dressing rooms and bursting in just in time to catch Biggert in the act of strangling Esmeralda and with his knife in his hand ready to cut her throat. He rescued her after a struggle. Then Biggert stood with his knife still in his hand and confessed to Craigie that he had carried out all "the Scorpion murders." Then before Craigie could stop him, he cut his own throat.

That was the end. Then Horatio said, *Well, what do you think?* And I said, *So don't we find out who killed Jamie the stagehand, and why?* And Horatio said, *No. And frankly I don't know who killed him. Anyway, who cares?*

I didn't say anything, but I can't wait to find out how Biggert will react when he sees the script.

I left shortly afterward. This evening has given me a lot to think about. There seems to me to be quite a lot of potential—as Horatio would say—in the script.

Friday

Horatio rang just now and invited me to come over to his place about eightish and watch the show on TV on Sunday evening while he goes to the shoot. Then he'll come back later and tell me how it went and I'll tell him what it looked like on the screen. I agreed to this arrangement, though as it happens, I have other plans for the rest of the evening.

It's all starting to fall into place very nicely.

SEPTEMBER

Sunday

Horatio let me in.

He was pretty busy getting ready to go to the "shoot"—as he called it. But he said he'd have time to watch the *Braes* before rushing off, so we sat down.

Just before the program started, there was an announcement. They showed a photograph of Auld Rab, and the announcer said he had just died. (I sneaked a glance at Horatio. He was *smiling!*) It was very odd, because when the show started, there was Auld Rab, large as life, and looking just as he always did. Then right at the end the lady who calls herself Roberta came in crying—though she must have been pleased really, even though he hadn't actually done disgusting things to her but to the real

Roberta—and said the "old gentleman" had just collapsed while he was helping old Mrs. MacGregor move her furniture. He'd been rushed to the hospital, and when the program ended, the whole village was waiting for news. But they'd just told us he'd died, for goodness' sake! They should at least try to get their lies straight.

It was pretty clear to me that he had been murdered. And my chief suspect is Murdo. He got his retaliation in first because he knew that Auld Rab was trying to murder him because he was blackmailing him over his various nasty little activities. I didn't bother to say this to Horatio, however. He's quite irrational about anything to do with Murdo. But as far as I'm concerned, Murdo—or Craigie, as he should really be called—killed that old man. And whatever the rights or wrongs of that, the fact remains that he deserves to be punished for it.

Anyway, after a few minutes Horatio hurried off to watch the shoot. As soon as he'd gone, I found his copy of the new story-book and popped it, still inside its box, into my bag.

I was just about to switch the TV off when a caption appeared with the words "News Flash." Then an announcer came on the screen and said, *In connection with tonight's episode of* Biggert, *the police have just announced a number of important clues in the so-called Scorpion murders for which they need assistance from the public. A blood-stained rubber glove, similar to the one in this photograph, was found near the body of Professor Moncrieff. Anyone who has any information about this is asked to contact the police. Moreover, Professor Speculand's attacker last Easter handed him a plastic replica of a scorpion. This came from a packet of the breakfast cereal called BrannyBrekkers. An identical object was found at the scene of the murders of both Professor Moncrieff and Professor MacMaster. And, finally, at the scene of the murder of Professor MacMaster, in Kinnoul Lane, the killer left this message written in the victim's blood in which the word cu-riosity was misspelled: "If you want to satisfy your curiousity about this, find Clarence Lovebone." Police are anxious to trace anyone whose name is Clarence Lovebone in order to eliminate him from their enquiries.* I knew that as soon as Horatio heard about this, he would put two and two together. But I was already prepared to act. I hurried back to my place and left the box containing his book there. (I'm going to be so busy, though, that I don't know when I'll have time to read the second half.) Then I collected my equipment and hurried to the lane. I was waiting in the right place by twenty past. Since the show ends on the hour, I reckoned Craigie would be along between about twenty and ten minutes to.

So I was a bit surprised when someone came running up the lane only about five minutes later. Anyway, he looked about the right height and build—tall and thin and he was wearing one of those d--n deerstalkers—so when he got near, I made myself ready and then jumped out and was just about to grab him when I realized it was none other than Horatio! (The silly hat fell off, as it happened.)

I don't know which of us was the more surprised. Of course, I tried to pretend I'd just popped out at him to give him a surprise, but he knew straight away what was up. (Though he hadn't heard the TV broadcast about the message.) Unfortunately, for one thing, he saw I had the rubber gloves on and spotted my other item of equipment before I could put it away. And I assume he guessed it was Craigie I was waiting for.

I know now exactly what happened back in Esmeralda's flat, though of course I didn't find this out until later: Biggert was so furious when he read the script just before the shooting was due to start that he went completely berserk and tried to attack Craigie—accusing him of putting Horatio up to it. And Craigie got so frightened, he just ran out of the flat and down the road in the opposite direction while some of the crew restrained Biggert. (Unfortunately.) Then Biggert turned on Horatio. I wish I'd been there to see it. He tried to punch him while the cameramen were holding him back. He was shouting, *I'll give you "little bandy legs and great jutting a-s." You f-----g double-crossing English c--t.* Horatio fled out of the flat and ran down Ruskin Lane with Biggert behind him.

Anyway, I didn't know any of that until later. Back in the lane Horatio and I had just had time to recognize each other when Biggert came pounding around the corner. Well, I was all hyped up already, and though it hadn't been at all what I'd had in mind, one has to be prepared to improvise. And he was a pretty objectionable type of person, to be absolutely frank.

It only took a moment. I had the gloves on, of course, so I didn't get splashed. Then I saw that Horatio was looking extremely odd. I sort of grabbed him and pushed him down the lane. As we hurried away, I noticed he hadn't picked up that silly hat of his. I didn't say anything.

I pulled him along the lane and into the next street and then the next one. Then I took him for a long walk. He looked so unwell, I could see he needed some fresh air. (Even so, we had to stop once for him to throw up.) And I felt I needed to point out a few "home truths" to him. I told him about the broadcast I'd just seen. Then I pointed out that, whether he realized it or not, he must already be a prime suspect in the cases of Professor Moncrieff and Professor MacMaster—not to mention the business with Professor Speculand—because of his link with all of them. And I suspected that the police were even trying to link him to the death of Dr. Bentley. (He shuddered when I said that, and I could see he knew I was right.) I said that sooner or later—if they had not done so already—the police would spot the links with *The Right Lines*: the throat cutting, the gloves, and the scorpion. I said that, of course, anybody could have read that book and then left those clues in order to frame him. But the allusion to Clarence Lovebone left at the scene of Professor MacMaster's murder was quite different, since he was the only person who knew what was in the new storybook. Plus his agent, of course, since he had sent the manuscript to him. And now he was the obvious suspect in the case of Biggert, since he was the person the deceased was last seen chasing along the lane. Then I mentioned about him dropping his hat.

He was very upset and panicky at first, but gradually he calmed down. He insisted we stick to the main streets, even though it would have been more prudent to stay in the lanes. I reasoned with him, and eventually he saw the force of my arguments. He said that if only he hadn't sent the manuscript to his agent, he'd be in the clear since—assuming his agent had not yet read it—he and I were the only people who knew what was in it and he had the other copy. So then I mentioned that in fact

I had taken it from his flat earlier that evening and hidden it somewhere. He was awfully upset to hear that. (I didn't say I hadn't had time to read it yet.) I suggested that we should both get some rest and said I was sure we'd see things more clearly and calmly after a good night's sleep. He nodded, but without speaking. He was still completely numb with shock. So much for that famous sangfroid of his.

I said the police might well be waiting for him if he went home. Or come for him during the night. (His face!) So I suggested he should book into a hotel just for tonight. He could work things out and then go home once he'd taken a few precautions. He took my advice, and I escorted him to a hotel near Central Station, booked him in under a false name, and left him there.

I've got him exactly where I want him. He can't move one way or the other. Now it's up to me to decide whether I turn him in by sending a copy of the manuscript to the police or keep him in a state of terror indefinitely for fear that I will do that.

Sunday Night
Got home exhausted. I'll have a wash and nap. I'll take the manuscript to work tomorrow and read the last part of it during the morning. It's always quiet Mondays. And then I can have a think about what to do next.

Monday Morning
Bible John! Bible f--king John! That pathetic, derivative plagiarizing amateur! He's gone too far this time. He has *really* gone too far.

I was so upset, I left the till open while I was in the back. Jerry came in and found it like that and was hopping mad, and we had a bit of a row. There was nobody in the shop, as usual, but he's always terrified of being robbed. He's so moneygrubbing. When I left for my dinner, I put the manuscript in the private case between *St. Ronan's Well* and *The Fortunes of Nigel.* It'll be safe there while I decide what measures are necessary.

Monday Dinnertime
This changes everything. Until I knew what was in the rest of it, I was quite happy to let the storybook be published in return

for his being convicted of multiple murder and spending the rest of his life in prison. But now I'm not prepared to let him off so lightly. Or to let that foul, dishonest libel be published.

I rang him at the hotel and suggested a deal. If he tears up the storybook and promises never to publish it, we'll both be happy. There will be no evidence against either of us, since it's only each other who knows the truth, and neither of us wants any of it to be made public. He not only agreed, but said he had already rung his agent to stop him reading the manuscript. (He hadn't started, luckily, or I'd have had a trip to London to face.) He had asked him to send it back by train (Red Star), so it should arrive late this afternoon. So I said I'd destroy my copy of it in his presence.

Of course, I realize full well that there's nothing to stop the little b-----d going to the police as soon as he gets the manuscript back and has destroyed it and has made sure I've destroyed my copy. Because once it no longer exists, then the most dangerous piece of evidence against him has gone.

How stupid does he really think I am?

I need to do an awful lot of thinking.

Monday Afternoon
Eureka! Brilliant! I'm a genius!

Seriously, it's absolutely perfect! One: I know him well. (Though hardly anyone is aware of that.) So that's worth one hundred. Two: It's superbly disguised. (That note.) Another hundred. So well that I don't even need an alibi! Three: And as for communicating, there's that note again. Another hundred. Three out of three! One hundred percent overall!

So I get the last laugh!

Later in the afternoon
After a great deal of cogitation, I think I've worked out the details.

What I'll do is, I'll suggest that he goes to the Red Star office at Central Station to collect the copy sent by his agent. Then he should tie it up in a tote bag with something heavy to make it sink, and take it to the footbridge over the Clyde. I'll meet him there. I'll tell him I'll bring the copy I took from his flat inside its box and that we'll drop both of them into the river. It'll be dark by then, so nobody will see us. I'll take that big rubber torch.

Monday Night
Got back very late and very tired. At least I've dealt with the problems. Though I say it myself, it went like clockwork. Nobody saw me on the bridge. Putting the torch inside the box was a brilliant idea. His face when I opened it!

Posted the note on the way home.

Just one more thing to dispose of tomorrow at the shop and I've finished. Golly, I'm tired.

N.B. I must remember to buy a television tomorrow.

Tuesday Morning
Got to G and P to find the shop shut up with two policemen outside. Jerry was in the van. He was in handcuffs and sitting between two burly policemen. He was smiling as if he was having the time of his life! He waved at me with his hands manacled together, but I pretended I was just walking past. Saw the policeman in charge and recognized him as that man with the short hair I've seen a few times recently. I just managed to dodge out of his view before he turned around. The van drove off, and I went into the little grocer's along the road, and Muhammad knew all about it. Seems the police forced their way in early this morning and then waited for Jerry to turn up. Apparently he was distributing imported magazines all over Scotland. Danish. I suppose he wasn't paying import tax. He'd do anything to save a few quid. I went back and just walked past the shop. When I looked in, I could see the place has been ransacked. I'll go back later.

Tuesday Afternoon

Gone! Everything! My West End observation notes! His b----y manuscript!

What happened was, I went back and found the place shut up and deserted. I let myself in. It was a terrible mess. Books and papers strewn everywhere. Then to my horror I found the private case was empty!

Blooming Jerry! His miserliness has ruined everything. D--n him! D--n him!

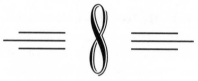

A Nice Touch

5th August

Dear Drummond,

      Congratulations on the publication of the new book. I hope you get wonderful reviews this time. Sadly, they really do affect how well a book sells these days. Thanks for sending me a copy. I'll read it as soon as I can find time. It looks absolutely wonderful. The jacket design in particular. People like tanks and guns on bookcovers, I believe. At least, at that end of the market.

Thanks, too, for letting me be one of the people "beta-testing" your new novel, as you put it. I'm intrigued that you've embarked on a new genre. I hope you have better luck with this fresh direction to your career. I can see why you might feel you'd got a bit stuck in a rut after six in the same genre. I must say, though, that you've entered what is probably an even more competitive field. As I know myself, the standard is high and it's difficult to think up ingenious new twists. May I say, without undue immodesty, that it's not as easy as it might look?

As I told you when you first mentioned sending me your current project, I don't beat around the bush when I'm asked for my opinion. Since you've warned me about your built-in bullshit detector, I can promise I won't mince my words. As you say, writing is too important for that. We're both professionals and we can be professional about it.

What follows here are just some hasty thoughts thrown onto the computer while reading your manuscript. (I'm just off to Paris for a few days for the French publication of *The Quintessence*, so I'm writing in great haste.)

I tend to feel that a whodunnit needs to pretty quickly bait the hook that catches the reader. You need the reader to suspect that there's a "corpse in the closet," as Hitchcock once put it. So I'm a bit concerned that by the end of the chapter we haven't had either a murder or an enigma. I know it can be part of the game to keep the reader guessing and then have a corpse suddenly fall out of the cupboard, but I think there's a danger of overplaying that hand. The reader wants you to try to outwit him all the time. He wants you to keep turning the tables on him.

Your hero, Farquhar, is potentially an interesting figure. With his gangling and skinny figure and his long, drooping mustache he's something of a modern Quixote. But while his reflections on literature and philosophy and on the way artists are exploited and abused in our philistine society are very thoughtful and profound, I have to say that they don't move the story forward much. (I seem to remember this was something the reviewers carped about in your war novels. Didn't one of them call the hero "Plato in combat fatigues"?) It's fair enough when he is in a bookshop, I suppose, but I found the discussion of Wittgenstein with the Chinese waitress frankly implausible. And, to be blunt, I'm not sure about your narrator's footnotes referring the reader to philosophical texts and earlier books of your own. Fiction is fiction and philosophy is philosophy. They don't mix. If it shows nothing else, the recent ludicrous example of Quaife demonstrates that, I think. If the man had stuck to Heidegger, he'd be alive now.

I notice the chapter is called a "Prologue," which implies that the main story is going to be something else. I think you need to get to it sooner.

Let me see more of it, please.

17th August

Dear Drummond,

No, in fact, I hadn't seen the piece by Tabby Squeill. Many thanks for sending it. I don't often buy *The Daily Scot*. And I certainly don't read that column in which—if you'll forgive me—she energetically massages the Scottish ego into a state of overexcitement every week.

You might have seen some earlier articles by Tabby about me which resurrect the ancient story (which I think I told you) about how I signed up with Tarquin Bone. I've no idea why the paper should take such a keen interest in me. I suppose I should be flattered.

I can't tell you why Tabby says, "The smooth-talking Oxonian is notorious for dropping people who have helped his career, and even going on to humiliate and ridicule them." Nor have I any idea who she means by "the most abused victim who in his innocence has failed to this day to recognize himself in the London-born novelist's grotesque caricature." Can you think?

As for calling my books "flashy, clever-clever, and meretricious in the most literal sense of the word," I can only say that I'll ask my publisher to quote her on the cover of the next one! I've looked up *meretricious*. It means "having to do with the sale of sex." So what's wrong with selling sex in my books? Selling sex is more than that skinny shrew could ever do!

Bad luck about the notices! I seem to be as unlucky with gossip columnists as you are with reviewers. Don't be discouraged. Reviewers are idiots, of course. Though I suppose I shouldn't really say that, since they've been so generous to me, on the whole. But they really don't matter. If a book is any good, it'll sell on its word-of-mouth reputation.

I'm sure every novelist has his ups and downs. You must know that better than me after seven novels. (Sorry about that! I forgot about the latest one! When is Gollancz bringing it out?)

The important thing is that your agent and your publisher have faith in your work in the long term. Frankly, the reviewers are neither here nor there.

As far as I know, in answer to your last question, it's about 1,800,000 by now. (That's all of them and foreign as well as English-language sales, of course.) Who would have expected it?

Best wishes,

P.S. You're quite right. You don't use the word *gangling* or *drooping.* Sorry.

28th August

Dear Drummond,
Thanks for the second chapter.

Well, well. What a steamy chapter this is!

First of all, I'm relieved that the story itself has started. Potentially, you have a lot of interesting material here with your hero, Jones, dreaming that he is going to enter the glamorous world of Hollywood stars by means of his screenplays now that the talkies have arrived and the cinema needs "real writers," and meanwhile haunting the bathhouses of Chinatown and being massaged by sexy young Chinese masseuses and getting stoked up into paroxysms of lust because he doesn't have any money to pay for sex when they offer it. So the image of his quivering organ slowly detumescing is quite poignant and also funny. But you still need something to happen!

I take it, by the way, that you've been doing some research on the saunas of Glasgow. It all reads very convincingly. I can't help wondering if Janet has read this yet and what she makes of it?

Moreover, I'm not sure that Athanasius Jones is quite the right character to bring out the potential in this material. It's hard for the reader to care about a round little voyeuristic figure living in a fantasy world of Chinese masseuses and Hollywood stars. And he doesn't display much inner mental life so far—apart from his sexual fantasizing. And on that topic, I'm not sure that you can use sex in this rather oblique and voyeuristic way in the genre you're trying to write now.

On a fairly banal but perhaps crucial point, I felt your portrayal of Los Angeles didn't quite ring true. I think it's San Francisco that has the big Chinatown, isn't it? And I believe Los Angeles doesn't have those steep hills with old-fashioned streetcars on rails. I'm pretty sure you only get those in San Francisco. When I was last in L.A. to talk to one of the studios about the rights to *The Quintessence,* I don't remember seeing them. But maybe you know L.A. better than I do.

My main point, though, is that the narrative still doesn't get under way fast enough. When does the action start? When does a body fall out of the closet?

What you say about Tabby is very interesting indeed. (I'll bet Ramsay McCoo wasn't supposed to tell you who writes the column! He must have been very pissed. Or should I say, more pissed than usual?) He used to write it himself, but since he's become literary editor, I suppose he's too busy. But now that I know it's Morag, I understand why the column has it in for me.

As a matter of fact, yes, I can tell you who Morag Frobister is. I'm surprised you haven't heard of her. She's nothing less than Scotland's only full-time literary agent. Or, rather, she was. She and I have had dealings in the past. There's a story there that I might tell you one day. So no wonder she's obsessed by my signing up with Tarquin.

On the domestic front, I've at last moved to Westbourne Gardens (to which letters should be addressed in future) and have been getting the house comfortable. It's far too large, I suppose, for just one person, but it's wonderful to have so much room. I love those big old places and I've always wanted to live in this part of town. The West End of Glasgow is as pleasant a place as anywhere in Britain, I reckon. I have a vast attic as well as an enormous basement. Speaking of which, I think you'll be impressed by the "torture chamber" I've installed down there. Next time you come to stay, we must have a go on the new exercise bike. I'm trying to get the paunch down after all those lunches and literary dinners in London!

Yes, thanks, it is going well and I hope to finish it within three months. Tarquin seems to be very excited about it and to think it will be much more successful than the first three *Smetterburns*. He's planning a rights auction as soon as I've got the final draft finished.

15th September

Dear Drummond,

Many thanks for sending me the next chapter. It arrived a bit late because you got the address slightly wrong. You probably wrote it at the end of a long day.

First, I must insist that I didn't mean to cause offense, and it's entirely my fault because I'm afraid I didn't make myself clear. I certainly think it's an interesting idea to inject some sex into a whodunnit. I've been doing something similar in my *Smetterburns*, as you know. But I think readers of whodunnits want action rather than fantasizing. At least, though, you're building up the sexual tension nicely. (I must admit I always felt the brothel scenes in the war books were inserted rather perfunctorily.)

Yes, something certainly starts to happen here when Jones gets rung up out of the blue by Zadonsky and summoned to his palatial mansion in Beverly—I think you'll find that's how it's spelled—Hills. Zadonsky is potentially quite an interesting character.

I quite like the scene where he insults his screenplay and literally rips it to pieces in front of a troupe of scantily clad starlets sprinkled around the pool. And I like the character of Blacker: a drunken, cynical screenwriter who despises the movie industry and yet needs to work for it to support his drinking and so is terrified of his producer's interest in a new writer. And his spite toward Jones comes out well. I like the depiction of Zadonsky exploiting Blacker's fears in order to show his power over him.

And Stetson is fairly interesting, too. You've brought out quite well the disparity between the self-assurance of this urbane, sophisticated actor and his underlying insecurity because his career is in difficulties because of the arrival of sound. This business about artists who have been wrong-footed by historical changes that are unforeseen and beyond their control is something that could really be quite interesting. And, again, Zadonsky's bullying, threatening, patronizing manner toward his biggest box-office star is intriguing.

But I think it's a little far-fetched to suggest that Stetson has been successful even though he can't act simply because he went to Yale and comes from an upper-class Boston background. And now he's been caught out by the arrival of the talkies, which have exposed his squeaky, posh voice. Frankly, I rather doubt if an Ivy League background was a very useful entrée to Hollywood, even in the amateurish twenties!

But when Zadonsky decides that what Jones needs to improve his writing is to get laid and then sends him off with ten dollars to his favorite bathhouse, the Blue Orchid, I found myself wondering if anything was going to follow from that? I think it needs to in order to strengthen the narrative thrust.

Of course you're right that Los Angeles has a Chinatown. I didn't really mean to say that it doesn't. But one certainly doesn't think of it as being as big and exotic as the one in San Francisco—full of Chinese bathhouses and restaurants and brothels and heroin networks run by the Triads. On that point, I must say I still have grave doubts about a historical setting. It's safe enough to set a novel in ancient Greece or medieval Italy because you can easily find out more than the average reader knows. But Hollywood—even in 1927—is the sort of thing lots of people know enough about to spot blunders.

I have a suggestion to make. As you know, I liked some of the Prologue quite a bit. The character of Farquhar is potentially intriguing, but I think you need to let him off the rein. Let him blossom. Have you thought of having him pop up at intervals throughout the novel commenting on the inner story? This would create an interesting contrast between the two worlds and the two characters. And that might be the place for his philosophical ruminations? Just an idea.

All the best,

18th September

Dear Drummond,

I called last night to explain, but you might not remember, so I'm writing. I'm sorry that when I said I always felt the brothel scenes in the war books were inserted somewhat perfunctorily, I used a rather clumsy word. In a sense, as you say, the perfunctoriness—or, as you say, "laconicism"—was part of the point: These are men at war who don't have time for the niceties, men facing death for whom a last fuck is important for its symbolic value more than its physical gratification. I agree with all of that.

Let me be quite clear, too, about your other point. When I used the word *pornography*, I didn't mean to imply anything more than, as you say, "healthy and thoroughly enjoyable interest in good, honest, straightforward sex." Farquhar visiting saunas and getting hand jobs and the odd fuck if he can afford it is all perfectly reasonable. And I'm sure it will help to sell the book. I'm afraid I haven't read either of the works you mention on the definition of pornography. Thanks for the article from *The Philosophical Review*. It looks interesting but rather heavy-going. I'll save it for now and tackle it when I've broken the back of the current novel.

And I'm sorry I failed to understand your perspective on Stetson and Blacker. Stetson's charm didn't strike me as at all sinister. And I can't say I saw the pride and hurt in Blacker. Just the booze and the self-pity. Will you have another look at that scene and see if you can bring these qualities out more clearly?

By all means send me the new chapter when you finish it. I should be back from Frankfurt by the 9th. (I'm taking a side trip to Munich to visit my German publisher and meet my translator.)

I look forward to seeing it.

10th October

Dear Drummond,

I've just got back from Munich. What a trip! The Oktoberfest! Don't miss it if you ever get the chance to go! (I had a most enjoyable time with my German translator, Heinrich. I was delighted to find that he speaks excellent German—though his English is dreadful.) Anyway, I returned to find your manuscript.

I'm intrigued that you'd already decided to introduce yourself (that is, Farquhar) as narrator throughout the novel popping in and out of the inner narrative. Great minds ... etc., etc. But maybe it's useful to know that a fellow professional thinks you're on the right track.

Let me see more, please.

1st November

Dear Drummond,

Thanks—if that's the right word!—for the clipping.

That woman has really gone too far!

She's absolutely wrong. My publishers are very happy with the way the *Smetterburns* are selling. And they're keen to publish the next one—so keen that Tarquin is getting them to bid against other publishers. (I must say, I've been very satisfied by the way Tarquin handles me.)

I'm amused by her saying, "Cyril Pattison's *Smetterburns* fail because they have none of the bravura that made his first three books so successful." I'm afraid it's just spite. Pure spite. The reason why Morag Frobister has it in for me is this:

When I was trying to get my first novel, *The Quintessence*, published, I got in touch with Morag. She was the only full-time literary agent in Scotland at that time. I was still teaching full-time then, but she got me one of those grants from the Glasgow Council for the Arts because she's a great friend of Arnold's. That let me take time off to finish it. Then she negotiated a deal with Cowgate. As you know, it became a best-seller and I made quite a lot of money. (And so did she!)

The Quintessence was a spy thriller of course, and I then published two more with Cowgate. Morag negotiated the contracts, and they both sold quite well. (They were *The Sensation Seeker* and *The Finger Man.*) But the ending of the Cold War two or three years ago made that genre obsolete very suddenly and they stopped selling. A lot of very competent writers who couldn't adapt fast enough found themselves without a market. It was a really Darwinian situation! I tried to mutate with my next book, which was a historical novel. Morag didn't like it and made very little effort to get Cowgate excited about it or to do any promotional work for it and she let Cowgate publish it very badly. So it flopped. As a result, I was pretty unhappy with the way Morag was handling me.

It was a pretty bad time for me. But it was then that I got my big idea: to take up crime by writing a series of whodunnits with a new twist. These, as you know, became the *Smetterburn* series. Morag told me she thought I should stick to Cold War fiction. She wasn't convinced when I tried to persuade her that I had a rather clever new formula for the series—a mixture of terror and eroticism—that I hoped would become addictive. She accused me at one point of trying to peddle "junk." Just then a big Dutch publisher contacted me about the first three novels. I asked Morag if she would agree to negotiate with them and split the commission fifty-fifty with me, but she became very indignant and said my suggestion was "disgusting" and "not her practice."

At that juncture Tarquin rang me. He said he had fallen in love with my work and wanted to know if I was looking for an agent. I sent him the new book, and he was very excited by it. So naturally I jumped at the offer to be handled by such a well-known agent. I know he's pretty young for a leading "player," but that just shows how bright he is. Moreover, he could supply lots of other services—foreign rights, movie rights, and so on. When I explained that I already had a relationship with Morag, Tarquin said he was prepared to share me with her. But when I put that to her, she was furious. She said I had to choose between him and her. Between a solid Scottish person and a flashy London wheeler-dealer. Well, of course I went with Tarquin, because he is brilliant at "distribution" and public-relations hype. Tarquin impressed me by stressing how much he believed that distribution was the crucial factor, and he had some interesting ideas about how to improve it.

I'd heard about him because of the superb way he handled the hype in the Prentice/Ireland case. At first he approached Prentice—or, rather, his lawyers—and they were ready to do a deal. Apparently Tarquin was talking about pretty large sums of money. But then he suddenly changed his mind. He had the vision to see that the other book was likely to be much more valuable, so he dropped Prentice and approached the other side. As they say, the rest is history. *Enough Rope* made a fortune.

When I told Morag I had decided to go with Tarquin, she was furious and started to put it about that *she* had dropped *me* because she disapproved of my cynicism in starting to write blatantly commercial and sexy whodunnits. No chance of a handout from the Glasgow Council for the Arts, I'm afraid. But then, quite honestly, I haven't needed one.

After losing me to Tarquin, Morag lost virtually all her other authors because, to be frank, I was her most prestigious client. Some of them also went to Tarquin. So you can imagine how she feels about him! She has an obsession about all the judgments about what's important in Scotland or what gets published here being made—she believes—in London. She's all the more bitter because she failed to make it there herself. Shortly after she and

McCoo got married, they went to London to make their fortune. She tried to get into publishing, but she only got as far as reading for a publisher. It didn't work out for him, either. (I believe the drinking had already started.) And so they came home with their tails between their legs. He got a job on *The Scot* and she took up agenting. When she lost me, she had to give that up, too. And that's when Ramsay found her something on the paper. You can get away with that sort of nepotism in Scotland in a way that you couldn't in London. And now he's wangled her the column! (Though I'd heard their marriage was pretty rocky.)

I don't at all care for these spiteful little stories and I wish there was some way of stopping the woman. I'd love to draw her claws. But she's careful never to say anything actually libelous about me, so I can't take legal action against her.

I'm sorry to hear about your own troubles with *The Armageddon Ultimatum*. I think Gollancz are crazy. As you say, they've made the investment in you in the last four books, so why should they throw away the profit now that it's about to be reaped? And, indeed, one wonders what your agent is getting her commission for if she can't keep your publisher enthusiastic about your work. If you're not happy with the way she's handling you, you might think about finding someone who can.

Best of luck. Write soon.

18th November

Dear Drummond,

Many thanks for sending me the revised version of the opening Los Angeles chapters and a couple of new chapters.

I really quite enjoyed the scene at the Blue Orchid with the young Chinese masseuse, Mo-Lak. I hope she will become an important character. It's interesting—and rather titillating—that she refuses to have "even the tiniest bit of sex" with Jones and, instead, tells him stories based on traditional Chinese folktales while she chastely but firmly kneads his ample flesh.

I'm glad that she at least finds him a little friend to provide other services for him. But Lam-Sae is a bit of a cipher and seems not to be quite "all there." Is she on something? Is that effect intended? Unless you build her up a bit, the reader will realize that she exists merely in order to tell Jones that Mo-Lak is working at the bathhouse because she is hiding from the mysterious "Mr. Big," who used to be her lover. But at least this means that at last the reader is hooked by the enigma: Who is this man and why is Mo-Lak frightened of him?

As far as the business of Morag is concerned, it would indeed be nice to see her get egg all over her stupid face in public. It would be hilarious if Ramsay had to sack his own wife! But I don't understand how your idea would work. She's certainly not going to publish anything just because *I* want her to. As I said, she's careful never to be actually libelous. And even if she wanted to be, the paper presumably employs a lawyer to check for libel. I'm afraid that one's a nonstarter.

How is the argument going with Gollancz? I think it's shameful that Sally refused to get involved. What does she get her ten percent for? And why hasn't she found you another publisher? I'm sure you're right that an agent is crucial to the success of a novelist these days. So I agree absolutely that if you don't think Sally is pulling her weight, you should certainly say so. Let me know how your meeting with her goes. And remember that she needs you more than you need her.

The answer to your question is that it's nineteen so far! But with Hebrew and Catalan on the horizon, too!

Anxiously awaiting more of the manuscript.

P.S. I'm sorry for getting the title of *The Armageddon Protocol* wrong. I was confusing it with *The Atlantis Ultimatum.*

26th November

Dear Drummond,

Just a note in response to yours.

I'm a little surprised she took it like that. Most unprofessional. It's surely the agent's job to help an author through a bad patch in his career. Frankly, you're better off without her.

I don't think I can help with finding another. Tarquin, as I think I told you, contacted me unprompted. He has mentioned that he's pretty busy and is taking on virtually no new clients at the moment, but by all means write to him and say you're a friend of mine. It can't do any harm. In the meantime I'll mention you to him myself.

How clever of you to get the rights to all your earlier books back! I'm sure my publisher wouldn't let me have mine. How did you manage it? As you say, that's quite a mouthwatering package to be able to offer a new agent: six novels and a seventh that's still virginal!

Good luck and send more of the manuscript when you can.

11th December

Dear Drummond,

I'm just about to dash to the airport. I'm going to Acapulco for Christmas again.

I'm sorry Tarquin was too tied up even to read your work. But it's certainly true that he is pretty busy, because, oddly enough, he has been asked to contribute a column to *The Daily Scot*. (The editor is an old friend of his.) Morag is so paranoid and hates him so much that she'll probably think he's doing this just to frighten her, though she has no reason to suppose that he even knows she writes the Tabby Squeill column. (As it happens, however, I told him.)

It's possible, I suppose, that Tarquin turned you down because he didn't fancy you. (I know people say that about him.) But I don't believe it. I can't say why he took me on, though I'm flattered—I think—by your suggestion. I continue, though, to believe it was my work that attracted him.

I suggest you just work your way through the *Writers' and Artists' Yearbook*. Frankly, I suspect one agent is as good as another. And who needs them anyway? After all, did Shakespeare have one? I'm sure you're right that the new book is going to mark the turning point in your career. Though I still think you need to do quite a lot of work on it.

On a lighter note, I liked the new chapter. It's a lovely idea that Jones works up Mo-Lak's stories into screenplays and that because her input has stiffened his narrative structure and characterization, Zadonsky gets very excited and buys them for lots of money. Don't worry. I don't think the reader will think Jones is stealing her work. That's how things are: One person has the talent to think of ideas but she doesn't know what to do with them, while another has the initiative to make something of them, and that makes him as least as creative.

I like the way Jones arouses the envy and hatred of Blacker now that Zadonsky is buying *his* scripts instead of Blacker's, and I particularly like the moment where Blacker drunkenly rounds on him and accuses him of ass-licking Zadonsky and trying to take away the living of real writers like himself with his slick commercial trash. We might disagree about this, because my view is that the cinema needs skilled craftsmen rather than brilliant but unreliable geniuses—who often turn out to be geniuses only in their own estimation.

Was I right to detect a hint that Zadonsky recognizes Mo-Lak's contribution to the screenplays? But that's ridiculous. How could he recognize her work? A Chinese masseuse who's probably illiterate!

It's a little confusing. And this brings me to my main criticism of the manuscript so far. It needs a firmer hand on the narrative structure to mold it into shape. Basically, you need to spend more time on plotting.

Also, I've now begun to feel that it's a weakness that Farquhar, who is potentially quite interesting when he pops up occasionally to comment on the Jones narrative, doesn't really connect with the story he tells. And since I'm still worried about the historical setting, I have a suggestion to make that would solve both problems. You might think about introducing Farquhar into the world of Jones and move it entirely into the modern period. Just a thought.

Many thanks for the good wishes. Don't worry. There's no chance of the nomination going to my head. I'm pretty cynical about the whole business of prizes, I think. Don't forget that I've been through quite a blitz of publicity and promotion already with the first book becoming an international best-seller. Keep your fingers crossed for me. The rest of the short list's pretty formidable, and a pal of mine who's one of the judges has warned me not to build up my hopes.

Indeed, I would love to see Morag sacked. I take your point about the need for someone else to plant the story on her, but I don't know who could do this. And the problem is that it would have to be to my discredit in order to make her want to publish it. And in fact to make her believe it, since it's a human characteristic to believe what we want to believe.

In haste,

15th January

Dear Drummond,

That's the final straw! After that the woman deserves everything she gets. (Thanks for showing it to me. I must start buying the damn thing on Saturdays.) To suggest that it's only because I went to Oxford and know all the right people in the "literary Mafia" that I've been short-listed! It's Scottish paranoia. All this stuff about the way that English mediocrities run the country because the Scots are "deserting their own bonny land for the bright lights and easy pickings of the decadent metropolis." The pickings were too hard for her!

And her accusation that "a fancy London agent" "stole" her Scottish clients is grotesque. And so is her allegation that I've stolen business from other Scottish novelists by "a series of cold-blooded hits masterminded by his debonair Svengali."

She has a fertile imagination. In fact, part of her problem is that she is a frustrated writer. She made a couple of suggestions to me about the first three books and became quite proprietorial when I adopted them. She even said something about going on the title page. When we had our bust-up, it emerged that she had grossly overestimated her input, and that was one of the things that made her so bitter.

Your idea about how to bait the hook to catch her is a good one. And I agree that the story you've devised is so preposterous that nobody but Morag will believe it. And in fact I can't quite imagine that even she would be stupid enough to fall for it. After all, the way we write is very different. I defy anybody to detect the hand of Gilchrist in *The Quintessence*.

When we pull the rug from under her feet and expose her, there'll be an awful stink. If there's any justice, she'll be snuffed out as a presence on the literary scene in Scotland. I hope you'll gain from the publicity. Frankly, I don't really need any more. I've almost had more than I can take. It's a two-edged sword, as you might find out one day.

Yes, Acapulco *was* wonderful—as always. I'm sorry it rained here most of the holiday.

Write soon.

3rd February

Dear Drummond,

I'm very sorry to hear about you and Janet. I'd always thought you were a well-matched couple. But, as you say, a creative artist is not the easiest person to live with, since he feels more pain than other people. Though I'm not quite sure I agree when you say the artist has to take the pain out on the person nearest to him.

It's a nuisance Morag wasn't at the Burns Society cocktail party. But you go to so many of these things, you're bound to run into her. You can't miss her: she's tall and thin and looks like Jeffrey Archer—only Archer doesn't have a mustache. The best thing would be to find yourself talking to her and only then—you pretend—find out who she was. She'd never suspect a trap if you can do it like that.

You mention that you met Arnold there and had a long chat with him. He's a man with a lot of power in the Scottish liter- ary scene, so I'm glad you're on good terms with him. If you get on the wrong side of him, you need never expect a grant from the Glasgow Council for the Arts. (Though I hope you'll never need one, of course.) I don't think he likes me much. He's always affable enough, in that vaguely menacing way he has, but I suppose he's a bit wary of a writer who doesn't need his handouts. Frankly, I think he finds successful writers rather threatening and prefers to have a circle of toadying me- diocrities around him who depend on his largesse. Of course, he sees himself as encouraging what he calls "real literature" by dispensing his grants to favored sycophants. I expect you heard him denouncing what he calls "commercial trash." But some people might argue that if a novel is any good, people will buy it, so public money just goes to subsidize the "uncom- mercial trash."

But the important thing is that the writing is going well. I like Jones's second visit to the bathhouse. And I hope we see more of the creepy bathhouse attendant Taw-Kwee, who has just started working there. But why is Mo-Lak so horrified when she sees him? And why does she accuse Jones of betraying her? Does this mean that Taw-Kwee is spying for Mr. Big? Has he followed Jones to the bathhouse? I'm getting a bit confused.

I'm amazed by the fact that Jones even thinks of Stetson as a possible suspect. The idea that he might have taken to crime after his career went into decline because of the rise of the talkies seems preposterous to me. It just makes no sense psychologically. Admittedly, you have a man who has become used to success, to money, to easy sexual conquests—by the way, why haven't you shown us Stetson's women friends when Blacker seems to be besieged by beautiful starlets?—and then suddenly it begins to slip away from him for reasons he has no control over: a new technology or a change in public taste. Under such circumstances an ordinary man might be driven to extreme courses of action in order to preserve what he has achieved. But a man like Stetson has too much pride, too much self-respect.

On another point, I take it from Taw-Kwee's high-pitched, lisping voice and effeminate features that he's a eunuch? (Is that plausible? Did they exist then? On that topic, once again, I think the historical setting is a problem, and I really do advise you to think seriously about switching it to the modern period.)

It's a nice surprise when Taw-Kwee suddenly offers Jones a "show" for a couple of dollars and it turns out to be an exotic exhibition that he watches through a two-way mirror. But at the risk of being taken for a fuddy-duddy, I have to say I think there might be some problems with taste here. I think a young girl massaging her naked father and finding he has a "stupendous erection" that she has to deal with without using her hands just might cause offense in these prurient and paranoid times when child molesting is getting such a bad press. Perhaps you should just omit mentioning her age so the reader can assume she's about fifteen?

I don't think I'm being a prude. My objection here is that it should be more erotic, since otherwise its tastelessness stands out somewhat nakedly. Make the reader too excited to remember to feel disgusted. And don't forget that the reader needs to identify and to some extent sympathize with the central character, even if he is presented as absurd and lecherous, and so on. So don't go too far and make Jones too contemptible.

Right at the end of the chapter, when Taw-Kwee asks him if he'd be interested in seeing a snuff movie, I thought you'd made a mistake. I had never thought of them as existing then— but on reflection I'm afraid they did.

Another point is that the villainous Taw-Kwee—though good fun—is perhaps just a bit too much of a stereotype—the corrupt Oriental—of the kind that people find offensive now. In fact, there's potentially a charge of xenophobia to be brought against your whole treatment of the Chinese element. That's another reason for thinking of switching the setting. What's wrong with Glasgow?

Send more as soon as you can!

Best wishes,

6th February

Dear Drummond,

Just a quick note to say I'm absolutely sure that you're not inserting what you rightly call "healthily erotic" passages just in order to make the book more commercial. I'm sorry you thought that was what I was implying when I said it would help to sell the novel. *I* don't think, either, that a writer should compromise his integrity. (I don't think anyone could accuse me of that. In fact, my refusal to compromise has got me into deep water more than once.) So if you feel the book needs those scenes, you must certainly go ahead and write them.

Write soon.

11th February

Dear Drummond,

Am writing in haste to say, Well done! I loved your description of her little piglet eyes rounding with amazement. I'd love to have seen you telling her not to breathe a word to anyone or it would ruin my reputation. I'm so glad Arnold called you out of the blue to invite you to that Glasgow Council for the Arts reception. (Did you talk to the Czech poet, by the way?)

I wonder if she has really taken the bait? And will she go too far if she does write the story up?

Incidentally, I mentioned to Tarquin our attempt to entrap Morag. I hope that wasn't indiscreet of me.

More of the manuscript, please.

15th March

Dear Drummond,

Thanks for the new chapters. The novel is certainly getting quite interesting with Mo-Lak's mysterious disappearance. I assume the sinister Taw-Kwee has something to do with that. Has she just fled, or has she been kidnapped or even murdered?

I have a theory about this. I suspect that, as I suggested before, Zadonsky, in some way that I don't understand, recognized from Jones's screenplays that he was getting his stories from Mo-Lak and got Taw-Kwee to follow him to the Blue Orchid. So that makes Zadonsky Mr. Big.

It's becoming quite intriguing.

I liked poor old Jones racking his brains to come up with a decent plot. And then the scene when he comes to Zadonsky to see what he thinks of it and the producer tells him it's junk, rips it up in his face, tells him he's sending for Blacker again, and then throws him out is really quite funny. And with a real sense of pain, too. (Though it is a repetition of the earlier scene. What is this obsession with people ripping his work to pieces in front of him?)

So now Jones has to find Mo-Lak! At last you've got a couple of quite engaging "hooks"—what has happened to Mo-Lak, and who is Mr. Big? And I'm sure you're bearing in mind the need to surprise the reader at the end. So I hope you've already decided who he is so that you can set up a nice surprise for the reader. Don't introduce some new character quite arbitrarily who turns out to be Mr. Big. You need to have something pretty good hidden in the closet in this kind of novel, I think.

Thanks for the enquiry about my own work. I'm so pleased with the way the new book is coming on that I'm urging Tarquin to start the auction even higher than he has suggested.

Looking forward to reading more.

25th March

Dear Drummond,

Well, well. So we both made it into the Tabby column. Though not the way we expected.

It seems to have backfired on both of us—perhaps you more than me. Sorry, old man. But you can see what a spiteful bitch she is. She's pretending to sympathize with you while actually milking the story for all the venom she can.

I really don't mind her crowing over the fact that I didn't win, but I don't much care for being called a "privileged and much-hyped English novelist whose most useful connection didn't quite manage to deliver the goods." I don't know who she means, though the implication is that she has Tarquin in mind, since immediately after that she mentions your being turned down by "a top London wheeler-dealer who claimed he already had too many clients."

I can't, I'm afraid, throw any light on who she is referring to when she says, "He's not too busy to spend time promoting a meretricious writer of slick whodunnits. No names, no pack drill. But it gets worse. For that same novelist advised him not to take on the hard working Scots scribe, Drummond Gilchrist."

On the competition again, thanks for the commiserations. It was a bit disappointing. My friend on the jury said one of the other judges had it in for me because I once reviewed him unfavorably. What a narrow, bitchy little world it is. I almost despair at times. Thank God for one's work!

Keep writing. Getting new batches of your manuscript is one of the things I most look forward to.

3rd April

Dear Drummond,

I'm intrigued that Morag rang you. As you say, that might mean she's suspicious or, on the contrary, that she has swallowed the hook. In which case maybe she *is* planning to run a story about me along those lines.

Thanks for the new chapter. I must say, I'm really intrigued by Taw-Kwee's remark that if Jones wants to find Mo-Lak, he should look for a forthcoming movie called *Minnie's Sticky End.* That sounds rather lubricious! Has she become an actress?

By the way, shouldn't Farquhar pop up again in the framing narrative about now?

Eagerly awaiting more.

Hello, it's me. Are you there? . . . Drummond? . . . Well, I just want to say thank you for setting Morag up so well. It was a good thing you warned me she might call. As you said, if I simply denied it, she wouldn't have printed it. I had plenty of time to find a form of words that would be appropriately ambiguous.

So when she rang, I professed to be astonished to hear from her and horrified that she's thinking of printing a story along those lines. I said plagiarism was the worst thing a writer could be accused of. I had my statement written out in front of me and I pretended to ad-lib it and to be really nervous and guilty. She seemed to fall for it. But we'll see, I suppose. I'd better not talk long, because I know this thing cuts out after about a minute. A package has just arrived from you, and it looks most seductive. I'll open it and start reading it this very . . .

23rd April

Dear Drummond,

I can't say I'm awfully amused by the new element in the novel. It doesn't seem very grateful on your part—or indeed very gracious.

I don't think you have a gift for caricature, frankly.

I enclose the manuscript—with no comments this time—and I wish you luck with the rest of it. Clearly you'll want to write it without any further help from me since you obviously find my advice so risible.

Yours,

30th April

Dear Drummond,

You sounded a little odd on the phone the other night. Had you been dulling the pain? Anyway, thanks for your long letter. I would be delighted to think that I've misunderstood your intentions.

I'm sure you can see it from my point of view. What most annoyed me about the scene in which Farquhar gets a long lecture from "Chartres Pettifer"—which is, in effect, taken from my letters to you—was the fact that Pettifer inflicts it, unasked, on Farquhar, who is portrayed as politely putting up with it. Not only that, but he describes it as Pettifer "ripping his work up and throwing it back at him"!

It seemed to me that instead of acting on my advice by improving the story, you'd simply incorporated it wholesale into the book with a few changes to make it look rather stupid. And I didn't much care for the portrait of Chartres Pettifer as worldly, oily, charming, well connected, pompous, two-faced, manipulative, and so on. Or the stuff about his cold and soulless emphasis on craftsmanship. Or the reference to his squeaky, posh voice. And if it comes to that, I am not below average height. Nor am I in the least plump! Though I admit that I'm far from being skeletal.

I think I understand the idea: That you dramatize my reactions and advice inside the framing narrative. But I don't care for it. See if you can use this letter!

At the same time, I'm pleased and flattered that you've found my advice so helpful so far. If I may say so, I think your novel has been improving as a consequence of our correspondence. But frankly, I don't see why I should do all the work. Giving you advice is one thing, but actually having my letters plagiarized and myself ridiculed is quite another.

Good luck with it, and I hope to see it in print one day.

Best wishes,

12th May

Dear Drummond,

You've really been very sly, haven't you? There was I thinking—I might as well admit it—that you were something of a literary naif, and all the time you've been laughing at me behind your hand. You've been playing games with me, you sly devil. Letting me offer my two cents worth of advice when you knew exactly what you were doing! What an idiot I feel!

But I've rumbled you. Suddenly I understood that I'd been

completely misreading your manuscript. And I grasped in a flash what you were doing.

Now I can admit that I thought you didn't know how to write a novel. Frankly, I thought most of what you were sending me was crap. I thought you hadn't managed to make the reader care about the characters. And that you weren't in control of the various enigmas in the plot. And that there were too many meandering, long-winded conversations full of self-indulgent pseudophilosophical drivel.

Then in a flash I saw the truth. Obviously I can't offer you any advice about how to write a novel, and it was arrogant of me to think I could. You know exactly what you're doing, and what looked to me at first like clumsy, pompous overwriting is deliberate. What you're out to do is to deconstruct the fictionality of the realist illusion. (Personally I rather like the realist illusion, but I know it's very unfashionable these days.)

There was I trying to "improve" precisely the things you're doing deliberately. Thinking that the narrator in the framing narrative, Farquhar, was much too pompous and pedantic for the reader to like or identify with, and I was even half afraid that it was based on you, Drummond. After all, there is a certain physical resemblance. On your more thoughtful, philosophical side. Now I see that the reader is *intended* to despise him. He's precisely *meant* to be a fictional portrait of a monster of vanity and egotism. And he's meant to be grotesquely over the top with his love of his own voice and his cracker-barrel philosophizing.

And I've been misreading the inner story, too. I can now confess that I actually thought that the pathetic, voyeuristic, fantasizing hero Jones, with his unhealthy interest in little girls, was another aspect of yourself.

Suddenly I grasped the fact that the real hero of the inner story is not Jones but Blacker. And he's a wonderfully moving portrait of a tormented, driven writer taking to alcohol to try to dull the pain of an outraged artist who sees his chance to create enduring works of art being taken from him by this nonentity, Jones. I'd thought Blacker was a pathetic, self-pitying, talentless failure. Now I see the grandeur of the man, a mighty half-ruined edifice that towers over the other characters.

I hope some of this is of some use. And please go on sending me more. Do you have a title yet, by the way?

16 May

Dear Drummond,

Many thanks for your generous letter paying tribute to my "perceptiveness," as you call it. I can't help detecting a note of irony—now that I'm alerted to it—because of the length of time it took me to realize that what I took to be your incompetent bilge—which I must admit I was rather enjoying feeling superior toward—was actually a complex and ironic post-realist work.

I'm intrigued that you're going to try to incorporate my letter into the text. There's a challenge!

I just wonder, though, at your complimenting me for being "perceptive." I wonder if it's not too much to ask of the average reader to detect the irony. After all, if I took so long to spot it, will he?

Thanks for sending back the manuscript that I returned to you in a fit of pique. I really like the scene where Jones goes to the seedy boardinghouse in Chinatown where Lam-Sae lives and she gives him a lovely long "massage." No, I didn't think there was too much about this. It's what the reader wants. And, incidentally, I've changed my mind about the advisability of switching the setting. I now think I was quite wrong to say you failed to convey the atmosphere of Los Angeles. Rereading it just now, I wouldn't have you change a word of it.

What Lam-Sae tells Jones about Mr. Big is interesting. (What's she on, by the way, to make her so indiscreet?) I'd already guessed that it is he who organized the sexual goings-on at the Blue Orchid—the "exhibitions" and the "parties" and so on. And that he largely controlled prostitution in Los Angeles. But I hadn't guessed he was also making blue movies. This suggests that he *is* Zadonsky, as I'd guessed. And I must say that hiding behind his work as a mainstream movie producer in order to produce and distribute sex films is a brilliant idea.

How intriguing that Lam-Sae tells Jones that Mo-Lak had some kind of connection with Blacker. What could be the link between a Chinese vice girl and a distinguished—if somewhat alcoholic—novelist? I can hardly wait for the next batch of manuscript.

And I think *The Year of the Talkies* is very good. It neatly brings together the Hollywood and the Chinese elements.

Hurry up!

19th May

Dear Drummond,

What a disaster!

Thanks for the clipping. In fact, several people called to tell me about the story the day it appeared, so I went out and bought the paper.

She's been cleverer than I expected—or the paper's lawyers have. It's pretty snide and nasty, but I'm afraid it stops just this side of libel. Unfortunately, she has that recording in which, with hindsight, I admitted too much, even though I was reading from my notes. The paper's lawyers must have listened to it and decided just how far they could go.

The way the story's written, I can't threaten to sue her as we'd intended, since we can't pull the rug from under her feet with a joint denial. I'm sorry I let you talk me into it. It's done me quite a lot of harm—if anyone believes it, which I don't suppose for a minute anyone will. Whereas you emerge from it quite well.

I imagine you've already written to the editor saying it's a pack of lies, so the best we can hope is that people believe you.

Let me see more of the manuscript. That's the thing to concentrate on.

3rd June

Dear Drummond,

I'm sure you have a good case morally, but it may not be the same in law. And it's a bit of risk to sue your own publisher. I'm sure you're right, and Gollancz failed to market the book properly or to put their weight behind it, and that's why it didn't do as well as it deserved. But if you lose the case, it could cost you a fortune, and if you win, you'll be notorious as the author who sued his publisher.

Why hasn't *The Daily Scot* published your letter yet? Incidentally, I asked Tarquin if he believed Tabby's story and he said he didn't. But I wonder if it's a coincidence that *Crime Monthly* didn't ask me to contribute to their roundup of *Books of the Year* as they have done for the last three or four years?

I like the new chapter very much.

The scene where Blacker struggles—rather incoherently—

through his pain to tell Jones the truth is very powerful. I never really thought he was Mr. Big. He's clearly a man of high and self-lacerating integrity. He's rapidly becoming the moral center of the book. As I see him, he drinks only to try to numb himself to the compromises he is being forced to make in prostituting his art to commercial pressures. It's his capacity to feel pain that makes him a writer—a real writer and not just a competent and bloodless craftsman. And on top of that, he has to watch men of less talent win the accolades, the pretty girls, and the huge financial rewards.

It's intriguing that he still won't say who "Mr. Big" is. I suppose it has to be Zadonsky. I must say, though, that I think that's a bit too obvious. Remember, we need a surprise to come popping out of that closet at the end. (But I must stop saying that sort of thing, because now I'm sure you know what you're doing.)

This whole sequence in which Blacker tells Jones about Mo-Lak's relationship with Mr. Big is very powerful. It has a quality of passion that is quite unlike anything in the rest of the novel. It's most impressive that you've enabled Blacker to speak so convincingly for an angry and embittered woman who has been abused and exploited by a brutal and unscrupulous man determined to build his career whatever the cost to other people. The voice of Mo-Lak as it comes through Blacker is uncannily convincing. Her struggle against Mr. Big's vice ring and his involvement in blue movies and his unsuccessful attempt to make her act in them are making her into the heroine of this novel—just as Blacker is becoming the hero. How intriguing that Mr. Big tried to force Mo-Lak into something—his "big idea"—that she refused to take part in. And then Taw-Kwee heard about it and got in touch with Mr. Big to help him pull it off with the help of his Triad connections and his grasp of "distribution" and public relations. I'm on the edge of my seat with excitement to know why Blacker tells Jones to go and ask Lam-Sae.

And I loved Blacker's description of how Taw-Kwee and Mr. Big, by bribing and threatening people in powerful positions and by cleaning out their rivals with a series of crude "hits," ended up virtually running vice in Los Angeles. I must say, though, that it comes as a bit of a surprise to find out that Mr. Big and Taw-Kwee fell in love with each other and started a passionate sexual relationship. I hadn't guessed that Mr. Big was gay—or bisexual, I suppose. (By the way, how sensitively you handle this issue given your own red-blooded heterosexuality!) And how horrible that he wanted Mo-Lak to join in his sex sessions with Taw-Kwee. (Incidentally, I've never heard the phrase "Dutch love" to mean a woman having sex with two men at once.)

No wonder Mo-Lak went into hiding to get away from Mr. Big. It's heartbreaking that she had to prostitute herself since her other "patrons" were too intimidated by Mr. Big to help her. But at least she managed to keep her dignity by working as a masseuse.

I'm sorry that Blacker tells Jones that Mr. Big has decided to have her killed, because she is becoming a more and more interesting and "strong" character. I suppose Taw-Kwee will be her murderer.

By the way, we still don't really know what the link is between Blacker and Mo-Lak.

I'm still pretty sure I've guessed who Mr. Big is. When Blacker talks about how he himself tried to help Mo-Lak, and says that although Mr. Big is shrewd and cunning, he is such a monster of vanity and egotism that he can be made a fool of and outwitted, I became pretty certain that it must be Zadonsky.

I can't wait for more of it.

15th June

Dear Drummond,

I'm intrigued to hear that Ramsay McCoo has been demoted from literary editor to Obituaries. It looks as if his career has been buggered. I wonder if it had anything to do with my mentioning to Tarquin that I knew that Morag writes the Tabby column? I've heard she's just left him too! Well, serves Ramsay right for being a piss-artist.

Many thanks for the new chapter.

I must say, if I hadn't known how ironic and sophisticated you really are, I would have had doubts about the scene in which Jones goes back to Lam-Sae's boardinghouse and sneaks into her bedroom and finds her lying half-naked on her bed and starts making love with her and only when he reaches climax realizes that she is dead. Surely if nothing else, he'd notice the strangulation marks around her neck? There are not many writers who could get away with a scene like that. And can you really strangle somebody with a length of film? I doubt it. Though it's a nice touch—I mean, in the sense of "witty"—that when Jones looks at the film, he finds what seems to be a clue. Maybe I'm being obtuse, but I can't work out the significance of the authors' credits on the strip of film being "Michael Blacker and Minnie Forrester." Though I see that this reminds Jones of Taw-Kwee's advice to look for a movie called *Minnie's Sticky End.*

Hurry up with the next batch of manuscript!

2nd July

Dear Drummond,

Jones going back to Blacker's house and finding him dead is a lovely surprise! And I was devastated that Jones finds a suicide note in which Blacker admits to being Mr. Big and to having killed Lam-Sae. I can't believe it! I don't want to believe it!

The way the chapter ends with Jones suddenly hearing someone coming up the stairs is really frightening.

I'm glad to hear that when your new agent read the book, he "fell in love" with it and signed you up immediately. You haven't yet told me who he is, though.

I have to say, by the way, that I don't understand why you haven't written to *The Daily Scot* to set the record straight. I can see that it's a little embarrassing for you to have to say you were joking, but think how embarrassing the whole thing has been for me. It's still not too late to write.

28th July

Dear Drummond,

The dénouement is superb. I loved the moment when the door slowly opens and—of all people!—Taw-Kwee comes into the room and tells the terrified Jones that he murdered Blacker on Mr. Big's orders because he was about to expose him. I knew he was courageous and honorable! And I was really pleased with myself when Taw-Kwee tells Jones that

Mr. Big recognized Mo-Lak's contributions to his scripts and ordered him to follow Jones. And so he took a job at the bathhouse and then kidnapped Mo-Lak.

And then you deliver another wonderful surprise when Taw-Kwee suddenly tells Jones he has fallen in love with him. Brilliant! I'd forgotten that Jones is so devastatingly good-looking. In fact, I'd remembered him as short and fat. And then Taw-Kwee tries to win him over to work with him and Mr. Big.

Jones is getting to be quite an interesting and resourceful character. It's really quite impressive now the way he deals with a dangerous Chinese gangster, declaring his passionate love for him. He shows how masterful he can be now when he refuses to say whether or not he will work with Mr. Big until he knows who he is. And so Taw-Kwee (because he has sworn not to speak his name) undertakes to show him Mr. Big at work.

It's a tremendous piece of writing when Jones finds himself smuggled into the studio lot that night. I loved the revelation that the men pretending to be night security guards are actually the cameraman and the sound technicians and so on who work on the porno films and snuff movies that are shot there at night. Ingenious! And I adored Jones crouching behind a piece of scenery and watching Mr. Big giving orders for the running of his drug empire. And I'm pleased with myself for guessing that it was going to be Zadonsky. The scene in which Mo-Lak is interrogated by him is very powerful. And now at last we learn the full story of her connection with Blacker: that they wrote Zadonsky's most successful screenplays in collaboration. So that's why Zadonsky recognized her contribution to Jones's work! And why his name and her *nom de plume* appear on the strip of film that Lam-Sae was strangled with! You've handled the plot complications very ingeniously. (And I must say, incidentally, that I think your plotting has improved enormously. There's a firm grasp on the material that I haven't detected before. It really stands up now.)

I hadn't guessed, though, that Mo-Lak also helped to produce and market the movies. And then the careers of Zadonsky and Stetson plummeted at the arrival of sound when their first talkie flopped because Mo-Lak's advice was ignored. It's really quite moving when, defiant in the face of imminent death, she talks about Blacker and how much they admired each other's work—

recognizing each other as real artists amid the crowd of greedy and talentless mediocrities flocking around Zadonsky and fawning over Stetson.

The sequence in which Jones watches the filming of the snuff movie is pretty strong stuff. My idea about the meaning of the title, *Minnie's Sticky End*, was certainly way off the mark. I was thinking of quite the wrong kind of "sticking." (Though I wonder why Taw-Kwee just happens to be carrying a poker and how he heats it up?) After being had frontward and backward and every which way by every man on the set, Mo-Lak's death must almost be a relief. Though one would prefer not to go in quite that manner. Yes, it's rather horrible, but it's also very funny. Don't tone it down.

How daring and unusual of you to have your hero stand by and see a major female character being murdered in a particularly gruesome way! You defy all the conventions in the boldest manner.

I loved the way Zadonsky, having watching Taw-Kwee kill Mo-Lak, then reveals that he knows he has tried to double-cross him and has him hideously tortured and killed in the same hideous way! So it turns out to be *Minnie and Taw-Kwee's Sticky Ends*!

Jones reveals a new and heroic aspect of himself when he seizes his chance while this is going on and steals the film from out of the camera and escapes. It's a brilliant idea because it means that he is using Zadonsky's own material to turn the tables on him.

Incidentally, I'm rather glad you've decided to cut all the sex with underage girls. Your women readers would not have cared for it at all, I suspect.

All the best.

14th August

Dear Drummond,

Well, what a surprise! You've taken my advice, but only after I've decided I was wrong. Though I think you didn't need to do it, I must say there is real wit and inventiveness in the way you've made the transfer from twenties Los Angeles to contemporary Glasgow. It's lovely the way the Hollywood movie industry becomes the Scottish literary scene with Zadonsky's studio turning into the Glasgow Council for the Arts. And Archibald (as you wittily call Arnold) *is* a bit of a Zadonsky figure—big, ambitious, paranoid, with a kind of bullying charm and surrounded by sycophantic writers toadying to him in the hope of getting his patronage. Though I can't quite see him running a string of brothels and making snuff movies! It's a nice touch the way Blacker becomes the novelist Ringan Gilhaize. And he's becoming more and more heroic and idealistic.

Making Taw-Kwee a London-based drug dealer and pimp who is mixed up in the metropolitan racket is a nice touch. I'm intrigued that you've kept him and Mo-Lak Chinese but made all the other characters Scottish—except for Stetson and Archibald, who become English. But Arnold actually *is* Scottish, so I'm puzzled that you've turned his equivalent in the novel into an Englishman.

I'm intrigued that you've done what I suggested ages ago and merged the frame and the inner story by making Farquhar and Jones into one character. And, as you say, now that Farquhar-Jones is tall and handsome (as well as courageous and high-minded) it makes perfect sense that Taw-Kwee falls for him.

Send me the last chapter as soon as possible, please. I can't quite see how some of the changes you've made are going to work out at the dénouement.

On a nastier subject. I'm sure you know that's a complete lie in Tabby's column. I never advised Tarquin not to take you on. Why would I do that? I can't imagine who could have told the spiteful bitch that. Apart from that—which harms me more than you—Tabby has given you quite a nice write-up. I wonder what she means when she says you are "now working with a collaborator." Does she mean me? Who told her? And if that's what she means, she lets me off rather lightly in view of her usual spite. And what do you make of "More about this very soon!"

Incidentally, nothing seems to have come of the idea of Tarquin writing a column. At least, I've not seen it if he has started one. I asked him about it in my last letter but he hasn't answered or returned my call. That's most unlike him.

Keep the manuscript coming!

By the way, what are you going to call it now that your original title—*The Year of the Talkies*—is no longer appropriate? I've got rather a clever suggestion. Why not call it *A Nice Touch*? It's relevant to a lot of the plot and it sounds sexy, and that certainly can't hurt sales.

17th August

Dear Drummond,

I've had a very strange letter from Tarquin. He talks in a rather enigmatic way about what is best for me and then mysteriously refers to "a conflict of interests" and being caught in "the backwash of my career." It's very odd. I've written a rather indignant letter.

I hope he doesn't believe that story we planted on Tabby! Could you write—or even phone—and tell him the truth? I'm sorry to have to ask you since I know he can't be your favorite person. I've been calling your number, by the way, but I only get your machine. (You seem to be out all the time these days.) Tell him it's a ridiculous allegation. Nobody who knows us as writers could believe for a moment that I would plagiarize from your work.

And while I'm on that topic, I might as well say clearly now that I don't know where you got the idea that the character of "Smidgett" in the *Smetterburns* is based on you. I can see a superficial resemblance in that you're both tall and slim with very splendid mustaches, but that's absolutely as far as it goes. I simply don't use real people as the basis of my characters—though I admit that there are elements of Morag in the neurotic woman who gets rather horribly murdered in the first *Smetterburn*.

Turning to the manuscript, I'm glad you've dropped Taw-Kwee being gay and the whole business of him falling in love with Farquhar-Jones. It's much better now that he has deserted Mr. Big simply for reasons of moral disgust. You've made him much younger and more innocent, haven't you? So now when he talks about Mr. Big, the reader feels a lot of sympathy for this naive youth who has been deceived, exploited, and abused by a sinister older man who is driven by greed and egotism.

The exchange in which Taw-Kwee tells Farquhar-Jones how he has become sickened by what Mr. Big was asking him to do is excellent. And his revelation about the chain of ostensibly respectable saunas run by Mr. Big that are really brothels was fascinating. I can see where your research has paid off! I wonder what the Glaswegian originals are for the establishments you call *Quin-too-sensual, Sensations,* and *Fingers!* Perhaps I shouldn't ask!

All that stuff about Mr. Big's drug-peddling activities is very vivid. So at last we find out what the mysterious "big idea" is that Blacker talked about: a distribution deal involving the new and highly addictive formula known as crack. I was really gripped to learn how Mr. Big has forced Taw-Kwee into tying up extortionate distribution deals all over the Glasgow area. I liked the business of Taw-Kwee standing up to him and telling him that the prices he was trying to extract from people hooked on his evil and addictive junk were extortionate! Brave, plucky little chap! And Mr. Big with his Triad connections and his metropolitan influence is emerging as a genuinely evil character.

When Taw-Kwee offers to take Farquhar-Jones to the place where Mr. Big does his evil work, I loved the way he leads him to one of the most fashionable streets in the West End of Glasgow. (I suppose it's Arnold's house in Lorraine Road? The journey there is almost too recognizable, as I know since I'm just around the corner in Westbourne Gardens. Have you ever been to one of his soirées, by the way? They are very civilized occasions.) I can't wait to find out what's going to happen. Presumably Archibald is going to be exposed. I'm sure I don't need to tell you how to avoid giving him the chance to bring a libel action!

I'm intrigued to know what has become of Pettifer? Have you dropped him in this version? Frankly, I'd be rather relieved if you had. And why have you decided to change the title to *The Quintain?* What does it mean?

Keep it coming.

24th August

Dear Drummond,

I've had an even stranger letter from Tarquin in which he says that he has tried to point out to me for a long time that I've overestimated the enthusiasm of the market for the new book. He says people aren't as addicted to my *Smetterburns* as I appear to believe. Then he ends by saying straight out that he has become convinced that he is not the right person to represent me and that I should approach another agent with the new novel! So I've been dumped!

Anyway, to the really important matter.

First, I'm fascinated that you've decided to make Taw-Kwee and Mo-Lak Scottish. Or, as I should now call them, Torquil and Moira. And it's a lovely moment when Torquil takes Farquhar-Jones into the basement of what I assume is Arnold's house and finds that it is fitted out like a torture-chamber-cum-studio with a video camera ready to roll. And then he hides Farquhar-Jones behind a rack disguised as an exercise bicycle so that he can't quite make out what's happening except for seeing Moira tied up.

I love the idea of the literature director of the Glasgow Council for the Arts making snuff movies with his drug-dealing boyfriend in order to kill off ex-mistresses! It's a wonderfully suspenseful chapter ending when Farquhar-Jones hears people coming down the stairs and then Archibald's voice (now speaking in broad Scots, I notice, so he's now Scottish after all!) emerging from the darkness. But what puzzles me is why he is talking about Chartres Pettifer? What is the relevance of all this stuff about how Pettifer's career has gone into decline because his novels have been exposed as plagiarized and no reputable agent will handle him now? What does Pettifer have to do with this?

I mean, it's clear enough, isn't it, that Archibald is Mr. Big and that it was he who put Torquil up to everything and brought together Farquhar-Jones, Moira, and Torquil?

By the way, I bought the paper today and I'm amazed at the blatant way that woman uses her column to hype herself: "Morag Frobister is going to astonish us all by revealing another facet of her multitalented personality." How does she have the nerve to promote herself so shamelessly? Is it a secret that she writes it? Even so, why does the editor let her get away with it? And I wonder how that connects with the story she says she's going to publish next week about "a wonderfully readable and witty thriller with an extraordinary real-life story of malice and deceit behind it."

I'd be grateful if you could call me up because I've still only been getting your answering machine.

P.S. I've looked up *quintain*, and it comes from the Middle Ages, when it meant "the target in jousting practice that the rider aimed at and that swung around and unseated him if he wasn't clever enough to get out of the way." Is that really the word you intended? Don't you think *A Nice Touch* is better?

5th September

You shit,

   I suppose you think you've been very clever. Your final revelation about Mr. Big certainly took me by surprise. But mainly because it's so absurd. I imagine you thought it was a neat twist that Archibald turns out to be a prisoner who's about to be murdered along with Moira. Well, it's just stupid. It doesn't work in terms of psychology. (Never your strongest suit!) Your absurd and venomous combination of Stetson and Pettifer doesn't work. "Chalmers Pettitson" simply has not been presented as the kind of person who would become a ruthless crack dealer running an empire of sex and drugs by the exercise of terror. And the business of him coming out of the closet and revealing that he is gay is equally absurd. I know what you're implying and it's a lie. If you publish the book in this form—if you manage to find a publisher!—I'll sue. Moreover, I didn't for a second believe that moment when Torquil turns on him and high-mindedly denounces him and summons Farquhar-Jones out of hiding and they heroically overpower him and set the other two free. The way Torquil—egged on by the others—then uses his heated poker on Pettitson to torture him to death is frankly sadistic. One of the nastiest scenes in a book that, to put it bluntly, is filled with sadistic fantasies that seem to have come from the mind of a deeply disturbed schoolboy.

  You talk about the pain of being an artist. What about the pain of reading your prose! When I think of the time I've spent trying to help you produce something readable! And how pleased I was when I saw signs that the thing was improving! But now you've got out of your depth. I couldn't help you even if I wanted to because, frankly, in literary terms you can't even swim.

Are you there, you cunt? I'll bet you're listening and you're too scared to pick up. I suppose you all think you've been very clever. You think you've had a good laugh at my expense. But it's blown up in your stupid faces.

Everyone I've spoken to thinks I come out of it better than you. They all think the story makes you look like a bunch of lying crooks. Nobody believes that ridiculous canaille *about me plagiarizing from you. Nobody who can tell good writing from trash! Even that little skunk Tarquin doesn't believe it, whatever he's told you. He just thinks there's a good opportunity for some nasty, spiteful hype of the kind he's so fond of. (And so what—by the way—if I did advise him not to touch you with a barge pole? I thought I was doing the double-crossing little rat a favor.) As for the idea of getting Morag to make a fool of herself by publishing the story—it was your idea, not mine! And the fact that you two got together to turn the tables on me just shows you up as a pair of two-faced sneaks.*

And now I've got a surprise for you! That's just what I intended. Of course I knew Tarquin had taken over the Tabby column, and I guessed what the three of you were up to. Especially when he suddenly dropped me as a client. Plus I could see your dreadful manuscript was getting better because someone was helping you. And you all fell into the trap and couldn't wait to show the world what a collection of gullible shits you are! Hah bloody hah! You've really gone and . . .

Me again, Gilchrist. I hate to disappoint you but none of you are going to make your fortune. Nobody's going to buy the book. One, because it's crap. And two, because the only reason for reading it is my letters, and if you don't take them out, I'll sue. I own the copyright.

I only wrote them because I was trying—God help me!—to improve your dreadful book. You ungrateful hypocrite! You have the nerve to accuse me of stealing ideas from Morag, and you cold-bloodedly picked my brains for your book. It's due to me that the book is worth anything at all. I don't have the words to describe how dreadful your other books are. You call yourself an artist. The only kind of artist you are is a piss-artist. I hope you choke on your own venom. All three of you! You accuse me of all sorts of things, but you're the ones who go in for Dutch practices! I hope next time you and that bitch give him head, you bloody well poison yourselves. And I hope he chokes to death sucking your . . .

CHAPTER

9

The Catch

I'M NOT PROUD OF EVERYTHING I'VE DONE—AS THIS AC-
count will more than amply demonstrate. But I will insist on
saying on my own behalf that I never behaved dishonorably. If I
made mistakes—and I readily admit that I made my share—it
was always because I did what at the time seemed to be the best
thing for the party, for the country, for my family, or for literature.

Since you probably saw me on that piece of film at what could
hardly be called the best moment of my life, I want to explain
how the scene it records came about and convince you to believe that it was primarily my good intentions that got me into
trouble. Plus, if I walked into a trap, it was largely one created
by my own ingenuousness.

I now know that the chain of events that led to my downfall
commenced that day in May four years ago when I had lunch
with Aubrey Sackville. I can't really explain why I kept up with
him. We had little in common. And there had always been
those rumors about his private life. Though I like to think I'm
a man of the world and as such pretty broad-minded. But we'd
met at launch-parties and on talk shows, and I suppose I enjoyed the old rascal's company, and he usually had some amus-
ing stories to tell. Plus he was chief fiction reviewer for *The
Daily Scot.*

But I can see that I'll have to write this like a novel. It's the only way I know how to tell a story.

We had agreed to meet at one of my favorite French places in Mayfair, situated on one of those little cul-de-sacs at the Berkeley Square end of Curzon Street. I arrived early because I'd left plenty of time, knowing that it was hardly the easiest thing in the world to find a space for a Bentley in that part of town. In fact, by an incredibly lucky fluke, I located a space almost immediately. (As it transpired, Sackville was late—a thing I detest, since punctuality is the politeness of princes and I happen to be privileged to know from personal experience that Royalty are never rude in that respect, unless they absolutely can't help it.)

The restaurant had French-style check tablecloths and high-backed chairs. The maître d', who was an old friend of mine and greeted me with an effusive smile, was a small, cheerful man with a high forehead and very little hair on his head. When he had shown me to my regular table and performed the usual servilities, the waiter came to take my drinks order. He had a long, nervous face and no more hair than the maître d'—but with a larger nose. I ordered an aperientive and sat and waited. I reflected that it was going to be very inconvenient if lunch went on late, because I had an appointment with my tailor that afternoon.

About twenty minutes later than the time agreed, Sackville breezed into the restaurant with such a self-satisfied look on his face that I knew there was something he was longing to tell me. He offered some offhand alibi for his unpunctuality as if he couldn't be bothered to come up with anything better.

I should tell you something about Sackville, I suppose, since he plays a not inconsiderable part in the story I am about to tell you, as will subsequently emerge later. Aubrey Sackville is a pseudoname, of course. You undoubtably know his real name, but our absurd libel laws prevent me from giving it here.

Sackville is a tall man with a rubicose countenance. He has a mane of white hair falling over his forehead and a somewhat protruberant nose and, though only in his early sixties, he has the eyes of a much older man. Everything about him is affected. his clothes are dandyish, and he talks extremely portentiously in a booming voice with a rich, plummy accent. But you know that because you must have seen him on TV.

His novels are always set in the most superior circles— aristocrats, landowners, cabinet ministers, big businessmen, and with a sprinkling of the most talented people from show business and the arts. They're intended to give the impression that he moves in those circles, though I happen to know he is hardly ever invited to dinner parties in the best houses in London, because I almost never see him there. The sad truth is he thinks he's Powell, but he reads like inferior Waugh. He is, to be blunt, a mid-list author.

We ordered the meal. I chose my favorite *cuise de cannard confit*, and Sackville ordered the *olivier de fillet de racsasse* on my advice. I don't mind admitting that good food is important to me and that I've always been something of a gourmand—if knowing the best and insisting on getting it makes me a gourmand. After the usual literary chat about what size advances particular agents were getting for their authors and which publishers had most recently been bought and which book-selling chains were doing best, the conversation became a little more personal. I had lunched the previous day with my agent, Tarquin Bone, and I commenced to talk, as one writer to another, about some of the rather exciting possibilities that were opening up for product-placement deals. I was just commencing to tell him about the implications of certain merchandising clauses in future contracts for the exploitation of commercial spin-offs, when we were interrupted by the wine waiter, who was small and balding but with piercing deep-set eyes. We ordered a bottle of Puligny Montrachet 1971, a very reasonable wine and not too heavy for lunchtime.

Hardly had the waiter gone when Sackville commenced to talk about his own books. He went on and on about them ad nauseum while I tried to politely hide the fact that I was almost totally disinterested.

When I was able to get a word in edgewise, I commenced telling Sackville about my new editor's very attractive marketing strategy. His approach was to focus on just a few authors at the top of the list and concentrate the company's resources on growing them. His intention was to increase my market share with each new title. I could justly say now that I was the brand leader, since I'd already overtaken Jack Sheldon and Robert Forsyth, and this financial year I was going to beat Sidney Higgins and

Frederick Ludlum. In short, I could now count on the brand loyalty of millions of readers all over the world.

Sackville said something like "No problems, then, dear boy? The past safely behind you?"

To be frank, I hardly noticed the significance of this remark or his tone of voice when he said it.

I said that my only problem was that I was not taken seriously enough as a writer and that my editor and I agreed that I needed to reposition myself up-market. We both felt that that was where the future lay, since I'd achieved market saturation at the more popular end of the range. And the eighties, we predicted, would be the age when the highbrow title would go mass-market.

I mentioned something about how badly I felt I was treated by the so-called quality newspapers, and told Sackville—maybe a little tactlessly—about a particularly vicious review of my last book by some sniveling lefty pansy in *The Observer* or some other socialist rag.

I remember that I said, "I'm realistic about myself, Aubrey. I know my limitations as a writer. I make no claim to be a Snow or a Sharpe, much less a Powell or a Le Carré. I welcome frank criticism of my work if I can learn from it and write better books as a result. But not spiteful carping and nitpicking."

I really meant that. I think I can honestly say that I'm less of an egotist than comparable novelists of my prominence. Though having said that, there aren't many, to be frank, that come into that rather exclusive category.

"Yes," Sackville agreed. "But you mentioned about Powell just now, and he is *sui genesis*. He and Proust are wholly and completely in a class of their own, my dear boy—a class that perhaps just the teeniest handful of contemporary novelists can be placed in."

That said, he sat back in that pompous, self-satisfied way he has. I knew he was thinking of himself, but I wasn't going to say anything to inflate his ego any more, so I continued, "Why have the so-called highbrows got it in for me? Is it just envy of my success? Or is it that they can't take my political views? Or that I write books that people actually enjoy reading instead of the pretentious drivel that they prefer?"

And Sackville took a deep breath and said, "Darling, I have

very little respect myself for those *grotesque* fellow novelists of ours who dance on the high wire of fashion at the command of the reviewer-ringmasters of the literary circus, albeit I am one who cracks the whip himself."

While I was trying to work that one out, he went on: "Frankly, Jeremy, why should *you* care about the reviewers? All right, my dear, I admit one has won the Booker and the Whitbread and had a South Bank Show on one's work and all of that."

I thought he was going to go on forever, listing his achievements. But then he came to the point: "Yet though you don't get that sort of attention, the fact remains that you're one of the most successful authors not just in this country but in the whole world. You're a public figure, you're looked up to by millions, you're a benchmark for your fellow novelists, and, above all, you make a hell of a lot of money. Certainly far more than I do."

I don't precisely remember his words, but that was certainly the gist of what he said.

And for some reason I replied, "All that's true, but I'd kill to have written one of your books. I'd kill to have written a book that got so-called highbrows in a flutter."

Now I don't know why I said that. To be totally frank, I was surprised to hear myself say it. I suppose it was the artist in me speaking. The truth is, I can't even read Sackville's stuff. Though I can see he's got something. I mean, I can see that he's quite a stylist. But I'm not sure that he has the ability—the basic straightforward ability—to offer the reader a rattling good yarn, which is an ability that, I don't think I flatter myself, I have in spades.

As soon as I'd said it, I regretted it. There was a silence. And Sackville took advantage of my frankness. He could easily have said something like: "Come off it. Your stuff is pretty good." But he didn't. He just looked at me and then he said, "We all have to do the best we can, Jeremy, my sweet."

I was a bit put out at that, to be totally truthful.

And then he went on: "The genre a novelist chooses to write in doesn't matter, dear boy. It's how well he does it. Speaking quite personally, I think Frederick Ludlum is really rather good-ish. His last one, *The Hauptmann Ultimatum*, was absolutely gripping. A gloriously old-fashioned *yarn*, my dear."

I could see exactly what he was trying to infer.

I told him pretty coolly that though I knew and liked Freddy, I hadn't had much exposure to his work. The truth was, I admitted, I had very little time for reading now, though when younger I had been a vociferous reader. Essentially, I was too preoccupied with promotional work and I had too many claims upon my time that I couldn't duck out of. That was the difference between us, I said. I wasn't a man of letters in the sense that Sackville was. For better or for worse, I was a man of the world with all the penalties—and, it had to be said, the advantages—that that involved.

I didn't spell it out, of course, but I don't mind admitting now that, to be completely frank, Sackville's work is much too bookish for my taste and for the tastes of most ordinary people. He writes books that are much more about other books than they are about the real world.

Sackville said, "It's *slightly* unfortunate you don't have more time to read, dearest boy, but you certainly do a lot of promotional work." Then he added spitefully, "But it can't be *quite* as exciting as what you were doing before. You must miss all that now. It must have been quite *marvelous* to have been at the very center of things!"

"On the contrary," I said, a bit stung at that. "I'm closer to the center of things than I ever was. I'm still considered pretty useful. Between you and I, my skills in language use have helped the party to massively upgrade its communication effectiveness. And I see a lot of the top people on a regular basis. In fact, I shouldn't really tell you this but last weekend I took the yacht out with a Very Important Person on board. The harbor was literally crawling with security personnel. So I think that shows that not much of the dirt flung at me stuck."

I could see that took him aback a bit. But he said, "Still, after all the excitement of public life, it must be *something* of the tiniest letdown having to earn your living by selling fiction."

"Well, I'm not doing too badly at it," I said. "That's the main thing."

I could see he didn't like that, though he betrayed no indication that he had taken my point.

"How did the last book do, darling?" he asked with a sort of sneer.

"Very well," I said. "Admittedly, not quite as well as the earlier ones."

"So I'd heard, my sweet," he said. "And how's the next one coming along?"

He said it with such a meaningful look that I wondered what he'd picked up.

In fact, the truth was that at that moment I'd hit something of a sticky patch in my career, both as a public figure and as a writer.

The first title I'd released, *For Richer, For Poorer*, had, of course, been a huge success and amply repaid the effort I'd put in on marketing and promotion. It's too well known for me to need to say much about it here, but you'll probably remember what it's about. The hero was a rising politician who, during a period in opposition, decided to go into business and accrue some money. Through his beautiful girlfriend he was introduced to a charismatic businessman of great charm and persuasiveness. He trusted this man and before long found that he had become involved in running a company that turned out to be fraudulent. His partner now offered him a choice: Either he could expose the company as crooked, thereby ruining both himself and thousands of small investors; or he could collaborate in maintaining the fraud for the sake of the ordinary, decent little people that had invested their life savings in it. After struggling with his conscience for many months, the hero took the decision to expose the fraud. Before he could do so, however, the truth emerged by another means in a blaze of publicity, and so it was easy for his enemies to claim that he had been covering the fraud up for his own purposes. And when the company collapsed, he discovered his partner had arranged things in such a way that he was left holding the bag. His partner and the girl disappeared. So the hero was deserted, in disgrace, bankrupted, and his political career was in ruins. He then picked himself up off the floor and fought to clear his name. At last he succeeded in showing that the whole thing was a KGB plot. The girlfriend that had involved him in the scheme and the charismatic businessman were both tools of the Soviets who had been instructed to find a rising politician and get power over him. Only his honesty in refusing to go along with the fraud had saved him. Then the KGB had unmasked the company as a fraud in a last desperate attempt to discredit him. (The businessman had forced the girl to return to the Soviet Union with him against her will, for she had fallen deeply and genuinely in love with her intended victim.) When this was fully revealed, his reputation was saved and his courage and honesty were rewarded with a place on the front bench.

I'd then capitalized on the success of *For Richer, For Poorer* with my next titles. *The Greater Glory* was the second novel, and a number of agents were involved with myself in putting the project together. It was about a man who, at the height of his political career, with a major cabinet portfolio and even the premiership itself within his grasp, suddenly gave it all up because he had a burning desire to write a novel. So he abandoned his ministerial post, gave up his seat in Parliament, and retreated to a cottage in the country where he wrote the novel— called *Let Not Ambition*—which was hailed as a masterpiece and won him the Booker Prize. But my book showed the cost of this and dealt with the impact of his decision, not only on his party, which was thrown into turmoil by his decision to leave politics, but also on his wife and on the woman that loved him passionately and that, by a cruel twist of fate, was married to the leader of the opposition.

Bone had organized a rights auction and it had been very successful.

And the last one, *The Cincinnatus Papers*, was about a great novelist at the height of his powers who dominated the country's intellectual and cultural life and was surrounded by beautiful women competing for his favor. The novel dealt with the choice he faced when the Prime Minister, in the middle of a political and economic crisis, suddenly asked him to accept a peerage so that he could enter the House of Lords and become Home Secretary. And so it behooved him to choose between the Nobel Prize for Literature, for which he was a front-runner and likely to win by producing just one more masterpiece, and on the other hand saving his country from a Communist plot that was being engineered by the KGB and put into effect through their puppets in the Labour Party and the media. Plus he knew that, with the Prime Minister under threat from his own party, the premiership itself was within his grasp.

The last one had, frankly, not done as well as I'd expected, even though I'd worked harder on it than on any other of my titles—a ten-city tour, twenty or thirty interviews, and any number of talk show appearances.

I was now in something of a dilemma because I'd sold the next two titles as part of a trans-Atlantic multititle deal. The sums involved were very satisfying as a mark of respect for a writing career that now spanned the best part of a decade and had achieved a not inconsiderable impact in the global context. The problem now was that I was having difficulty coming up with the material to actually produce new titles. I hadn't, to be frank, told the whole truth to Sackville in inferring that it was merely lack of time that was preventing me from completing the next one. The truth was that at times I felt that I'd said what I had to say in the books I'd written. I didn't have much more to say. I certainly didn't have the prolificacy of, for example, Sackville. In short, I sometimes wondered if I'd burned myself out as a writer.

I wasn't exactly short of money, but I needed to generate more cash from the advance on the next title because my cash flow was beginning to cause me no small degree of concern. Of course I had lots of capital but most of it was tied up in land and investments. Plus I liked a high standard of living, although I was never one to flout my wealth. Despite that, my lifestyle extorted a certain cost: the house in Chester Square, the place in the country adjacent to Oxford, the boys' education, my staff, the Bentley, my wife's Lamborghini, the boat, and so on. My wife had impeccable taste and therefore was dressed by the top designers, Balmain and Bob Mackie, both of whose services did not exactly come cheap. The life of a major literary figure was no cheaper, I'd discovered, than that of a leading politician: restaurants, nightclubs, flowers, little gifts of jewelery, the rent on a small apartment in Fulham, and so on.

So when Sackville asked me about progress on the next title, I decided I really didn't want to get into that subject at that precise moment. And certainly not with him.

"Fine," I said. "The only problem is simply finding the time to produce the material."

He said, so offhandedly that I didn't notice the implication at the time, "My dear, *is* that a problem?"

I said I was anxious to come up with a title that would force the literary editors to take me seriously. I needed a wholly new kind of book, I told him. In effect, I needed a new image.

"I don't think the objection is to the *kind* of novel you publish," he said with that smarmy smile. "After all, there are beyond peradventure novelists that work wholly and completely within a genre but who are nonetheless taken *absolutely* seriously."

Beyond peradventure! That's the way he talks! And writes, too.

"I have in mind," he went on, "writers such as Le Carré. Deighton. P. D. James."

"I don't know their work at firsthand," I said.

"Perhaps you should," he replied. "After all, Jeremy, one can't expect to stay ahead if one doesn't keep an eye on the competition. And I think you'd be impressed by the quality of some of their plotting. That's something the reviewers have just had the *tiniest* tendency now and then to find fault with in your work, isn't it?"

I sat and smiled at him without saying anything. I knew what he was up to and I wasn't going to let him have the satisfaction of seeing that he was getting to me. I was very familiar with the ploy that people adopt toward me when they tell me how successful I am while at the same time running down my books out of sheer envy.

My appetite seemed to have gone and I left most of my food uneaten. But I never was a veracious eater.

He went on: "May I suggest, as one writer to another, that your plots are sometimes just the tiniest bit lacking in wit?"

Wit? In a plot? I literally had no idea what he meant and I told him so.

"I mean," he went on, like he was speaking to an idiot, "that they tend to be to just the *slightest* degree predictable. They develop with just a *little* too much inevitability from the initial premise."

"What point are you trying to make?" I asked him, somewhat sharply. To be frank, he was beginning to aggravate me. I can take constructive criticism on the chin as well as the next man, but this was just spiteful abuse. I didn't at all care for the way he was inferring that I didn't know my craft. I pride myself, and not without reason, on my ability as a yarn spinner. I don't think the millions of devoted readers that buy and read my books can all be too stupid to know quality—real quality—when they're offered it.

"*Tout court*, you need some ingenuity," he said. "That's what I mean, darling. What you want to write is a twister—a story with a really clever twist." He sat back in his chair cradling his glass and said, "Find yourself a good little twister, dear boy."

The patronizing little shit!

Well, I soon wiped the smile off his face.

"By an extraordinary coincidence," I said, "it happens that I have already written exactly what you're describing."

He looked pretty surprised at that, I can tell you.

"It was the first novel I ever wrote," I went on. "A work, I might say, of my apprenticeship. It was about a man being cheated by a con man, and it had a clever twist in the plot so that the reader is taken in by the con man as much as the hero is."

"What was the story?" he asked.

So I told him.

I didn't tell him everything, of course. You dare not trust another novelist not to steal your good ideas. The whole story is this. It was right after that bit of bad luck that led me to withdraw from my political and business interests. I holed up in a flat in Chelsea I had managed to salvage from the wreckage of my personal fortune, and there I sat down and wrote a novel that was loosely based on the experience. I might as well admit that this was hardly the best period of my life. I'd lost everything: my political career, my seat in Parliament, my business career, most of my wealth, my marriage, my mistress, my good name. Everything but my self-respect and my belief in myself. When the novel, which I called *The Sting in the Tail*, was finished, I asked friends of mine who the best publishers of fiction were. They all told me Chatto and Warburg, so I sent it to them. I waited anxiously to hear their reaction. Nothing. At last, after two weeks without hearing a word, I had to call them up and pull a bit of rank. (After all, I was still a well-known figure.) Then one morning a few days later back came the manuscript, and with it was an incredibly offensive letter rejecting it—a letter that the author later had reason to regret having written. A letter that was highly unprofessional in its quite gratuitous spitefulness, not to mention the way it kicked a man who was already on his knees.

Well, at that point in time things looked pretty chronic. You have to remember how my enemies on the left were crowing over my downfall, as they saw it. But I wasn't going to give in that easily. It would have pleased too many people that I despised. Undaunted by this spiteful rebuff, I sat down and decided to try again. And in effect I pulled myself out of the mud and turned the bad publicity around so that it worked in my favor. I turned the tables on my enemies. The wonderful idea I had this time was to write a novel that would appeal to the public's interest in what had actually happened to me. I exploited, if I may permit myself this somewhat rotund phrase, the lure of the lived fact. I calculated that people would want to read my side of it and see what I had to say in my defense. Instead of a novel that was only loosely based on my experiences, as the first one had been, I wrote one that was as factual as I could make it. So I worked closely with a libel lawyer of my acquaintance and wrote an account of what had happened that was as close to the facts as he would allow it to be. This, of course, was the novel that became *For Richer, For Poorer.* I sent it to André Gollancz, since people told me they were the next best to Chatto and Warburg. As has become a matter of public record, it was a huge success. Nothing less than the biggest-selling first novel since *Gone with the Wind.*

When I had the next novel ready, I went back to Chatto and Warburg. Now of course I had access to the managing director and the editorial director. I said to them that I'd like them to publish me in future, since they were the top fiction publisher. But if I was to be associated with them, I would want them to employ only people of the highest caliber. And frankly someone that could turn down a manuscript by a writer of the proven quality of myself was not someone they should be happy to be employing. They agreed with me and took the appropriate steps. And they've been my publisher ever since.

Sackville seemed very interested in this story and asked me several questions about it.

Then, as we were at the cigars-and-liqueurs stage, he said, "I suppose what your story about *For Richer, For Poorer* shows is that the old saying is true: No publicity is bad publicity."

"It's not so simple," I said somewhat indignantly. "The same story can be presented favorably or unfavorably. The media will simply choose whichever looks like the best copy. So the whole art of public relations is to know how to bait the hook. Give them their story but leave them just enough work to do to make them think they've got there theirselves. As a matter of fact, I was saying exactly that to the Prime Minister when we lunched together in Downing Street last week."

And that's when Aubrey Sackville's eyes gleamed and he seized his chance to blatantly drag into the conversation the "rabbit from the hat" that he'd been keeping up his sleeve.

He said, "Talking of Downing Street, dearest boy, I shouldn't really tell you this, but it'll be in the papers the day after tomorrow when the Birthday Honours are published, so what the hell. And it *is* rather a divine piece of news. The fact is, one has been given a knighthood. A KCB."

Frankly, I was surprised. He's done nothing for the party. I don't know if he even belongs to it. Or even votes for it, come to that. Not only that, but there had always been those rumors about his private life. I wasn't sure whether to believe them or not. I thought not, but you can't always tell. Altogether, I have to say I was very surprised. I certainly hadn't been consulted about it. That's for sure. Though I tried to look like I already knew.

I even said, "As a matter of fact, the Prime Minister mentioned to me about it the other day. I wasn't sure if you'd been officially informed, or I'd have said something about it."

"Thanks, dear boy," he said, looking like he didn't believe me.

But the truth is, it wasn't really so surprising that Sackville had got his K. He's regarded as a serious "literary" novelist, whatever that means. Frankly, to my way of thinking the whole thing is a total fraud. He's part of the "Eng Lit" mafia. If your face fits and you know the right people and do the right things, then you're a serious literary writer. Even if all you've published is a so-called sensitive first novel or some portentious little sheath of love poems. If you're successful in the sense that ordinary book-reading members of the public purchase your product in not inconsiderable quantities, then there's no way you'll ever win a literary prize or be reviewed in the so-called serious papers. I'm delighted to say, at that time I'd never been short-listed for a literary prize, let alone won one. If you merely write books that millions of people buy and get thumping good entertainment from, then you're a lowbrow, a potboiler. Either you're not reviewed at all or else you're reviewed in a tone of condescending superiority.

Then he asked me if I'd "got anything this time." I felt he was sneering at the OBE I got four years ago.

So I said, "The convention is, as you know, that the more worthwhile honors are given to mark the end of someone's contribution. I think the Prime Minister feels that my contribution is very far from being over. In fact, to be frank, she was kind enough to say so when we had lunch."

That was pretty much the truth. And it was certainly true that I hadn't ruled out the option of returning to politics in the not too distant future. I felt enough time had passed.

If my own fortunes were at a low ebb, still it was a good time for the party and thus for the country. We had just won the 1979 general election and done so under the most powerful and charismatic leader since Churchill. That had given me some reason to hope that my opportunities for public service were far from over. But although I had waited by the telephone for a week after the election, no call had come from Downing Street. At our luncheon, however, the Prime Minister had told me she would "adore" to have me working for her, and I had come away filled with optimism and enthusiasm.

"Surely there's absolutely no *question* of your returning to politics after that business you were mixed up in, my dear?" Sackville said, smiling bitchily in his inimicable way.

I indignantly refuted that. I reminded him that no charges were ever brought against me. People tend to forget that, and it makes me very angry. I had been naive and I had been unfortunate in my choice of business partner. That was all.

"You can't be gullible enough to believe everything you read in the press, can you?" I asked in amazement. I don't think he liked me saying that.

I told him that if the Prime Minister ever decided that I could be useful to the party or the country, then I would be honored and flattered to place my services at her disposal whatever the cost to myself personally in financial terms.

"And all you expect in return is a K or even a peerage,"

Sackville said venomously. Then he went on: "Frankly, darling, if it's a title you're after, you'd better stick to fiction. I imagine you have a better chance of getting one for services to literature."

Then he smiled in a way I didn't care for at all.

I said with considerable dignity, though I was beginning to get not a little exacerbated, "Do you find that possibility so comical?"

"Come on, sweetie," he said. "It can't be difficult to turn out your books."

"Then why haven't you tried?" I asked. "I don't notice your books stacked up on the airport bookstalls or heading the bestseller lists across the civilized world."

That got him.

He said: "I got my K for contributing to literature, not helping the balance of trade."

He was really put out now!

I said, "I see. You'd write my sort of books and make a fortune except that you can't bring yourself to stoop so low."

"Something like that," he answered.

"Frankly, I've been a bit naive," I admitted bitterly. "I simply hadn't realized how much you envied me."

"Me envy you!" he exclaimed.

Now he revealed his true colors. He turned red and almost shouted, "What the hell do you have that I should envy? Your books are badly written trash. They're a fucking joke. I can't think of any half-decent writer in the country that would change places with you."

"You'll apologize for that," I said softly but grimly.

Then he said with a sneer, "I don't know why you're so offended, darling. You don't actually write them yourself anyway."

Now he had really gone too far.

This vile rumor had been circulating ever since I released *For Richer, For Poorer*. Frankly, I think people just couldn't believe that someone that had achieved a not inconsiderable degree of success in one field (politics) would be able to succeed in another—and one so different as literature.

At this moment the maître d', who was small and balding, came hurrying over on his short but surprisingly nimble legs to ask if everything was all right.

We were both so angry by now that we ignored him.

"You can't be stupid enough to believe that incredible lie!" I exclaimed.

"Oh it's credible," he said. "It's credible, darling, because it's the literary equivalent of embezzlement."

Well, that was it. I have always prided myself on never losing my temper unless a situation got completely out of control. But on this occasion his affrontery was more than I could endure.

I got up and leaned over him. He cringed like he thought I was going to hit him. But I put my mouth up against his ear and whispered something very unpleasant that I'd been told about his personal life. He literally blanched.

Then I slapped down on the table a fifty to cover the meal with a generous tip, and left the restaurant with the little maître d' hurrying after me to ask if anything had been wrong with the meal or the service.

It was only five or six weeks after that lunch that the manuscript arrived. It had been pushed through the mail drop of the front door of my London house and was marked "By hand." I receive numerous manuscripts from would-be authors. Any successful author will tell you the same. In most cases I send them straight back. I would have done the same with this one, only there was something about the cover letter that caught my fancy. And I was intrigued by the title.

> *18 Mafeking Terrace*
> *Walthamstow*
> *Tel: (01) 806 3737*
> *12th June*

Dear Mr. Prentice,

I am taking the liberty of sending you the typescript of my first novel, *The Twister*, in the hope of benefiting from your advice about finding a publisher. I have followed your career as a novelist with great interest for a number of years and I think I have learned much from it. I intend to become a successful author, and your example has been an inspiration to me. I will frankly admit that I have no taste for the grotesque posturings on the high wire of literary fashion of some of our most "serious" novelists, who are so terrified of the banality of a large readership. I hope you will find my novel a respectful imitation—might I even say an *hommage?* Allowing for stylistic differences, I'd like to think that it could almost be mistaken for one of your own novels.

I know nothing about publishing or agents or contracts, so would be grateful for any advice you might feel disposed to give me.

You will be the first person to read this typescript, and I have no intention of sending it to anyone else until you have read it. If you do not have the time, may I ask you not to pass it on to your publisher or agent but to return it to me or destroy it.

Yours in anticipation,

William Henry Ireland

I sat down and read the manuscript as soon as I could find the time in an unbelievably busy schedule. This is the story I read:

The novel was about a young and penniless aspiring author called Thomas Chatterton who had written a thriller with a political setting. This was the first novel he had finished and he had never published anything. He sent it to a well-known and highly successful writer of similar novels—thrillers with a political background. In the cover letter he proposed that they should meet to discuss it if the best-selling novelist liked it. The successful novelist was a cabinet minister who was well known for writing novels in his spare time. His name was Godfrey Bellamy.

Bellamy was the Secretary of State for Defense and therefore the person in the government that was negotiating a crucial top-secret deal that was vital to the defense of the country. (In the part of the novel that dealt with the world of politics, Ireland revealed his obvious lack of firsthand knowledge of the inner workings of government. But there was nothing here that couldn't be fixed by someone with the requisite expertise.)

Bellamy read the manuscript—which was called *The Sting in the Tale.* I was, of course, struck by the coincidence that it was almost identical to the title of my first and unpublished novel. Bellamy liked it enough to suggest to Chatterton that they should, as suggested by the younger man, meet for lunch. At that meeting he told Chatterton how much he admired the novel. Chatterton explained that he was married with a young family and that he desperately needed money. His job as a clerk in the planning office of a London borough provided him with barely enough to keep his wife and children. Plus he had a glamorous and demanding young mistress. These were the preliminaries to his main point: He made to Bellamy the astonishing proposal that he, Bellamy, should publish the book as his own and that they should share the profits.

Bellamy was taken aback by this, and his first instinct was to dismiss the suggestion out of hand. But Chatterton pointed out to him that his readers were avidly waiting for a new title from him. Had he the right to go on disappointing them simply because his ministerial responsibilities were taking up so much of his time? This made Bellamy stop and think. The relationship between an author and his readers was a wonderful one, he reflected, in the way it took on a life of its own like a plant or a tree, but like a plant it needed careful watering or it would commence to pine and fade. Chatterton's views chimed with his own, and the young man now put his finger on something that Bellamy had himself pondered when he asked, How long would even Bellamy's devoted readers stay loyal without another title of his on the bookshop shelves?

Chatterton said he was sure that the cabinet minister would insist upon a thorough rewrite of the manuscript in order to give it the inimicable quality of a Bellamy title. In fact, he would probably want to do this personally. He was sure that Bellamy would not abrogate his ultimate responsibility for the text, because it was his name on the title page. And that, ultimately, was what his readers were buying: the Bellamy brand name. If Bellamy was satisfied that the title was of adequate quality to fully justify that brand name, then there could be no sense in which he was cheating his customers.

Bellamy had reservations, but eventually Chatterton succeeded in convincing him that there was no risk involved. Bellamy admitted that he had been far too preoccupied with great affairs of state to find the time to knock off a novel. And after some reflection, he had to confess to himself that he couldn't see any catch.

Before agreeing to the deal, Bellamy insisted upon certain

conditions. He made it clear that his integrity and artistic conscience required that there should be some changes to the story and to the title and so on before he could contemplate its being published under his name. Chatterton readily accepted all the changes. One of them was that the title of the novel should be changed from *The Sting in the Tale* to *The Twister*.

The negotiations required several meetings. It so happened that at one of them Chatterton arrived with his beautiful young girlfriend. Although he left her to wait outside in his Nissan 200SX, she came in because she was naturally anxious to meet so distinguished a literary and political figure as Bellamy. She was fantastically beautiful with exquisite limbs and feet, and seemed awed and fascinated by the fame of the older man.

Well, Bellamy was a man who was not at all immune to female charms, and before long he had secured her telephone number, dined with her at his favorite intimate little French restaurant, and taken her back to his Westminster pied-à-terre. To his delight the girl was as eager for lovemaking as he was, and within minutes they were making passionate love and he soon brought her to a shuddering climatic organism. She left soon afterward. And as he tidied the room in which her perfume still lingered in the air, reminding him of the pleasures her youthful body had given him, Bellamy decided not to see her again. It would have been unfair to the girl.

Bellamy continued to meet Chatterton to negotiate with him, taking care not to let him know that he had seduced his girlfriend. Having finalized a number of artistic changes, the two writers came to an agreement about money. Chatterton insisted that it was to be paid in cash with no witnesses present. Bellamy was only too happy to agree. Everything went like clockwork.

As he had decided, Bellamy's affair with the girl was not continued after their one passionate lovemaking session. It was like she realized that to continue to see him would throw her life right off balance, and that was not a risk she was prepared to take. He found himself trying to forget her in the arms of other women, yet she haunted his memory strangely. The novel was published and met with considerable critical acclaim. For the first time, Bellamy's work was taken seriously by the literary editors of the so-called quality newspapers. The public, too, bought it in large quantities, the fact that it was written by a cabinet minister giving it an extra degree of piquancy.

Then one day—months after their last meeting—the girl came to Bellamy and made it clear that she wished desperately to give herself to him. Against his better judgment, he gave in, since she looked so attractive standing there in a low-cut dress and shoes that left much of her feet bare with her little toes peeking coyly out. When they had made love passionately and at length, she seemed reserved and quiet. He, on the other hand, was enervated and refreshed by their lovemaking as he always was. At last she said that there was something she had to tell him. She was in an impossible position because she had to betray either the man she loved and venerated (Bellamy) or the man to whom she owed several years of happiness (Chatterton) and whom she respected as a human being. But because she had fallen passionately in love with him, it was behoven upon her to tell Bellamy the truth.

"It's a sting," she told him. "You have been led into a trap. Thomas is not what he seems. He is an agent for the KGB, and the novel was written by them in Moscow."

"Why," Bellamy exclaimed, "that explains a lot. It explains why it contains errors of the kind that the KGB would make about the workings of a democratic society."

The girl nodded and went on: "I'm sure you understand the purpose of the sting. The KGB will expose you as a plagiarist unless you do what they want. The price of their silence will be that you must betray your country over the secret defense deal."

The fact that she knew of the existence of this highly secret deal was proof enough for Bellamy that she was telling the truth.

Now in tears, the girl—whose name was Annabel—told him it was too late for him to save himself. He must be aware that he was in a hideous situation. Either he betrayed his country to its enemies and caused it incalculable harm or he allowed himself to be humiliated and disgraced in public and his political and literary careers would both be at an end at a stroke. Plus his wife would find out that he had had an affair. And how would she react to finding herself married not to a man admired by millions but one humiliated and disgraced?

But to her astonishment Bellamy appeared unmoved. When

she expressed surprise at his calmness, he told her that he was safe, since he had already taken steps to protect himself from being blackmailed and destroyed by Chatterton. And this was the ingenious twist that Ireland's manuscript exploited.

When they had made love again, Bellamy explained to the astonished girl why he wasn't worried about Chatterton's "trap." Some fifteen years before this time he had written a novel—his first—whose setting and cast of characters were very roughly similar to the one that Chatterton had offered to him. The plot was, of course, totally different, although it was also a political thriller involving a cabinet minister and featuring blackmail and so on. It had never been published. Its title was *The Twister*. When he had finished it, he had showed it to a distinguished political figure with an interest in publishing. This was none other than Sir Harold MacLennan. He had liked it but had urged him not to publish it at that particular time.

So, Bellamy now explained to the astonished girl, he had not been as naive as Chatterton and the KGB had imagined. For when the issue of his publishing Chatterton's book under his own name first arose, he had contacted this distinguished elderly figure and reminded him of that manuscript, saying he thought the time had now come when he could safely publish it. The old gentleman, whose mind was as sharp as a razor, had confirmed that he remembered *The Twister*'s title, characters, and setting very well—but not so well that he would remember that the novel recently published under that name was not the one he had read fifteen years ago.

Bellamy went on to inform the girl that this was why he had told Chatterton he wanted to make just a few changes for artistic reasons. In short, he had insisted upon Chatterton changing the title, the names of the central characters, and some of the incidents in the story just enough to fit that unpublished manuscript. All he had to do now to escape the blackmailing trap sprung by Chatterton was to cite no lesser an authority than Sir Harold as a witness. The old gentleman would be prepared to say in public—in a court of law if it came to that—that he recalled reading *The Twister* some fifteen years ago, and Sir Harold was nothing less than the most respected elder statesman in British public life.

The girl appeared relieved, and when they had made love

again and he had brought her to another series of shuddering organisms, she left him. I quote again from Ireland's manuscript:

> When the girl had gone, Bellamy stood looking out the window. He had told her the truth, but not the whole truth. He remembered it now and smiled as he recalled his conversation with the old gentleman all those years ago. There had been no need to tell the girl the whole of it.
>
> "Don't publish it," Sir Harold had said. "I'm not saying it isn't a decent enough piece of work, but it will harm your career. You wouldn't be taken seriously as a politician. If it was totally top-notch, that might be a different matter. But frankly it's not. For one thing, the plot doesn't hang together that well. I don't read much of this kind of thing myself, but I'd say it's too damned implausible."
>
> Bellamy had asked, "Do you mean the business of the Master of the Queen's Musick being a KGB agent?"
>
> The old man had looked at him piercingly with those steel-blue eyes that had once impaled the blustering leaders of the Soviet Union like so many frightened rabbits and, just like he hadn't heard him, he had said, "As a novelist, you've still got a lot to learn. Whatever you may be in politics, in literature you're no Trollope."
>
> "I respect your judgment, sir," Bellamy had said. "But I'm sure you'll agree that if I don't publish the book and take the brickbats that follow, I won't learn from the experience. I'm prepared to risk a little humiliation."
>
> The old gentleman had paused.
>
> "I respect that," he had said after a while. "And I can see you're determined. (You're a very determined young man.) So I'm going to do something that might be damned stupid. I'm going to take the risk of divulging something to you I learned on Privy Council terms. I'd get into very deep water if it ever came out. Do you understand?"
>
> "I do, sir," Bellamy had replied. "I'm very grateful. And I give you my solemn word that no power on earth will make me betray you."
>
> "There is a serious obstacle to publication," Sir Harold had then explained. "The idea of a prominent KGB agent being employed by Her Majesty as a senior member of Her Household is not too improbable to publish. The truth is, it's too sensitive to publish—at least in a novel by someone in your exalted position."
>
> Bellamy must have betrayed his astonishment at this for the old

gentleman had quickly gone on: "I am not at liberty to say any more at the present moment except that you must take my word for it that there are grave considerations of national security—not to mention the danger of causing serious embarrassment to the highest in the land."

In short, Bellamy reflected now as he stood gazing out the window at the London skyline, he had anticipated nothing less than the scandal involving Sir Quintin Parrott, the distinguished composer and Master of the Queen's Musick who was in fact a Soviet agent. He was one of that generation of homosexual Communist sympathizers usually known as the Homintern, recruited at Cambridge in the 1930s, who had cold-bloodedly betrayed hundreds of our agents to their deaths. The Queen was deeply embarrassed, but the government dared not expose him or even secretly dispose of him because that would signal to the Soviets that his role as an agent was known.

That was one of the finest scenes in Ireland's manuscript. After this the novel moved rapidly and somewhat implausibly toward its climax. The crucial thing was that Bellamy had not foreseen that the girl would be forced by Chatterton to reveal what he had told her about the precautions he had taken against being blackmailed.

The following weekend Bellamy was a guest at the country house of none other than Sir Harold MacLennan himself. This had come about because he had gone to Sir Harold to ask him to be prepared to give evidence and to "refresh the old gentleman's memory."

Bellamy happened to go into the library just before lunch and to his horror found the former statesman laying dead on the Persian rug. His killer was still standing there with the gun in her beautiful hands—for it was none other than the girl, Annabel. She was standing there with her feet quite bare.

When she saw him, she threw herself into his arms. In floods of tears she told him she had been forced to commit this murder by Chatterton and his superiors in the Russian Embassy. She had stolen into the house in bare feet. Bellamy debated within himself whether to hand the girl over to the authorities and thereby try to save himself from ruin. But looking at her tearful face, he knew he could not betray her. So when they had made passionate love, he allowed her to escape, telling her he would give her an hour before he alerted the rest of the household to the terrible tragedy.

Left alone with the body of his witness, Bellamy saw that he was trapped and his political hopes were over. Here in this great mansion where prime ministers had settled the future of nations, his own ministerial career had ended. At last, with a trembling hand, he pressed the bell that brought the white-faced butler to the door.

What he had feared soon occurred. A few days later his alleged plagiarism was gleefully exposed in one of those left-wing highbrow newspapers that get many of their stories—and most of their income—from Moscow. It was backed up with ample documentation and an interview with Chatterton, masquerading as the innocent victim of a literary theft. So it was behoven upon Bellamy to resign his high office, taking leave of a sympathetic monarch at a brief but moving ceremony at the palace. As an added source of pain, he had to look on while the defense interests of the country were adversely affected by his alleged misdeeds. Moreover, his party lost the general election, which shortly followed at least partly as a consequence of the publicity campaign whipped up by the hyena media against Bellamy.

In the final pages of the novel Bellamy, abandoned even by his wife after the revelation of his affair with the girl, gazed out of the window of his Oxfordshire mansion into the garden and then took his father's shotgun and put an end to his life. He had taken the most honorable way out.

When I had read the manuscript, to be frank I was deeply impressed. Granted, there were things that needed changing—glaring faults of youth and ignorance that cried out for the hand of an older and more mature craftsman. Above all, the final sequence—for all that the closing chapter describing Bellamy's suicide was well written and deeply moving—was all wrong. Everything I knew about politics and life told me that a man of Bellamy's gifts and experience—a cabinet minister, a best-selling author, a man with an irresistible fascination for women, in short, a man of the world—would not have behaved like that. These reservations apart, I saw that this was exactly the "twister" I had been looking for. If Ireland had failed to fully exploit the potential of this story, yet the artist in me recognized what could be done with it.

Plus I saw the Ireland manuscript as an opportunity to edge my name a little up-market. For with this material, I felt I had the opportunity to convincingly demonstrate that I could write well—as well as the best of them.

One element in the manuscript that I certainly didn't care for because I thought it was too clever by half was that the novel that Chatterton had written, *The Sting in the Tale*, followed almost exactly the plot of *The Twister* itself. In summary it was this:

An obscure and penniless young man called Thomas James Wise wrote a political thriller and sent it to a best-selling novelist who was also a successful politician with a place in the cabinet and who was called Giles Honeyford. Wise proposed that Honeyford should publish it as his own and that they should share the profits. All of that was pretty much as in *The Twister* itself. The two novels diverged sharply, however, at the point where Wise's girlfriend told Honeyford that Wise was about to blackmail him on behalf of the KGB. At that point, instead of having his own defenses against blackmail already in place— which was the cleverest element in the plot of Ireland's own novel—Honeyford had no defense against Wise. In a pretty banal bit of writing, Honeyford therefore decided to murder his blackmailer, and from this point onward the novel's only interest lay in his attempt to do this without incriminating himself.

All of this was, as I think is very clear even from my brief account of it, much weaker even than the ending of Ireland's novel, since it sacrificed the clever twist and instead introduced the highly improbable notion of a highly placed political figure attempting to commit murder.

However, the method of murder was quite well thought out. It centered on sailing and used this setting pretty well—with the important reservation that it was quite clear to me as a yachtsman of no small experience that Ireland knew not the first thing about boats and had made a basic and ludicrous blunder.

This was how it worked: Honeyford arranged to meet Wise on some pretext, and since their meeting had to be secret, it was not unreasonable to suggest a lonely place. After carrying out some careful recces, he chose an isolated country pub a few miles inland from the port of Weymouth. Honeyford kept his yacht, *The Cock-a-Hoop*, at Poole, about six or seven hours' sailing around the coast, and just before his appointment with Wise he sailed his boat to Weymouth, leaving his car at Poole.

Honeyford had sailed in and out of Weymouth a number of times, so he knew the harbor well. But he had not done so for several years, and then it was in a different boat, so he was unlikely to be recognized or remembered on this occasion. He docked at the town quay and was just in time to catch a bus to the pub, since he had carefully reconnoitered the area and knew the routes and times of the infrequent buses. There he met Wise, who had come by car. Honeyford told his victim that he had been dropped at the pub by a friend. When the meeting was over, Wise—as Honeyford expected—offered to drive him back to Weymouth. When the two men got there, Honeyford invited Wise on board to look over his boat.

It was low tide, so as they clambered down the twelve-foot ladder from the quay, Honeyford warned Wise to be careful. He didn't want him to slip and break a leg! Once they were aboard, Honeyford suggested they go for a brief sail. Wise agreed.

Because it was a little breezy, Honeyford gave Wise a pair of sea boots and some oilskins. So he took off his shoes and put on the boots instead, and then donned the oilskins over his own clothes.

While he was doing this, Honeyford suddenly exclaimed that he had lost his keys and must have dropped them in the car. So Wise lent him his car keys, and Honeyford went back to where the car was parked on the quay. Unseen by Wise, he left on the front seat of the car a typewritten suicide note: "I'm very sorry for any inconvenience I might cause."

Then the two men sailed out to sea. When they got around the corner and into the bay, the sea became quite choppy because the wind was stronger than expected. Honeyford told Wise the boat was carrying too much canvas and they should get some off her. They would change down to a smaller sail.

For what he had in mind, Honeyford had to get his man out of his sailing clothes. So he asked Wise to go out on the foredeck and change the sail while he stayed in the cockpit to steer, since they were sailing out of the harbor past various buoys. As Honeyford had anticipated, Wise got wet through in spite of the oilskins and boots. When they were safely out at sea, it was therefore not at all surprising that Honeyford should invite Wise to go into the galley to change.

While he had his boots and the jacket off, Honeyford—who was peering in at him from the cockpit—called out to him to come back on deck immediately.

"You've left a halyard flying loose!" Honeyford shouted. (In fact, of course, Honeyford had seized his chance to open it himself when Wise went below.)

He asked him to go forward and secure the halyard while he continued to steer. While Wise was balancing himself to do this, Honeyford seized his opportunity and swung the wheel hard down. He had intended to throw his victim off balance and topple him into the sea, but Wise managed to hold on.

"Sorry, old man," Honeyford shouted. "I didn't catch that wind shift."

He saw on Wise's face a sudden expression of fear and realized that he had aroused his intended victim's suspicions. But, remembering the other man's ignorance of boats, he had an idea for making Wise bring about his own nemesis.

So he suggested to the much-rattled younger man that they change places.

"You take the wheel," he called out. "You'll be safe here. I'll look after that halyard."

Wise gratefully came aft and took the wheel.

So Honeyford went forward and made himself busy with the lines while the boat was heeling and bouncing, smashing into the waves as a yacht does when it's close-hauled and going to windward.

Then, watching the sea and choosing his moment carefully, he called out to Wise imperiously: "You're not steering up to the wind. Come to starboard."

He did a pantomime with his arms to indicate what the other man should do, and Wise obediently turned the wheel hard in the appropriate direction so that the boat tacked through the eye of the wind. Instantly the mainsheet snapped quickly across and caught Wise off balance. He only had one hand on the wheel. Then, as the boat came through the wind, she heeled suddenly the other way, helped by a timely gust.

Just as Honeyford had hoped, Wise was pitched overboard. As

he went over, his hand flailed wildly for the guardrail but missed, and he was launched into the icy water.

Calmly Honeyford came back to the cockpit and started the motor. The west-going tide was commencing and he knew that Wise would be swept into the race and drowned somewhere off the Portland Bill—that is, if he wasn't killed by the cold first. And so he coolly sailed back to Poole. Nobody there knew or cared where he had been, and his car was waiting for him. A day or two later Wise's body was washed up in Lyme Bay, as Honeyford had expected. Meanwhile, of course, his car and the suicide note had been found at Weymouth. All the evidence indicated that he had gone there with the intention of taking his own life. It was assumed that he had walked along the shore looking for a quiet place to do it unobserved and had probably gone into the water at Chesil Beach, where the current would quickly pull him out into the race. The police had no reason to question this reading of the evidence.

The net effect was that Honeyford had published a best-seller and eliminated the only man who had the power to blackmail him—and he had done it without any possibility of detection. Honeyford had committed the perfect murder.

This was much more satisfying than the ending to Ireland's novel itself in which Bellamy committed suicide. What was particularly attractive about this was to see the victim turning the tables on his blackmailer. Yet a murder by a man in Honeyford's exalted position struck me as damagingly implausible. Already the writer in me was beginning to see how the best things in the two stories could be combined.

Once again, Ireland had got a good story but had marred it by his lack of technical expertise. It was just like the way his inadequate grasp of politics marred the story of Bellamy and Chatterton. Here he had made a silly blunder that nobody that really knew about yachts would make. I suspected that he had learned everything he knew about writing from books.

I called Ireland and suggested we should meet for lunch. Sounding surprised, he agreed, and I named a restaurant pretty much off the beaten track in a little corner of Soho. (To be frank, it was one I'd used a few times for assignations where absolute discretion was necessary.) I was particularly anxious to have no witnesses to this meeting.

When he came in, I quickly apprised him. Visually, he was perfectly innoculous. He seemed like a man who would be fairly complacent if handled properly. He looked like exactly what I took him to be: a clerk in the planning office of a London borough. He was a small man, slightly built with thinning hair and a worried expression. He had a small nose and surprisingly large ears. The restaurant was anything but an expensive place, but it looked to me like he wasn't used to even that standard of food and service. He sat down and we made small talk before anything was said about his typescript, which laid on the table between us.

All the time that we talked, I was assessing him without giving him any indication of what I was doing. I like to think I'm a good judge of character. It comes from my training as a novelist. It became clear to me that he was a bit of a dreamer. He was obviously quite intelligent, but not what I'd call clever. His knowledge of the world was fairly limited. And he tended to live in a world of books. As I had suspected, he had no agent and was clearly unfit to represent himself. I felt that he wouldn't be too difficult to deal with.

I could see he was on tenterhooks to know what I thought of his novel, and in order to frighten him a bit, I said to him, "You don't know much about yachts, do you?"

He readily admitted that he had based Honeyford's murder method on a report he had read of an inquest—or perhaps it was a trial—mentioning about someone that had died accidentally while sailing a yacht. He had fallen overboard because he had turned the wheel too far and the boat had tacked through the eye of the wind. (This confirmed my impression that in Ireland I was dealing with a talented amateur.)

I told him I had guessed as much, since I had spotted an enormous howler.

He asked what it was, but I told him he was going too fast.

When I felt I had kept the poor young fellow on tenterhooks for long enough, I patted the manuscript and said, "You've certainly got some talent. Some of this is quite Prentice-esque, if I may say so."

He was almost pathetic, so manifest was his gratitude and relief, now that he knew that I had a good opinion of his novel.

I cautioned him that there were problems but told him I

thought I could make something really quite good of his material. It would need quite a lot of work, but I felt that the potential was there in the story and the characters. I said I was prepared to give his material my most full-hearted support.

He took a long time to understand what I meant. At first he seemed to be amazed, and then, when he had overcome his initial astonishment, he professed to be high-mindedly outraged. He talked a great deal about artistic integrity.

I told him he could get up and walk out of the restaurant right now and nothing more would be said. He had no way of proving that I had made the suggestion I was now putting to him. Or he could stay where he was and very probably become a rich man.

He stayed, but he continued to protest, saying I was planning to perpetuate what he called "nothing less than a calculated and cynical fraud upon the reading public."

I told him as mildly as I could that I had no intention of perpetuating any sort of fraud. Firstly, my readers—my many readers—were avidly awaiting a new title from me, and I had only proposed this because of my desire not to disappoint them. The relationship between a writer and his readers is a very wonderful and a very precious one, I told him. And I said I hoped he would someday come to appreciate that himself.

Secondly, I pointed out that no deception would be involved since my name on the cover of a book was nothing more nor less than the guarantee that it was of a certain type and quality—just like a trademark or brand name. How the title came into existence was of no more concern to a reader than it was to me to know how my Bentley had been made. The trademark itself was a warranty of quality.

Thirdly, I personally would not profit financially from the book in any way whatsoever. My main motive was to expose the Communist agents from the so-called Homintern of the 1930s that were still occupying positions of power in British society. And my share of the proceeds from the book would go straight to the party's treasurer to boost campaign funds for the next election. (Had things not turned out as they did, that would certainly have been what would have happened to the money, after a deduction to cover my expenses and the cost of my time.)

And fourthly, his material was going to have to be thoroughly revised anyway to give it the distinctive quality of a Prentice title, so the process of composition would not be very different than my usual one.

Normally, I explained, I would write a two-page design specification of a new title, and then my researchers would block in the prose. Naturally, I did not abrogate my ultimate responsibility and took complete charge in person of the quality-control process. As such, I would keep requiring rewrites until the product matched the quality my readers are entitled to expect. After all, it's my name that goes on the cover and that's where the bucks stopped. I pointed out that the same procedure was followed in the studios of the great masters such as Michelangelo and Raphael, who would sketch out the overall design and then have assistants paint in the details. He nodded, and I saw that I had persuaded him. In this instance however, I continued, Ireland had done the developmental work on the original concept and what I was therefore proposing was simply to buy the manuscript as it stood. This was no different than a manufacturing company buying in from a supplier materials of a quality that it would cost it an uneconomic amount of time and money to produce itself. In short, I was offering to make an outright purchase of Ireland's raw background research.

He agreed to this in principal, provided other conditions were satisfactory. Before we got down to discussing details, I warned him that there would have to be extensive changes to his material—some for artistic reasons but others, frankly, for commercial reasons. I explained that I wanted to change the novel's title and the names of some of the major characters, and I wanted to make some changes to the story. The book's title was to be *The Sting in the Tail.* And I wanted the names changed in this way: Annabel to Anita, Sir Quintin Parrott to Sir Cecil Reckitt, and Godfrey Bellamy to Geoffrey Sadleir-Brown. Ireland readily agreed to the changes of title and names, but said he would not agree to a deal until he knew precisely what changes to the story I was planning to make.

I found this proprietorial attitude rather irritating and, frankly, unbusinesslike, but I had no choice but to exceed to his request.

"For example," I said, "the girl doesn't come alive as a character. We need to know more about her past and her relationship with Chatterton."

He agreed that I was right about this.

I said I would make the most straightforward changes of this kind and would think about what needed to be done to improve the structure of the book. So we arranged to meet again at the same restaurant in a couple of weeks to discuss them again.

I mentioned to him that he was very welcome to bring a girlfriend along, but he said nothing.

I told him that absolute secrecy was essential. Nobody else must know that me and him had ever been in communication. Ireland insisted that he fully appreciated that it was in his interests as much as mine to keep quiet about his role in furnishing some of the raw material for the title, because my readers would not buy the book unless they knew I was the author.

I wasn't taken in by this. I knew Ireland, however unworldly he was, must have realized that he could make more money out of blackmailing me than out of sharing the profits on the book.

In the three weeks that followed, I worked hard. Damned hard. I wrote every single word of the new material myself. I was not prepared to entrust any of the rewriting to one of my assistants because of the need to ensure absolute secrecy.

I took the trouble, moreover, to do some "product-placement" deals. (I pride myself that I'm one of the first authors to have spotted the potential of this exciting new marketing tool.)

As far as the larger question of the plot was concerned, I knew that I had to make some major structural changes. But at this junction I was stumped and couldn't see my way clear to the solution. It was, however, fairly easy to rewrite the love scenes between Bellamy (now to be called Sadleir-Brown, of course) and Chatterton's girlfriend: As they stood, they just weren't convincing. To be totally frank, I wasn't sure that Ireland knew much about women, that he knew what a woman really wanted. And as I had said to him, the girl needed to be more fully described and better developed as a character. In these days of "women's lib" a writer can't any longer get away with treating women as nothing more than beautiful sex objects in his books.

When I'd finished with the scene where Bellamy invites the girl back to his flat, I was really quite pleased with it. This is how it now went:

His wife and children were out of town at his Oxfordshire country house. He was alone with the girl. And now, like so many young women, she didn't know whether she was going to give herself to him or just torment him with her beautiful young body.

He had resource to his well-stocked drinks cabinet, and as they toyed with their glasses of Snodgrass's Royal Cognac—the brandy that's drunk by connoisseurs—in front of the roaring log-fire, the conversation turned to literature.

"I've read all your books," she said. "I suppose you know they're fantastic?"

"I've never believed that until this moment," he answered, gazing at her with frank admiration.

She was tall and blond with legs that seemed to go on forever until ending in two exquisite feet. Her face had the classical elegance of a Dior model. Her demeanor was proud, and she met Bellamy's gaze with an unswerving gaze of her own.

When he made his interest in her clear, she backed away, saying haughtily, "A man that will betray his wife will betray his country."

"Betrayal!" he echoed. "I'd be betraying myself if I didn't make love to you."

"Oh, God, Godfrey," she sighed. "What an irresistible man you are."

With that, she fell into his arms.

"Why are you here?" Bellamy suddenly exclaimed, while he was kissing her slender neck and bare shoulders. "A beautiful young woman like you? You could have any man in London at your feet."

She raised her beautifully sculptured head and looked at him proudly: "You're a powerful man. Don't you know that, Godfrey? I like power. It turns me on."

She brought her rubicose lips up to his, and they kissed passionately and with total abandon. Within moments she had slipped out of her elegant clothes—except for her high-heeled shoes, which were a vivid red—and was laying in all her beautiful proud young nudity on the stylish sofa, though her delicate feet, coyly peeking from the shoes, were still on the ground. He gazed at her slender body with frank and unconcealed delight. He bent over the girl and gently eased each foot in succession from its hiding place and then began passionately kissing her exquisite toes.

"Plus," she added with her eyes glittering with desire, "plus you're an Artist. A Great Artist."

Moaning with excitement, he pulled off his own clothes. She gasped.

"Oh," she said, "you're so big. Will you be gentle with me?"

As he made love to her, she moaned and twisted with pleasure. Her whole body throbbed with passion. She came convulsively again and again. And then again.

Afterward he laid prostate and drained beside her, and they smoked quietly, sharing a packet of Worcester King Size cigarettes, the coolest, longest smoke in the world.

Breaking the meditative, intimate silence that hung between them, Bellamy said to her, "Tell me about your relationship with Chatterton."

Her beautiful features darkened. She turned her lovely head slightly aside and said softly and wistfully, "He never made love to me so powerfully and yet so tenderly. In fact, we don't make love often now. And it was never as good as between you and I. Not even in the beginning." She gasped and then said in a voice choked with sobs, "He never made me come."

"What, never?" Bellamy asked in disbelief.

"No, never. For one thing, his penis is too small. Only four inches."

I liked that scene. It managed to suggest a great deal. Personally, I've never subscribed to the modern desire for explicitness, believing, with the Great Victorians, that you can write a highly erotic scene without using four-letter words. I deplore the recent trend for so-called literary writers to get down into the gutter and reveal what they do sexually.

I made several more improvements to the manuscript and, when the three weeks were over, went to the rendezvous with Ireland.

He arrived alone.

I said to him, "You haven't brought anyone?"

He smiled enigmatically and said, "I don't think you really want to meet my lover."

I said, "Oh, yes I do."

But he changed the subject rather clumsily.

I showed him the changes I had made, and to my surprise he was somewhat negative about them. Presumably from envy. He accepted them in the end, however.

Now we turned to the crucial structural changes that would still have to be made. The major change would have to be to the whole business of Bellamy telling the girl how he has taken precautions to prevent Chatterton from blackmailing him, and then being betrayed by her when she tells Chatterton and he has MacLennan murdered.

I told Ireland quite bluntly, "The cabinet minister wouldn't be so stupid and gullible as to trust the girl and so put into her hands the power to undo him. It's just not in character. The man is clearly fantastically clever and resourceful. He's a man of the world. He's had dealings with beautiful, dangerous women and knows just how far to trust them. Take it from me. I know that milieu."

Seeing that he looked doubtful, I added, "Believe me, readers are not like the Red Queen, who made herself believe six impossible things before breakfast in order to improve her credibility."

Ireland admitted that he had had reservations about the ending of the novel himself. He couldn't work out a satisfactory ending, he said, and seemed happy to hand it over to a more experienced writer.

He said, "I admit that it's a little clumsy that you have two old men figuring in the plot offstage—Sir Harold MacLennan, who is the distinguished witness who is murdered by the girl on Chatterton's orders, and Sir Cecil Reckitt, the Master of the Queen's Musick, who is a Communist spy."

I agreed. I felt that it was encouraging to see so inexperienced a writer being prepared to learn from an old hand.

We both wracked our brains for several minutes.

Then I remember he said, "What do you think of the names? Should we swap them around so that the old statesman is called Reckitt and the ex-Communist spy is MacLennan?"

"No," I said somewhat impatiently. "It needs something much more fundamental than just playing about with names."

Frankly, it seemed to me that Ireland was obsessed with names. He had the typical intellectual's obsession with words. I on the other hand have always been an action man.

We carried on thinking.

Then Ireland broke in upon my elucubrations, saying, "If only it were Reckitt that was killed instead of MacLennan, then Bellamy could publish the novel with no danger to national security."

When Ireland said that, suddenly it came to me in a flash. The answer was staring us in the face. I looked at him, but it was quite clear from his blank expression that he had no idea of the importance of what he had just said.

I now explained it to Ireland. My—frankly—brilliant idea got rid of the problem that Bellamy was naive in trusting the girl. Instead, it relied on the much more satisfactory idea that Bellamy didn't in fact trust her. Everything was the same, I explained, down to the moment when Bellamy told the girl about his distinguished witness who had read the similar story written by Bellamy years before and was prepared to give evidence to that effect. But in my version, Bellamy, as a man of the world, was clever enough to be suspicious of her, and so instead of revealing to her that this witness was the retired statesman, Sir Harold MacLennan, he told her it was the distinguished composer Sir Cecil Reckitt, whom he knew from Sir Harold himself to be a KGB agent.

The girl reported this back to Chatterton, and he murdered Reckitt without first consulting his paymasters in the KGB. In what I flattered myself was a nice twist, Chatterton was then himself killed by the KGB, which had come to the conclusion that he had betrayed them by murdering one of their most illustrious and best-placed tools. So in effect by the end of the novel Bellamy has pulled off nothing less than to trick the KGB into killing two of its own most dangerous agents.

When I explained this to Ireland, he said he wished he'd had the know-how to think of it himself. He said it was witty and elegant.

I now went off and rewrote the book along the lines I had proposed.

Ireland and me met again a couple of weeks later, and once again he arrived alone. Now, before anything else, we at last talked terms.

At first he said he wanted half of the royalties, but I told him that was an inappropriate formula when we were dealing not with a collaborative production but the purchase of material to be reprocessed. He accepted this point and pretty soon agreed to an outright purchase. We then settled on a figure. (He didn't seem to be particularly interested in the financial aspect, and at the time, I put this down to his somewhat head-in-the-clouds outlook.) I stipulated that I would pay the amount agreed in cash to him personally and with no witnesses present. He asked for used notes and suggested the meeting take place on Platform 3 of Victoria Station.

All we had to do now was to finalize the manuscript. It was strange that having agreed so easily on the financial arrangements, we ran into trouble over the revisions.

At first it seemed to go well. He accepted the new material we'd already discussed with no objections. But he took an irrational dislike to an entirely new sequence I'd written. I explained to him that I had always been worried about the flatness of the portrayal of Bellamy's relationship with the girl. One of the things that didn't emerge enough was her true feelings about him.

I said to him, "I feel strongly that this young woman was so fascinated by this sophisticated, worldly older man that she couldn't keep away from him. When he rejected her, because after Chatterton's murder of Reckitt he knew that she was a KGB agent and working to destroy him, her love would turn to hatred and she would try to kill him. And she'd do it by poisoning—an essentially female method of murder."

Ireland rejected this out of hand, saying that I was misrepresenting the girl. She wasn't savage and vindictive but a pathetic pawn who was wholly in the power of Chatterton. And then he said that in addition to that, he had what he called an "artistic distaste" toward poison. He said it was old-fashioned and reminded him of Dorothy Sayers and Agatha Christie.

We appeared to have reached deadlock and we became quite heated. Now I had to pull rank a little, and as a result Ireland became unpleasantly aggressive. He said that we had agreed to collaborate together on the revisions and he warned me rather nastily that if I betrayed him over this, then the whole agreement was subject to revision.

I didn't at all care for his tone and manner and told him so in no uncertain terms. I reminded him just whose name and reputation were going to be the book's selling point. Eventually he saw sense and calmed down. Then we got back to work.

Frankly, the plain truth was that I absolutely had to have poison feature in the plot, as I'll explain in due course. Now I had another bright idea and suggested as a compromise that I would drop the girl trying to poison Bellamy. But in exchange for this, it should be the girl rather than Chatterton that killed Sir Cecil Reckitt. She could do it by winning his confidence and then poisoning him. She escaped but was caught in some way by Bellamy and confessed to him what she had done.

Ireland commenced again to talk about how little taste he had for poison. He kept saying that poison was unsubtle and "not witty"(!). And then he referred to what he called a "monograph" entitled something like "The Principals of the Perfect Murder in Detective Fiction: Notes Towards a Logical Matrix" by some Scotch philosophy don, which apparently said that to use poison in a whodunnit was "cheating"! (I've read it since then, since I've had the leisure. And it has some interesting ideas.)

I was getting pretty exacerbated. I could see he wasn't the kind of person you could negotiate with and then stick to an agreement. So finally I said to him, "All right, no poison then. I promise."

Although I had told him I would give way to him about the ending, I knew in my heart that Ireland was wrong and I was right. I knew it as an artist. (Plus I needed poison.) The ending I had suggested was the right one. And it was my name that would appear on the cover.

And so I revised the manuscript along the lines that Ireland had tried to veto. For the murder of the Master of the Queen's Musick, I wrote a scene in which the girl went, unbeknownst to anyone, to Sir Cecil Reckitt posing as a Ph.D. student who was interested in writing about his work. When he offered her a drink, she slipped poison into it. She watched him die slowly and in considerable agony and then sneaked out of Buckingham Palace by a side entrance. As a result Chatterton's superiors in Moscow came to believe he had betrayed them. He was quickly kidnapped by the KGB, and the girl knew that they were now looking for her. She realized that she had been outwitted by Bellamy. And so in the final scene she came to Bellamy's flat, waited for him, and when he arrived, pulled a gun on him.

Almost hysterical with grief, the girl explained to Bellamy that if in the first instance Chatterton had forced her to seduce and betray him, yet the truth was that she had genuinely fallen in love with him. Now she was going to kill him and then herself because she knew she could not live with him and could not bear to think of him with another woman. Gently but persuasively Bellamy coaxed the gun from the hand of the weeping girl. He made passionate love to her and then, with tears in his eyes, handed her over to the authorities to be deported back to Russia, shuddering to think of the fate that awaited her there.

The publicity generated by the murder of a distinguished member of the Queen's household—although his identity as a KGB agent was not, of course, revealed—was huge, and Bellamy consequently made a fortune from the novel. And now, of course, he did not have to give any of it to Chatterton.

In the leadership contest within his party that took place soon afterward, Bellamy became leader and premier. In a rather nice final chapter the reader saw him being given a high honor by Her Majesty the Queen for having rid the country of two of its leading enemies—one of whom was personally embarrassing to Her Majesty. It was nothing less than a CH (Companion of Honor), which is in the personal gift of Her Majesty. And one that leaves such lesser honors as a KCB far behind in the shade. And then, to his inexpressible delight and pride, she was graciously pleased to tell him that on his retirement from political life—which she was generous enough to say she hoped would be far in the future—she would honor him with a hereditary earldom instead of the usual life peerage given to outgoing premiers!

For the sake of greater plausibility, I also rewrote the scene when Bellamy remembered his conversation with Sir Harold MacLennan about his first unpublished novel, and it now went like this:

> Bellamy smiled as he recalled his conversation with the old gentleman all those years ago when he had asked him his opinion of his first, unpublished novel:
> "Don't publish it," the old gentleman had said.
> Bellamy had blushed: "You think it isn't good enough, sir?" he asked somewhat timidly, for he had admired and venerated the elder statesman of his party from boyhood.

It was the older man's turn to blush.

"On the contrary," the much-lauded parliamentarian had snorted indignantly. "It's too damn good. That's the trouble. It would finish your career in politics. And I would really hate to see that happen. You're a fine young man," the elder statesman had said and then, his voice wobbling slightly, he had added, "You remind me of myself at your age." After a pause and a sniff he had continued: "You see, you'd be seen as a professional novelist, not a politician. A man that can write as well as you just wouldn't be taken seriously as a politician. Look at Disraeli. Plus the Tory party never has trusted an intellectual and certainly not an intellectual that writes fantastically brilliant novels."

I delivered the manuscript to my publisher, explaining that writing a novel of that type was a career first for me. When he had read it, he was even more excited about it than usual. He said that it added a whole new dimension to my work and that nobody could dismiss me now as a writer of mere potboilers. Frankly, I was a bit put out at that because I didn't think anybody had. And he'd certainly never said so before.

Then a few weeks later my agent called me with some fantastically exciting news: My publisher had decided to enter the title for the Booker Prize! The highest honor in fiction writing. And even to be short-listed was a gratifying achievement.

As if that wasn't enough, a few days after this was announced, the Prime Minister summoned me to Downing Street. That was not completely surprising, since I had been invited to receptions and luncheons and so on quite often. This, however, was to be a meeting simply between the two of us with only her senior personal assistant present. After some friendly small talk, she suddenly asked me if there was anything in my private or professional life that was likely to be exposed and cause a scandal. I assured her that this was not the case. (The truth is there were only a few very minor sins that I was sure she would consider venereal if they ever came out.) And then it was that to my delight and amazement she invited me to take on the role of her personal media and public-relations adviser, though she told me she was afraid this would mean that I would have even less time for writing. I told her that I was prepared to sacrifice even literature for the sake of the party and the country. She said she was sure my sacrifice would be widely appreciated.

A general election was imminent, and I was therefore kept pretty busy for the next few months by my new responsibilities. The election was just about to commence when the novel was released. To my delight, the reviews were the best I'd ever had. Plus the book was reviewed by papers that had previously ignored my work.

About a week after publication, Ireland broke all the rules agreed between us by telephoning me. The things that he said about my changes to the text hurt. Frankly, it hurt a lot to be accused of literary incompetence by a mere nobody. A man that had never published a novel in his life. And he made sarcastic remarks about the book being short-listed and said how much he'd love to win the Booker Prize. Him! As if *he'd* written the novel!

And then the little twister commenced to tell me how he was working on a "project" (as he called it) about an unknown author that lures a best-selling novelist into a trap! Of course, I assumed straight away he was writing another novel and was threatening to tell a lot of lies about me.

But I was not afraid of anything he could do. And now the time has come for me to explain why I was confident that I had outwitted him. It had been quite apparent to me from the moment I had received the typescript through the post that there was the distinct possibility that Ireland himself might do what Chatterton did when he tried to blackmail Bellamy. Nobody could blame me for taking measures to forestall any such move by Ireland. Indeed, it would have been reprehensibly negligent not to have done so.

Now, it happens that some years ago I wrote a novel that I never released. (This is the one I mentioned about to Aubrey Sackville and that was called *The Sting in the Tail.*) After reading the manuscript Ireland had sent, I looked in my files to see if I still had any correspondence from Chatto and Warburg, the publisher to whom I had first sent it and that had rejected it. I found there were two letters from them. In the first they had merely said they felt they were not the right house to publish the manuscript and would not be able to do it justice. I had written back asking why not, since everyone had told me they were the most prestigious and so I could see no reason why they would not be able to handle it effectively. In reply an editor had sent me a letter enclosing a report on the manuscript. At the time, I had been pretty furious. But I now saw to my delight that these documents described the novel with just the right mixture of detail and vagueness I needed.

Just for the record, here is the report:

> This manuscript is an attempt at the genre of political thriller. Its central figure, Sadleir-Brown, is "tricked into committing or collaborating with embezzlement," as the author puts it.
>
> Sadleir-Brown is a "brilliantly clever" young man who has worked his way from a "humble suburban background" to the highest counsels of the Conservative party. He is "handsome, sophisticated, a man as comfortable in morning dress at Ascot or in tails at Covent Garden as he was in a Norfolk jacket and Wellingtons out with a gun on a Highland estate." Having worked for several years in the City as a merchant-banker and thereby "accrued adequate wealth to comfortably enjoy a high standard of living" for the rest of his life, he has idealistically gone into politics and won a safe seat in a Sussex constituency.
>
> But now, during the period when his party is in opposition in the seventies, he decides to go into business. He does so not in order to make money, since he already has "an ample sufficiency" but, as he explains to a close friend, "in order to broaden my range of understanding of British commercial life." While he is looking around for something, he meets an attractive young woman, Anita, over cocktails at an embassy reception. Anita is a "fantastically beautiful" South American girl who was Miss Bolivia in 1973. She works as a political journalist. Soon they are having an affair. Anita introduces Sadleir-Brown to her father, who is, rather surprisingly, an English businessman called Cecil Reckitt. Reckitt is the managing director of a small financial investment house specializing in offshore trusts. Sadleir-Brown is attracted by the company, which he believes to be "a fantastic advertisement for capitalism and very advantageous to the small investor." And he has spent much of his professional life selflessly promoting the merits of capitalism as a guarantor of individual freedom. When

Reckitt invites him onto the board, he readily accepts. He waives any fees and stipulates that he make no money at all out of his connection with the company. To his delight, the company successfully exploits Sadleir-Brown's name to attract thousands of small investors to the business of equity-ownership for the first time.

For several months all seems to be going well. But then the girl begins behaving oddly. She makes strange remarks to Sadleir-Brown that he fails to understand. She is trying to warn him. Suddenly she tells him quite explicitly that he should not trust his partner, her ostensible father. The next time he meets her, he is horrified to find her injured, and although she insists she has had a fall, he gets her to admit that she has been beaten up. The quality of the writing can be judged from this scene:

> *"Who has done this to you?" he gasped.*
>
> *"Darling," she moaned in her exotic foreign accent, "I can't tell you. Don't ask me."*
>
> *Her injuries excited him to bursting point, especially her delicate little toes peeking out of the plaster that encased her right foot, and a moment later they were making love wildly, passionately, tearing off her bandages and reaching new heights of pleasure as he mounted her again and again.*

Anita tells Sadleir-Brown that she was instructed to strike up an acquaintance with him and lure him into an affair. She has done this for the KGB many times. But this time she has fallen madly in love with him and as a result she is now betraying her masters. She tells him that he has become the victim of a KGB "sting." She is an agent and her so-called father is not her father at all but a Soviet colonel in the intelligence service. To his horror, she confesses to him that in her capacity as a KGB agent, she has slept with many of the leading figures in British public life: newspaper editors, ministers, talk-show hosts, rock stars, bishops, peers, etc. She has done this in order to collect information to enable her KGB superiors to blackmail them.

Because she has gone too far in trying to warn Sadleir-Brown, Reckitt finds out what she has done and she is enticed to a secret rendezvous to which Sadleir-Brown is also lured. There she is poisoned by the KGB and dies rather slowly and very painfully. This all happens in the presence of Sadleir-Brown, and he is secretly photographed at the scene in a way that makes it look as if he poisoned her. So the KGB's sting threatens not merely to end his political career but also to land him in prison for many years.

Acting on what she has told him, he discovers that Reckitt has been committing fraud on a massive scale. All the money invested by thousands of little people has evaporated. He is placed in a dilemma: cover it up and try to keep it going in order to prevent the company's collapse, or blow the whistle.

Sadleir-Brown adopts the former course and so he tries to cover up the fraud for the most high-minded of reasons, but in doing so he unwittingly performs actions that can later be used against him to make it look as if he was committing fraud for his own benefit. Despite his efforts, the company goes down and thousands of people lose their investments.

Reckitt has so arranged things that he is in the clear while Sadleir-Brown is left to take responsibility. He is made bankrupt and instead of trying to save anything, voluntarily surrenders his private fortune, even though it is safely in a Swiss bank account. Despite this act of altruism, he has to give up his parliamentary seat. He goes to prison, a man publicly humiliated but borne up by the knowledge that his conscience is clear.

That was a fair enough summary of the novel, so it was all the more surprising that it was rejected. This was the letter that accompanied the report, and it was very offensive and highly unprofessional in its quite gratuitious spitefulness:

Dear Mr. Prentice,

Thank you for your letter, which, I'm afraid, reveals something of a misunderstanding of my previous communication.

I don't usually send my report to the author or take this amount of time over a manuscript that I'm rejecting, but in your case— unusually—I know who the author is. I realize that things have not been easy for you recently, and I admire your attempt to salvage something from the wreckage.

I strongly feel, however, that you will be wasting your time in attempting to write a novel based on your experiences, and I don't like to think of you doing that. I believe you underestimate the amount of skill and—yes, talent—required to write a publishable novel. I suggest you find a good ghostwriter and tell him your story. Stay as close to the facts as you can and try to exploit what I might call, in a somewhat Jamesian phrase, the lure of the lived fact. People will be interested to read your side of the story.

Although presenting your experience in the form of a murder story with a political setting is an attractive idea, I think there is a real problem of credibility. Sadleir-Brown's naïveté in getting involved with the fraud is, frankly, not believable. I simply don't accept that a successful politician would walk into an ambush as foolishly as he does. (Not even a trap baited with so attractive a character as you've intended the girl, Anita, to be.) And I similarly failed to believe in his altruism in declining to be remunerated for his time and efforts. I also found the revelation that the highly respectable and very English Cecil Reckitt was a KGB agent rather improbable. I'm afraid readers are not as obliging as the White Queen in Alice *who improved her credulity by making herself believe six impossible things before breakfast.*

I also found clumsy and improbable the secret meeting at which the Soviet agent is murdered. Moreover, the description of the victim's slow death is horrible. To be blunt, I don't at all care for your poisonous ending.

The signature was illegible, and after all these years I had forgotten the writer's name. But the letterhead was that of the publisher. I called Chatto and Warburg up and told them I was planning to revise for publication a manuscript I'd sent them many years ago. I wanted to know if they had any correspondence about it. Plus I wanted to know if they still had their copy.

They promised to search for these things and called back a couple of hours later to say they had found the letter but they had failed to find their copy of the manuscript, which, they assumed, must have been returned to me according to their invariable practice.

That was perfect. And so I had gone ahead and got Ireland to change the novel's title and characters' names to match the ones mentioned in the letter, which would therefore constitute proof that I had written the novel many years ago. Now, it should be clear that the reason I had to have poison feature in the plot was that it was referred to in the letter.

It's now beholden upon me to describe actions that might seem at first sight difficult to understand. But I felt morally justified in taking extreme measures. I had no doubt in my mind that I was the effective author of the title. I had taken an overwritten manuscript, marred by blatant mistakes in fact and with a clumsy ending, and using the skills of a master craftsman, honed it into shape and given it an ending that brought it to a thumping climax. I was in every important sense, as Shakespeare says, the "onlie begetter" of the property.

Now, it was clear to me that Ireland was going to falsely allege that he was the author. It was a kind of murder he was threatening me with—the murder of an artist's soul.

He had left me no option. I had totally no desire to take the action I did, but I was forced to neutralize him. It had nothing to do with the money. I could easily afford to pay him what we had agreed. But Ireland was trying to steal my literary glory, and I could foresee that his claim would have a superficial plausibility—particularly for those sections of the media that had long been conducting a vendetta against me. And now that I was playing a prominent role on behalf of the party, I had to think of its interests as well as my own. Even though Ireland's charge of plagiarism would be defeated in a court of law once I produced the letter from Chatto and Warburg, the mere accusation would make a nasty stink, and many would believe the charge. I could see the amount of damage that the fallout from the affair would do to the party and even to the Leader.

I knew only too well—none better—what a double-edged sword publicity could be. The very hacks that were ready to fawn on you one moment would stab you in the back the next and, like sharks smelling blood, drag you down into the gutter whence they come from theirselves.

I also want to make clear that what happened had absolutely nothing to do with the fact that the Booker Prize was within my grasp. I owe it to myself to say that I had a much less selfish reason for taking the course of action I did—misguided though I now see that it was.

So I laid my trap. I had to plan everything very carefully because, as that Scotch philosopher says in his little book, even the cleverest people can be tripped up by something stupid happening unpredictably. (Very wise words, as I have to admit in retrospect.) Determined, therefore, not to act precipitously, I planned it all very carefully, and I must admit that it was pretty ingenuous, if I say so myself. First I phoned Ireland and invited him to meet me in a pub not far from Chichester, which I had previously reconnoitered. I got him to come down by telling him that that was a good, quiet place for us to meet to discuss the differences between us.

I drove down to Littlehampton early in the morning and sailed my boat around to Chichester Harbor. From there I took a taxi to the pub. Ireland came in his car. We had a pleasant meal and a few drinks, and when I mentioned that I had to get a taxi back to the harbor, Ireland offered to drive me there.

When we reached the harbor, I invited him on board to have a look around. It was a fine day but rather choppy. I asked him if he fancied a sail and he said yes.

While he was putting on the waterproofs and sea boots, I told him I'd remembered that I'd left my newspaper in the car, so I borrowed his keys and went back for it. Then we sailed out into the bay.

I got him to sit in the bow, and so pretty soon he got soaked through. Then I invited him to come aft to the cockpit and gave him a drink—a Scotch, I recall—and we chatted while I steered.

I have this clear mental picture of him. He was sipping his drink and swinging his legs as he asked me these questions, smiling smugly at my answers.

Well, I suppose you remember how it went.

I said to him, "What about this project you told me you were working on?"

"What project was that?" he said with that irritating smile he had.

"The one about the best-selling novelist that's lured into some sort of trap by an unknown writer," I said.

"Oh, that," he said. "Let's talk about that some other time."

"I think we'd better talk about it now," I said.

"Well, I'm heavily involved in it," he said. "In fact, I'm working on it right now. You see, I work in TV."

"You're not a planning clerk?" I asked.

"Did I ever say I was?" he said.

That made me think. No, he never had.

Then I said, "You must be getting cold in those wet clothes. Why not go below and change?"

But he just smirked at me.

Then he said, "Do you want me to steer?"

"Yes," I said. "But you'd better change first."

He gave a sort of spiteful smile and said, "Did you remember the note?"

I pretended I didn't know what he was talking about and said nothing.

Then with an insufferable snigger he said, "I assume you left it in my car when you went back for your newspaper? Did you really think it would work?"

"What?"

"A man being thrown overboard by steering through the eye of the wind?"

"I've seen it happen," I said.

Frankly, I didn't like the turn the conversation was taking.

Then he said, "You think I don't know much about boats, don't you?"

"Yes," I said. "Nobody that sailed would have made that silly mistake you made."

Then he smirked again and said, "You mean, the one about it being high tide when Honeyford and Wise go on board the yacht, and then not long afterward it's a full west-going tide?"

I was pretty surprised, I must admit.

"I've sailed all my life," he said. "I have enough certificates to cover a wall."

"If you knew it was wrong, why did you write it?" I asked.

"You really haven't grasped it yet, have you?" he said. "That was part of the bait."

I told him I had no idea what he was talking about.

"If you hadn't got me here today," he said, "I was going to come forward to denounce you for having plagiarized *The Sting in the Tail*. Imagine the field day the papers would have had with that!"

I nodded grimly.

"Then you'd have produced that letter from Chatto and Warburg," he continued. "And claimed that it proved that you'd written the novel nearly ten years ago. The press would have loved all that."

I was paralyzed with astonishment.

"That's when you would have got a nasty surprise," Ireland said. "You remember that lunch you had with Aubrey Sackville when you told him about having had a novel called *The Sting in the Tail* rejected? Well, he got in touch with Chatto and Warburg and found out who had been the editor—the one you got sacked—and contacted him."

He grinned at me, cradling his glass and swinging his legs.

"It was *you!*" I exclaimed in a brilliant flash of illumination. My writer's intuition had helped me to see what he was implying.

He nodded.

Now I understood. He'd been the editor sacked for incompetence after I'd moved to Chatto and Warburg. He'd been nursing a grudge against me for years!

"So I was going to announce a press conference," he explained gloatingly. "And reveal to the world's press that I'd written the letter and could prove that it referred to a different novel than the one you've just published."

"How?" I asked, half guessing even as I put the question.

He sniggered and took his time before he said, "Because I'd produce the original manuscript that you sent to Chatto and Warburg and that I've still got. And it has your handwritten revisions."

I clasped my head in my hands. So that was what had happened to the publisher's copy!

"By now the media would have been in a lather for more revelations. And probably a general election would have been approaching, so you can imagine the amount of interest in all this that *The Mirror* and *The Guardian* would have been taking. I don't suppose you'd still be the Prime Minister's media adviser by this stage! And about now we'd hope to screen the TV documentary that I've been working on. This would tell the whole story. And there would be one further and dramatic revelation."

He looked at me: "Can you guess what it is?"

I shook my head.

"Aubrey Sackville was going to appear and announce that it was he who wrote the book."

"Sackville wrote it?" I gasped.

"He tossed it off in a couple of weeks. And he baited it with that business of Honeyford murdering Wise on board his yacht because he knew you had a yacht and he hoped you'd be stupid enough to try to use that method to kill me. I helped him on all the yachting business. I said I didn't think even you would be such a sucker as to swallow it, but evidently I was wrong."

My mind reeled. Once again, I had been made the victim of a sinister conspiracy.

"But why were you and Sackville collaborating?" I cried. "What's the connection between you?"

He smiled, and it came to me in a flash.

I shouted: "You're . . ." And then I said the word I had whispered into Sackville's ear in the restaurant.

He grinned at me shamelessly and said, "The girl in the story was based on me."

I was horrified by his insauciance as he made this revelation.

"But why did Sackville do all this?" I demanded. "When he could make more money publishing the novel under his own name?"

"Could he? Without your brand name on the cover? That's all that distinguishes your books from hundreds of titles churned out by nobodies every year. Could he have made more than by feeding the story behind the book to the media the way I've described? Think of the serialization rights. We've got the top agent selling them. Anyway, it was revenge Sackville wanted more than money. Both of us, in fact. And we're going to make a lot of money as well."

"Sackville might," I said, "but not you."

"What do you mean?" he asked.

And for the first time his cocky look wavered.

"Well," I said. "I didn't, as a matter of fact, think the business with the wheel would work. I didn't think you'd be stupid enough to fall for it."

"You didn't?"

I remember the expression on his face. He didn't like me saying that at all. Not at all.

"No," I said. "So I didn't intend to rely on it."

"What were you planning to do?" he asked in a sort of choking whisper, and I could tell his mouth had gone dry.

"I've done it," I said. "That Scotch."

He looked at the glass, and I swear he turned white.

"Dimethylethylene," I said. "Quite tasteless. And completely untraceable. It breaks down into pure alcohol. If they even do an autopsy, they'll think you drank a couple of bottles of Scotch to give yourself the courage to walk into the sea."

Then I remember he practically shouted, "You idiot! Where did you get that from?"

"A little chemist's shop in Manchester," I said.

"No," he shouted. "I meant, where did you get the idea?"

"It was in my original manuscript," I said. "Don't you remember? The girl is poisoned by the KGB. You said in your letter that you didn't like the poisonous ending. That's why I had to put into the novel the girl poisoning the old traitor. I had to have poison."

And he sort of shouted, "No, you didn't, you idiot! You didn't have to use real poison. That phrase could be read metaphorically!"

Then his voice dropped right down, and he said almost as if to himself, "I never had a taste for poison."

"Look," I said, feeling quite sorry for him. "You might as well jump overboard. You're dead anyway. But before you do, tell me something I don't understand. Why did you decide to tell me all this now? I mean, it's going to spoil your strategy for selling the story to the media." Then I added tactfully, "Spoil Sackville's, that is."

"On the contrary," he said. "It's going to be the centerpiece."

Then he corrected himself: "Was going to be."

Then he sort of laughed and said, "I suppose it still will be. Aubrey will make even more now. It'll be a wonderful piece of television."

Well, as everyone knows, he showed me the microphones and cameras that were hidden in various places on the boat, and he explained how our conversation was being transmitted to a mobile recording studio on the coast.

He said, "Smile, you're on TV." And then he explained, "We even had a camera placed in the car to shoot you placing the suicide note."

Then he commenced to feel the effects of the stuff.

Well, I don't want to go into the rest of it. It's hardly the most enjoyable thing in the world to watch a man die slowly and in agony, even if he is someone that has done you a grave wrong.

The stuff was supposed to be quick and painless, but frankly it really wasn't. At least, it didn't seem so to me. Just before he died, he said a funny thing. He sort of grinned—though he was in pain—and said, "And it was the *White* Queen."

After that he couldn't talk for quite a long time. But it was over at last. After debating within myself, I eventually decided to stick to the original plan and toss the body overboard in the hope that Ireland had been lying and that the cameras were fakes, or that if they were real, then for some reason they had not been transmitting. (The worst of it was that I had to pull off his sea boots and waterproofs to fit the way he was supposed to have committed suicide.) But of course the whole world has seen the film of me doing all that and then sailing my boat into harbor and being met by a posse of police officers and newsmen.

As you'll be able to imagine, I've had some pretty nasty experiences since that day on the boat. I won't dwell on them, because I'm not one to indulge in self-pity or waste time on pointless speculation about how things might have been done differently in the past than how they actually were.

It was a stroke of luck, really, the first trial being abandoned when the judge died suddenly. It gave me time to write a brief for my defense team. That was the first draft of what you've been reading. It will eventually be part of an autobiographical account of my life, which I flatter myself might be of no little interest. (I had a most unpleasant experience, incidentally, when Tarquin Bone, one of the top literary agents in the country, first fawned on me to get the book and then dropped me when he decided there was more money to be made out of Sackville's lying account of the affair than mine. But I'm not bitter.)

I'm not asking for sympathy. That's not my style. I just want people to know the truth. And, after all, this isn't the first time I've been knocked to the ground and trampled on. Just like before, I've kept on fighting and I'll be back again.

In a way I'm glad the whole long process of the successive judicious appeals is at last over. Frankly, the outcome shook my faith in British justice—the most fantastic in the world, as I still continue to believe. But I am confident I will eventually be vindicated one day.

I'm getting on pretty well here, all things considered. I'm

treated with quite a lot of respect. They've made me librarian, which is nice. The job is fairly sedimentary and leaves me plenty of time for writing. (I also work two afternoons a week in the cobbler's workshop, which I find fantastically gratifying.) The library is surprisingly good, and has almost all the novels of yours truly. I'm catching up on the great writers and already thinking about beginning a new novel. I don't want to say too much about it yet, but the hero is a man who is framed by his political enemies and has a furious struggle to clear his name and get out of prison in order to win back the love of the women in his life.

Of course the media have had a field day. They're pretty good at kicking a man when he's down. What most annoys me about the whole thing, though, is that people think I was made a fool of just because they saw me looking pretty uncomfortable on their TV screens that day on the yacht. In fact, the truth is I was too clever by half.

10

A Review from *The Daily Scot*

TRULY MIGHT THE AUTHOR OF THIS WORK CLAIM, IN THE words of the inimitable Oscar, that he put his genius into his life and reserved merely his talent for his art. It was to murder that his genius and his talent were alike devoted, but his greatest triumphs lay—alas for both his victims and his readers!—in the real thing rather than the fictional kind.

As a practitioner of what De Quincey called "one of the fine arts," the author of *Down on Whores* murdered with wit, with flair, and with originality, and kept his adopted city in a state of high excitement for many months. As a practitioner of whodunnits, he killed without inspiration, without excitement, and without purpose, and must have bored to death more readers than he killed.

While his fictional plots were plodding and derivative, the webs he spun to entrap his victims and baffle the police were possessed of genius. He struck again and again within his own neighborhood of Glasgow, and his victims were people closely connected with him, and yet he was never even a suspect.

Demonstrating a quite marvelous gift for improvisation, he playfully began to imitate—or, rather to parody—a television serial that happened to be being broadcast at the time. Finally he even succeeded in writing an episode of that serial that was intended—by the authorities—to entrap the killer. Instead, he turned it into an ambush for the man he had chosen as his final victim—the actor who played the detective pursuing the fictional killer! And then, with admirable sangfroid, he lured this unfortunate into his trap and killed him just around the corner from the cameras.

Your reviewer, of all people, must be permitted to point out that this is the second case in recent times of a novelist turning to murder. And in a somewhat tasteless and meretricious attempt to exploit this adventitious topicality, the publishers have put on the back cover the plaintive line *"I wish I'd written it!"* *(Jeremy Prentice)*. Poor as it is, yet it lies far beyond the abilities of the author of *Too Clever by Half.*

And it *is* poor. For in terms of murder, the author of *Down on Whores* does not measure up to Christie (Agatha) as a writer, albeit he gloriously outranks Christie (John Reginald) as a killer. And his achievement grows in stature posthumously, since to the respectable tally of four, two more victims have recently been added.

For he is now known to have murdered yet another colleague in his university's Department of Philosophy, one William Bentley. (It seems that the two philosophers had once nursed for each other a more than Platonic *tendresse* but later quarreled over a student Ganymede in whom they were both interested.) This was an absolutely *brilliant* murder—near to being perfect—which went undetected for several years because of the quite marvelous ingenuity with which the killer managed to disguise Bentley's death as suicide.

It seems he also murdered the colorful immunologist Professor Dugdale for a motive that is presumed to be connected with the famous Galvanauskas Affair, in which the two men were on opposite sides. Shortly before he himself died, Dugdale is believed to have engineered—by means of a feline boobytrap!—the death of a laboratory assistant with whose wife he was having an affair. For some time that "love tangle," as the tabloids have joyfully called it, misled the police into bringing charges against another of the wife's lovers. (Charges against him have been dropped, and the file on the case closed.)

Many have assumed that remorse drove Horatio Quaife to make his own quietus. The more cynical view of the police, on the contrary, is that he realized that he had betrayed himself by dropping his deerstalker with his name in it at the scene of his final murder. Lacking even the tiniest element of literary insight, our blundering bobbies have wholly and completely failed to perceive that, on the contrary, this was a last, gloriously Wildean gesture: He left his Holmesian calling card as a way of saying that without that "clue" the police would never identify him. And, surely, after that wonderful last murder scripted by himself and almost broadcast live on television, he knew he could never reach those aesthetic heights again.

No, it was neither remorse nor fear that led him to end his life but boredom. One sees that clearly in the wonderfully deadpan laconicism of the suicide note that he posted to the police before throwing himself into the river Clyde, for these are the words not of a frightened or penitent suspect but of an artist who, having alike tasted the bitterness of failure and savored the aroma of triumph, has grown weary of his calling:

> I'm sorry I killed so many people. I admit that it was somewhat tasteless—and certainly very inelegant. I suppose I was obsessed with the idea of the perfect murder. But what can I do now?

The manuscript of this novel was bizarrely found during a police raid on a pornographic bookshop that rejoiced in the rather divine—and appropriately Rabelaisian!—name of "Gargantua and Pantagruel." It was rescued by a literate police officer (*o rara avis!*) who, presumably because he was known to be bookish, had been assigned to the Obscene Publications Division. He recognized it as an unpublished sequel to Quaife's first novel, *The Right Lines,* when he spotted in the hero's name—"Clarence Titheradge Lovebone"—a link with the don turned detective-hero in that earlier book.

The manuscript was found in a dark corner of the shop in a large box upon which was marked in bold letters "Complete Works of Sir Walter Scott—edition of 1897 (pages uncut): £40." Under the benign though unwitting protection of Scotland's greatest novelist reposed the sole copy of this novel and, beyond peradventure, there it might have lain for many a long year. The mystery of how it came to be there has so far remained unsolved. With it was a list of addresses in that area of Glasgow indicating windows to watch—presumably for the selection and entrapping of future victims!

After all this the novel itself is sadly thin. In a desperate act of self-plagiarism it uses the idea in Quaife's first novel of a philosophy don investigating an actual murder. In this case Lovebone—the great-nephew of Clarence Titheradge in the first novel—investigates the so-called "Bible John" killings in Glasgow in the late 1960s. In so doing he encounters a man called Mungo MacSporran who is an amateur astrologer with "a passion for murder" and who works, oddly enough, in a bookshop called Keats and Chapman that sells pornography under the counter.

MacSporran is described—in one of the novel's rare moments of inspiration—as a strange little man "with child-molester eyes" and "a drooping gray mustache like two grubby lambs' tails." This distinctly unprepossessing individual has, like Lovebone himself, a link with the earlier novel in that he is the grandson of the driver of the train that took the participants in the Killiecrankie Mystery on their fateful journey to the cliff where Mrs. Armytage died. MacSporran turns out to be obsessed with the idea that his grandfather—a fanatical and teetotal Calvinist, given, Lovebone alleges, to demonic outbreaks of drinking and priapism—killed Mrs. Armytage for the most high-minded of reasons. MacSporran is also obsessed, it is eventually revealed, with the notion that his grandfather was none other than Jack the Ripper—"the first and greatest of serial murderers," as he calls him. Eventually Lovebone unmasks this grotesque figure as, quite absurdly, "Bible John" himself. For, piling implausibility upon improbability, it turns out that the repressed fantasist MacSporran is trying to carry on what he believes is his grandfather's noble work of "ripping whores." (To the challenge that the women he has murdered were not prostitutes, he ripostes, in his grandfather's tones of Calvinist fanaticism, that any woman who goes to a dance is a whore.)

Even had one not known the identity of the author, it would have been clear that this novel is the work of a man who was not merely obsessed with murder in the abstract but who took enormous pleasure in the real thing. The descriptions of killing inspire some of the best passages, and the novel's very faults arise, surely, from a dissatisfaction with merely verbal murder.

One wonders which impulse came first—the murderous or the fictional. Was Quaife murdering as a way of doing research for his fiction, or was he turning into novels his murderous urges and activities? Indeed, a thought occurs as one pens these very words. Could the novel—feeble as it is—be a final irreverent tease? A playful hint intended to help the police clear up a still-unresolved series of killings? One wonders, *tout court,* if our estimable officers of the peace have investigated the whereabouts of Horatio Quaife during the "Bible John" murders?

Auberon Saville

APPENDIX

Henri Galvanauskas's "Lo(o)sing the Signifier: Silence, Wordlessness, and Desire in Kipling's 'The Tongueless Boy' ": A Summary by Graham Speculand

Galvanauskas began by showing that the text of Kipling's story, "The Tongueless Boy," is phallic. For here, in one of his most important contributions to human understanding, Galvanauskas demonstrated that both a text and a reader must always be either "phallic" (master) or "emasculated" (victim). And he showed that there must always be a contest for authority in the struggle between a phallic reader and a phallic text. (The emasculated side of the equation need not detain us: The emasculated reader experiences pleasure in the acceptance of the authority of the phallic text, while the emasculated text yields everything to the reader immediately and without prevarication.) The phallic reader attempts to master the text by forcing it to make a "voluntary sacrifice" by which it accepts his authority. Similarly, the phallic text tries to entrap and to betray the reader by such strategies as remaining silent or lying or equivocating through the use of ambiguity.

This is how Galvanauskas expresses this crucial idea of the phallic text's resistance to being mastered, and I quote from the original transcript with my own emendations in square brackets in order to convey the corrupt nature of the transcripts of his seminars that were then in circulation:

> What is this gap, this silence, from which the phallic text speaks and yet is silent? What is it but the text's phallus?

What but, precisely and exactly, that phallic moment from which it has spinned himself like a disavowal, a lay [lie]. For what is a phallic text if not a lay [lie] which has to be demasked, his strategies witted out? [That is, *outwitted.*] Behind it lays [lies] the desire which is not the desire of the author for the author as Barthes has told us, is dead. (Consult also *Aphorism 28*: "Barthes is dead.") Nor any more the desire of the analyst-master, for the analyst-master has no desire other than, precisely, the desire that he demask the text. It is, rather, the desire of the text [*le désir du texte*]. In what, then, does it consist, the defeat, the mastering of this desire that we have designed [that is, *designated*] the desire of the text? It follows that it is by means of a wound, a rapture [rupture?]. From this wound, this gap where the analyst has demasked, has emasculated the text, or rather has extortured the text's own voluntary sacrifice, the text now, tongueless and aphallic, outters [utters] his truth-which-is-only-that-by-being-manifestly-a-lie. So much explains himself.

Since this text is phallic, Galvanauskas went on, it is duplicitous and untruthful. And so it constitutes a threat to the authority of the phallic reader. Yet, properly interrogated (or, as he liked to express it, "interrorgated") and induced to make its "voluntary sacrifice," the now no longer phallic text can be made to speak the truths that the analyst knows it holds (back).

Galvanauskas pointed out that at the center of Kipling's story is the idol through which the high priest speaks. The fact that the idol is silent until it is spoken through, Galvanauskas suggested, and the references to the enlarged "part" stolen by the boy, indicate that it has no tongue but that it "speaks" through its phallus. He took this as a metaphor for the self and the fact that truth is uttered not by the tongue (lingua) but by the instrument of desire (lingam).

There is, therefore, no unified self that knows itself and the world and that speaks with full knowledge of itself. Instead, one is always "spoken through" by the voice of desire. In short, there is no objective truth. And so all ideas of the self, free will, moral choice, morality, and so on he showed to be nonsense, demonstrating that there was only conflict with its consequences: power, will, struggle, capitulation, penetration, orgasm, and death.

The first conflict in the text is between Huxtable and the subprefect. And Galvanauskas pointed out that the anthropologist has come to the official not in order to invoke the authority of English political power (the raj) in the hope of averting the death of the boy. Rather, he has come precisely to lure its representative into a trap in which it will demonstrate its own futility and irrelevance by a display of blundering powerlessness. The subprefect falls into the trap because he believes that his task is to unmask the "truth" and that this is all that is necessary to resolve the situation satisfactorily.

And so the two men return to the village, where the subprefect, as has been stated, attempts to use Western logic to "save" the boy. He fails miserably, thereby destroying his own authority. The way is now open for a second and crucial struggle to be staged between Huxtable and the high priest.

For Galvanauskas this was the heart of the text, since he saw it as an account of the contest for authority that is central to all relationships.

What is at stake is the leadership of—authority over—the tribe. The high priest maintains power by speaking through the idol, and so his power is now threatened by the loss of its phallus, which is the Signifier of Authority. He is bent upon killing the boy because he is planning to sever his phallus and give it to the idol in order to restore the lost part and thereby regain his own authority.

But there is another conflict at issue. This arises from the challenge and betrayal involved in the relationship between the anthropologist and his boy servant. Galvanauskas's reading stressed the struggle of wills between master and servant and pointed out how the boy had been asserting his authority in defiance of his master: The boy had been late serving dinner—he has tried to starve his master. The boy has worn his master's long black gown—he has been trying to usurp his master's place. Finally he has stolen the crucial part of the idol in a blatant bid for power over the tribe and over his master. He has taken nothing less than the Signifier of Authority.

Given that there is no objective truth, there is always and inevitably a struggle for mastery of signification, which is to say "authority." All human relationships—personal as well as political—are based on a struggle for authority of this kind. And so every relationship involves a hierarchy in which only one party has authority at any given time. (This hierarchy is always unstable and, as we will see later, may be inverted.) Authority always derives from possession of the Signifier of Authority, which is the phallus. This is true of every relationship: master/disciple, analyst/analysand, interrogator/interrogee, bourgeoisie/proletariat, and—as we shall see later—reader/text.

Authority, as we have seen, derives from possession of the phallus because: "While the tongue can only lie, only the phallus 'speaks' the Truth of Desire" (*Aphorism 8*). (Hence, incidentally, Galvanauskas showed that "Woman is tongueless" [*Aphorism 9*]. That is, she has no phallus and therefore does not speak. This was why women were literally not allowed to speak during his seminars and analysis sessions. Women can, however, be "spoken by the truth" when their lack of a tongue is remedied by the presence of the Signifier of Authority.)

So, returning to the contest for authority, there is always a conflict over meaning, which is also a struggle for authority. This can be seen clearly in the conflict between analyst and patient, who, by being "in denial" and refusing to answer the analyst and tell him "the truth," is challenging his authority. The context between the anthropologist and his servant boy in Kipling's story is just such a conflict. So it raises in an acute form the whole question of interrogation to which Galvanauskas had devoted so much of his career and which had aroused so much controversy.

As is now well known, Galvanauskas developed a theory based on what he called the "paradox of disavowal." This was the idea that the only truth is that which is disavowed and so it is only when subjects lie that they reveal the truth.

When subjects lie, they do what the phallic text does: They elaborately disguise what they are trying to conceal, and those disguises can then be shown up, penetrated, dismantled, and the truth revealed. But this truth is not readily comprehensible, for it can be read only by a master, one who understands and has "the key."

Faced with a subject who would not speak—or a text that would not yield unambivalently its meaning—Galvanauskas discriminated between two kinds of challenge to his authority: silence and wordlessness. Silence is the ability to speak but the refusal to do so, and is therefore the phallic strategy of a rival authority. Wordlessness is the inability to speak and is the strategy of power that is emasculated.

This approach was the basis of Galvanauskas's famous interrogation technique. Essentially, this involved adopting the two opposite strategies of "silence" and "wordlessness" and switching arbitrarily and suddenly between them.

In the former, the interrogator remains silent and the interrogee has to talk. (This is merely an exaggeration of traditional therapeutic procedure.) In the second, the interrogee is not permitted to talk—and is sometimes even gagged—while the interrogator demands speech, even shouting and making threats of physical violence, which are sometimes acted upon.

Interrogation is crucial in Galvanauskas's thinking because of the inevitability of betrayal. For he insisted that to exist is to be betrayed, since we exist for others only by virtue of what we betray of ourselves to them. He showed that the hierarchy (phallic/emasculated, master/servant, etc.) is always unstable and capable of being inverted because of "betrayal," in which the weaker party tries to "steal the phallus," that is, to evade and undermine the stronger. And so all authority—especially that of the analyst—is faced with betrayal.

Galvanauskas showed how betrayal functioned in Kipling's story. The boy's "betrayal" in stealing the idol's part constituted a challenge to his master's authority, for everything is at stake in this act of blasphemy. The idol—representing power, authority, and control—stands in for the anthropologist, so that by defacing the idol the boy has challenged authority by an act of betrayal of his master. It is an act of double betrayal, since the theft endangers the anthropologist's work among the tribe. Galvanauskas argued that in much the same way every analysand challenges the authority of the analyst when he or she remains "in denial" and attempts a betrayal of the analyst and the destruction of his work, for the patient reasons thus: If the analyst can be defeated in this particular case, then all his work comes into doubt. So the analyst must control and dominate the patient, who will otherwise destroy him.

Betrayal by the Other expresses itself, among other ways, through what are called "jokes." The text mentions that the boy was fond of jokes and suggests that the taking of the part from the idol was in some superficial sense intended as a joke—or "prank," as Huxtable calls it. But Galvanauskas pointed out that this excuse is often used to mask or defend an act of blasphemy, and he would have none of it. The taking of the phallus was in truth no joke but a bid for authority, for as Galvanauskas pointed out, "There are no jokes" (*Aphorism 66*).

By this he meant that there are no jokes that do not betray profound meanings about the desire of the joker, and a joke is always a threat, an expression of aggression. If you joke about my death or my being injured, that betrays the fact that you desire it. So "jokes" are disguised acts of aggression that try to reverse the hierarchy of authority.

Now comes the crucial point, which is the apparent paradox at the heart of Galvanauskas's work and probably its most controversial aspect.

The boy is like the text itself—evasive, silent, traitorous. He is first silent out of willfulness when he refuses to acknowledge his guilt, and then he becomes wordless once his tongue is removed because he is now unable to speak.

At the point in the text where the boy's tongue is cut out by the high priest in order to facilitate confession, Galvanauskas quoted what he called the key sentence in Kipling's story: "The tongue was cut out first because the tribe believed that in such cases it was for the gods to speak and not the merely mortal tongue of the accused person."

Every text, Galvanauskas has demonstrated elsewhere (*Dits II*, pp. 165–66), has a point at which it simultaneously is absurd and also attempts to remain silent on the subject of its own absurdity, to evade the reader and conceal its internal contradictions. This notion of speech with the tongue cut out is where that point occurs in this text. At this stage the Signifier has become lost or, more accurately, "loosed." It can be found elsewhere in the text in the "part" which the boy has stolen from the idol. The text is evasive, but it is clear that it is the idol's phallus that is at issue and that therefore becomes an equivalent for the boy's tongue.

Since they have been brought together by these two acts of defacement, we should compare the situation of the idol and of the boy. And we should compare them in two states: Before (1) and after (2) the act of desecration that each undergoes.

In State 1 the phallus of the idol is grotesquely enlarged, and it, rather than the tongue, is the part through which the idol allegedly "speaks," so that we can say: Phallus = Speech. In State 2 the idol has lost its phallus and, equipped only with a tongue, has lost its power of speech, so that we can say that the possession of a tongue debars it from speech, or: Tongue = Not-Speech. When the boy is being interrogated in State 1, he has lost his tongue and does not speak, so that we can represent his situation thus: Not-Tongue = Not-Speech. We shall return to the boy's second state in due course.

The high priest has as his desire the regaining of the part, and so he commands the boy to tell him where the part is hidden or he will cut off his penis. He thinks he will win and defeat Huxtable whatever happens, since he is planning—if the boy does not tell him where the part is hidden—to take the boy's phallus and give it to the idol. The anthropologist, having watched the failure of his colleague in trying to use the discredited rationalism of the West, correctly perceives what needs to be done.

This is where Galvanauskas's Theory of Pleasure was demonstrated. Galvanauskas dismissed the conventional notion of pleasure as pleasurable and showed that pleasure is a "voluntary sacrifice" involving pain and submission and obedience in the face of authority.

Now that the idol has been blasphemed, what is required is nothing less than that its authority be reestablished. For this a "voluntary sacrifice" is necessary so that a transfer may be effected whereby the idol is restored. The part of the boy that must be cut off is precisely the part that the idol is missing.

To understand this, we must return to the schema and attempt to supply the missing fourth term, which is the second state of the boy:

Idol:

  1 Phallus = Speech
  2 Tongue = Not-Speech

Boy:

  1 Not-Tongue = Not-Speech
  2 Not-Phallus = Speech

A glance at the schema shows us that the final term must be: Not-Phallus = Speech. The anthropologist perceives this and makes his crucial intervention in order to bring this condition about.

We have seen the conflicts depicted in the text between the stronger and the weaker: Huxtable/subprefect, Huxtable/boy, and Huxtable/high priest. The relation between the reader (interrogator) and the text (interrogee) enacts this same conflict.

The phallic text must sacrifice itself to the power of the critic and be emasculated and thus made to speak like the tongueless boy.

In what does the intervention of the anthropologist then consist, Galvanauskas demands? It consists precisely in the fact that at the critical moment he remains silent. When the foolish subprefect attempts to force him to speak in order to prevent the tribal magician from carrying out the next stage of the ritual disfigurement, the anthropologist instead wisely chooses to exercise "the authority of silence." The high priest consequently cuts off the boy's penis—for though it is not named, who can doubt that this is the part of the body referred to?

I quote here from the text of the original transcript as I first read it in 1986:

> As the boy regards death, tongueless, aphallic, his limbs cut off, his eye (I) now perceives the authority of his master. For the anthropologue (and remember that he *is* an anthropologue) has made his decisive intervention—the intervention of silence. And occurs now the climactic moment—the moment of the wordless gesture of submission, of respect, of even love that the boy makes to his master: "He opened merely the mouth and then gyrated the obscene stump of his severed sexual organ." In this gesture—and who can doubt that it is a literal climax, that the boy, shortly, ejaculates?—the truth is revealed—not the illusory truth that the subprefect seeks about the identity of the thief but the truth of the boy's acceptance of his master's authority. He has pleasure in accepting the authority of Huxtable just as the text capitulates to the authority of the reader, and the analysand to the authority of the analyst. After this there is no more for the boy to express, and so, having manifested himself in "a-language-that-is-a-silence," the text has no further use for him.

In the same way the phallic reader emasculates the phallic text and forces it to speak—to speak not in any literal sense but to utter what he, the reader, desires it to say.

There have been some trivial objections to Galvanauskas's reading of the text, which I will briefly mention here.

Galvanauskas has been accused of having failed to understand the text's irony. The best answer to this is "Irony is always unimportant" (*Aphorism 17*). But let us concede for the sake of the argument that there are a number of issues in the text that are "ironically" concealed.

One critic has suggested that Galvanauskas's reading misses the implication that the anthropologist is actually not that at all but more probably a missionary. Also that he has been having a homosexual relationship with the boy. And, above all, that he, rather than the boy, is the person who has stolen the idol's "part." The same critic has suggested that this is what he puts in the subprefect's mailbag rather than an account of the affair, as Galvanauskas assumes. And so the irony is that Huxtable allows the innocent boy to die in order to protect himself. Another critic has argued that Galvanauskas has failed to understand that the high priest's purpose in torturing the boy is not to get him to speak but to force Huxtable—over whom, as a British subject, he has no political authority—to confess that it was he who stole the part. Even if these pettifogging objections are accepted, that fact would not change in the slightest way the thrust of Galvanauskas's reading, which is not concerned with notions of "guilt" or "innocence" but solely with the conflict of desire in the power relationships involved.

INDEX OF NAMES

AL-SADDIQI, HAROUN: He is mentioned in Chapter 4, "The Medicine Man," as the author of "The Bait." (A story that resembles this is Chapter 5, "The Trap.")

ANDRO: A character in *Gargunnock Braes* in Chapter 7, "An Open Mind." He is a lorry driver.

ANGELINA: A character in *Biggert* in Chapter 7, "An Open Mind." She is the girlfriend of McIlhargey.

ANITA: This is both a character in Prentice's first and unpublished novel, and the new name of Annabel in the manuscript novel that Ireland sends to Prentice in Chapter 9, "The Catch," when it is published under Prentice's name.

ANNABEL: Chatterton's girlfriend in the manuscript novel that Ireland sends to Prentice in Chapter 9, "The Catch." (When the novel is published under Prentice's name, the name is changed to Anita.)

APPLEYARD: The Major gives this as the name of the victim in his story, "The Stairs," in Chapter 2, "The Wrong Tracks."

ARBUTHNOTT, PROFESSOR: A character in *Biggert* in Chapter 7, "An Open Mind." He is a professor of reptilian zoology.

ARCHIBALD: In Drummond Gilchrist's manuscript in Chapter 8, "A Nice Touch," this is the name given to the literature director of the Glasgow Council for the Arts, who is really called Arnold.

Armageddon Protocol, The: In Chapter 8, "A Nice Touch," this is the seventh and most recently completed of Drummond Gilchrist's novels, and it is so far unpublished.

Armageddon Ultimatum, The: Pattison refers to this as a novel by Drummond Gilchrist in Chapter 8, "A Nice Touch," actually meaning *The Armageddon Protocol.*

ARMITAGE, LAVINIA: The author of the manuscript discussed in Chapter 3, " 'The New Surgeon at St. Oswald's.' " And in Chapter 7, "An Open Mind," Sholto finds what seems to be a revised version of this manuscript published as *The Throat Surgeon.* He develops a theory about the identity of the author and her relation to Jack the Ripper.

ARMYTAGE, MRS.: A character in Chapter 2, "The Wrong Tracks." She also appears in Horatio Quaife's *The Right Lines,* which is mentioned in Chapter 7, "An Open Mind."

ARNOLD: The literature director of the Glasgow Council for the Arts in Chapter 8, "A Nice Touch."

Atlantis Ultimatum, The: In Chapter 8, "A Nice Touch," this is one of Drummond Gilchrist's six published novels.

AULD RAB: A much-loved character in *Gargunnock Braes* in Chapter 7, "An Open Mind." (Fraser Pittendrigh is the actor who plays him.)

"BAIT, THE": This is what Speculand calls the Moorish tale in Chapter 4, "The Medicine Man."

BARTLETT, SHEILA: The older nurse in Chapter 3, " 'The New Surgeon at St. Oswald's.' " who is a rival for the handsome surgeon's affections.

BEARDSLEY, AUBREY: A character in the play *The Importance of Being Jack,* in *Biggert* in Chapter 7, "An Open Mind."

BELLAMY, GODFREY: The central figure, a cabinet minister and best-selling novelist, in the manuscript novel that Ireland sends to Prentice in Chapter 9, "The Catch." (When the novel is published under Prentice's name, the name is changed to Geoffrey Sadleir-Brown.)

BENTLEY, WILLIAM: The young lecturer in philosophy at Glasgow University in Chapter 4, "The Medicine Man," and Chapter 7, "An Open Mind," who is mentioned in both chapters as having committed suicide as a result of the Galvanauskas affair. Another perspective on his death is given in Chapter 10, "A Review from *The Daily Scot.*"

Biggert: A police serial in Chapter 7, "An Open Mind."

BIGGERT, GUTHRIE: The detective chief inspector of the Glasgow police who is the central character in *Biggert* in Chapter 7, "An Open Mind."

BLACKER, MICHAEL: The screenwriter in Drummond Gilchrist's manuscript in Chapter 8, "A Nice Touch."

BLUE ORCHID: The sauna at which Mo-Lak works in Drummond Gilchrist's manuscript in Chapter 8, "A Nice Touch."

BONE, TARQUIN: The famous literary agent who is mentioned in Chapter 8, "A Nice Touch," as Pattison's agent and in Chapter 9, "The Catch," as Prentice's.

CALUM: A character in *Gargunnock Braes* in Chapter 7, "An Open Mind." He is Roberta's twin brother—as has only recently been learned—and Horatio tells Sholto he believes he is her lover and the father of her child, Jacqueline.

CAMERON: A character in *Gargunnock Braes* in Chapter 7, "An Open Mind."

CAVALLI: A restaurant owner and father of Fiammetta in *Biggert* in Chapter 7, "An Open Mind."

CELTIC TWILIGHT, THE: A pub much patronized by the Glasgow literati in Chapter 7, "An Open Mind."

CHATTERTON, THOMAS: The young would-be novelist who writes to Godfrey Bellamy asking him to read his novel in the manuscript novel that Ireland sends to Prentice in Chapter 9, "The Catch."

CHERRYMAN: The actor who is murdered during a performance of the play *The Importance of Being Jack*, in the first episode of *Biggert* in Chapter 7, "An Open Mind."

Cincinnatus Papers, The: Prentice's most recently published novel in Chapter 9, "The Catch."

CONRAD, JOSEPH: He is mentioned in Chapter 4, "The Medicine Man," as the author of *The Black Heart*—a text that Galvanauskas cites.

CRAIGIE: A character in *Biggert* in Chapter 7, "An Open Mind." He is an assistant to D.C.I. Biggert.

Daily Scot, The: The Scottish national paper mentioned in Chapter 1, "An Obituary from *The Daily Scot*," in Chapter 7, "An Open Mind," in Chapter 8, "A Nice Touch," and in Chapter 10, "A Review from *The Daily Scot*."

Diaeresis: This is mentioned in Chapter 4, "The Medicine Man," as the academic journal in which Speculand publishes his essay on the Arab tale.

Diarrhea: In Chapter 7, "An Open Mind," Sholto refers to an academic journal of this name.

DONALDA: A character in *Gargunnock Braes* in Chapter 7, "An Open Mind." She adopted Roberta after she and her twin brother, Calum, were given up for adoption by their real mother.

Down on Whores: The title of Horatio Quaife's new book. The title is not mentioned in Chapter 7, "An Open Mind," but the novel is the subject of Chapter 10, "A Review from *The Daily Scot*."

DRIVER, THE: The driver of the train in the Killiecrankie Mystery, which is recounted in Chapter 2, "The Wrong Tracks." Sholto reveals in Chapter 7, "An Open Mind," that the driver was his great-uncle Hamish.

DUGDALE, WILLIAM HERBERT: The distinguished scientist who is Pierre L'Angelier Professor of Immunotoxinology at the University of Glasgow and is the subject of Chapter 1, "An Obituary from *The Daily Scot*." He is mentioned in Chapter 4, "The Medicine Man," and in Chapter 7, "An Open Mind." Another perspective on his death is given in Chapter 10, "A Review from *The Daily Scot*."

DURRANDS: The Major gives this as the name of the officer who gives the fatal map to Maddocks in his story, "The Stairs," in Chapter 2, "The Wrong Tracks."

EDWARDS: The victim in the judge's story in Chapter 6, "The Accusation."

ELLIOTT, MONA: Mrs. Armytage gives this as the name of the heroine in her story, "The Masque," in Chapter 2, "The Wrong Tracks."

Enough Rope: This is mentioned in Chapter 8, "A Nice Touch," as the title of Auberon Saville's book about the Prentice affair.

ESMERALDA: A character in *Biggert* in Chapter 7, "An Open Mind." She is an assistant to D.C.I. Biggert.

FANSHAW, VALENTINE: Mrs. Armytage gives this as the name of Randolph's friend in her story, "The Masque," in Chapter 2, "The Wrong Tracks."

FARQUHAR: The character in the Prologue and framing narrative in Drummond Gilchrist's manuscript in Chapter 8, "A Nice Touch."

FARQUHAR-JONES: The new name for the character who is a combination of Farquhar and Jones in Drummond Gilchrist's manuscript in Chapter 8, "A Nice Touch."

FIAMMETTA: A character in *Biggert* in Chapter 7, "An Open Mind."

Finger Man, The: The third of three spy thrillers that Cyril Pattison published with Cowgate in Chapter 8, "A Nice Touch."

FINGERS: A sauna in Glasgow mentioned in *The Importance of Being Jack*, in *Biggert* in Chapter 7, "An Open Mind." Trevor works there and it is patronized by the actor playing the Prince of Wales. The same sauna appears in Drummond Gilchrist's manuscript in Chapter 8, "A Nice Touch."

FIONA: A character in *Biggert* in Chapter 7, "An Open Mind." She is a young woman who works in the laboratory of Professor Arbuthnott.

For Richer, For Poorer: Prentice's first published novel in Chapter 9, "The Catch."

FORDYCE, SIR RANDOLPH: Mrs. Armytage gives this as the name of Isadora's fiancé in her story, "The Masque," in Chapter 2, "The Wrong Tracks." Sholto has a theory about him in Chapter 7, "An Open Mind."

FORRESTER, MINNIE: Jones sees this name on the credits on the piece of film with which Lam-Sae has been strangled in Drummond Gilchrist's manuscript in Chapter 8, "A Nice Touch."

FROBISTER, MORAG: The writer of the "Tabby Squeill" column in *The Daily Scot* in Chapter 8, "A Nice Touch." She is a former publisher's reader and literary agent. See also "Mo-Lak" and "Moira" and Chapter 3, " 'The New Surgeon at St. Oswald's.' "

GALVANAUSKAS, HENRI: The world-famous psychoanalyst in Chapter 4, "The Medicine Man." He is also mentioned in Chapter 7, "An Open Mind."

GARGANTUA AND PANTAGRUEL: This is mentioned in Chapter 10, "A Review from *The Daily Scot*," as the name of the bookshop in the West End of Glasgow in which the manuscript of *Down on Whores* was found.

Gargunnock Braes: A soap opera in Chapter 7, "An Open Mind."

GICQUIAUX, JACQUES: He is mentioned in Chapter 4, "The Medicine Man," as the author of *The Mystic Medicine Man: Henri Galvanauskas in Lithuania 1940–41 and Paris 1977–84.*

GILCHRIST, DRUMMOND: The novelist who is addressed in the letters that form Chapter 8, "A Nice Touch."

GILHAIZE, RINGAN: The is the new name in the Glasgow setting of the novelist who was the Hollywood screenwriter Michael Blacker in Drummond Gilchrist's manuscript in Chapter 8, "A Nice Touch."

GLADSTONE: A character in the play *The Importance of Being Jack,* in *Biggert* in Chapter 7, "An Open Mind."

Glasgow Clarion: The local paper mentioned in Chapter 7, "An Open Mind."

Glasgow Tribune: The local paper mentioned in *Biggert* in Chapter 7, "An Open Mind."

Greater Glory, The: Prentice's second published novel in Chapter 9, "The Catch."

GUARD, THE: This is the guard of the train in the Killiecrankie Mystery, which is recounted in Chapter 2, "The Wrong Tracks." See also Chapter 1, "An Obituary from *The Daily Scot.*"

GWENDOLYN: Mrs. Armytage gives this as the name of her aunt in her story, "The Masque," in Chapter 2, "The Wrong Tracks."

HAMISH: Sholto refers to his great-uncle Hamish in Chapter 7, "An Open Mind," as having been the driver of the train in the Killiecrankie Mystery, which is recounted in Chapter 2, "The Wrong Tracks."

HONEYFORD, GILES: The central figure, a cabinet minister and best-selling novelist, in the manuscript novel that Chatterton sends to Bellamy in Chapter 9, "The Catch."

HUXTABLE: The Parson gives this as the name of the anthropologist in his story, "The Scapegoat," in Chapter 2, "The Wrong Tracks."

Importance of Being Jack, The: The play written by Maturin and being produced at the Citizen's Theater in *Biggert* in Chapter 7, "An Open Mind."

IRELAND, WILLIAM HENRY: The young would-be novelist who writes to Jeremy Prentice asking him to read his unpublished novel in Chapter 9, "The Catch."

ISADORA: Mrs. Armytage gives this as the name of Randolph's fiancée in her story, "The Masque," in Chapter 2, "The Wrong Tracks."

JACQUELINE: A character in *Gargunnock Braes* in Chapter 7, "An Open Mind." She is Roberta's child—possibly by Calum.

JAMIE: A character in *Biggert* in Chapter 7, "An Open Mind." He is a stagehand working on the play *The Importance of Being Jack* and is killed in the second episode.

JANET: Farquhar's wife in Chapter 8, "A Nice Touch."

JENNY: A character in *Gargunnock Braes* in Chapter 7, "An Open Mind." She is the mother of the child, Shona, who is killed by Andro's lorry. Horatio develops a theory about this.

JONES, ATHANASIUS: The character in the inner story in Drummond Gilchrist's manuscript in Chapter 8, "A Nice Touch."

KELLY, MARIE: The young nurse who is the central character in Chapter 3, " 'The New Surgeon at St. Oswald's' " And in Chapter 7, "An Open Mind," the same name is mentioned again.

KILLIECRANKIE MYSTERY: This is the subject of Chapter 2, "The Wrong Tracks," and is discussed in Chapter 7, "An Open Mind."

KIPLING, RUDYARD: He is mentioned in Chapter 4, "The Medicine Man," as the author of "The Tongueless Boy," on which a paper, apparently by Galvanauskas, is in circulation.

LAM-SAE: The Chinese masseuse who works with Mo-Lak at the Blue Orchid in Drummond Gilchrist's manuscript in Chapter 8, "A Nice Touch."

LATIMER, MARCIA: The silent young lady who was the companion of Mrs. Armytage. She appears under that name in Horatio Quaife's *The Right Lines*, which is mentioned in Chapter 7, "An Open Mind." She is not named in Chapter 2, "The Wrong Tracks," where she is referred to as the silent or mute young lady. The resemblance to the name Magnus Lorimer is presumably coincidental.

Let Not Ambition: The title of a novel written by a character in *The Greater Glory* in Chapter 9, "The Catch."

LEVAVASSEUR: A former disciple of Galvanauskas who has allegedly plagiarized from and betrayed him. He is mentioned in Chapter 4, "The Medicine Man."

LORIMER, MAGNUS: A student mentioned by Horatio in Chapter

7, "An Open Mind." Auberon Saville refers to him in Chapter 10, "A Review from *The Daily Scot.*" The resemblance to the name Marcia Latimer is presumably coincidental.

LOVEBONE, CLARENCE TITHERADGE: The detective don who is the hero of Horatio Quaife's *Down on Whores* in Chapter 7, "An Open Mind." He is the nephew of Clarence Titheradge, who appears in Quaife's *The Right Lines.*

M'LAY: A character in *Biggert* in Chapter 7, "An Open Mind." He is a criminal whom the actor playing Oscar Wilde in *The Importance of Being Jack* meets in a bar and with whom he steals cars. M'Lay is also involved in a conspiracy with Trevor.

MacLENNAN, SIR HAROLD: The Tory elder statesman who advises Bellamy against publication in the manuscript novel that Ireland sends to Prentice in Chapter 9, "The Catch."

MacMANGAN, SCOTT: The actor who plays D.C.I. Biggert in *Biggert* in Chapter 7, "An Open Mind."

MacMASTER, ANGUS: The professor of philosophy at Glasgow University who is the Galvanauskas Institute's chief enemy in Chapter 4, "The Medicine Man." He turns out to be Horatio's enemy in Chapter 7, "An Open Mind."

MacQUARRIE, JACK: The surgeon in Chapter 3, " 'The New Surgeon at St. Oswald's,' " who is nicknamed Jock the Ripper.

MacSPORRAN, MUNGO: The name of the character based on Sholto MacTweed in *Down on Whores.*

MacTWEED, SHOLTO: The diarist who writes Chapter 7, "An Open Mind."

MADDOCKS: The Major gives this as the name of the officer who was probably the murderer in his story, "The Stairs," in Chapter 2, "The Wrong Tracks." He is described as "something of a scholar in various of the native tongues."

MADDOCKS, RICHARD FAWCETT: The translator from the Arabic of Chapter 5, "The Trap."

MAGGY: A character in *Gargunnock Braes* in Chapter 7, "An Open Mind." She is Andro's wife.

MAJOR, THE: A character in Chapter 2, "The Wrong Tracks." He also appears in Horatio Quaife's *The Right Lines*, which is mentioned in Chapter 7, "An Open Mind."

MATURIN: The author of the play *The Importance of Being Jack*, in *Biggert* in Chapter 7, "An Open Mind."

MAUREEN: A character in *Gargunnock Braes* in Chapter 7, "An Open Mind." She is Calum's daughter.

McALWEENIE: A Scottish poet who appears in Chapter 7, "An Open Mind."

McCONVILLE: A Scottish novelist who appears in Chapter 7, "An Open Mind."

McCOO, MORAG: The publisher's reader who reports on the manuscript in Chapter 3, " 'The New Surgeon at St. Oswald's.' " See also Chapter 8, "A Nice Touch."

McCOO, RAMSAY: The literary editor of *The Daily Scot* who is mentioned in Chapter 7, "An Open Mind," and in Chapter 8, "A Nice Touch."

McCRUM, MRS.: A character in *Biggert* in Chapter 7, "An Open Mind." She escapes from "the Scorpion" and can identify him.

McGINNITY: A character in *Biggert* in Chapter 7, "An Open Mind." He is a taxidermist who works in the lab of Professor Arbuthnott.

McILHARGEY: A character in *Biggert* in Chapter 7, "An Open Mind." He is the theater critic of *The Glasgow Tribune* who unfavorably reviews the play *The Importance of Being Jack* and is killed by a scorpion.

McPHILEMY, JOOLS: The actor who plays Craigie in *Biggert* and Murdo in *Gargunnock Braes* in Chapter 7, "An Open Mind."

Minnie's Sticky End: The snuff movie in which Mo-Lak is to be killed in Chapter 8, "A Nice Touch."

MOIRA: A character in *Gargunnock Braes* in Chapter 7, "An Open Mind." She adopted Calum.

MOIRA: This is the new name in the Glasgow setting of the character who was previously called Mo-Lak. See also Mo-Lak and Morag McCoo.

MO-LAK: The Chinese masseuse who works at the Blue Orchid in Drummond Gilchrist's manuscript in Chapter 8, "A Nice Touch." See also Moira and Morag.

MONA: See under "Elliott, Mona."

MONCRIEFF: A philosophy lecturer at Glasgow University in Chapter 7, "An Open Mind."

MURDO: A character in *Gargunnock Braes* in Chapter 7, "An Open Mind." He comes back to the village after training as a vet. The actor who plays him is Jools McPhilemy, who also plays Craigie in *Biggert.*

Nice Touch, A: Pattison suggests this title to Drummond Gilchrist for his manuscript in Chapter 8, "A Nice Touch."

OSCARS, GAVIN: Sholto writes of an academic scandal involving this individual in Chapter 7, "An Open Mind."

PARROTT, SIR QUINTIN: The Master of the Queen's Musick, who is a KGB agent in the manuscript novel that Ireland sends to Prentice in Chapter 9, "The Catch." (When the novel is published under Prentice's name, the name is changed to Sir Cecil Reckitt.)

PARSON, THE: A character in Chapter 2, "The Wrong Tracks." He also appears in Horatio Quaife's *The Right Lines*, which is mentioned in Chapter 7, "An Open Mind."

PATTISON, CYRIL: The author of the letters that make up Chapter 8, "A Nice Touch."

PEDDIE, ARCHIBALD: The author of *Scotch Mysteries* in Chapter 7, "An Open Mind."

PETTIFER, CHARTRES: Drummond Gilchrist's version of the name Cyril Pattison in his manuscript in Chapter 8, "A Nice Touch."

PETTITSON, CHALMERS: This is the new name in the Glasgow setting of the two characters who were previously called Stetson and Pettifer in Drummond Gilchrist's manuscript in Chapter 8, "A Nice Touch."

PITTENDRIGH, FRASER: See under "Auld Rab."

PRENTICE, JEREMY: The former cabinet minister and best-selling novelist who writes Chapter 9, "The Catch."

PRIMROSE: The prompter for the play *The Importance of Being Jack*, in *Biggert* in Chapter 7, "An Open Mind."

QUAIFE, HORATIO: A philosophy don at Glasgow University who writes about detective fiction and who appears in Chapter 7, "An Open Mind."

QUIN-TOO-SENSUAL: A sauna in Glasgow mentioned in Drummond Gilchrist's manuscript in Chapter 8, "A Nice Touch."

Quintain, The: This is the eventual title of Drummond Gilchrist's manuscript in Chapter 8, "A Nice Touch."

Quintessence, The: The first of Cyril Pattison's novels and the first of three spy thrillers that he published with Cowgate in Chapter 8, "A Nice Touch."

RAB: See under "Auld Rab."

RANDOLPH, SIR: See under "Fordyce, Sir Randolph."

RECKITT, CECIL: This is both a character in Prentice's first and unpublished novel and the new name of Sir Quintin Parrott in the manuscript novel that Ireland sends to Prentice in Chapter 9, "The Catch," when it is published under Prentice's name.

Reflection, The: Speculand says in Chapter 4, "The Medicine Man," that Washington Irving plagiarized the story he calls "The Bait" for his *Tales of the Alhambra* under this title.

Right Lines, The: Horatio Quaife's first book on the Killiecrankie Mystery, mentioned in Chapter 7, "An Open Mind."

RITCHIE, PROFESSOR: A distinguished immunologist who is the author of the obituary that is Chapter 1, "An Obituary from *The Daily Scot.*"

ROBERTA: A character in *Gargunnock Braes* in Chapter 7, "An Open Mind." She is the village postmistress and, it is revealed, the twin sister of Calum. The actress who plays her leaves the show in order to play the actress in *Biggert*, who plays Ellen Terry in *The Importance of Being Jack.*

ROBERTSON: The murderer in the judge's story in Chapter 6, "The Accusation."

ROUGHEAD, WILLIAM: The author of *Unsolved Scottish Crimes*, mentioned in Chapter 7, "An Open Mind."

RUDOLPH, SIR: The deceased laird who owned Killiecrankie Castle in Chapter 2, "The Wrong Tracks."

SACKVILLE, AUBREY: The pseudonym invented by Jeremy Prentice in Chapter 9, "The Catch," in order to conceal the identity of a distinguished novelist.

SADLEIR-BROWN, GEOFFREY: This is both a character in Prentice's first and unpublished novel and the new name of Godfrey Bellamy in the manuscript novel that Ireland sends to Prentice in Chapter 9, "The Catch," when it is published under Prentice's name.

SALLY: Drummond Gilchrist's agent in Chapter 8, "A Nice Touch."

SAVILLE, AUBERON: The author of the review in Chapter 10, "A Review from *The Daily Scot.*"

SCORPION, THE: A serial killer in Chapter 7, "An Open Mind," both in reality and in *Biggert.*

SENGA: A character in *Gargunnock Braes* in Chapter 7, "An Open Mind." She is the wife of the village's minister and the person who knows who is the real mother of the twins, Roberta and Calum.

Sensation Seeker, The: The second of three spy thrillers that Cyril Pattison published with Cowgate in Chapter 8, "A Nice Touch."

SENSATIONS: A sauna in Glasgow mentioned in Drummond Gilchrist's manuscript in Chapter 8, "A Nice Touch."

SHOLTO: See under "MacTweed, Sholto."

SHONA: A character in *Gargunnock Braes* in Chapter 7, "An Open Mind." She is the child of Jenny and is killed by Andro's lorry.

SICKERT, WALTER: A character in the play *The Importance of Being Jack*, in *Biggert* in Chapter 7, "An Open Mind."

SMETTERBURN: The leading character in a series of novels by Cyril Pattison in Chapter 8, "A Nice Touch."

SPECULAND, GRAHAM: The author of Chapter 4, "The Medicine Man." He is a professor of English Literature at Glasgow University and has published *Unmasking Strategies of Desire: Texts, Power, and the Phallus in the Work of Henri Galvanauskas* and the three-volume collection of essays by Galvanauskas, *Dits*. He has also written the essay on the Arab story published in *Diaeresis:* "Pleasure, Authority, and the Phallic Text: A Galvanauskasian Reading of al-Saddiqi's 'The Bait.'"

SPENCER: A character in *Biggert* in Chapter 7, "An Open Mind." He is the director of the play *The Importance of Being Jack*.

STETSON: The Hollywood star in Drummond Gilchrist's manuscript in Chapter 8, "A Nice Touch."

Sting in the Tail, The: This is the title both of the first novel Prentice ever wrote (which has remained unpublished), and of the manuscript novel sent him by Ireland that Prentice publishes under his own name.

Sting in the Tale, The: In Chapter 9, "The Catch," this is the original title, in the original version of the novel that Ireland sends to Prentice, of the novel that Chatterton sends to Bellamy. Bellamy insists that it be changed to *The Twister*, since that was the title of the unpublished novel he showed to Sir Harold MacLennan.

STOKER, THE: He appears in Chapter 2, "The Wrong Tracks."

SWINBURNE, ALGERNON: A character in the play *The Importance of Being Jack*, in *Biggert* in Chapter 7, "An Open Mind." He was originally played by Cherryman, but, after his murder, the actor who had been playing the tiny role of a London policeman took over the part.

TABBY SQUEILL: The gossip column in *The Daily Scot* in Chapter 8, "A Nice Touch."

TARQUIN: See under "Bone, Tarquin."

TAW-KWEE: A Chinese drug dealer and pimp in Drummond Gilchrist's manuscript in Chapter 8, "A Nice Touch." See also under "Bone, Tarquin."

TEN BELLS: This pub is mentioned in Chapter 3, " 'The New Surgeon at St. Oswald's.' " A famous tavern of the same name is mentioned in Chapter 7, "An Open Mind," as being involved in the case of Jack the Ripper.

TERRY, ELLEN: A character in the play *The Importance of Being Jack*, in *Biggert* in Chapter 7, "An Open Mind." She is a rival of the Countess of Warwick for the Prince of Wales's attentions. The actress playing her is at first the actress who played Roberta in *Gargunnock Braes*, but she leaves the production in order to take on a role in the soap *Tillieknock Nuik*. The actress who replaces her is later entrapped into killing the actress playing the Countess of Warwick.

Throat Surgeon, The: The novel Sholto finds, which is written by Lavinia Armitage. See also Chapter 3, " 'The New Surgeon at St. Oswald's.' "

Tillieknock Nuik: The soap opera in *Biggert* in Chapter 7, "An Open Mind."

TITHERADGE, CLARENCE: The detective don in Horatio Quaife's *The Right Lines* who is mentioned in Chapter 7, "An Open Mind."

Too Clever by Half: The reviewer in Chapter 10, "A Review from *The Daily Scot*," mentions this as the title of Jeremy Prentice's book about his experiences with Ireland and "Sackville."

TORQUIL: This is the new name of Taw-Kwee in the Glasgow setting in Drummond Gilchrist's manuscript in Chapter 8, "A Nice Touch."

TREVOR: A character in *Biggert* in Chapter 7, "An Open Mind." He is a masseur in the sauna Fingers, and he and M'Lay are involved in something there that requires video cameras.

Twister, The: In Chapter 9, "The Catch," this is the original title of the novel that Ireland sends to Prentice (which Prentice renames *The Sting in the Tail*). It is also the new title of the novel that Chatterton sends to Bellamy in Ireland's manuscript since Bellamy insists that it be changed to this since it was the title of the unpublished novel he showed to Sir Harold MacLennan.

VALENTINE: See under "Fanshaw, Valentine."

WARWICK: The Countess of Warwick. A character in the play *The Importance of Being Jack*, in *Biggert* in Chapter 7, "An Open Mind." She is the mistress of the Prince of Wales.

WISE, THOMAS JAMES: The young would-be novelist who writes to Honeyford asking him to read his unpublished novel in the manuscript novel that Chatterton sends to Bellamy in Chapter 9, "The Catch."

Year of the Talkies, The: This is the original title of Drummond Gilchrist's manuscript in Chapter 8, "A Nice Touch."

ZADONSKY: The Hollywood movie producer in Drummond Gilchrist's manuscript in Chapter 8, "A Nice Touch."

CHARLES PALLISER, the author of *The Quincunx* and *The Sensationist*, has taught English literature and creative writing in Britain and the United States. He lives mainly in London.